"Jamie Ford is a first-rate novelist, and with *Songs of Willow Frost* he takes a great leap forward and demonstrates the uncanny ability to move me to tears."
—PAT CONROY

"With vivid detail, Jamie Ford brings to life Seattle's Chinatown during the Depression and chronicles the high price those desperate times exacted from an orphaned boy and the woman he believes is his mother. *Songs of Willow Frost* is about innocence and the loss of it, about longing, about the power of remembered love."
—NANCY HORAN, author of *Loving Frank*

"Ford's boundless compassion for the human spirit, in all its strengths and weaknesses, makes him one of our most unique and compelling storytellers."
—HELEN SIMONSON, author of *Major Pettigrew's Last Stand*

"A beautiful novel . . . William's journey is one you'll savor, and then think about long after the book is closed."
—SUSAN WIGGS, author of *The Apple Orchard*

"One of those rare books that move right into your heart and stay there . . . a delight to read [that is] destined to become a book-club favorite."
—ANNE FORTIER, author of *Juliet*

"Characters so full of passion and courage that we cannot help but follow them into the pages of history."
—JEAN KWOK, author of *Girl in Translation*

"Ford weaves another rich tapestry of history and family drama in this cliff-hanging tale. . . . Hope and fate, laughs and tears: *Songs of Willow Frost* has it all."
—IVAN DOIG, author of *The Bartender's Tale*

BY JAMIE FORD

Songs of Willow Frost
Hotel on the Corner of Bitter and Sweet

Songs of
Willow Frost

Songs of
Willow Frost

A NOVEL

JAMIE FORD

BALLANTINE BOOKS TRADE PAPERBACKS

NEW YORK

2014 Ballantine Books Trade Paperback Edition
Copyright © 2013 by Jamie Ford
Map copyright © 2013 by David Lindroth, Inc.
Reading group guide copyright © 2014 by Random House LLC

Published in the United States by Ballantine Books, an imprint of
Random House, a division of Random House LLC,
a Penguin Random House Company, New York.

BALLANTINE and the HOUSE colophon are registered
trademarks of Random House LLC.
RANDOM HOUSE READER'S CIRCLE & Design is a registered
trademark of Random House LLC.

Originally published in hardcover in the United States by
Ballantine Books, an imprint of Random House,
a division of Random House LLC, in 2013.

LIBRARY OF CONGRESS CATALOGING-IN-PUBLICATION DATA
Ford, Jamie.
Songs of Willow Frost: a novel/Jamie Ford.
pages cm
ISBN 978-0-345-52203-0
eBook ISBN 978-0-345-52204-7
1. Orphans—Fiction. 2. Orphanages—Fiction.
3. Mother and child—Fiction. 4. Actress—Fiction.
5. Hollywood (Los Angeles, Calif.)—Fiction.
6. Psychological fiction. I. Title.
PS3606.O737S66 2013
813'.6—dc23   2013011007

Printed in the United States of America on acid-free paper

www.randomhousereaderscircle.com

9 8 7 6 5 4 3 2

Title-page image: © iStockphoto.com

Book design by Victoria Wong

*This book is for my mother,
whom I used to call every Sunday night.*

I lost the angel who gave me summer
the whole winter through.
I lost the gladness that turned into sadness,
When I lost you.

—Irving Berlin, 1912

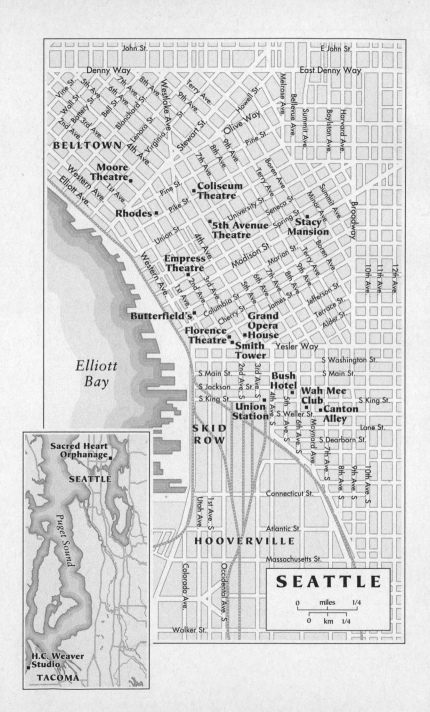

Songs of
Willow Frost

Sacred Hearts

卍

(1934)

William Eng woke to the sound of a snapping leather belt and the shrieking of rusty springs that supported the threadbare mattress of his army surplus bed. He kept his eyes closed as he listened to the bare feet of children, shuffling nervously on the cold wooden floor. He heard the popping and billowing of sheets being pulled back, like trade winds filling a canvas sail. And so he drifted, on the favoring currents of his imagination, as he always did, to someplace else—anywhere but the Sacred Heart Orphanage, where the sisters inspected the linens every morning and began whipping the bed wetters.

He would have sat up if he could, stood at attention at the foot of his bunk, like the others, but his hands were tied—literally—to the bed frame.

"I told you it would work," Sister Briganti said to a pair of orderlies whose dark skin looked even darker against their starched white uniforms.

Sister Briganti's theory was that bed-wetting was caused by boys illicitly touching themselves. So at bedtime she began tying the boys' shoes to their wrists. When that failed, she tied their wrists to their beds.

"It's a miracle," she said as she poked and prodded the dry sheets between William's legs. He watched as she crossed herself, then paused, sniffing her fingers, as though seeking evidence her eyes and hands might not reveal. *Amen,* William thought when he realized his bedding was dry. He knew that, like an orphaned child, Sister Briganti had learned to expect the worst. And she was rarely, if ever, disappointed.

After the boys were untied, the last offending child punished, and the crying abated, William was finally allowed to wash before breakfast. He stared at the long row of identical toothbrushes and washcloths that hung from matching hooks. Last night there had been forty, but now one set was missing and rumors immediately spread among the boys as to who the runaway might be.

Tommy Yuen. William knew the answer as he scanned the washroom and didn't see another matching face. *Tommy must have fled in the night. That makes me the only Chinese boy left at Sacred Heart.*

The sadness and isolation he might have felt was muted by a morning free from the belt, replaced by the hopeful smiles the other boys made as they washed their faces.

"Happy birthday, Willie," a freckle-faced boy said as he passed by. Others sang or whistled the birthday song. It was September 28, 1934, William's twelfth birthday—everyone's birthday, in fact—apparently it was much easier to keep track of this way.

Armistice Day might be more fitting, William thought. *Since some of the older kids at Sacred Heart had lost their fathers in the Great War, or October 29—Black Tuesday, when the entire country had fallen on hard times.* Since the Crash, the number of orphans had tripled. But Sister Briganti had chosen the coronation of Venerable Pope Leo XII as everyone's new day of celebration—a collective birthday, which meant a trolley ride from Laurelhurst to downtown, where the boys would be given buffalo nickels to spend at the candy butcher before being treated to a talking picture at the Moore Theatre.

But best of all, William thought, *on our birthdays and, only on our birthdays, are we allowed to ask about our mothers.*

BIRTHDAY MASS WAS always the longest of the year, even longer than the Christmas Vigil—for the boys anyway. William sat trying not to fidget, listening to Father Bartholomew go on and on and on and on and on about the Blessed Virgin, as if *she* could distract the boys from their big day. The girls sat on their side of the church, either oblivious to the boys' one day out each year or achingly jealous. But either way, talks about the Holy Mother only confused the younger, newer residents, most of whom weren't real orphans—at least not in the way Little Orphan Annie was depicted on the radio or in the Sunday funnies. Unlike the little mop-haired girl who gleefully squealed "Gee whiskers!" at any calamity, most of the boys and girls at Sacred Heart still had parents out there—somewhere—but wherever they were, they'd been unable to put food in their children's mouths or shoes on their feet. *That's how Dante Grimaldi came to us,* William reflected as he looked around the chapel. After Dante's father was killed in a logging accident, his mother had let him play in the toy department of the Wonder Store—the big Woolworth's on Third Avenue—and she never came back. Sunny Sixkiller last saw his ma in the children's section of the new Carnegie Library in Snohomish, while Charlotte Rigg was found sitting in the rain on the marble steps of St. James Cathedral. Rumor was that her grandmother had lit a candle for her and even went to confession before slipping out a side door. Then there were others—the fortunate ones. Their mothers came and signed manifolds of carbon paper, entrusting their children to the sisters of Sacred Heart, or St. Paul Infants' Home next door. There were always promises to come back in a week for a visit, and sometimes they did, but more often than not, that week stretched into a month, sometimes a year, sometimes *forever.* And yet, all of their moms had pledged (in front of Sister Briganti and God) to return one day.

After communion William stood with a tasteless wafer still stuck to the roof of his mouth, waiting in line with the other boys outside the school office. Each year, Mother Angelini, the prioress of Sacred Heart, would assess the boys physically and spiritually. If they passed muster, they'd be allowed out in public. William tried not to twitch or act too anxious. He attempted to look happy and presentable, mimicking the hopeful, joyful smiles of the others. But then he remembered the last time he saw *his* mother. She was in the bathtub of their apartment in the old Bush Hotel. William had woken up, wandered down the hall for a glass of water, and realized that she'd been in there for hours. He waited a few minutes more, but then at 12:01 A.M. he finally peeked through the rusty keyhole. It looked as though she were sleeping in the claw-foot tub, her face tilted toward the door; a strand of wet black hair clung to her pale cheek, the curl of a question mark. One arm lazily dangled over the edge, water slowly dripping from her fingertip. A single lightbulb hung from the ceiling, flickering on and off as the wind blew. After shouting and pounding on the door to no avail, William ran across the street to Dr. Luke, who lived above his office. The doctor jimmied the lock and wrapped towels around William's mother, carrying her down two flights of stairs and into a waiting taxi, bound for Providence Hospital.

He left me alone, William thought, remembering the pinkish bathwater that gurgled and swirled down the drain. On the bottom of the tub he'd found a bar of Ivory soap and a single lacquered chopstick. The wide end had been inlaid with shimmering layers of abalone. But the pointed end looked sharp, and he wondered what it was doing there.

"You can go in now, Willie," Sister Briganti said, snapping her fingers.

William held the door as Sunny walked out; his cheeks were cherry red and his sleeves were wet and shiny from wiping his nose. "Your turn, Will," he half-sniffled, half-grumbled. He gripped a letter in his hand, then crumpled the envelope as if to throw it away, then paused, stuffing the letter in his back pocket.

"What'd it say?" another boy asked, but Sunny shook his head and walked down the hallway, staring at the floor. Letters from parents were rare, not because they didn't come—they did—but because the sisters didn't let the boys have them. They were saved and doled out as rewards for good behavior or as precious gifts on birthdays and religious holidays, though some gifts were better than others. Some were hopeful reminders of a family that still wanted them. Others were written confirmations of another lonely year.

Mother Angelini was all smiles as William walked in and sat down, but the stained-glass window behind her oaken desk was open and the room felt cold and drafty. The only warmth that William felt came from the seat of the padded leather chair that had moments before been occupied, weighed down by the expectations of another boy.

"Happy birthday," she said as her spidery, wrinkled fingers paged through a thick ledger as though searching for his name. "How are you today . . . William?" She looked up, over her dusty spectacles. "This is your fifth birthday with us, isn't it? Which makes you how old in the canon?"

Mother Angelini always asked the boys' ages in relation to books from the *Septuagint*. William quickly rattled off, "Genesis, Exodus, Leviticus . . ." on up to Second Kings. He'd memorized his way only to the Book of Judith, when he'd turn eighteen and take his leave from the orphanage. Because the Book of Judith represented his own personal exodus, he'd read it over and over, until he imagined Judith as his forebear—a heroic, tragic widow, courted by many, who remained unmarried for the rest of her life. But he also read it because that particular book was semiofficial, semicanonical—more parable than truth, like the stories he'd heard about his own, long-lost parent.

"Well done, Master William," Mother Angelini said. "Well done.

Twelve is a marvelous age—the precipice of adult responsibility. Don't think of yourself as a teenager. Think of yourself as a young man. That's more fitting, don't you think?"

He nodded, inhaling the smell of rain-soaked wool and Mentholatum, trying not to hope for a letter or even a lousy postcard. He failed miserably in the attempt.

"Well, I know that most of you are anxious for word from the outside—that God's mysteries have blessed your parents with work, and a roof, and bread, and a warm fire, and that someone might come back for you," the old nun said with a delicate voice, shaking her head as the skin beneath her chin shook like a turkey's wattle. "But . . ." She glanced at her ledger. "We know that's not possible in your situation, don't we, dear?"

It seems that's all I know. "Yes, Mother Angelini." William swallowed hard, nodding. "I suppose, since this is my birthday, I'd just like to know more. I have so many memories from when I was little, but no one's ever told me what happened to her."

The last time he saw her he'd been seven years old. His mother had half-whispered, half-slurred, "I'll be right back," as she had been carried out the door, though he might have imagined this. But he didn't imagine the police officer, an enormous mountain of a man who showed up the next day. William remembered him eating a handful of his mother's butter-almond cookies and being very patient while he packed. Then William had climbed into the sidecar of the policeman's motorcycle and they drove to a receiving home. William had waved to his old friends, like he was riding a float in Seattle's Golden Potlatch Parade, not realizing that he was waving goodbye. A week later the sisters came and took him in. *If I had known I'd never see my apartment again, I'd have taken some of my toys, or at least a photo.*

William tried not to stare as Mother Angelini's tongue darted at the corner of her mouth. She read the ledger and a note card with an official-looking seal that had been glued to the page. "William, because you are old enough, I will tell you what I can, even though it pains me to do so."

That my mother is dead, William thought, absently. He'd accepted that as a likely outcome years ago, when they told him her condition had worsened and that she was never coming back. Just as he accepted that his father would always be unknown. In fact, William had been forbidden to ever speak of him.

"From what we know, your mother was a dancer at the Wah Mee Club—and quite popular. But one day she made herself sick with bitter melon and carrot-seed soup. When that didn't work, she retired to the bath and tried performing . . ."

Performing? His mother had been a singer and a dancer. "I don't understand," he whispered, unsure if he wanted to know more.

"William, your dear mother was rushed to the hospital, but she had to wait for hours and, when they did get around to her, the admitting physician wasn't entirely comfortable treating an Oriental woman, especially one with her reputation. So he had her remanded to the old Perry Hotel."

William blinked and vaguely understood. He knew the location. In fact he used to play kick the can on the corner of Boren and Madison. He remembered being frightened by the ominous-looking building, even before bars were added to the windows and the place was renamed the Cabrini Sanitarium.

Mother Angelini closed her ledger. "I'm afraid she never left."

WHEN WILLIAM FINALLY arrived at the Moore Theatre on Second Avenue, the younger boys had forgotten about their mothers and fathers in the rush to spend their nickels on Clark bars or handfuls of Mary Janes. Within minutes their lips were smeared and they were licking melted chocolate off their fingertips, one by one.

Meanwhile, William struggled to shake the thought of his mother spending her final years locked away in a nuthouse—a laughing academy, a funny farm. Sister Briganti had once said that if he daydreamed too much he'd end up in a place like that. *Maybe that's what happened to her.* He missed his mother as he wandered the lobby, looking at the movie posters, remembering her taking him to old photoplays and silent films in tiny second-run theaters. He recalled her arm around him, as she'd whisper in his ear, regaling him with tales of his grandparents, who were stars in Chinese operas.

As he lingered near the marble columns in the lobby, he tried to enjoy the moment, greedily palming the silver coin he'd been given. He'd learned from previous years to save it and follow the smell of melting butter and the sound of popcorn popping. He found Sunny, and they put their money together, splitting a large tub and an Orange Crush. As William waited to be seated, he noticed hundreds of other boys from various mission homes, institutions, and reformatories. In their dingy, graying uniforms they looked shrunken and sallow, frozen in line, a fresco of ragpickers. The prisonlike uniforms the other boys wore made William feel awkward and overdressed, even in his ill-fitting jacket and hand-me-down knickerbockers that hung eight inches past his knees. And as he sipped his drink his gullet pressed against the knot of black silk that barely passed for a bow tie. But despite their differences, they all had the same expectant look in their eyes as they crowded the entrance, buzzing with excitement. Like most of the boys at Sacred Heart, William had been hoping to see *Animal Crackers* or a scary movie like *White Zombie*—especially after he heard that the Broadway Theatre had offered ten dollars to any woman who could sit through a midnight showing without screaming. Unfortunately, the sisters had decided that *Cimarron* was better fodder for their impressionable young minds.

Gee whiskers, William thought. *I'm just happy to get away, happy to see anything, even a silent two-reeler.* But Sunny was less enthusiastic.

When the bright red doors finally swept open, Sister Briganti put her hand on his shoulder and rushed Sunny and him to their seats.

"Be good boys and whatever you do be quiet, keep to yourselves, and don't make eye contact with the ushers," she whispered.

William nodded but didn't understand until he glanced up and saw that the balcony was filled with colored boys and a few Indian kids like Sunny. There must have been a separate entrance in the alley. *Am I colored?* William wondered. *And if so, what color am I?* They shared the popcorn and he sat lower, sinking into the purple velvet.

As the footlights dimmed and the plush curtains were drawn, a player piano came to life, accompanying black-and-white cartoons with Betty Boop and Barnacle Bill. William knew that, for the little boys, this was the best part. Some would barely make it through the previews, or the Movietone Follies. They'd end up sleeping through most of the feature film, dreaming in Technicolor.

When the Follies reel finally began, William managed to sing along with the rest, to musical numbers by Jackie Cooper and the Lane Sisters, and he laughed at the antics of Stepin Fetchit, who had everyone in stitches. He laughed even harder than the kids in the balcony. But silence swept the audience as a new performer crooned "Dream a Little Dream of Me"—staring wistfully into the camera. At first William thought, *She looks like Myrna Loy in* The Black Watch. But she wasn't just wearing makeup, she was Chinese like Anna May Wong, the only Oriental star he'd ever seen. Her distinctive looks and honeyed voice drew wolf whistles from the older boys, which drew reprimands from Sister Briganti, who cursed in Latin and Italian. But as William stared at the flickering screen, he was stunned silent, mouth agape, popcorn spilling. The singer was introduced as Willow Frost—*a stage name,* William almost said out loud, it had to be. And best of all, Willow and Stepin and a host of Movietone performers would be appearing LIVE AT A THEATRE NEAR

YOU, in VANCOUVER, PORTLAND, SPOKANE, and SEATTLE. Tickets available NOW! GET 'EM BEFORE THEY'RE ALL SOLD OUT!

Sunny elbowed William and said, "Boy, I'd do anything to see that show."

"I . . . have to go" was all William could manage to say, still staring at the afterimage on the dark screen while listening to the opening score of *Cimarron,* which sounded farther and farther away, like Oklahoma.

"Keep on wishing, Willie."

Maybe it was his imagination. Or perhaps he was daydreaming once again. But William knew he had to meet her in person, because he had once known her by another name—he was sure of it. With his next-door neighbors in Chinatown, she went by Liu Song, but he'd simply called her *Ah-ma.* He had to say those words again. He had to know if she'd hear his voice—if she'd recognize him from five long years away.

Because Willow Frost is a lot of things, William thought, *a singer, a dancer, a movie star, but most of all, Willow Frost is my mother.*

Feeling Is Believing

꿈

(1934)

When the movie ended William clapped politely; everyone did—all but the little boys who startled awake, blinking and rubbing their eyes as the houselights flickered. Sunshine spilled in as ushers opened the double doors. William and Sunny followed the rest as they wandered out, two by two, huddling on a nearby streetcar platform, beneath a rare blue Seattle sky. The temperature had dropped, and clouds drifted over the Olympic Mountains on the horizon. William laughed as Sunny found an old cigarette butt and pretended to puff away, trying to blow smoke rings with his breath as older kids squeezed into the middle of the pack, hoping to find shelter from the wind that blew discarded leaflets and handbills down the street like tumbleweeds and thistledown.

William could smell seaweed drying on the mudflats of Puget Sound, but he also detected the aroma of shellfish and broth. His mouth watered as he looked around, noticing Sister Briganti arguing with a bootblack across the street who was passing out newspapers to men who stood in line for free bread and soup. William counted at least eighty souls before the line reached the corner and snaked around the building. The silent men looked as though they were dressed for church, in wool suits and knit ties, but beneath their hats and scarves he could see that most hadn't shaved in days, or weeks. *I wonder if any of our fathers are in that line,* William thought.

"That was the best movie ever," Sunny said, looking up at the lighted marquee, calling William's attention away from Sister Briganti's polite bickering.

Aside from the prairie scenes with thousands of men on horseback, he'd been utterly bored with the movie, distracted by thoughts of Willow and his ah-ma. He struggled to remember her face, sleeping in the bathtub, or singing on the silver screen, fearful that he'd forget one or the other. His mother was like a ghost, like Sunny's water-vapor smoke. William could see her clearly, but there was nothing to grasp.

"It was okay, I guess," he mumbled, then recalled that Sunny had once mentioned that he was part Cherokee, like some of the characters in the film. But how could he like a movie in which Irene Dunne called the Indians "dirty, filthy savages"? Then William vaguely remembered the movie's hero, Yancey, defending the tribe and their stolen land.

"I'm glad you found something you liked," William told him and nodded absently as a piece of yellow paper stuck to his shoe. The handbill was for the Movietone Follies and featured pictures of Stepin, Willow, and some comedian, Asa Berger, with dates for their northwest road show, including Seattle appearances in two weeks. Since both of his coat pockets had holes in them, William folded the paper and tucked it into a rip in the lining of his coat. He remembered his mother's cheerful voice, the sound of her heels on the wooden floor, the sweet-smelling perfume his ah-ma used to wear. His memories were suddenly present and alive, and if this were a dream, he mused, he didn't want to wake up.

William blinked when he heard a trolley bell ringing somewhere down the hill. He watched as Sister Briganti tromped back across the street, newspaper in hand. She slapped the cigarette butt from Sunny's mouth and swore, shaking her head, glaring at the newspaper as though she were witnessing some mortal sin. She tore the newspaper in half again and again, then tossed the scraps into an overflowing garbage can. "Judas Priest!" she snapped. "First the unions, now the communists—I never thought things would get this ba—"

William turned to follow Sister Briganti's line of sight as she looked past him toward a paperhanger in tattered coveralls. The workman had unrolled a huge four-sheet poster of Willow and Stepin and was gluing the panels with wheat paste to the side of a boarded-up brick building. The two of them stared at the man and the giant advertisement featuring a Negro and a Chinese woman. Then William turned, his eyes met hers, and she looked away, as though embarrassed. She quickly clapped her hands and snapped her fingers, ordering everyone to line up single file to board the streetcar.

On the ride home, William watched Seattle roll by, house by house, block by block. He ignored the vacant buildings and the squatters in the park. Instead he longed for his mother, he longed for Willow, as he noted all of the movie houses and storefront theaters along the way—counting sixteen before they left downtown proper. The marquees were so inviting, so majestic, so dazzlingly colorful, like gateways to magical worlds, where the flicker of a cinema projector had brought the spirit of his mother back to life. He was so captivated, so lost in the neon reverie, that he hardly noticed all the shantytowns, the billboards calling for strikes and protests, or the missionary kitchens in between, handing out free bread to bearded skeletons.

"WELCOME HOME, BOYS," the motorman said as he slowed to drop everyone off near the end of the North Seattle Interurban Line. He rang a brass bell, eliciting a palpable groan from nearly everyone onboard, drowning out the whir of the electric motor and the crackle of blue sparks that flickered from the trolley pole overhead.

As William descended the muddy steps of the streetcar, he joined Sunny and the others and glumly walked past the convent and the sacred grotto, up the lane toward the five-story brick-clad villa of Sacred Heart. He trudged along with everyone else, knowing that the best part of his birthday was officially over. But something else, something new, was just beginning.

"Back to the Villa on the Hilla," Sunny joked.

William didn't laugh, still lost in his thoughts. In reality he knew that his stately home was a kindly, loving, flower-adorned prison even though there were no guard towers—no barbed wire or barking dogs at Sacred Heart. Some of the older kids even lived on their own in quaint rows of Craftsman-style cottages with porch swings and hummingbird feeders. From atop Scottish Heights, he could smell the coal fires to the south, he could hear the boat horns and train whistles, see the city, appearing through the morning fog and disappearing in the moorish twilight. But on any given day, the panoramic views of Puget Sound and Lake Washington were William's only access to Seattle. *And if Sister Briganti has her way,* he thought, *it will be another year before we set foot outside of these wooded acres.*

As William walked past the hedgerow and white picket fence that was all that separated him from the outside world, from Willow, he couldn't help but notice how scalable the palings were, even for the scrawniest of boys. But the gates were never locked. It was the words of parents that kept most of the orphans here—the silken bondage of a mother's promise, "I'll be back by Christmas, if you're a good boy." Those mythic words, laced with happy-ever-afters, became millstones come January, when ice deckled the windows and the new boys stopped counting the days and began crying themselves to sleep, once again. After five winters at Sacred Heart, he'd learned not to hope for Christmas miracles—at least for nothing greater than a pair of hand-me-down shoes, a book of catechism, and a stocking filled with peanuts and a ripe tangerine.

As he approached the villa, the girls of Sacred Heart came pouring out of their cottages and barracks to greet them. They'd spent the afternoon decorating the common areas with crepe paper and hand-painted signs, and he could see (and smell) fresh angel food cakes cooling on the windowsills. The boys would do the same for them on July 15, when the girls all celebrated their collective birthday in honor of Mother Francesca Cabrini. The intrepid nun who founded the orphanage had once longed to serve a mission in the Orient. But she died somewhere in the Midwest, almost twenty years ago, long before William had even been born.

Following them in a wheelchair was the one boy who'd been left behind. His name was Mark *something,* but everyone called him Marco Polio, even though his matchstick legs had been malformed by rickets.

Marco and the girls all wanted to know what the movie was like—many had never been to one. They wanted to know about everything *out there.*

"Did you go to the Curiosity Shop at Colman Dock and see the jawbone of a whale?" a girl with long braids asked.

"Did you see the window displays at Frederick and Nelson?" Marco chimed in, "Did you try a Frango milk shake?" The question drew excited oohs and aahs from the girls, who'd been given Frangos last year from a kindly docent who always came bearing chocolate and flowers.

"What about the totem pole in Pioneer Square?" a girl in the back asked while waving her hand, prompting Sunny to frown and retell the story of the stolen icon, though no one cared to listen.

William noticed that everyone continued asking questions except for Charlotte, who stood on the porch of her cottage and held on to the banister. In her other hand was a white cane she'd been given by the Seattle Lions Club. She cocked her head toward the setting sun, her ear turned to the chatter of boys and girls mingling on the wet, grassy courtyard.

"I wish I could have been there," she said, still looking at the sun as William approached, her freckled cheeks turning pink in the cool breeze. "I'd do anything to get out of this place—to feel the city up close."

William stared at the faded blue of her milky eyes as her hair swept back and forth. "There was a player piano that worked like magic and a huge Wurlitzer organ—the music was tops," he said. "You'd have liked it."

He watched as she smiled and nodded in agreement. How Charlotte always recognized him was something of a mystery. He wore shoes virtually identical to those of the other boys, bathed with the same soap, but perhaps something about his walk, his gait, gave him away. William had even tried sneaking up on her once in the grotto, but she called his name before he got close. Maybe it was because the other boys were so hesitant—her damaged eyes spooked most of them. Or maybe it was because the other boys rarely spoke to her at all.

"I brought you something."

She turned to the sound of his voice, holding out her hand as he placed a bag of fresh saltwater taffy in her grasp, folding her fingers around it. She crinkled the bag, brought it to her nose. "Peppermint," she said.

William smiled and nodded. "It's your favorite." He'd played jingles with the other boys last week and had won enough pennies to buy her a small taste of the outside world.

"Happy birthday," she said, shrugging. "You know what I mean . . ."

"I don't even remember when my real birthday is anymore," William confessed, remembering a party with his mother, long ago. "Sister Briganti won't tell—she says that when I'm adopted, I'll want to celebrate that day as my new birthday."

"You don't sound like you believe her," Charlotte said. "She's a holy vessel, she's not supposed to lie." Charlotte unwrapped a piece of taffy and offered it to him.

He thanked her and popped it into his mouth, tasting the sweet, chewy mint, feeling guilty for having already eaten three pieces in a fit of nervous tension on the ride back from Second Avenue. He'd spent the last few years resigned to the fact that he would never be adopted. *A white family would never have me,* William almost said. *And it's doubtful that a Chinese family would adopt a child so unlucky. No one is coming for me.*

"How was your birthday visit with Mother Angelini?" Charlotte blinked as she asked him.

William looked up, noticing that the blue sky had turned into a mash of thick, gray rain clouds. "No letters," he sighed, but Charlotte knew he wasn't expecting one. "Though I did hear a story about my mother."

Neither of them spoke for a moment as a whistle blew from the steam plant next door. Charlotte paused, and he knew she was giving him an out—an opportunity to change the subject or to speak about something more pleasant.

"She means well," William said.

Charlotte frowned wearily. "This year she told me how I lost my eyesight." She shook her head slowly and tucked her hair behind each ear. "I always thought I'd been born this way, but Mother Angelini told me about how the nurses accidentally put fifty-one-percent silver nitrate into my eyes after my mother gave birth to me, instead of the normal one percent. They were trying to prevent some kind of illness, I guess, but instead they burned my eyes. But at least that explains why I dream of colors, and light, and tears. It's weird to know that I saw the world once, if only for a few minutes, then shadows for a few years, before everything went dark. That also explains why I can never cry, no matter how sad I feel. Because my tear ducts were seared shut."

William knew that Charlotte and he had both been here for more than five years and both lived with similar expectations—that is to say, neither of them had any. They'd been pinned down with thumbscrews of truth, preferring the monotony of melancholy to the nauseating highs and lows of hope and inevitable disappointment.

"Mother Angelini told me my mom was taken to a sanitarium—an asylum. She didn't come out and say it, but I guess that's where she's supposed to have died."

Charlotte stopped chewing for a moment. For a girl without the benefit of eyesight, she was terribly perceptive.

"But . . . you don't believe her, do you?"

How can I? William scratched his head and furrowed his brow. "I . . . I *saw* her today—well, not in person, but I saw someone at the movie—on the screen, that looked just like her," he said. "I know how it sounds—totally crazy. I wanted to tell Sunny, anyone—even Sister Briganti. But no one would ever believe me."

"I believe you, William."

"How can you?"

"Seeing isn't believing. Feeling is believing."

She reached out and patted his coat, finding the space above his heart, where the handbill was safely tucked away. "I feel you."

One Man's Family

卍

(1934)

Because it was still the boys' birthday, the orphans were given the night off—no chores, no cleanup duty, nothing but free time in the parlor, where the Philco was tuned in to *Amos 'n Andy* on Portland's KGW, instead of Father Coughlin's show on CBS, which was Sister Briganti's favorite. William thought it was nice (though mildly alarming) to hear their headmistress chortle and laugh as she listened to the show, instead of watching her frown and scowl, nodding as Father Coughlin railed against the communists and socialists, who he said were ruining the country and prolonging economic hardships. He watched as she sat back and closed her eyes, smiling, even though she had a copy of Coughlin's newspaper, *Social Justice,* folded in her lap. On the table next to her sat two empty bottles of Rainier beer. *Farewell, Prohibition,* William thought. Even though during the Noble Experiment, everyone knew she had a secret stash that she enjoyed on special occasions. Seattle was always a foggy, rainy city, but during the temperance movement the county had remained especially wet.

Wind and rain pelted the windows as William sat on the wooden floor with Charlotte, working on a simple jigsaw puzzle of the Holy Family. He listened to the comforting crackle and pop of the fireplace and the soft tumblers of dice as other kids played Parcheesi.

Charlotte had found the all-important edge pieces and had success-fully completed the border, leaving William to work his way into the center. Looking at the stained-glass scene depicted on the box top, he could already tell that they were missing a handful of impor-tant pieces. But he kept working anyway, toward an incomplete picture. As he stared at the empty space he allowed himself to wonder—*Why did you leave me? Why didn't you write?* The lonely years had been easier to endure when he'd imagined his mother dead. He hurt and he grieved, but that sorrow was less heartbreak-ing than the thought of his ah-ma alive and well, leaving him behind like a stray dog.

"What did she look like?" Charlotte asked. She sat back and crossed her legs, covering them with her dress, dusting off her hands. "The woman you saw on the movie screen. What did she look like? I mean, how did you know it was her? Was she stunning, like you?" she joked.

William shrugged, oblivious to Charlotte's flirtations, and pawed through the loose pieces. "She looked . . . Chinese." Then he real-ized that Charlotte had no idea what a Chinese person looked like, or a black person, or Indian, or Italian—she didn't even know her own skin color.

"She had bright eyes, with long eyelashes and shoulder-length hair that was curled at the ends. And she looked . . . rich. But my mother was poor." *We were poor,* William recalled, *even before the Crash and all the jobs went away.* "My own mother had . . . long fingers, with wrinkly knuckles that made her hands look much older than the rest of her." He looked at his own fingers, which were the same way. "And when she'd fall asleep on the sofa, I used to sit and watch her breathe, her chest rising and falling—just to make sure she was still alive. She looked so peaceful, but she was the only fam-ily I had. I was always afraid of losing her. I hated the thought of being alone. But the lady today, it was her voice that I recognized most. Her singing voice."

"Did your mother sing to you?"

William nodded, slowly. "Sometimes. At bedtime she'd sing Chinese lullabies that I barely understood, or a British tune that went: 'Isn't this precious darling of ours / Sweeter than dates and cinnamon flowers.' I can hum the rest, but I don't remember the words. It was a long, long time ago . . ."

"You're lucky. I hardly remember my mother at all. I used to try and remember what her voice sounded like. Like mine, I guess, but wiser."

He knew that Charlotte's mother had died a few years after she'd been born. And like William, she never mentioned her father. He wanted to ask more, but he'd learned that, in the orphanage, it was better not to pry about things not freely spoken.

As *Amos 'n Andy* ended, he looked up at Sister Briganti, expecting her to begin shooing them off to bed, but she'd fallen asleep. Her head slumped back and her Franciscan habit draped over the chair like a pile of brown laundry. As he exchanged glances with Sunny, who was in the corner playing tiddlywinks with Dante Grimaldi, and the other kids in the room, the unspoken sentiment was *Play on.*

William continued to sort puzzle pieces as the radio announcer introduced the local businesses that would be sponsoring tonight's episode of *One Man's Family.*

Sister Briganti snorted twice but didn't wake up, even as thunder rolled in the distance and the electricity flickered off and on, causing a few of the kids to gasp and squeal, while Sunny made ghostly booing sounds.

"But before we begin"—the announcer spoke in a droll, monotone voice, fading in and out with the encroaching storm—"I'd like to introduce tonight's very special in-studio guest, an up-and-comer who's come home to the Great Northwest with Hollywood glitter on her shoes. Not since Bing Crosby and the Rhythm Boys left Tacoma have we had such local talent hit the big time."

William froze, staring at the radio, a puzzle piece dangling from his fingertips.

"And now she's back for a limited series of engagements, on loan to us from the Fox Movietone Follies. Ladies and gentlemen, here's the China doll to top them all, the Asian sensation from Seattle, Weepin' Willow Frost."

I don't believe it, William thought, as he sat spellbound while Willow and the announcer exchanged pleasantries.

"Now, Miss Frost . . ."

"Please, just call me Willow."

"Ah, Willow it is," the announcer said. "I'm curious about your 'Weeping' moniker. I wonder if you might be able to share with us the story behind that."

"Oh, I dread that nickname," she said in a modest, polite way that barely masked how tired she seemed of this question. "It makes me sound like such a sorrowful person all the time. But the truth is, an old friend . . ." She hesitated. "An acquaintance of mine gave me that name after a walk-on appearance. I had just learned some unpleasant news and forgot my lines for a moment. My eyes welled up, and by the time I remembered my part, I was crying. I sobbed my way through the script—luckily, it was a sad scene. I ended up getting discovered afterward—that was my first film."

"Some would call that fate," the announcer said. "Or was it just good acting?"

There was an awkward pause. William wasn't sure if the weather was affecting the broadcast or if she really was uncomfortable talking about her big break.

"It was just luck. Pure and simple," she said quietly. "A year later I was on a set in Studio City trading lines with Ronald Colman and Tetsu Komai in *Bulldog Drummond*. And here I am now . . ."

"And here you are, and we are delighted to have you." The announcer brightened and introduced Willow and the station's call letters once again.

"That's her," William whispered to Charlotte. Then he looked across the room to Sunny, who stared back and gave him a thumbs-up as a piano played on the radio and Willow began singing "Dream a Little Dream of Me."

"This is so booooring," a boy said from across the room. "Somebody get up and change the station to KJR."

"Yeah, let's listen to *The Shadow,*" someone else chimed.

"The Shadow knows this is boring," another boy teased.

"Don't touch the radio," William blurted. "Please!"

"Hey, you heard this already this afternoon . . ."

"I want to hear her too," Charlotte said, waving her cane.

Dante was about to touch the dial when William leapt to his feet, his heart racing as he shoved him out of the way. Dante tripped over a footstool and tumbled noisily to the floor. Some of the boys laughed, a few of the girls too.

"Hey!" Dante wailed as tears welled in his eyes. "What'd'cha do that for?"

William stood in front of the speaker, listening intently, his heart pounding.

"William Eng!"

He didn't need to turn around. He recognized Sister Briganti's voice immediately. She must have stirred awake in all the commotion. William glanced over his shoulder and saw her looking at her wristwatch, then at everyone who hadn't yet gone to bed.

"William—come here!" she snapped. "The rest of you—upstairs."

He felt her pinch his elbow as she dragged him away from Charlotte, away from the radio to the foyer. Sister Briganti opened the door to the cloakroom, smacked him on the head, and shoved him inside.

"If you can't behave, we'll have to separate you from the rest . . ."

"I'm sorry, I didn't mean it," he protested. "I just wanted to listen to the radio a little bit longer—you have to let me hear the radio." *I need to hear Willow Frost.*

Sister Briganti paused and rubbed her forehead as though considering his plea, but then she slammed the door. William stared down at the sliver of light beneath the door and at the glimmer from the keyhole. It too went dark as he heard a key being inserted and turned, locking him in for the night. He felt for the back wall, found it, and slumped down, coming to rest on a pile of old shoes and galoshes. The entire closet smelled of wool coats, wet leather, and mothballs. He banged his head against the wall until he heard the radio fading in and out as the announcer was interviewing Willow again.

"And so you grew up just north of here," the announcer said.

"I did, I grew up in Washington—in Seattle's Chinatown, but I left years ago," she said. "I never thought I'd go back, not in a million years."

"And why is that?"

William strained to listen as she paused. He waited in the darkness, eyes wide open, his ear to the door, hearing the tatter of rain lashing the building.

"I . . . I didn't have any reason to, I guess. I didn't have a reason to stay."

The volume faded as Sister Briganti turned the radio off with a disappointing click, then the lights. William heard footsteps in the dark as she trudged upstairs.

Alone Together

꾀

(1934)

Like most of the boys, William had spent a night or two in the cloakroom. Sometimes it was warranted, like the time Sister Briganti caught him pitching pennies in the chapel. Other times it was merely a case of being in the wrong place at the wrong time. But as far as punishments went, spending a night in the closet wasn't as bad as being locked in the boiler room, which was hot, even in winter, and redolent of the fiery, sulfuric Hell the sisters warned everyone about. And the place was so noisy that no one could hear you cry or scream. William remembered that Sunny had once been caught fighting and spent three days locked up down there. Sunny never threw another punch, not even when the two boys were working on an old crystal radio kit donated by the Boy Scouts and Dante walked by, flipped the box over, and said, "I've got a new name for you: Sunny Mess-maker." Dante laughed as the pieces—wires, tuning knobs—scattered and the delicate cat's-whisker receiver was broken. Without that fine-tipped wire, the homemade radio would never work. One of the girls expected a fight and ran to get a teacher, but Sunny didn't say a cross word, he just stared out the window as black coal smoke belched into the sky.

But like so many orphans, William most feared being alone. *It's just one night,* he reasoned. After five years of sleeping in the same room with two dozen other boys, the absence of snoring, giggling, whispering, even the squeaking of old bedsprings, left nothing but the sound of the timbers shifting, pipes groaning, and the storm winds rattling the windowpanes. The unsettling sounds of emptiness, the chords of solitude, caused William to feel a rise of panic as the echoes of a grandfather clock chiming somewhere two stories above reminded him just how long that night would be.

I didn't have a reason to stay. Willow's words echoed in his mind.

In the darkness he shoved aside the shoes and boots. He pulled down two woolen coats and, like some feral creature, tried to create a makeshift bed. But the tinkling of metal hangers and the swaying shapes in the dark kept him awake. Plus he thought he heard footsteps, or light tapping. *It's just the creaking of floorboards,* William thought. *This building is new and still settling.* He knew it was doubtful that Sister Briganti had changed her mind about his punishment— if anything, she'd forget about him until someone needed a raincoat or until he wet the floor, whichever came first the next day.

He pulled down another coat and was using it as a blanket when he heard the unmistakable sound of a key rattling in the lock. He reached up and felt the doorknob turn, then jumped back.

"William," a girl's voice whispered as the door cracked open.

"Charlotte?" he asked the shape in the dark. Then he felt her hand touch his arm as she crawled in next to him, sitting with her back against the wall, her knees up, her cane in front of her. He poked his head out into the blackened hallway. A faint glow came from down the corridor. A night-light flickered off and on as the rain pounded and lightning flashed. He heard a loud rumble in the distance as he closed the door. "What are you doing here? How did you . . . ?"

"Sister B leaves the key in the candle drawer in the hallway, I always hear her put it away," Charlotte said, her voice quavering. "I . . . I don't like nights like this, especially in my cottage. Sometimes I come down here and hide when the weather is this bad." She sniffled and wiped her nose on the sleeve of her long flannel nightgown.

"It's . . . just a thunderstorm," William said. "We're in a big building. It's completely safe. Even if the power goes out . . ."

Lightning flashed beneath the door, illuminating Charlotte as she pulled her knees tighter against her chest and thunder rattled the building. He wrapped a coat around her even as she flinched.

"Would it be better if I left you alone?" he asked, unsure of where he might go.

She shook her head. "Please stay."

"Are you afraid of the dark? It's okay if you are . . ." As soon as he said it he realized what a ridiculous statement that was. He was about to apologize . . .

"I'm not afraid of the dark."

"The storm will pass, I promise . . ."

"I'm not afraid of the storm either."

William sat in the darkness, confused, but relieved to have her company—anyone's company. Charlotte had been his best friend and, until Sunny arrived, his only friend. He scooted over and sat next to her. She leaned into him, resting her head on his shoulder. Then she reached up, hung her cane from the rack overhead, and offered him part of the coat. He wrapped it around the two of them as her shoulders shook. She was wet, trembling and shivering.

"What are you so afraid of?" *Besides the storm, the teachers, the whippings . . .*

Silence. He felt her slowly shake her head and inhale deeply, exhaling as though she were completely fatigued, exhausted.

"My mother used to light candles and sing whenever the power went out," he said. "She told me the thunder was applause, the lightning, Heaven's spotlight. I would climb into bed next to her and she'd wrap her arms around me until I fell asleep."

"You're so lucky, William."

For a moment he actually felt that way, then, and now, to no longer be so alone.

"After my mother died," Charlotte whispered, "it was just my father—he always came into my room on stormy nights—'just to make sure I was okay.' He hardly said a word. I couldn't see him, of course, but I knew who it was."

William paused, not fully comprehending what she was saying. He had always wondered what happened to her father. Before he could ask, she changed the subject.

"I have to leave this place—soon."

"Why? You've been here longer than I have . . ." *And who would take you?*

"They're going to send me away," she said. "They say I don't belong here anymore. They're going to send me to a special school for people like me. Sister B says it's time I was with my own kind."

William swallowed and chewed his lip. He remembered the past few summers, when farmers from the Yakima Valley would come to Sacred Heart and adopt the strongest boys or, occasionally, the prettiest girls. William knew then that no one would ever adopt a blind girl, no matter how comely she might be.

"But, where would you go?" he asked. "Maybe the special school isn't so bad. They could teach you how to read with your fingers . . ."

He felt her shaking her head.

"I know all about that place. My father used to threaten to send me there if I didn't do as I was told or if I said anything bad about him. They have you sit in a room and make brooms all day. That's all they ever do, until you're too old to do anything else. And if you refuse or complain they send you to a lockup."

That was the one good thing about Sacred Heart. Despite children's worst indiscretions, Sister Briganti would rarely cast them out. William had heard rumors that the state paid the school a fixed amount per child, so to the sisters a crowded orphanage wasn't a complete tragedy.

William didn't know what words he could offer that might comfort Charlotte. If the sisters thought that a special school would be better for her, their decision would be irrefutable. And where else could she go? She didn't have any other options.

Charlotte drew a deep breath and let it out slowly.

"I want to go with *you*," she said.

"And where am I going?" he asked, though he had a vague idea—a wistful dream, a hope, an unmade plan.

"I want to go with you to find her."

"Willow?" William asked as he caught the scent of Charlotte's floral shampoo, a welcome respite from the dank-smelling closet. After living in the boys' sweaty dormitory for so long, he was suddenly aware of how much he missed the comforting smell of perfume, the fragrances of home.

"Your mother."

"I don't even know who that woman really is. Sister Briganti might be right, I could just be letting my imagination get the better of me." *This mirage probably happens to everyone at some point,* William thought. *The joyful dreams of sad, lonely children are difficult to wake up from.*

Charlotte pulled down another coat and draped it over them. She leaned into him as he listened to the rain and her breathing until he thought she'd drifted to sleep.

Then she stirred, just for a moment. "Think about it, Willie. We both have nothing, and nobody wants us," she murmured. "So that just means we have nothing to lose."

William stared into the darkness, wondering if this was how Charlotte perceived the world. Then he realized she probably didn't see *anything*. So instead, she saw the world through her imagination—which had to be better than real life.

He listened to her breathing until she fell into a restless sleep, twitching and occasionally crying out, softly.

Pigs Get Fed

(1934)

When William woke, Charlotte was gone, like his mother, leaving him to wonder if she'd ever been there at all. A janitor let him out, and William stretched his tired legs, then limped back to his dormitory, his back aching as he went about his day.

That night he was grateful to sleep once again in his own bed, where all week long he dreamt of the Movietone Follies and each sunrise he woke up, torpidly searching for the sad melodies of songs with long-forgotten lyrics. As he counted the rain-soaked days and his mornings with dry sheets, inching closer on the calendar to when Willow Frost (he couldn't quite call her his mother) would be performing, he thought about Charlotte's desire to run away. *There is nothing here. And no one is coming for us, no one at all.* He knew she was right, but still, he hesitated.

When he rolled over in bed he stared at Willow's picture; then he sat upright, scratching his head as the others brushed their teeth and got dressed. Some of the boys had regal, sepia-toned portraits of themselves with their parents displayed prominently on their nightstands. But all William had was the dog-eared photo from the handbill that he'd placed near his bed in a frame crafted from Popsicle sticks and rubber cement. Looking at the photo, he was convinced they had the same eyes, the same chin. In his memory, his ah-ma's nose had rounded slightly to the left. He couldn't tell from the head shot because Willow was showing her good side, backlit Hollywood-style, but he remembered that unmistakable bend. And in turn, he wondered what she would remember about him. He was little and remembered less. She was a mother. *How could a mother forget?* he wondered. *How could a mother leave her child behind?*

AFTER BREAKFAST HE grabbed his books and hurried upstairs to his classroom, where thirty-five children crowded into neat rows, boys on the left, girls on the right, two to each desk—all but Marco, who seemed to relish having his own space, even if it was a wheel-chair in a corner at the front of the room.

William wedged himself into a wooden seat in the back, next to Dante, who was twice his size but clumsy and loping like a big dog that didn't know how enormous he really was. "Sorry about the other night," William whispered. "You can punch me in the arm if you wanna get even."

"No need." Dante shook his head. "A night in the cloakroom is punishment enough. Too much if you ask me."

Dante had grown tired of the sisters calling him Danny. "Too Irish," he'd said, and now he wanted to be called Sawyer, in homage to his late lumberjack father. For a big son of a lumberjack, Sawyer cried an awful lot.

Instead of listening to Sister Seeley go on about arithmetic, William stared out the window, watching autumn settle upon Sacred Heart like a blanket of wet magnolia leaves. He calculated how he and Charlotte could get away to the 5th Avenue Theatre, the Pantages, or the Palace Hippodrome—wherever Willow would soon be appearing. He'd never been inside any of those venues but had always marveled at the posters on the street; even the old ones that were faded and peeling still thrilled him with images of ice-skating couples, animal acts, magicians with spangled waistcoats, and child performers like Dainty June Hovick—the Darling of Vaudeville. *Admission is usually twenty-five cents,* William thought. But Willow's show might cost a bit more. He had a whole dollar in coins, hidden beneath a rock in the grotto, but with four-penny flophouses now advertised as two bits a night, plus trolley fare and transfer on top of that, they wouldn't last a week in the city. *And winter is just around the corner.*

"You're still thinking about that show, aren't you?" Sunny whispered from his desk across the aisle. William shook his head. "You get caught, they'll kick you out for sure. They'll sell you to a poor farm that'll make this place look like Heaven on Earth."

Heaven, William realized, *some kids actually love this place.* Which only made him wonder how bad their lives must have been on the outside. But as a Chinese boy who always struggled to fit in, he knew he didn't belong here. From the way the other kids looked at him and called him *chink* to their mortified reactions when he told them his favorite snack was barbecued chicken feet. Tommy Yuen had known it too. This was not their kind of paradise. *Though Sunny is right.* Just last month they'd learned that the board of trustees had voted to expel all the colored kids—sending them to the King County Poor Farm, down by the rills of the Duwamish River. There they'd be indentured workers until they turned twenty-one, without the possibility of placement or adoption.

William feared the poor farm even though he'd only seen it through the nickelodeon of his imagination, cranked to high speed by the stories Sister Briganti shared. "The poor farm isn't a place of charity, it's a den of iniquity. When you're sent there they publish your name in the newspaper for all the world to see," she'd said. "When you recite your bedtime prayers, give thanks that you're not bunking next to grown men—drunkards, layabouts, and stew bums—the lot of them cursing, fighting, and causing trouble. Or some rapacious old beaucatcher, probably touched in the head. They'll steal your shoes while you sleep, just to make a pot of soup with the leather."

William blinked as Sister Seeley caught him daydreaming.

"Willie," she said. "Why don't you come to the board and solve this equation for us?" She held out a piece of chalk and cocked her other hand on her hip.

William walked to the front of the classroom and stared numbly at the blackboard, still thinking of how he could possibly manage outside, with or without Charlotte. *Was it worth the risk?* As he felt the piece of chalk in his hand, he missed the way his mother had helped him with his schoolwork when he was in the second grade. She'd been so cheerful, so content, and so incredibly proud. He vaguely remembered echoing those feelings. He wondered if he would even recognize that kind of love and adoration anymore. Everything was muddled now. He regarded the chalkboard. Somehow life had become a story problem, and William was terrible at math.

"WE SHOULD DO it—we should run away," Charlotte whispered to William at lunchtime, half-daring, half-pleading. "We could team up." She spoke with such enthusiasm, such ridiculous, impractical confidence—the way a little kid would see Mount Rainier peeking through the clouds eighty miles away and blurt, "We should climb it."

William wasn't so convinced. At Sacred Heart he could never get *enough* time with friends, but out in the real world, he'd be her eyes, her caregiver—her protector. She was his best friend, but he wasn't sure if he could handle that much responsibility. *I don't know how I'd provide for myself,* he worried. He wished he had someone to call on, but most of his ah-ma's relatives had died from the Spanish flu, and the only cousins whose names he could remember had left years ago.

William asked, "Do you have anyone that could help us?" He watched as she felt the edge of her plate and turned it clockwise, eating and wiping her chin with a napkin.

"I have some relatives," she said. "But I'm the *white sheep* of my family."

He didn't quite understand as he regarded Charlotte's fair skin and ginger hair.

"I'm the only normal one. My father and all his brothers are behind bars on McNeil Island." She smiled as she spoke, tucking her spoon into a heap of crab-apple pudding. William wasn't sure if she was happy that her father was imprisoned or happy with her dessert. "And my grandma has her hands full taking care of my grandpa, who lost his wits in the Spanish war. I don't know if she'd help us. I know she'd feed us, but she'd probably turn around and bring us right back here."

Sister Briganti constantly reminded them that there were starving children out there, despite the fact that those kids still had able-bodied parents—times were that bad for everyone. William looked down at his sandwich and frowned. *Tomato.* He'd eaten tomato sandwiches every day since August. Soon, they'd switch to zucchini for the winter months, which only made him long for tomatoes again. Lunch seemed like a wide, colorful variety compared to breakfast, which was always oatmeal. He hated the warm mush because he was next to last in line and had to pick out the weevils that settled at the bottom. Sunny, who was dead last, refused his porridge one morning. He told the sisters he wasn't hungry and stared back defiantly. That got him a whipping for being obdurate and a double helping the next day. He ate it without bothering to pick out the bugs, then threw up all over one of the sisters. William didn't bother to ask if Sunny did it on purpose.

William shook his head. "I don't know—I don't like it here any more than the rest, but it sounds awfully tough out there." *And who knows what might happen if we got caught? Sister Briganti would probably make us say the Hail Mary a thousand times and then still send us to the poorhouse.*

"Well, I'm leaving, William—with or without you. And I'm not coming back," she said and then paused as though waiting for his reaction. "Ever."

William took a bite and chewed the stale bread. "But . . . how will you live? What're you going to do, steal lead from chimneys? Sell fruit on the street?" A girl in her condition, leaving, running away—it seemed like such foolishness. But even as he said those words of doubt, he felt an overwhelming admiration—for her courage, her *blind* ambition. She wasn't about to settle for making brooms or sewing buttons on coats for the rest of her life. *Surely if a sightless girl wasn't afraid . . .*

"We'll find something," she said, staring at nothing, yet smiling at everything.

Or someone, William thought. *If Willow is my ah-ma, she has to take me back, doesn't she?* She probably figured that another family had adopted him—case closed, William reasoned. *Why else would she leave me here? When she realizes I'm her long-lost son, we'll send Mother Angelini a picture postcard of the two of us in front of the Hollywoodland sign.* William pictured the prioress dropping dead of a thrombosis right there in her office. But he also imagined something darker. He struggled to contain his fears, his doubts that were just below the thin icy surface of hope—lurking beneath was the possibility of finding out that she really didn't want him at all.

Before Charlotte could press her argument, a wave of silence rippled through the lunchroom as Sister Briganti appeared, ruler in hand. She glided past, saying, *"Porci pinguescunt porcis adepto mactatos,"* in a cheery, singsong voice. The Latin aphorism meant Pigs get fat, hogs get slaughtered, and was supposed to be about working hard and avoiding sloth, but she said it only in the cafeteria, much to her own amusement, an inside joke between her and the Holy Ghost.

"I have a most special surprise for you after lunch," she said. "So eat up, little piglets. Don't dillydally. Don't lollygag. Don't miss out."

As children whispered and scraped their plates, William heard a truck rumbling up to the porte cochere in front of the school. A horn honked as though on cue.

"Probably a slaughterhouse on wheels," Sunny remarked as he walked by. "I saw one of those back home on the reservation. They march pigs up a ramp and then a giant blade chops their heads off."

A girl at the next table overheard Sunny and said, "Ewwww . . ."

Because of Sunny's deadpan voice, William was never sure when he was joking. And when he playfully punched William in the arm, Sunny still didn't smile.

"When you clean your plate you may come outside," Sister Briganti announced with a snap of her fingers; tucking the ruler up her sleeve, she glided out the door. William hurried to finish his sandwich and gulped it down with a tin cup of warm powdered milk. He stood up and felt a hand on his shoulder as Charlotte found the crook of his arm and let him lead her out the front door and down the stairs with the rest of the herd. In their excitement they didn't even stop to get their coats or hats.

Idling in the courtyard was an enormous truck with the words KING COUNTY painted on the door. The rear of the truck was enclosed like a bus but windowless, though there were shuttered panels on each side. William watched as a mysterious ramp extended from the back to the mossy grass, like the gangplank of a steamship.

He explained what he was seeing to Charlotte, and she nodded along and fidgeted with her cane. Then he felt someone tap his other arm.

"I told you so," Sunny said, making oinking noises and snorting like a pig.

William knew he was joking—he had to be, but the truck made him nervous nonetheless. He held out hope that it was a traveling act, like the puppet show put on by the Junior League or a brass ensemble.

Sister Briganti motioned to the driver, who turned the engine off.

Much to William's surprise, a young woman with short brown hair stepped out of the cab, smiling and waving, peering at everyone over her spectacles. She peeled off her driving gloves and adjusted her hat.

"Since we can't go to the library," Sister Briganti said, "the library has agreed to come to us—they call it a bookmobile. This is Miss Fredericks."

William didn't quite understand until the librarian rolled up the shuttered panels to reveal hundreds of books. There were even folding step stools for the shorter kids. Some of the children clapped and squealed so loudly that they scared the birds from the trees overhead. Then Miss Fredericks climbed up the ramp and wheeled down a squeaking metal cart filled with picture books. One of the sisters rolled it toward the infants' home as everyone lined up, standing on tippy-toes, peering over each other's shoulders to get a better look. William forgot about his mother for a moment as he spied books by Defoe, Dickens, Hawthorne, and Longfellow, and countless other names he didn't recognize. And there were entire shelves dedicated to Oliver Optic, Horatio Alger, and even the Hardy Boys. There were also pamphlets on modern evils. Sister Briganti thumbed through one called *Orgies of the Hemp Eaters* and another one about teetotalism. Until last year Prohibition had outlawed alcohol for as long as William could remember, which only confused him the first time he tasted wine during communion. *God must have handpicked exceptions,* he thought.

William's excitement grew as the line shortened and smiling, delighted children began wandering off, books in hand, finding places to sit and read. William had been to the public library only once before, on a field trip, and even though he wasn't allowed to check out anything, he never forgot how it felt to wander in and see books on shelves as high as the ceiling. *The library is like a candy store where everything is free.*

Sunny, Charlotte, and he took a step closer.

"Please pick something out for me, William," Charlotte said as she tapped her cane. "I'd love for you to read it to me."

William patted her arm. "I will, I promise," he said. Then he felt someone grab the back of his shirt, almost popping off his back collar button.

Sister Briganti pulled Sunny and him aside. "Not until the kitchen is clean," she said sternly, raising her eyebrows as she marched them back toward the cafeteria.

"Yes, ma'am," they replied in unison. As they walked, William turned back and saw Charlotte looking dejected, leaning on her cane and staring in the direction of the bookmobile. The librarian smiled uncomfortably and politely ignored her.

At the orphanage everyone took turns sweeping floors, scrubbing toilets, washing dishes, and doing laundry. In all of the excitement, William had forgotten his assignment for the day—kitchen cleanup. As Sunny donned an apron and began washing the dishes, William hauled out the trash, each of them working faster than usual, afraid that the marvelous library on wheels would leave while they labored.

William dragged the garbage cans behind the main building, where he separated the refuse into large bins. One was for normal garbage. The other was filled with vegetable peels, apple cores, and other food scraps that local pig farmers would pick up and use for slop. He was so excited about the bookmobile that he began to think Sacred Heart wasn't so bad. *Maybe it's safer if I just write to her*, he reasoned. *If she knows I'm here she'll come for me. Dear Willow Frost . . .*

Then William looked into one of the bins and saw a familiar face on a crinkled piece of paper—his photo of Willow, covered in eggshells and soiled coffee grounds. He fished it out with a stick, then wiped the image clean with his shirttail, doing his best to dry it off, smoothing out the wrinkles. He surmised that Sister Briganti didn't approve of the glamorous photo and had crumpled it. *She must have tossed it out with the morning garbage.* William gently folded the damp picture and slipped it into his pocket. Then he snuck back into the dormitory and regarded the blank spot where his Popsicle frame had been. Alone he sat at the foot of his bunk, where he took out the picture, which still smelled of rotting fruit. He gazed at the strange, mysterious woman and whispered, "Why, Ah-ma?" as the ghost of his mother stared back.

Checking Out

꒰

(1934)

William spent most of that cold, drizzly Saturday afternoon stuck inside, atop a stepladder as he cleaned the third-floor windows. The tender skin on his fingers had wrinkled and pruned as he dipped sponges, again and again, into wooden buckets filled with vinegar and water. He gazed through the spotless glass as he wiped the surface dry with old newspapers. He admired the lofty view, staring through the fog toward Chinatown, trying to remember the smells of the Tai Tung Restaurant, the taste of sesame on oily chow fun noodles, and the sound of his mother's voice. *I have to leave,* William resolved. He'd been driven to distraction by the thought of Willow coming to town and then vanishing before he ever had an opportunity to look into her eyes, searching for answers to his brokenhearted questions. As William regarded the panorama of mist and tall buildings, he noticed his own reflection—the shape of his face, his chin, which mirrored that of the mysterious woman he'd seen on-screen. He watched the light change in the polished glass as he tried to divine his future, a Gypsy peering into a crystal ball, seeking substance from shadow. Then Sister Briganti walked by and barked at him for daydreaming, lollygagging, and for wiping his hands on his breeches, where he'd left inky fingerprints and streaks of yesterday.

William cleaned up and met Charlotte after dinner in the study lounge. She needed someone to read her history assignment for her, so William had volunteered, as he always did, even though he still struggled with the big words and complicated, Western-sounding names. As he read aloud, he looked about, knowing he was Charlotte's only option for help because the other kids acted so queer around her. When others read to her, they'd increase the volume of their voices as if she were deaf, or phrase things in simple terms as if she were dim. Sitting next to Charlotte, William remembered all the times a new boy would arrive, how that boy would turn his head when he saw her strawberry-red hair, only to quickly lose interest when he noticed her cane and those wide, milky eyes, which never found what they were searching for.

"When do you want to do it?" Charlotte asked.

"Shouldn't we keep working on history?"

"This place will be history once we leave."

William hesitated, then shrugged, closing the book in his lap as he looked around to make sure no one was listening in. "Well, according to the newspaper, the Movietone Players begin their run next Friday at the 5th Avenue Theatre. I think we should look for the best opportunity, for the best weather, but the later in the week the better."

Charlotte nodded.

The closer to curtain, William reasoned, *the less time they'd have to fend for themselves before the big show.* Plus that allowed him a few more days to save crackers, biscuits, and bread crusts from every meal. He had a bounty wrapped in a large piece of cheesecloth left over from the kitchen. The scraps would be enough to feed them for a week. Their bellies would never be full, but they wouldn't starve, at least not right away.

"I still don't know how we'll make it on our own." *We need money,* William thought. *We won't last more than a week . . .*

"I'll beg if I have to," Charlotte said. "I'm not too proud."

It may come to that, William worried, as he recalled the streetcar ride back from the theater and the dozens of men he saw with signs, seeking food, seeking work, seeking shelter. Sunny had once talked about being hired by a downtown apartment manager to run from room to room, twice a day, sniffing beneath the doors for the smell of gas. People were out of work and starving. The pitiful conditions got so bad that hundreds had committed suicide, all over the city. William remembered his mother's pale, limp body and shuddered. He could never do that job. With any luck they could sell newspapers—that's what most of the kids his age seemed to do. But Dante used to work as a newsie. He said it was a terrible job and that he constantly fought with the other kids over territory. Dante finally quit after showing up late and seeing a group of newsboys standing in a semicircle peeing on his bundle of papers.

"I have about a dollar saved up," William said. "How much do you have?"

"Four dollars and fifty cents."

William sat upright. "How'd you get that much?"

"My grandma sends me a dollar for every birthday. I've saved most of it—what is there to spend it on?"

William sat back, wide-eyed. He wasn't sure what was more surprising—that Charlotte had that much money or that Sister Briganti actually let her keep it.

ALL WEEK WILLIAM bided his time, looking for the best opportunity. Then on Thursday morning, while walking to class, he noticed the other kids carrying their library books. He couldn't help but smile when he realized the bookmobile was coming back that afternoon. He sat in Sister Briganti's religion class, listening to her drone on about Moses and Exodus as he waited impatiently for her to turn and address the blackboard. That's when he slipped a note to the boy next to him, who passed the folded piece of paper along to the girl who shared a desk with Charlotte. The note asked the girl to whisper, "Let's check out during library. Meet me in the grotto."

William watched as the girl quietly delivered the message then looked back at him and shrugged, somewhat confused. Charlotte merely turned her face to the boys' side of the room and slowly nodded her head, trying not to smile as Sister Briganti cleared her throat to get everyone's attention.

William snuck away from lunch and gathered up his knapsack and a few belongings—his hat, scarf, mittens, and an extra pair of socks. What he couldn't take, he hid in Sunny's cubby along with a brief note saying goodbye and that he'd write to him when he could. Then he slipped down to the grotto and retrieved the coins he'd hidden. There was a single stick of fragrant incense left smoldering in a rusty brazier. He thought about his long-lost mother, about Willow and Charlotte. He even thought about kneeling and offering a half-hearted prayer, but then he waved the smoke away. The state had required William to be christened when he was little, but whatever faith was to be had in that strange ceremony, he'd never found it.

When he heard the soft tapping of Charlotte's cane, he turned and saw her wending her way toward him. After five years, she'd learned to navigate the school grounds with relative ease, as long as she stuck to the brick-lined paths. Charlotte was known to spend time in the grotto, so it was doubtful that anyone would suspect a thing if they saw her there now.

"I'm here," William whispered as he brushed pine needles from a stone bench. They sat together, both grateful that it wasn't too cold or raining.

"Are you ready for this?" she asked.

He shook his head—grateful she couldn't see his doubt. "Ready if you are."

She nodded and smiled, beaming as though this were the best day of her life.

"We'll wait until everyone is distracted by the bookmobile," William said. "That's when we'll head to the gate and then to the nearest streetcar platform. I'm not sure when the car comes, but we can probably keep walking south, in the direction of downtown, and it'll pick us up somewhere along the line—we just need to get farther away in case . . ."

"In case Sister B comes looking for us. Do you think she'll even notice?"

William wasn't sure. No one had seemed to care or even mention Tommy Yuen when he'd vanished. *Maybe there were too many sheep in the flock,* William said to himself. *If one or two went missing, did anyone even bother?*

They both looked skyward as birds whorled above them. William saw a flock of petrels heading south; then scores of smaller birds vacated the trees, beating their wings in sudden retreat as a loud diesel engine rumbled and pinged. William heard brakes squealing from down the lane. *Perfect timing.*

"It's here, get down," he said.

As the bookmobile clattered to a stop in the rear courtyard, William peeked through the greenery and saw dozens of cheering children descending the school steps. He could hear Sister Briganti commanding them to stop behaving like animals, snapping her fingers and barking at them to line up in an orderly fashion.

"Now's our chance," William said. Then he stood and looked over the hedge toward the school entrance and the unlocked gate, which was all that stood between them and whatever waited *out there.* His hope vanished as he saw two sisters near the gate and one of the custodians. One sister stayed near the entrance while the others walked along the fence as though searching for something, or someone.

"Why aren't we going?" Charlotte asked.

Not possible. Not fair. William hesitated, trying to process what he was seeing.

"There's someone down there," he said in disbelief. "Did you tell anyone we were leaving? Did you accidentally say anything . . . ?"

"I didn't tell a soul—I swear, who would I tell?"

William rubbed his temple. *It must have been me.* He worried as he remembered the note he'd passed. The girl who'd whispered to Charlotte must have told someone, who told someone else, and that gossip had eventually reached the ears of someone in charge.

"William Eng!" a woman called through the trees, from the direction of the school.

"It's Sister B," Charlotte whispered. Her voice was laced with panic.

William's heart pounded. His first thought was to make a break for it. He could sprint through the trees until he reached the fence— then up and over. *I can outrun any of the sisters, probably the janitor as well. But what do I do about Charlotte?* he fretted. *I can't leave her behind.*

"It's okay," Charlotte said softly, calmly.

"It's not, this nixes everything . . ."

She reached out and took William's hand. "We can just tell her we came here—to the grotto—to spend some time alone."

"Doing what?" William asked, furrowing his brow.

She stared in his direction with her other hand on her hip. She raised her eyebrows. "You know—what boys and girls sneak off *for.*"

William blushed. He understood, grateful that she couldn't see his face.

He was about to agree with that plan when he peered through the trees and saw the librarian, Miss Fredericks, pushing the wheeled cart of picture books toward the infants' home. And he caught a glimpse of Sister Briganti marching down the brick path.

We can do this. "There's still a chance. Do you trust me?"

"Of course."

"Then I have another idea. We're gonna crawl through the hedges." He took her wrist, and they both got on their hands and knees. He instructed her to hold on to his ankle and follow him as they burrowed their way like rabbits through the thick hedgerow and the next, until they were standing near the lane between the school and the gate.

"Are we going to run now?" Charlotte asked, brushing leaves and needles from her sweater. She gripped her cane and stepped downhill toward the gate.

"No, we're going to ride." He took her hand and quickly led her back toward the school and the bookmobile.

He heard Sister Briganti arrive in the grotto. "William Eng— I know you're out here somewhere. And Miss Rigg, you know I'll find you too, and when I do . . ."

Charlotte covered her mouth and giggled as Sister Briganti began shouting angrily in Italian. "*Ho il mio occhio su di te e* Malocchio *troppo!*"

The only word William recognized referenced something about the *evil eye*. He imagined the statuary of saints wincing and covering their ears.

With Miss Fredericks gone and most of the children on the other side of the bookmobile, William led Charlotte through the driver's door. The outside panels had been raised on the opposite side, and most of the kids were focused on the rows of books, or had their heads down, lost in stories of pirates or runaway slaves—all but Sunny, who stood in the back of the line, waiting impatiently. William saw his eyes widen in shock when they spotted each other through the passenger window. *So long, Sunny,* William thought as he put his finger to his lips and led Charlotte into the back of the truck, behind the enormous shelves where there were boxes and crates of books. He found a large, wheeled bin, half-full with hard-bound books. He and Charlotte climbed inside, digging their way to the bottom, their legs tangled together as they covered themselves as best they could with copies of *Pudd'nhead Wilson, The Prince and the Pauper,* and *Huckleberry Finn.* William waited, in that uncomfortable heap, his heart racing and his temples throbbing with fear and excitement.

"This is an adventure worth writing about," Charlotte whispered.

Before he could agree William heard the librarian return, banging up the ramp with the cart. He took Charlotte's hand, and they quietly slumped down as deep as they could. He felt the book cart slam against their bin, and heard Miss Fredericks locking the wheel so it wouldn't roll. The librarian said something about needing some coffee, then shoved the ramp back into the bookmobile and closed the door, leaving them in shadows. William pushed the books aside so he and Charlotte could breathe and have a little more room, untangling their legs, though she didn't seem to mind.

He peeked up from the bin and saw the librarian climb into the driver's seat, start the noisy engine, and then light a cigarette, tossing the match out the window before rolling the window back up. William clenched his teeth as he heard her grinding the gears. Then the bookmobile lurched and cigarette smoke drifted into the back as the truck pulled forward, turning through the circular drive, heading back down the lane to the city streets and away from Sacred Heart.

On the wall William noticed a poster that read, BOOKS ARE WINDOWS TO THE WORLD. *Windows?* he thought. *This is an exit door, on wheels.* As the bookmobile pulled onto the city street and sped up, William felt Charlotte squeeze his hand.

She whispered, "Sister Briganti once said that all great stories of love and sacrifice have a moral—it's up to us to find the lesson hidden inside."

William didn't know if his story had a moral to it. Honestly, he didn't care. He was going to find Willow Frost. All he wished for was a happy ending.

Scars on First Avenue

꒭

(1934)

William climbed out of the dusty bin and sat on the floor near the rear of the bookmobile, struggling not to sneeze. He breathed slowly, trying to relax, inhaling the scent of paper, glue, and printers' ink. He peered through the rear window as they rolled by the stately brick buildings of the University of Washington, cruised through the Broadway hilltops, and then headed down Pike Street into the heart of Seattle's business district. Much to his surprise the streets seemed more crowded than when he was out on his birthday, not just with cars and trucks but with people—scores of men, some in army uniforms, were filling the streets, slowing traffic to a crawl. Charlotte felt his arm and tapped his shoulder; then she pointed behind her head in the direction of Miss Fredericks, who had stopped at an intersection and was talking to a traffic cop. William overheard the librarian asking if there was a better way to get to Boeing Field. William had never seen the new airport, but he remembered riding the interurban line all the way to Meadows Race Track, where he and his mother often went when he was just a toddler. As William listened in, he had a vague recollection of curlicues of cigar smoke and the smell of horses sweating on a hot summer day. He remembered his mother pointing out a giant red barn across the river.

"That's where they make airplanes," she'd said, much to his bewilderment. "Some can even land on the water. Then they go . . ."

He'd watched as she made a zooming sound and pointed to the sky. Sister Briganti had once told them that Charles Lindbergh had landed there a few years back, but William wasn't convinced. *I don't know what to believe anymore.*

William felt the bookmobile lurch into motion as Miss Fredericks pulled onto a side street, which was filled with more cars and people. He peeked through the rear-door window and saw a mounted police officer galloping toward them, blowing his whistle. *He's seen us.* William tried not to panic as he glanced in all directions for another exit, a better place to hide, anything, just as the policeman veered around them, slowly trotting through the crowded street. William heard the roar of an enormous crowd. He looked back and saw Charlotte looking just as worried as he was.

"What is it?" she whispered.

"I don't know, but we might as well leave now." *While we can.* "I don't think this rig is going anywhere anytime soon."

William felt Miss Fredericks pull the bookmobile over to the side of the street. She honked the horn and then stepped out onto the running board to get a better look.

"Now's our chance." William opened the rear door and was overwhelmed by a flowing river of men—thousands, a huge column marching past them toward Pike Street, tromping in worn leather heels. The men leading the march carried huge painted banners that read, WE WANT CASH RELIEF, MORE CALORIES AND LESS WORMS IN RATION BOXES, and BUILD THE SUBWAY FOR JOBS. The pedestrians on the sidewalks, an assortment of businessmen dressed in suits and women in pleated skirts, quickly got out of the way.

William helped Charlotte exit the back of the bookmobile, then donned his knapsack and took her free hand as she walked with her cane outstretched in front of her. Fortunately even the most boisterous of those in the crowd still had the civility to recognize a little blind girl and stepped aside or tipped their caps even though she couldn't see their courteous gestures. They tried walking against the tide of marchers but were like helpless fish struggling to swim up-stream. *It's a protest march,* William realized. *We're lucky it hasn't broken into a full riot.* He took Charlotte's arm and turned her around, going with the flow of bodies until they reached the main avenue; then they slowly peeled off toward the packed sidewalk. He led her up the steps of an apartment building, someplace safe where he could get a better look. He watched as veterans in uniform, some missing arms and legs, hobbled by on crutches shouting for the bonuses they'd been promised. Then someone blew a whistle and the chaos took on a more orderly shape as the marchers began singing in unison, "Don't scab for the bosses. Don't listen to their lies. Us poor folks haven't got a chance, unless we organize."

"It's a rally of some kind—like an angry parade," William said. "Soldiers demanding back pay and all kinds of men marching for jobs. Women too."

From his perch atop the steps, William looked up and down the broad avenue for a boardinghouse, but all he saw were banks, shoe stores, druggists, and an odd assortment of diners, sausage carts, and popcorn wagons. He glimpsed a large sandwich board with a poster he recognized, the same one he'd seen on his birthday.

"Let's go this way," he said, leading Charlotte through the crowd to the painted image of Stepin Fetchit, Willow Frost, Asa Berger, and an all-girl orchestra called the Ingénues. As William noted the venues and showtimes, Charlotte pulled away from him and walked toward the sound of a player piano.

William looked up at the sign. "*Le Petit,*" he said. "It's a penny arcade."

"Let's go inside."

William hesitated, then shrugged and led her through the swinging doors.

"It smells like candied apples," Charlotte said, smiling.

And cigarette smoke, William thought, as his eyes slowly adjusted to the dimly lit parlor with walls covered in red velvet wall-paper. There were rows of nickelodeons showing adventures, comedies, and grown-up movies about what the butler saw. There was even a sports parlor with brass Mutoscopes where you could watch Jack Dempsey fight Gene Tunney for a penny a round. William remembered visiting an arcade like this years ago, but that place had been sparkling new and crowded with children, as well as men and women standing elbow to elbow, impatiently waiting in line for their turn at a Moviola. This place had newer machines but was completely vacant.

"Another day, another rally in the street," a man said from behind a counter with neat rows of candy jars and bins of popcorn and boxes of Cracker Jack. "We're lucky the Silver Shirts weren't out there causing a ruckus. That's all we need, common folk getting bloody in the streets. Been more than ten years since the general strike and things are worse now than they were back then." Coins jingled as he shook his waist apron, redirecting the subject. "You kids need some change?"

"I can't, William. But you should . . ."

William looked around. "I don't think we have a penny to spare . . ."

"Live a little. You can see. I can't. Do it for me."

William reluctantly agreed and fished out a handful of pennies. He bought Charlotte a bag of cotton candy, and she held on to his arm as he wandered past the rows of movies and newsreels, reading the strange titles aloud.

"Sorry, kid, the only new flicks we got are work films—we get 'em for free from Uncle Sammy." The proprietor sat back, dipping into a tin of wax that he applied to the tips of his wide mustache.

William passed on a movie by Jimmy Durante titled *Give a Man a Job*. "Do you have any movies with the lady on the poster?" he asked.

"Willow? I figured you'd ask something like that," the man said.

Why, because I'm Chinese? William thought.

"Especially after her making the tabloids this morning." The man showed him the front page of *The Seattle Star,* which featured a photo of Willow in a voluminous fur coat, being greeted at Union Station by the local theater critic Willis Sayre and a gaggle of Seattle dignitaries. They were flanked by two police officers on motorcycles. Stepin was seated behind one of the uniformed men, mugging at the camera. Everyone looked enthralled. William echoed that sentiment as he stared at the newspaper. She looked so much like his mother. *She looks like me,* William thought yearningly. *And I look like her.*

The proprietor spoke up. "I don't have any of her new movies, but take a look at the machine on the end there. She ain't listed in the credits, but I think Weepin' Willow is in there somewhere, as an extra, I guess. Give it a whirl."

William felt Charlotte squeeze his arm.

He read the placard on the machine. "It's only three minutes long." Then he stood on the footstep, dropped a penny in the slot, and slowly turned the crank as a light came on and the title flickered in black and white. *"The Yellow Pirate,"* he said.

"Do you see her?" Charlotte asked.

Not yet. William didn't answer. He was absorbed in the simple story of a Chinese merchant who sold his cargo and then returned, dressed as a comical bandit, and attempted to steal it back. He failed and was quickly killed, losing his Oriental daughter to an American sea captain—but she didn't look like Willow. There were only three main actors and a handful of extras; many of them appeared to be the same people, only their costumes had changed from scene to scene, and only a few were women. William stared, trying not to blink, his eyes watering as he waited to catch another glimpse of the women who stepped in and out of the background. Then the movie ended.

"Did you see her?"

"I don't know," William mumbled, rubbing his eyes. "It all moved so fast and was too blurry at times. I don't know what I saw."

"Then watch it again," the man said.

William began to wonder if this was just a ploy to milk them of every penny they had. Ploy or no ploy, it worked. With Charlotte's blessing, he watched the movie five more times, each time catching a glimpse of a woman in the background who looked like someone he once knew. But he couldn't be sure. The more he wanted the actresses to be his ah-ma, the more they began to resemble her. Each time his imagination projected memorable features onto the figures that quickly entered and then exited the scene. He gave up before his imagination ran away with him and the women on film began to speak to him directly, waving and calling his name.

WILLIAM AND CHARLOTTE still needed a place to spend the night. The man at the penny arcade handed them a card on their way out that read, "All You Downtrodden Ones call 354 Rockwell, Sister Mary's Mission."

"Not passing judgment on your character," he said. "But just in case, the mission home is probably the safest place to rest your head."

William stared at the card as they walked down the street.

"I don't think we can, William," Charlotte said. "Not a good idea. The sisters at the mission might just send us back to the orphanage."

William doubted that anyone at Sacred Heart would even want them back, but he agreed that the mission wasn't worth the risk. So they walked down Skid Row, where First Avenue curved around Pioneer Square. Through a haze of dust and coal smoke he could see the street spilling like a river onto the mudflats south of the city, where hundreds of ramshackle homes and clapboard shacks were pieced together with scrap lumber and tar paper. A hand-painted banner hung across the road that read: WELCOME TO HOOVERVILLE. WHERE LIFE IS STRIFE. As the wind blew northward he could smell sawdust, urine, and despair.

That's where we don't want to end up, William fretted. *Pioneer Square is bad enough.* Instead of busy merchants in three-piece suits and fine hats, they now stepped around unemployed millworkers and bankrupt shirttail farmers who drank in the street and vomited in the gutters, cursing and swearing.

Charlotte pinched her nose at the smell but didn't complain.

Amid the discouraging sights, sounds, and smells, William saw a polished sedan that stood out like a shimmering pearl in a rotting oyster. An old, uniformed chauffeur sat stoically behind the wheel as the sleek car glided by, heading uptown. Rich children in elegant clothing rode in the back and made slant-eyed faces, pointing at Charlotte and him as though they were monkeys on display in the Phinney Ridge menagerie. William watched them go and looked around. If anyone regarded him as a lost Oriental, they didn't show it. The people William saw, those living and dying in the streets and alleyways, couldn't see past their own despair or their next meal.

As clouds rolled in, William crossed the intersection of King Street. He pondered finding a room back in Chinatown—someplace familiar, maybe even at the Bush Hotel, but those places near the train station seemed too expensive. So he kept wandering, avoiding establishments that were near burlesque houses like the Rialto or tattoo parlors, frowning at the many signs that read NO INDIANS. He'd once been mistaken for an Indian boy and worried that someone would complain and have them tossed out. Most of the doss-houses, like Father Divine's Mission, the Boatman Hotel, and the Ragdale Home for Working Men, didn't allow women or children. And vice versa for the women's homes. More out of desperation and necessity than because of price or location, and because the sun was setting, William finally settled for a flophouse at First and Yesler that wasn't so discerning.

"How much is it?" Charlotte asked.

William read the sign. "Twenty-five cents for a room, fifteen for a bed, and slings for a nickel. I'm not sure how you want to do this."

She took his arm and paused as though acknowledging his unspoken thought—which was that neither of them wanted to be alone. "I'll share a room."

William led her down the concrete steps from the street into a tiny alcove beneath the building, where an old man with baggy eyes and a wrinkled, windburned face sat behind a glass, sipping coffee and playing solitaire with an old deck of cards. William slid a shiny quarter beneath the smudged window. "One room, please. One night."

The man looked up and did a double take, then nodded as though checking off a Chinese boy and a blind girl from the list of strangers that had visited. He took the quarter, examined it, and slid back a key. "We don't normally allow boys and girls to share a room, but seeing as how she . . ." The man pointed to Charlotte's eyes, then waved his hand in front of her, just to be sure. "Room Seventeen." He went back to his card game.

"It's not much," Charlotte said, smiling. "But it's home."

Until tomorrow, William thought. *Then what?* All day long they had lived in the moment, not thinking too far ahead. They both seemed to know the quiet, lurking reality that if they couldn't reach Willow, and even if they did and she wasn't who William thought she was, or worse, if she rejected him entirely, then they'd be out on the street for real. Left to fight for meals with other homeless kids. Left to sleep in vestibules and doorways with their shoes on, for fear of having them stolen in the night.

As they descended a lightless, garbage-strewn stairwell into a basement warren, William realized that this flophouse wasn't much better. The rooms had been subdivided again and again into spaces barely large enough for a bed and a locker. The walls didn't even touch the ceiling. Instead, chicken wire had been used to bridge the gap, leaving everyone breathing the same air in the rooms, where he could hear tubercular men and women coughing and a baby crying. Everything smelled like cigarette smoke and body odors. As they passed a shared bathroom, William noticed a sign with a calendar nailed to the door instructing residents to avoid flushing during high tide because the toilet would back up. *Lucky us. The tide is out.*

"It's not so bad," Charlotte said. "We can survive anything for one night."

William wasn't so confident.

"Besides, everyone knows that Blacks and Indians have it worse."

"You're starting to sound like Sister Briganti," William said, as he remembered the nun's many baleful tales of *the least among us.* Stories of families sleeping in windowless rooms without heat or blankets. Where men with ripe sores on their legs and lice crawling their bodies drank homemade gin to stay warm.

William shuddered at the thought. Then he found their room and he shuddered again. Room 17 had a single lightbulb that hung precariously from the ceiling. The walls were covered in graffiti and an assortment of salacious artworks, some drawn with pencil or ink, others carved into the wood. William heard a cat somewhere, wailing, probably at mice—or rats.

"I know you must think this place is dreadful, and it probably is," Charlotte said, "but it'll be okay, William—it's only temporary."

For the first time since he'd known Charlotte, William actually felt like he was the one living with a handicap, being sighted in a place like this.

He barred the door and she took his hand, searching with her cane until she found their bunk. The bedding was nothing more than a quilt of soiled, moth-eaten rags, so thin, so rough and foul-smelling that Charlotte peeled it back and shoved it in the corner. William broke out the bread and crackers, and they both nibbled on some of each. Then they huddled face-to-face on the squeaky bed with all of their clothes on, their hats too. They used their coats as blankets.

"Are you still glad you came along?" William asked, apologetically.

Charlotte removed her left mitten and slipped her hand into his, lacing their fingers together for warmth and comfort. "I haven't been this happy in a long time. There's not a place I'd rather be right now."

William still didn't know what she had to be so joyful about.

They sat in their tiny hovel, listening to the snoring, breathing, coughing, and the rhythmic squeaking of mattress springs somewhere in the basement.

"We'll find her, William. You have to feel it."

Of that he was fairly confident. *But what if she doesn't want me?* he thought, keeping his fears to himself—bracing his heart for one final rejection. As the Moviola at the penny arcade faded into memory, as he strained to remember the show at the Moore Theatre, her image blurred and became warped, distorted by his feelings of abandonment. *What if she doesn't care?*

"My mother died when I was little," Charlotte said. "But I remember her holding me—I remember feeling safe and happy and content. I didn't even know that I couldn't see; my whole world was nothing but those feelings."

She squeezed his hand.

"What's your earliest memory of *your* mother?" Charlotte asked. "The very first one?" She moved closer, their knees touching.

William closed his eyes and tried to remember. Sounds came first, and then smells. "My earliest real memory," he said, "is of lying on my back, staring up at the tin ceiling of what must have been our apartment at the Bush Hotel. I was wet and warm from a bath in the kitchen sink, and the towels felt cold and rough against my bare skin. I remember my nose twitching from the scent of ammonia or detergent, and I couldn't stop giggling and kicking my feet as my ah-ma cleaned my belly button with a Q-tip."

"That's a sweet memory."

He smiled.

"She would say in Chinese, 'Don't be a wiggle-worm.' Whatever else she said to me I've forgotten, or lost, along with most of my Cantonese. And I remember hearing live music on the radio, and the window—it was dark outside, except for the moon, so it must have been my bedtime. Ah-ma sat me up and I wobbled as she stretched and tugged this nightshirt over my head that must have been too small because I recall my ears throbbing afterward. I don't even know if that actually happened. I was little. It's been so long. I barely remember anything. I might have imagined it all."

William paused and cleared his throat. Then he went on, speaking more slowly.

"But there was another time I've never forgotten, years later, I was older . . . maybe five, I'm not sure . . . she was helping me get dressed and I heard a knock on the door. She turned and walked away. A man's voice was shouting something . . . in Chinese, and my mother shouted back even louder. I heard glass breaking. Then my world turned sideways, the ceiling became the wall, and the wall became the floor. My head hit something, and everything went dark. I wanted to cry but couldn't inhale, or exhale."

"Who was that man?" Charlotte asked.

Was that my father? "I . . . don't know," William said instead. He chewed his lower lip. "But I touch the side of my head whenever I think of that moment, even to this day." He removed her hand from their shared mitten and guided her fingers to a crease on his temple, just below his hairline.

"That's how I know it's a real memory," he said. "Because I still have the scar."

He closed his eyes and felt Charlotte run her soft, delicate fingertips along his old wound that had been so neatly hidden.

"We all have scars, William. You. Me. I'm sure Willow has more than her share."

She gently kissed his blemish, then wished him good night.

Velvet Rope

(1934)

William and Charlotte woke the next morning and turned on the light, to the vociferous complaints of their neighbors in the next room. They quickly turned off the bulb and gathered their meager belongings. William could barely knot his tie in broad daylight, yet somehow Charlotte and her amazingly dexterous fingers managed to craft a perfect bow in the gloaming. Eager to leave, they left the flophouse midmorning, shooing away a flock of pigeons that had been picking at earwigs crawling on the cold steps that led up to the street. The sidewalks were less crowded than the night before, though there were now men of every age, sleeping in gateways or raggedly snoring beneath nearby bushes with sheaves of old newspaper stuffed into their coats to stave off the crisp, damp Puget Sound air. How they remained asleep was a mystery, especially as the Salvation Army marched by, banging their loud bass drums. They formed a semicircle in the square, where the brass instruments lit into a heaven-splitting hymn that William barely recognized as "Solemnize Our Every Heart." Charlotte grinned from ear to ear as the two of them sat on a vacant bench and listened to the men and women in their strange, bright uniforms playing bugles, trumpets, cymbals, and trombones. Before the song was over a stout woman passed a tambourine among the crowd asking for donations for the poor and downtrodden. William regarded the homeless men sleeping in the gutters and put in a nickel.

William thought his companion should eat as they walked uptown, so they stopped at a lunch counter and ordered shredded wheat with cream, sprinkled with salt, and shared a cup of Ghirardelli chocolate. He let Charlotte have most of the hot cocoa and barely touched the cereal. His stomach was a knot of excitement and anxiety. As he glanced around the diner, he worried that grownups might question why they weren't in school, but then he looked outside and saw dozens of kids their age, many younger, shining shoes, delivering newspapers, and sweeping up in front of stores. *Public school is free,* William thought, *but even that has become a luxury some can't afford.*

At the counter, William asked a stranger for directions, then guided Charlotte toward the new Skinner Building, where the 5th Avenue Theatre was impossible to miss. Its glowing red and yellow neon sign must have been four stories tall—William spotted it from three blocks away and squeezed Charlotte's hand. Plus flashing signs for KOMO and KJR adorned the roof, along with towering radio antennae, which broadcast NBC Red and NBC Blue. But his heart quickened even more when he saw the entrance to the theater and its Chinese motif—layers of gold and jade, with massive, studded double doors painted burgundy, the threshold guarded by a pair of giant Foo dogs. Each golden canine was at least a foot taller than he or Charlotte.

"Is this the place?" she asked.

William looked up at the lighted grand marquee, which read: SEATTLE'S OWN WEEPING WILLOW FROST. PLUS: STEPIN FETCHIT— THE WORLD'S LAZIEST MAN. FEATURING ASA BERGER AND THE FOX MOVIETONE PLAYERS, WITH THE INGÉNUES. Stepin was a bigger star and had been in dozens of movies, but Willow, a local hero, had managed top billing.

"Without a doubt," William said. He'd forgotten that the 5th Avenue was a *Chinese* theater, at least on the outside. Somehow it was fitting that Willow would be performing here. It was the audience that would appear out of place.

William took Charlotte's hand and showed her how to touch the ball within a Foo dog's mouth. "You're supposed to rub it for good luck."

"Do I make a wish?"

"You can if you want."

Charlotte closed her eyes and furrowed her brow. Then she smiled.

"We should get in line," William said as a crowd gathered, everyone waiting for the box office to open. William's eyes widened when he saw that the theater was showing movies—some with Willow, though most of them, like *Show Boat* and *The Galloping Ghost,* featured Stepin. There was also an anthology, showcasing some of the other performers who would be appearing live, once in the afternoon and once for the final show of the evening. As much as William wanted to watch the other movies, he knew that they needed to save their money. So he didn't mention the other shows as they lined up and bought tickets from a blond woman for the matinee, which cost thirty cents apiece, half the price of the evening show.

As he stared at the posters and portraits of Willow in her elaborate gown and dramatic makeup, he wondered what he'd say to her. *Will she remember? And if not, will I be forced to beg for answers?* She was famous and he was nothing. He began to doubt, suddenly bereft of hope, contemplating what he'd do if she weren't his ah-ma. *What then?* He'd be on his own, but at least he wouldn't feel so rejected. There was strange comfort in that.

WILLIAM AND CHARLOTTE spent the afternoon skipping from store to store, savoring the freedom they'd been starving for back at the orphanage. They wandered like curious dogs with broken leashes. They lingered at Mozart's Cigars until they were kicked out for loitering. And they played downstairs in the Bon Marché's vast toy department, where Charlotte delighted in touching and squeezing the stuffed bears. They even tried on hats at Best's Apparel, until a customer mistook William for an Indian and a security guard was roused to chase them off. Neither of them seemed to mind. The city was noisy, and smelly, and fragrant, and even though poverty and joblessness had consumed whole boarded-up neighborhoods, the downtown district was alive. Plus, there were storefront theaters on almost every block—sometimes three or four in a row, showing second-run talkies, newsreels, cartoons, and a mix of silent photoplays. Motion pictures seemed to be the only business that was thriving.

By the time they got back to the 5th Avenue Theatre, William's legs were tired and his feet sore from walking in shoes one size too small. But that discomfort diminished with each minute that ticked away, bringing them that much closer to showtime. As they waited, some of the people in line gave them queer looks or commented under their breath, especially when they saw William's Oriental face or Charlotte's cane. William ignored them.

And when the ornate doors finally parted, everyone fell silent.

"What is it?" Charlotte whispered.

"It's . . ." William blinked as his mouth hung open. "It's . . ." He was at a loss for words. As the crowd marveled, William took Charlotte's hand and walked through the entrance into another world. They sank into the lush carpet of the lobby, promptly greeted by usherettes in Mandarin costumes of red, blue, green, and gold. The walls were draped in shimmering ribbons of crimson and jade. And as they entered the massive theater, William felt as though he were setting foot in China's Imperial Palace, overlooking the landscape of his ah-ma's wildest fairy tales. He looked up, in awe, gushing his amazement as he beheld an enormous, lavishly sculpted five-toed dragon that had been carved across the center of the high, deckled ceiling. An opulent pearl chandelier dangled from the creature's gaping mouth.

"From all the gasps I'm hearing, I take it this theater is quite impressive," Charlotte said, squeezing his hand. "I can feel this place—the way it smells, the way the air moves, the way our voices carry. It must be huge."

While waiting in line William had overheard someone mentioning that the 5th Avenue had nearly three thousand seats, but he'd never envisioned a place this large. The interior resembled the Temple of Heaven he'd once seen in *National Geographic*. The décor felt like a confirmation, a sign that Willow was indeed sent from somewhere on high.

It's the most breathtaking place I've ever seen! William thought. But he said, "It's so fantastically . . . ornate." As he led Charlotte to their seats, he struggled to figure out how to describe such rich colors to a sightless girl. "The curtains are blue velvet, like the sky at night, the golden pipes from the organ stand tall above the arch of the stage, it's huge, but with fine details in every corner. And it's all . . . Chinese."

"Like your mother."

Like Willow. William had never seen anything this majestic, this exotic, even within the few square blocks of Chinatown. "And the people here to watch the show, they're all . . . white." The contradiction left him feeling strangely proud.

Charlotte closed her eyes and beamed as the pipe organ filled every corner of the theater with sound. "Now I can see it," she said with a smile.

William watched as patrons found their seats while the main floor filled up, almost to capacity. He felt himself drifting between two worlds: the austerity of his childhood, the orphanage, the poverty of Pioneer Square—and the magical realm of the stage, with its decadence, its overwhelming opulence. Most of the other people in the audience wore suits or dresses, but no one was twinkling with sequins or dripping in diamonds. Some were dressed no better than he was, in his old jacket and tie. But everyone seemed rapt, nearly bursting with excitement. The theater was an escape and an amusement—a welcome, celebratory respite from the harsh, cold reality outside.

As the houselights faded and the audience clapped, William imagined that they had all stepped into Charlotte's world of sound and music and infinite space. But then a spotlight illuminated a dashing fellow in a dark tuxedo.

"Laaaaaaadies and geeeeeeentlemen, children of all ages, shapes, sizes, flavors, and levels of sobriety . . ."

William recognized him from the advertisements, even before he introduced himself as Asa Berger. He cracked a few jokes and then broke into song and dance as the curtains parted to reveal the Ingénues, who began to play. William didn't quite know what to make of them. They were fantastic, though strangely comical at times as one of the girls strutted across the stage in glittering heels while playing an ivory accordion.

The all-girl orchestra was followed by an act billed as Straight and Crooked Magic, in which a magician named Blackstone made a birdcage vanish, leaving a squawking canary in the hands of Pete, his jocular assistant. For their finale they made a lightbulb levitate from a table lamp. The radiant orb flew above the audience while the musicians in the pit played "I Know That You Know." As William described the illusion to Charlotte, the man sitting behind them said, "I hear Thomas Edison himself is trying to figure out how he does that." Magic made William nervous. He hoped it was just a trick.

Blackstone was followed by a duo who performed "Indian Love Call" from the hit musical *Rose-Marie*. A broad-shouldered man dressed as a member of the Royal Canadian Mounted Police rode in on a wooden horse and sang to a blond woman dressed as an Indian maiden. William couldn't help but think about Sunny, who would probably change his name to Sunny Does-Not-Approve.

After that a high-kicking dance number called "Hot Cotton" took over the stage. William counted sixteen leggy ladies in enormous feathered hats and floor-length tutus that were nearly transparent. The men in the audience whistled and hooted.

Asa, who had the crowd rolling with laughter, introduced each performance, though most of the jokes were beyond William's level of appreciation.

Finally, the emcee said, "Well, folks. It's that time, time to reintroduce you to a local doll who's done the extraordinary, the nearly impossible—she's been able to put up with *me* for two months on the road!"

"This is it," Charlotte whispered.

This is it. William sat spellbound as Asa teased and the audience chuckled while timpani drums rolled louder and louder and louder . . .

"Here she is—the one you've been waiting for, from the silver screen to the airwaves above us, and finally to the grandest stage on the West Coast, I give you the one, the only, the inimitable, Miss . . . Willow . . . Frost!"

Charlotte clapped wildly and cheered, more than the rest of the audience, who seemed interested but less enthused. William became a statue, a gargoyle staring at the slender figure in a lavender gown with flowers in her hair. She began to sing, softly, deftly, in a whisper that quieted the audience, as the orchestra followed her lead.

A pair of sailors shouted, "Take it off, sweetie!" and "How much for a private dance?" prompting a male usher to ask them to refrain.

I should have rented a pair of opera glasses, William thought, because from his seat in the middle of the theater he couldn't see her face or define her features. But something about the way she carried herself, her walk, looked familiar. She seemed profoundly stylish,

standing out as the one Chinese performer in a Chinese theater—
but in a modern dress, before a modern audience. She sang her version of "Dream a Little Dream," her voice rising and rising until the
rich, powerful notes filled every corner of the theater and people
began clapping, cheering. William caught his breath.

"*That's* her?" Charlotte whispered.

That's her. The hair stood up on the back of his neck as William
recognized her voice. And when the song ended he watched as Willow blew kisses and waved while the audience continued their lusty
applause and Asa whisked her away.

It has to be her. It has to be.

Then Asa was back, only to trip over a shadowy figure sleeping
onstage, just below the following spotlight. The crowd roared when
Stepin Fetchit sat up, yawned, stumbled to his feet, and dusted himself off. He looked elegant yet comical in a skimmer and coonskin
coat. "Man, is it showtime already?" Stepin scratched his head.
"My hotel is right across the street, so I called me a cab. When I told
the cabdriver to take me to the Fifth Avenue Theatre, he said, 'But
it's right over there,' and I said, 'I know, hurry up, I'm gonna be
late!'" The audience laughed and clapped while he stripped off his
long coat to the sound of a scratchy trombone. Beneath the fur he
wore a tuxedo covered in purple sequins. The tuxedo's tails touched
the floor.

"How do you like my outfit?" Stepin asked as the audience
clapped and whistled. "I bought it from Rudy Valentino." The men
groaned as the women cheered. "He wore it on his wedding day. He
and the bride both wore *lavender*!" The audience roared, but William didn't understand the joke. "Brother, it's good to be here—we
just rolled in by train. You know, I love riding the train, which is
much better than traveling in the South. You know how we travel
in the South?"

Asa yelled from offstage, "No, how do you travel in the South?"

William listened numbly as Stepin paused, drawing the audience in. "Fast. At night. Through the *woods*! That's how a colored man travel in the South . . ."

The audience ate up the comedian's jokes, laughed at his pratfalls, marveled at his dancing, was surprised by his singing, and begged for more. He even took a turn conducting the orchestra, directing them through a medley of Mozart and ragtime.

But William didn't smile. He hardly noticed. He sat spellbound, staring into the wings of the stage and the back of the house, hoping to catch another glimpse of Willow Frost, his ah-ma, whoever she was.

For the grand finale all of the performers, including Willow, came back onstage. William was still mesmerized by seeing and hearing her in person, along with the other living, breathing movie stars—figments from the silver screen, walking, floating across the stage like ghosts from his haunting, faded daydreams. Then the curtains sighed.

As the houselights came on and the usherettes appeared, William sat staring at the stage. *You have to come back.* Charlotte took his arm, and he reluctantly led her up and out onto the sidewalk, where a man with a cart was selling bunches of flowers and directing autograph seekers to the stage door, tucked in the alley. William thought about how much the flowers must cost, then shrugged and bought a small clasp of purple and blue.

"They smell lovely," Charlotte said. "For your mother?"

"For Willow," he said. Then he led his friend around the block to where the stage door was crowded with reporters and other fans, some of them holding their own bundles of flowers or elegantly wrapped gifts. Together they waited patiently behind a doorman and a velvet rope. William could hear the band playing, tuning, and clearing their valves for the evening performance while an airmail plane droned overhead. Then he heard clapping and cheering as performers began to mill out, the musicians, the Ingénues, the dancers—all of them smiled and waved, hugged the locals they knew, and graciously accepted gifts before they were ushered toward a queue of waiting taxis. William heard a crashing sound, like glass breaking, and then Asa Berger burst through the door. Ever the showman, he posed for the cameras and shook the hands that stretched beyond the velvet barrier. William touched the comedian's sleeve and could smell alcohol on his breath, even from an arm's length away. William looked at Charlotte, who had her nose scrunched though no one else seemed to mind. He smiled as the comedian stumbled back to the door, unsure if the clumsiness was all part of Asa's act. The man held the door open for Willow and then Stepin. William's heart pounded in his chest. He rubbed his eyes as blue flashbulbs popped again and again in the shadows of the alley while reporters peppered the headliners with questions.

She's right here! William thought. *So close I can almost touch her.*

He held on to Charlotte as they struggled near the rope to keep from being pushed aside by pale women with ruby lips who gushed over the black showman and the many Caucasian gentleman admirers who offered their flowers to the coy Chinese actress. William watched Willow accept several of the bouquets, smiling graciously as if each gift were of singular importance. Then she handed them to Asa, whose arms were quickly filling up. He pretended to collapse under their weight.

As Willow turned to leave, William blurted, "Wait!" He waved frantically from behind the velvet rope, standing on his tippy-toes, desperate to make eye contact with the woman who turned and smiled knowingly, as though comforted to see a young Chinese fan with flowers. "Aw, morning glories are my favorite—how did you know?"

She was inches away, but he couldn't speak. *I've always known. Don't you know who I am?* The words stuck in William's throat. He could barely think. This was his moment, but he stood paralyzed by the thought of rejection. Was it better to keep hoping, dreaming, than to be disappointed forever? He looked up with desperate eyes, watching as her wide Hollywood smile, her perfectly painted face, shrank into an aspect of stunned, devastating sadness. William offered the flowers, and she took them slowly, raising them to her nose, staring back at him over the wide, bluish petals.

A reporter interrupted. "Miss Frost—can I ask you one more question?" He spoke as he scribbled in a small notebook. "How's it feel to be back in Seattle?"

Willow didn't answer. She didn't move. She closed her eyes, tightly, then opened them and looked toward the sky as tears traced her soft cheekbones. She wiped the wetness away and sniffled, half-hiding behind the flowers.

Everyone, even the chattering newsmen, fell silent, all of them hanging on her answer, as though this dramatic pause were merely the foreshadowing calm before a typhoon of song and melody and heartrending drama—as if her entire life were an act.

"It's . . ." She seemed to be searching for the words. "All so, *unbelievable . . .*"

"And how is that, Miss Frost?" another reporter asked.

William stared into her eyes as she gazed back. He was close enough to see his hopeful reflection in the murky hazel. The rope was all that separated their two worlds.

"It's the people," she said. "Not just the fans, but the familiar . . ."

"When did you leave?"

"Five years ago."

"And do you still have family in the area?"

You do, Ah-ma. I never left. I've been here all this time.

William watched as she slowly, almost absently, shook her head and whispered something so softly that he almost didn't hear her say, "How could I . . ."

"Miss Frost," the reporter said.

"Could you repeat the question?" she asked, wiping away more tears.

"I was asking about your family. I know you grew up here. I was wondering if they were planning to come to any of your performances—I was curious as to what they must think—family, friends, relatives. I'm sure they're incredibly proud of all of your success and how far you've come. Miss Frost?"

Charlotte whispered in William's ear, "Get her autograph."

As though waking from a dream, William blinked, once, twice, and then took out the folded, dog-eared photograph and handed it to the movie star whose likeness it bore. He watched, spellbound, as she held the paper, regarded it for a moment, and then quickly scribbled her signature with an ornate fountain pen. She handed the autograph back and paused for a moment as a reporter snapped a picture of the movie star and the young boy, staring at each other from opposite sides of the plush red velvet rope. He took the photo with both hands, then looked up as the woman stood gazing back at him. She didn't let go until a taxi driver blared his horn and revved his engine. William sank beneath the padded shoulders of his jacket as Asa flashed Willow his wristwatch and pulled her away.

She hastily said, "This was the best performance of my life. One I will never, ever forget—for as long as I live. And if there were any friends or old fans in the audience, I hope they can forgive me . . . for being away so long."

William found his voice as she turned her back toward him. "Ah-ma?"

She paused while her companions, Stepin and Asa, climbed into the taxi.

"You were wonderful," William said in Chinese.

Willow hung her head. It started to rain, and thick, heavy droplets dotted her cape and cloche hat. She peered back over her shoulder and then stepped into the car, wiping a tear from her cheek as the door closed and they pulled away.

William stood like a statue placed on a muddy shore, sinking deeper and deeper as the current washed away the sand beneath his feet. While the assortment of reporters, well-wishers, and stargazers slowly drifted elsewhere, he remained transfixed, holding Charlotte's hand, wondering what exactly had happened.

"Was it really her?" she asked. "Was Willow . . . you know . . ."

William drew a deep, weary breath. He jogged his memory as he looked at Willow's autograph and ran his fingertips across her signature, which was written in Chinese. He recognized the characters: *Liu Song.*

Greenroom

꒦

(1934)

William and Charlotte sat in the alley long after the crowds of fans and reporters had drifted away, slowly, like cotton in the air. To William, it seemed as though everyone else had someplace to go, someone to be with, some duty to attend to. He, on the other hand, couldn't move, couldn't leave. He sat on the dirty, broken pavement, his shoulders against the stage door, waiting. *I have no place else to go.*

"She'll come back," Charlotte said. "There's another show tonight, and another tomorrow and the next day. We could leave and return an hour before the evening performance. That would give us plenty of time . . ."

"I'm not leaving," William said, crossing his hands in front of his chest. He had tried banging on the door, hoping that some stagehand might hear and let them inside. William hoped that he'd be able to sneak into his ah-ma's dressing room and wait for her arrival. But they only attracted the attention of an angry old custodian, who told them to scram—shooing them off with his mop. Eventually the rumblings from inside the belly of the theater quieted, matching the soundlessness of the vacant alley.

"We can't wait forever," Charlotte argued politely. "What if we get arrested for truancy or, worse, vagrancy? They'd split us up for sure."

William listened as he noticed the wending cracks in the concrete, covered with moss and tufts of long-dead crabgrass. He followed the cracks to the garbage-strewn mouth of the alley and watched a group of old men shamble by with hand-painted picket signs resting on their shoulders. William's English was spotty at times, but even he noticed the misspellings on the placards. And the men, they looked like they'd worn the same clothes for weeks, and their unshaven faces and windburned skin revealed the relentless sorrow of their days. *No one will even notice us,* William realized. *We're invisible—no value, no trouble to anyone.*

As the minutes became hours, William and Charlotte huddled together and passed the time talking about food and songs, about family and unfulfilled wishes. She even held his hand, tucked her hair behind her ear, and rested her head on his shoulder as William watched the long afternoon shadows creep down the red-brick walls and wrought-iron fire escape that had been painted yellow. Eventually the colors of the alley faded and darkened, like a bruise on a piece of rotting fruit. Occasionally they'd doze off, one or the other, sometimes both, napping amid the unkind smells left behind by roving animals and stray humans, their respites interrupted by the wails of sirens or the clanging of a trolley, and finally the slamming of a car door.

William squinted down the alley toward the sunlit street as the yellow blur of a taxi pulled away. He nudged Charlotte, then realized she was already wide awake.

A man in an overcoat stalked toward them, his face hidden beneath the brim of his fedora. He tipped the hat as he stopped in front of them, but William's tired eyes were slow to adjust to the shade of the alley and he couldn't see the man's face clearly.

"What do we have here?" the man said as he waved his hand in front of Charlotte's vacant eyes. "Lemme guess, you're a new act—Chinky and Blinky."

It's the comedian. William recalled the voice. *Asa—something . . .*

"Is that you, Mr. Berger?" Charlotte asked, timidly.

"Slow down, honey. My father is Mr. Berger. My friends call me Asa. You can call me . . . Sir Handsome Bloodworth the Third, Lord of the Alley, Sultan of Sloth, and the Patron Saint of Blind Runaways and Lost Celestials—no offense, kid."

The man spoke so fast that William had a hard time understanding. He helped Charlotte to her feet as they dusted themselves off. William buttoned his jacket and straightened his bow tie. "Is it showtime already? What time—"

"Why, you kids looking for work?" Asa interrupted. "Or just taking a napping tour of Seattle's finest alleys?" The man paused, hands out as though waiting for laughter or applause, but the only sound they heard was from a fat tomcat that mewed from atop an overflowing garbage can. The comedian shook his head and mumbled something toward the sky in a language William didn't understand.

"We're waiting for Willow," Charlotte blurted as she held on to William's arm.

"She's my mother. That's why she cried when she saw me," William stated with all the vigor of a deflating party balloon. *I think that's why, at least.* He found the autograph and showed it to the comedian.

"Wow." Asa snorted. "Conclusive proof. Except for all I know this says, 'Free Chow Mein on Sundays.' What else you got? After all, kid, Willow's an actress—the tears are part of her shtick; she cries at the drop of a hat, any hat."

William couldn't answer.

"C'mon, kid, we get stuff like this all the time. I mean, you know Stepin has a way with the ladies, and Yours Truly is no slouch when it comes to affairs of the . . . uh, affairs of the . . . ah, screw it—just affairs. I mean, we're the ones looking over our shoulders for angry fathers and cuckold husbands, but Willow Frosty with kids—that's rich. Um, let me ask you this in all seriousness—are you two kids related? What I mean to ask is, does Little Orphan Optic here know she's not from the Far East? And I'm not talking about Long Island."

William shrugged through another awkward pause.

"We're both from around here . . ." Charlotte corrected. "From Sacred Heart . . ."

"I'm from Chinatown. My mother was Liu Song Eng—her name means *Willow*. We lived at the Bush Hotel on South Jackson. My mother was taken away five years ago and I was sent to an orphanage . . ."

William watched as Asa stretched into an exaggerated yawn. "Yeah, yeah, I'm a sucker for a sob story. You want in for free, c'mon in. You wanna tell fairy tales, save it for the rubes. You can wander around backstage until showtime—then off you go, my little Irish twins. Don't tell anyone, though, or they'll start these crazy rumors that I'm some kind of a nice guy." He handed them each a ticket from his billfold and then banged on the door, first with his fist, then he kicked it several more times for good measure.

A large man in a ratty black sweater opened the door, looked at his watch, and grunted "Good evening" to Asa. William watched as the man in black propped the door open with a chair and sat upon it, looking them up and down.

"That's Chuckles the doorman—Mr. Personality, that guy," Asa said as he led them inside and down the hallway. "That's the stairway to the voms that will take you out to your seats. Stay out of the way of anyone in black—those are stagehands and union guys. That's the greenroom. I suggest you wait in there, and don't steal the silver. I'll be in my office taking my medicine."

Medicine, William thought. He watched as Asa walked into a dressing room across the hall. The comedian looked out of place against the gold-flecked wallpaper, sitting beneath a crystal chandelier. Asa found a bottle of whiskey with a ribbon around the neck, poured a mug of cold coffee into a trash can, and opened the bottle, hands shaking as he poured. William could see the man's Adam's apple rise and fall with each gulp. Then he set the mug down, looked into the mirror, turned and met William's gaze with sad, bloodshot eyes, and slammed the door.

William and Charlotte sat in the greenroom—which wasn't green at all—surrounded by bouquets of flowers, baskets of fruit and hard rolls, and a silver tea service steaming with fresh coffee. They were afraid to touch anything, certain that someone would see them and kick them out at any moment. But when a stagehand popped in with a clipboard and asked who they were with, they held up the tickets Asa had given them. The stagehand's suspicious eyes softened when he saw Charlotte's white cane, and he shrugged and walked on. *Thank you, Charlotte,* William thought. *No one doubts the intentions of a blind girl.* Charlotte suggested he read something to her, but the only thing he could find was an old newspaper. The headline was about a high school girl named Frances Farmer who won a trip to Russia with an essay entitled "God Dies." William spared his blind friend the article but nodded in agreement.

He sat back and watched a small parade of theater workers and performers breeze in and out of the greenroom. Some he recognized from earlier in the day. Others were new, like a ventriloquist with a dummy that played the bagpipes, and an old man who arrived with a chimpanzee in a tuxedo. And each time he heard a commotion in the hallway he expected to see his ah-ma and each time he was disappointed. Eventually he heard the musicians in the concert hall tuning up for their performance and began to worry that Willow might never show up. Then he heard flashbulbs popping and laughing from the alley. He peeked down the hallway, expecting Willow, but instead it was a black man in a finely tailored suit.

William hesitated. At first he thought the man was an usher. Then William recognized him. "You're Mr. Fetchit, aren't you?" William noticed the man had a daily racing form from Longacres tucked beneath his arm, along with a copy of *Ulysses.*

"Call me Lincoln." He shook William's hand. "Lincoln Perry. You know there's a place here in town called the Coon Chicken Inn? I thought everyone in the Great Northwest was better than all that." He turned his head and cursed. "Say, are you an acrobat or something? Man, I hope you're not performing tonight—kids always steal the show. Bad enough I have to share the stage with that damn monkey . . ."

"We're here for Willow," Charlotte said, waving her cane.

William watched as Stepin looked at them quizzically. "That so?" the man said. "Well, she's here. Though I don't think she'll be hanging out in the greenroom. She's in one of her blue moods. When she's down like that, we all just leave her be. She's in her dressing room." Stepin pointed. "But if I were you, I'd enter at your own risk."

"She's here?" William blurted.

"She's been here for thirty minutes—down in the basement. That's where all the ladies' dressing rooms are, in case you were wondering."

"But Asa told us to wait here . . ."

Stepin waved his hand. "That man don't know his last name half the time. He came home from the war all shell-shocked—went from receiving the Croix de Guerre for heroism in the trenches to years in a funny farm. Now he's Mr. One-liner and all that. Somehow it makes sense, I guess."

Charlotte interrupted. "Go, William. Just go."

William thanked the man and promised Charlotte that he'd be right back. He thought about what he could possibly say as he ran downstairs, going against the flow of glittering dancers and corseted showgirls, who barely noticed him. He found there was no carpeting in the basement, and the cement floor seemed to radiate cold. At the end of the cluttered hallway, past racks of clothing, props, and set pieces, he saw a star painted on a door. Written in chalk was the word *Willow*. William straightened his jacket and drew a deep breath, tasting talcum and tobacco in the air as he gently knocked. No answer. He knocked again, harder this time. Still no answer. He looked around the hallway and then opened the door, which creaked on rusty hinges, announcing his arrival. He peeked inside and saw the actress sitting in the windowless room, perched before a mirrored vanity, staring at her reflection through a haze of smoke. The cigarette in her hand had nearly turned to ash. He spied the ashtray, which was overflowing.

"Sorry, Asa dear, I can't go out there tonight," he heard Willow say. "I don't care what they're paying me. Please tell them to take it up with the Screen Actors Guild. I can't play this town—the rain is bad for my voice."

But your voice sounds perfectly fine. William stood in the doorway staring. He noticed that she wore a different dress from earlier in the day but sat barefoot. Up close, her glittering jewelry looked like painted glass and her sable wrap looked dead, a lifeless slice of brown carpet. She sat staring at the lighted mirror, which was broken and splintered. Her glamorous composure seemed wrinkled and faded, discarded and stained, like the photo he kept in his coat.

"Who are *you?*" she said as she caught his silhouette in the mirror.

I didn't have a reason to stay. He heard her words from the radio interview all over again. "I'm . . ." *Scared to know why you left me behind.*

William heard the din of footsteps upstairs on the worn wooden floor, and the skittering of high heels, the clicking of tap shoes. He watched as she stubbed out her cigarette and slowly turned around. When her eyes met his, it was as though they were both staring at the ruins of a broken promise. Her grace had vanished along with her glamour. The dark circles of her eye makeup stood out against her pale skin. This woman—his mother, who was barely thirty— seemed a million years old and weary beyond reckoning. She gazed at him unblinking, while a single black tear wandered down the hollow of her cheek, coming to rest at the confluence of her lips, which trembled.

"It's really you," Willow said, "isn't it?" She took a deep breath and then another, struggling to collect herself. "You've grown so much . . ."

"It's William," he said, nodding, "William Eng."

She looked as though she'd been slapped. "Please, don't say that name."

"William?"

She shook her head, slowly. "Eng."

"But you're Liu Song *Eng,* aren't you?"

She bit her lip. "Don't call me that either."

"What should I call you . . . Willow? They told me you were dead, but you're right here—you're my mother, aren't you? You're my ah-ma."

With those words she seemed to shrink onto the floor, sinking to one knee, arms open, outstretched, hands limp as though reaching for something she dared not grasp—as though her every hope might be laced with poison.

William melted into her arms, a swirl of familiar fragrance and memory, her embrace, the terrible way her body shook as she sobbed, the warmth of her tears on his cheek, on his neck, the pain, hauntingly familiar.

She ran her fingers through the hair on the back of his head as he tried not to cry. "I'm so sorry, William . . . I'm so sorry . . . so sorry." She rocked him back and forth, the way she had when he was just a toddler.

He felt her kiss his cheek and his ear. "I'm so sorry. I've thought about you every day, wondering—who you were with, what you'd remember about me."

"But how could I forget?" William asked.

She let go of him, gently fixing his collar and touching the buttons on his shirt, as though she'd dressed him herself and was about to send him back out into the world. She touched his cheek as she spoke. "The person I was back then, she's dead, William. The person you knew is buried in sorrow and shame. The mother I was, Liu Song, she didn't have a chance. She didn't even have a choice. So I let her die. And all that was left was the person on-screen, onstage. Willow, who just kept going . . ."

But you are both. "Willow is just a stage name."

"It's how I've survived, William. Willow saved me."

Yes, but from whom? "Then why didn't you come back for me?"

She paused and motioned for him to close the door. Then she asked him to lock it as well. She fished out another cigarette, put it to her mouth, hesitated, and then put it away. "There's so much you don't know. You were just a little, little boy."

William swam through the memories of his years at the orphanage—years of loneliness, years of longing. Then his mind flashed upon her flickering image on-screen, the movie posters and radiant lifestyle. *You have everything.*

When William had dared to hope that Willow was indeed his mother, he'd imagined this moment, the tears of joy, the embrace, the life they would have together. This was nothing like that. These were tears of sadness. "What couldn't you explain to me?"

"All I knew was that I couldn't give you the hideous life I had then—I wouldn't wish that upon anyone. And I couldn't give you the life I have now, for your own protection. I couldn't even give you a decent name. I couldn't give you anything that mattered."

"But you have it all." William gestured to the dressing room, the theater itself. "You are wealthy—famous! Everyone loves you. What don't you have?"

"I don't have what matters most."

Your son, William thought. *I'm right here.*

She whispered so softly he barely heard her. "Forgiveness."

"What more is there to forgive?" William asked. Then he had a terrible realization, that maybe she was unable to forgive herself.

She motioned for him to come closer, and she took his hands. She slowly examined them. The years he'd spent working in the laundry or pushing a mop at Sacred Heart hadn't smoothed his long, wrinkled fingers—they still had the same hands, old hands. But where his were warm, hers were cold, frozen. He felt her let go and then watched as she stared into her empty palms as though reading lines on a map, searching.

And then, while music began to play from somewhere upstairs, somewhere far away, she spoke to him of family and fathers.

Songs

回

(1921)

Liu Song Eng walked home from Butterfield's, where she worked after school as a song plugger. Singing in front of the store wasn't a bad job, per se. With her voice—her thunderous contralto—she managed to earn a nickel for every page of sheet music sold. But her looks drew unwanted attention from passersby, especially when she wore her mother's chevron tabard dress. Matronly women squinted their eyes at Liu Song and pursed their bee-stung lips. Grown men stopped dead in their tracks when they heard a tearful Mamie Smith ballad coming from Liu Song's seventeen-year-old body. They leered, looking her up and down, then slowly back up again. Even the prim Seattle beat cops seemed to linger nearby, palming their batons and making jokes about a stiff breeze as she fought to keep the chill wind from blowing up her slip. Meanwhile, Old Man Butterfield sat inside, where it was warm, smoking his pipe and flitting his long fingers across the chipped ivories of an old, upright piano, which, unlike the pianolas, wasn't for sale. He could have let one of the new autopianos do all the work, but Liu Song suspected that he liked to play as much as she liked to sing. To Liu Song, the lonely old man seemed wedded to his music. He'd never married and rarely even talked about women, except to comment on their shoes.

"Don't make the same mistakes, Liu Song. Don't be alone with a man—any man—not until you're married." Those were the last words her mother ever spoke to her.

Liu Song shrugged at the thought. She wasn't afraid of being alone with her boss, but she dreaded the thought of being alone, without her true family. As she crossed the street she fastened her coat's collar button. She tied her favorite scarf around her neck and wrinkled her nose because the wool smelled like cherry-vanilla tobacco. She longed for the comforting sound of her mother's voice. Liu Song knew her mother had once performed onstage but couldn't recall ever hearing her sing, not even a sad lullaby.

When Liu Song rounded the corner into Chinatown, she saw her stepfather and two other businessmen smoking and talking in front of the Quong Tuck Company. She recognized him from two blocks away by the expensive Oxford bags he wore. As she crossed the street she thought his stout frame and round belly looked ridiculous in those baggy English trousers, especially next to the businessmen in their three-piece suits.

"Hello, Uncle Leo," she said cordially as she passed by.

Her stepfather didn't fancy the idea of having a daughter and had insisted on being referred to as *uncle*. He flicked his cigarette butt into the gutter and spat on the sidewalk, then turned his back and continued talking.

You're not my uncle, Liu Song thought, *or my father. You're just a laundryman.*

Liu Song's real father had been a theater director and a Cantonese opera star, but his company in Seattle had foundered when the Spanish flu forced him into temporary retirement. Despite quarantines, he died from the Grippe—the same disease that took her brothers and crippled her mother.

She wished she could have seen him perform, just once, but girls were not allowed back then—not good girls, anyway. And she loved his stories.

"One time during the seventh month, when I was just a boy apprentice, our troupe traveled to a remote village and gave a grand performance," her father had often told her. "But when we woke in the morning, the village had completely vanished—we were standing in an empty meadow. We'd been entertaining ghosts!"

His story about the ghost village was her favorite, and sometimes when she sang, at home, at school, or in front of Butterfield's, she imagined his ghost watching, nodding approval or offering instruction.

As Liu Song wandered down Canton Alley and into her family's apartment in the East Kong Yick building, she was overwhelmed by the smell of camphor—a reminder that the only real ghost in her life was her bedridden mother. The beautiful woman Liu Song's father had called My Joyful Goddess had lost her hearing when a fever ruptured her eardrums during the influenza epidemic. She couldn't sing, could hardly speak, and rarely communicated now. It was a strange miracle that Uncle Leo had even married her, but she still had her looks, and Chinese women were few, so he took them in. Liu Song's mother had cooked, cleaned, and done everything Uncle Leo expected from an obedient wife, except provide him with a son. As her health failed as well, Uncle Leo administered a variety of treatments, which only brought on a withering storm of seizures. Each time, a part of her mind faded—her memories disappeared. Her mother was a wildflower, transplanted into a bed of sand, losing her natural color and fragrance. Her vitality gone, she seemed to age rapidly, beyond her years.

"How are you today, Ah-ma?" Liu Song asked as she took off her coat and peeked into the bedroom her mother shared with Uncle Leo. It was a rhetorical question, for comfort—an aspiration of normalcy. Liu Song filled a teakettle and put it on the stove before returning to her mother, who was awake and struggling to sit up in bed. Liu Song watched as her mother looked around as though momentarily bewildered. Then she looked at Liu Song and smiled. She closed her eyes, puckering her lips emphatically.

Liu Song kissed both her mother's cheeks, then licked her thumbs and rubbed in the residual lipstick, rouging her mother's sallow complexion.

"Did you eat?" Liu Song asked. She motioned as though scooping imaginary rice from an imaginary bowl with a pair of imaginary chopsticks.

Her mother shook her head slowly, then nodded, wide-eyed.

Liu Song went to the kitchen and returned with a bowl of cold rice and a spoon. She struggled to smile when her mother's hands shook violently as she reached for the dish. Despite her relatively young age, and as much as she wanted to try, her ah-ma was well past the point of being able to properly feed herself.

"I'll do it, Ah-ma. It's okay, I'll do it."

As her mother crossed her arms and gripped her nightgown to control her spasms, Liu Song saw red welts and bruising—fresh rope burns. Liu Song lifted the stained sheets at the foot of the bed and saw that her mother's ankles had been tied as well. And the brass around the bedposts looked polished.

"Who did this to you?"

Liu Song had offered to—no, she'd insisted she would—quit school and stay home to be her ah-ma's full-time caregiver, but Uncle Leo had said no. He said *he* would take care of her, as he always had, with a strange brew of herbal remedies, which failed. When Dr. Luke was finally called, he diagnosed Liu Song's mother with Saint Vitus' dance—a rare affliction for a woman her age. But her peculiar convulsions, her jerking and twitching, never went away—her health grew worse until there was little anyone could do. A nurse who used to come by to check on her condition had eventually stopped coming.

"Did Uncle Leo do this?"

Liu Song gently touched her mother's wrists as she jerked them away.

"Did he do this to you?" she pleaded, her words falling on scared, deaf ears as she found a jar of Pond's cold cream and gently rubbed the salve, which smelled of witch hazel, onto her mother's bruises. Liu Song asked again, pointing to a framed photo of her stepfather that hung on the wall. Years ago her real father's portrait had occupied that space. Her mother stared blankly at the photo, and then looked toward the door, blinking, and she smiled with trembling, cracked lips. She made a sound that was lost somewhere between a laugh and a cry.

"Get out," Uncle Leo said, as he appeared in the doorway, holding a bottle of camphor oil. "I need to give your mother her medicine."

"She hasn't eaten," Liu Song said, pointing to her mother's body, which must have weighed less than ninety pounds. "Can't you see she's starving?"

"Leave the food. I'll take care of it."

Liu Song stared at Uncle Leo. This was the same man who had helped sponsor the local Go-Hing festival—a carnival to raise money for famine relief in China.

"Make me some tea." He glared back, unblinking, as the kettle whistled in the kitchen. "Do as I say, Liu Song *Eng*." He emphasized his last name, which she was now burdened with, like an animal branded for life.

Liu Song turned to her mother, who was nodding slowly as she reached up and wrapped her bruised, trembling arms around her, pulling her close, whispering in her ear.

"I'm s-s-s-so . . . sorry," her mother said.

The teakettle blared.

Liu Song felt her ah-ma release her and exhale slowly, raggedly. She watched as her mother sank into her pillow and closed her eyelids tightly, as though shutting out the world. When Liu Song stood to leave, her stepfather was still staring at her body, appraising her appearance in her mother's chevron tabard dress. He grunted and then stepped aside, closing the bedroom door behind her.

Flower Girls

口

(1921)

After school, Liu Song rode the streetcar from Franklin High over to Butterfield's, where she stood beneath a leaking umbrella and tried to sing, "Blue days, all of them gone . . ."

She forgot the rest of the lyrics when she caught her reflection in the rain-streaked storefront window. She looked so much like her mother, especially in the dress. She couldn't remember the last time her mother had worn it. All she could think of now was her wisp of a parent, tied to her bed, mute, delirious, and slowly starving.

Mr. Butterfield continued playing the chorus to "Blue Skies," then the bridge, then back to the chorus as Liu Song struggled to sing, "Never saw the sun shining so bright . . ." She lowered the umbrella and felt the rain on her face.

"I'm sorry, Mr. Butterfield."

The old man stood up from his piano just inside the front of the store, tucked away behind the red-velvet curtains of the window displays, which Liu Song had helped arrange—Leedy drums, polished brass instruments, and a life-size statue of Nipper, the Victor Talking Machine Company's canine mascot. The ceramic dog stared with his head tilted, one ear perpetually cocked, toward a new Victrola in an expensive Chippendale cabinet. Mr. Butterfield cracked his knuckles, then patted his pocket, looking for his three-finger cigar case. "Take a break, sweetheart," he said. "It's a slow afternoon anyway."

Liu Song stood in the doorway, where the air was fresh, watching flivvers and Model Ts roll by. She counted scores of cars. Their noisy, clattering engines and blaring horns scared a team of horses pulling an old carriage in need of fresh paint. The coachman steered to the side of the street to let them pass.

Liu Song felt a dizzying wave of melancholy because her father had once owned a tree-green landaulet—an old model, with gas-powered headlights. Liu Song remembered going for bumpy, wild rides on Sunday afternoons to Green Lake and Ballard, sitting on the fender and eating ice-cream floats. Now Uncle Leo owned her father's motorcar. He rarely drove it and, when he did, he never put the rear top down, not even on sunny afternoons when the weather was perfect. As Liu Song lingered in the past, she felt as though her memories were quicksand and she was sinking deeper and deeper.

"There's fresh coffee," Mr. Butterfield interrupted, yelling from the back room. "And a flask of cognac, if you need something a bit warmer."

Liu Song shook her head. Her parents had never allowed her to drink alcohol, not a sip or a taste, even before Prohibition. And she certainly wasn't going to sample some home brew that was probably mashed by hand in someone's basement. She ignored the offer, pretending she didn't hear.

As she looked down the avenue for paying customers, she saw a familiar face—her best friend, Mildred Chew, walking with her mother, stepping around puddles.

Liu Song smiled and waved. She had a lot in common with Mildred. They were both American-born, to naturalized parents. They both had to work after school, instead of going to the Chong Wa building to learn city Cantonese. And they both envied the rich kids who always went after class to Dugdale Field, where they watched the Seattle Indians play doubleheaders, eating popcorn and salted peanuts while the poor kids watched from the cabbage patch up the hill.

Mildred didn't wave back. And her mother looked unhappy.

When they stopped in front of the store, Liu Song said, *"Neih hou ma?"*

Mildred's mother was shorter than Liu Song by a foot. She looked Liu Song up and down, shaking her head and ignoring her polite greeting.

"I'm sorry, Liu—" Mildred said in English.

Mildred's mother shushed her, then spoke in Taishanese. "It's come to my attention that you're the daughter of that *opera singer*." She spat the words in her thick dialect, as though the thought of Liu Song's mother left a bitter taste in her mouth. "Where I come from, the only women who hang around the theater are *courtesans*. And you yourself stand here, shamelessly working the street."

Liu Song didn't understand. Most of the locals loved Yuet Kahk. But she remembered her father's darker stories, about when he was a boy and how Cantonese opera had been banned by the Ch'ing dynasty and performers had been slaughtered. She never asked, but she knew that was why her apprentice parents came to America on tour and never went back. They knew some harsh feelings were slow to change—even after decades, or thousands of miles, even after the Manchus began to allow Peking opera in the north.

Liu Song tried to be polite. She didn't want to argue. She bowed her head in deference. "I just sell sheet music, by the page . . ." she said in English, then Chinese.

"You should be home taking care of your family, not out here skulking around like the flower girls over in Paradise Alley." Mildred's mother jerked her thumb in the direction of South Washington Street, where Lou Graham's brothel had operated before she'd been run out of town. Now girls, some of them Liu Song's age, doused themselves in perfume and wrapped their bodies in crepe de chine, selling flowers on the corner. But everyone knew that what the girls were really selling was negotiable.

"*Dui m'ji,*" Liu Song said. "I'm sorry if I've offended . . ."

"Stay away from my Mildred—*she's a good girl!*"

Liu Song stood there, speechless. As a car passed, the driver whistled at her.

Mildred's mother raised her eyebrows and cocked her head, resting a fist on each bony hip. "Mildred doesn't need friends like you in your . . . *flapper dress.*" She swished her hand in the air as though brushing away a bad smell and then turned on her heel and stormed off, cursing in Taishanese as she stepped in a mud puddle.

Mildred slumped her shoulders and mouthed, "I'm so sorry." Then waved goodbye as she followed her mother.

THE RAIN HAD stopped by the time Liu Song got off work, but the sky was still a perpetual mass of gray. Gaslights on each city block flickered to life, illuminating oily rainbows that swirled down fetid gutters and storm drains clogged with rotting leaves.

The attitude of Mildred's mother explained a lot. Especially at school, where Liu Song hung out at lunchtime with the other Chinese students, who were kind and polite, but not exactly close. And they rarely asked about her home life or her ailing ah-ma. At first Liu Song thought it was because so many of them had also lost relatives to the Grippe, or in the Great War. But her classmates never dropped by, or talked about visiting. And not once had she been invited to any of their parties or get-togethers.

"They're jealous of how beautiful and talented you are," her mother had scribbled in Chinese on a writing slate when Liu Song first entered Franklin High.

Maybe she's right, Liu Song had thought. High school was filled with silly pettiness at times. But when Liu Song sat uninvited to the first tea dance and later the Winter Banquet, she realized that there was something unspoken between her and her peers.

Only Mildred came to visit. Only Mildred had spent time with her these past few years. But Liu Song realized that was probably because Mildred had transferred from the Main Street School Annex in junior high and didn't know a soul.

As Liu Song walked down Canton Alley to her apartment, she longed to smell her mother's cooking, to hear her mother's voice, to feel gentle hands braiding her wet hair once again, to communicate with someone who understood her pain, and her loneliness. Liu Song was so different; from an unorthodox family, she didn't seem to fit in anywhere, and she longed for approval. She craved validation. Her strength was her voice, but to most in her neighborhood, her gift was a crippling malady—a chronic weakness that made her unsuitable for marriage. And a Chinese woman without a husband was worth nothing.

When Liu Song reached her front step, Uncle Leo was coming out the door. He offered her a large box, overflowing with her mother's belongings.

"Take this to the garbage," he said. "Your ah-ma won't be needing these things anymore. And I can't sell any of this. Who would buy?"

Liu Song stared at the box in disbelief. She could smell her mother's lilac perfume on an old scarf. And she felt the finality of Uncle Leo's callous gesture as she regarded an old brush, filled with her mother's hair, which in recent days had been falling out in clumps. Liu Song's fingers trembled as she touched the dress her mother had worn the last time she had been strong enough to leave the house, which seemed like a lifetime ago. Everything here was laden with sentiment but held no monetary value—Leo must have kept those things, or gambled them away.

"But . . . all of this belongs to my family," Liu Song said. She nearly broke down sobbing as she realized she didn't say, *belonged to my mother.* The tightness in Liu Song's chest, the lump in her throat, made her feel as though she'd already lost her ah-ma.

Uncle Leo dropped the box onto the pavement. He pulled up his suspenders and flared his nostrils. "Fine," he barked. "Choose one thing to keep. But the rest . . ." He waved his hand dismissively. "All bad luck."

Liu Song picked up the box and slowly walked down the alley as she heard Uncle Leo slam the door. She saw a pile of her mother's possessions, the remnants of her family, good and bad memories, strewn among yesterday's refuse.

Your superstitions haunt the both of us, Uncle, Liu Song thought.

She set the box down next to the rest of her mother's belongings and knelt on the wet, mossy pavement, amid orange peels, fish bones, and tattered cigarette butts. She reverently touched her mother's old possessions as if they were alive—her blouses, her hats, shoes, slips, books, trinkets and curios from the theater.

Choose one thing.

Liu Song nodded when she found her mother's vaudeville case—a cracked valise filled with stage makeup, headpieces, satin footwear, and assorted costume jewelry. The leather was spattered with used coffee grounds. She wiped it clean with her bare hands.

The case had been an engagement present from her father and was stamped with ports of entry—Seattle, Vancouver, Los Angeles, and San Francisco, mementos of a time when her parents were barely out of their teens. They'd traveled from city to city with a troupe of 130 other performers—catering to audiences of migrant workers and high-minded Caucasian socialites who wanted to indulge in something exotic. Liu Song dug through a box and found her mother's final costume, the elegant gown with long tassels, shimmering sequins, and silver beads. She carefully folded the embroidered silk and tucked it into the suitcase, along with a small photo album, old letters—as much as would fit. She knelt on the case to close it. Then buckled it shut. She thought about taking more things, but Uncle Leo would probably just burn them if he found them. In his mind it was bad fortune to keep anything so personal, because after death they might draw the spirit back.

Inside, the apartment smelled like pungent dried herbs, old incense, and the ever-present camphor oil. Her mother hadn't moved at all from when Liu Song left that morning. She adjusted the blankets and pillows to prevent bedsores, talking to her mother as if she could hear—as if there was a chance that she would come back to the world of the living. She noticed round mirrors on the windowsill, on the dresser, on the nightstand—mirrors her parents had used to symbolize a perfect marriage were now being used to ward off unwanted spirits. Uncle Leo was preparing for the worst. Whatever was happening to her mother, good or bad, would be reflected, magnified.

Liu Song pressed her face to her mother's cheek. She felt heat from a rising fever and a wisp of her ah-ma's breath on her ear. Liu Song closed her eyes wearily as she avoided looking into the mirrors.

Glory of Mourning

(1921)

Liu Song didn't weep when Uncle Leo woke her up a week later and told her, "Your mother is in Heaven." She didn't whimper as she sat at the table and watched the undertaker bring in a pine casket while her breakfast grew cold. She didn't even shed a tear as she dressed her mother's frail body in an old gown she'd saved for this sad occasion, an elegant slip of ivory that now seemed three sizes too big. She did everything a dutiful, obedient, loving daughter was expected to do—without fuss or complaint. She brushed her mother's remaining hair and carefully applied her makeup. She wore black for the wake and hung a dark wreath on the door. She burned incense and joss paper all day, sending riches to her mother in the afterlife. And she broke her mother's favorite comb, placing half in the casket and keeping half for herself. She left the crying to the wailers. Uncle Leo had hired a trio of old women with missing teeth who were famous for their ability to sob for hours at a time, at great volume, shedding real tears.

As she sat in their living room and tried to block out the baleful noise, Liu Song wished her father and brothers had been given such a wake, but they weren't even given proper funerals. They'd been laid to rest without caskets, since there were none to be found in the city. Instead, a truck had taken their bodies from a temporary morgue at the old city hall and delivered them to a potter's field somewhere south of town, just past the county line. They were buried along with others who had died from influenza, without ceremony, in a massive unmarked grave.

Liu Song remembered that her father had been a pragmatic man. He always made sure he and his family wore their gauze masks. But he'd been stricken with fever and began coughing up blood two days after the Armistice celebration, when thousands of drunken revelers had taken to the streets without protection. Her brothers had died two weeks later, prompting her uncles and aunties to sell their belongings and flee with her cousins to Reno, Nevada, and Butte, Montana. Some even went back to China, leaving her alone with her widowed mother, grieving in a city overflowing with bodies, infected with mourning, prone to fevers of panic and despair.

Now she was even more alone, as Uncle Leo's relatives, associates, and business partners came and paid their respects. To Liu Song they were a parade of strangers, who didn't shy away from commenting in her presence.

"She didn't even give him a son," one woman complained bitterly.

"How terrible it must be," another woman said, "to inherit a daughter who doesn't carry your own blood, from a shameful mother with such bad luck! Who would want to marry Leo now—with her family's ghosts around?"

"Maybe he'll send the daughter away—marry her off quickly," a man replied. "She's too tall—her eyes too big, but there are so few girls, he'd get a nice dowry."

Liu Song thought about her mother's final words and her final warning as she weighed which might be worse: being stuck here, alone with Uncle Leo, or being betrothed to some unknown man, haphazardly chosen by her stepfather. She stared at the framed portrait of her mother and found no answers and little comfort.

"Ah, look at her." A woman pointed at Liu Song. "She's so

skinny. She must be a terrible cook. No one will want her, and Leo will probably starve—that poor man."

That poor man, Liu Song thought.

She heard laughing and cursing, and looked out the front window, watching as Uncle Leo and a group of men in shirttails and suspenders tossed dice in the alley. Her uncle had a fat pile of silver dollars and a wad of folding money in front of him as he knelt on one knee, chewing a cigar. He rolled again, smiling as the other men groaned and shook their heads, reaching into their billfolds for more cash.

Liu Song knew that it was customary for at least one person to remain awake nearby to guard the body and that men sometimes played poker and faro, mah-jongg or cribbage—anything to stay vigilant. And while Uncle Leo was extremely traditional and very superstitious by nature, she'd never heard of the husband taking on that responsibility, or enjoying it so much.

She put her head in her hands, wondering how her mother had been able to marry such a man. But after the run-in with Mildred's mother, Liu Song finally understood—that most Chinese, even in America, regarded a woman onstage as no better than a prostitute. Her mother probably couldn't even find a job as a maid. What choice did she have? She gave up performing, pawned her dreams, and finally lost her voice.

"*Hahng'wúih?*" Someone spoke. Then he switched to English. "I hope you don't mind if I practice my American?"

Liu Song peeked through her fingers and saw pristinely polished wingtips. Then she looked up at a man in a dark wool suit and striped tie, which made him seem older than the youthful appearance of his clean-shaven face. She blinked, rubbing a bit of mascara from the corner of her eye. "Excuse me?"

The young man spoke fluently but with a strange accent. "You must be Liu Song. I could tell by the resemblance. Your mother was the most beautiful woman in Chinatown. The most talented too, if you don't mind my saying."

Much to her surprise, the curious man offered to pour Liu Song a cup of tea. She held the warm porcelain teacup with both hands as she noticed that the sleeves of his dress shirt hung open at the wrists. He'd removed his cuff links, all jewelry, in fact, out of respect for the dead. His simple manner was a stark contrast to the older women, who wore pieces of carved jade and decorative hatpins, dabbing the corners of their eyes with monogrammed lace.

"If I may introduce myself, I'm Colin Kwan." He exhaled and looked as grief-stricken as she felt. "I'm . . . humbled by your staggering loss."

Liu Song regarded the man and said, *"Do jeh."* And then, "Thank you," as she nodded in solemn appreciation.

"We've never actually met, but I was one of your father's understudies. I came here from Hong Kong. I trained with him." Colin cleared his throat, then removed his fedora and ran his finger along the brim. "It didn't . . . work out the way I had hoped."

Liu Song invited him to sit down and thanked him as he poured more tea into her cup. From the corner of her eye she regarded his Chinese features, his dark hair, which was neatly parted to the side and slicked back. "Your accent, is so unusual . . ."

"Ah, that. My English teacher was a colonial, originally from Bristol, England. Perhaps I sound more Anglo when I speak my American, yes?"

Liu Song nodded again, smiling slightly at the musical cadence of his voice. She looked around the room and realized that they were probably the only ones here who spoke English well enough to carry on a conversation. She found strange comfort in that.

"The man was an excellent teacher, but I learned a great deal more in the short time I worked with your father. And I was fortunate enough to see your mother's remarkable performance at the Grand Opera House, before it burned down, of course."

Liu Song's heart ached. "Her *only* performance."

"That too. Still, it was . . . magnificent . . . groundbreaking."

"I wish I could have been there."

Liu Song remembered staying home with her brothers that night, four years ago, when her mother took the stage amid a kaleidoscope of giant silk flags and twirling swords—the first woman to appear in a Chinese opera in Seattle.

"It was my father's idea. He was so excited when he saw the film version of *Zhuangzi Tests His Wife,* where Yan Shanshan played the servant girl. He thought he would do one better and actually have a *woman* play the Widow of Zhuangzi."

A moment of silence lingered between them, and Liu Song wondered if Colin felt the biting irony as well. Her mother had played a woman whose husband faked his death to test her loyalty, to see if she would remarry. Liu Song took another sip and then stared into her half-empty teacup, watching bits of peony swirl and settle to the bottom.

The wailers began crying again in earnest, one of them tearing her clothes.

Liu Song looked at Colin as he jumped in his seat and then fanned himself with his hat. His other hand patted his heart. Liu Song tried not to laugh. She sat back in her chair and exhaled, long and slow, relaxing, remembering what it was like to be happy. Since her father had died, she'd barely known comfort or contentment.

"I brought a few things for your mother, out of respect for your father." He reached into a leather briefcase and withdrew a small statue of T'ang Ming Huang, the patron saint of Chinese opera. He held it up for her approval. She nodded and watched him place the clay figurine on the shrine near the casket, next to offerings of food, money, and smoldering joss paper.

"And I've had this for some time, but I'd rather it belong to your family now." He held out an opera mask with both hands. "It was . . ."

"My mother's." Liu Song took the mask, gently, looking at the ornate design—dramatic features painted in red, green, and black.

"This is the one she wore . . ."

"As Zhuangzi's wife," Colin said with a polite smile.

Liu Song touched the wooden mask as though she were caressing her mother's cheek. She brought it to her nose, and for a moment she thought it even smelled like her mother's perfume, or at least the greasy black eye makeup that she wore.

"The art director took ill," Colin said. "So I offered to take it home and replace the straps on the back. I was eager to do anything to impress your father. But then the fire—I know your father looked for another venue . . ."

"And then the quarantines."

Colin frowned and nodded. "I was unable to return it. I sent letters to Leo—your stepfather. I told him that I had something that belonged to your mother, but either he never received the missives or he never bothered to reply."

Liu Song knew the answer. She thanked him, then excused herself for a moment and walked to her mother's open casket, lingering, looking at her ah-ma's hands. Her fingers, which had been long and graceful, now looked aged, withered. Liu Song reached out to touch them, but stopped an inch away when she felt the absence of warmth and noticed that her mother's favorite ring had been removed—the ring that she had been given by Liu Song's father after they were wed. Her mother had continued to wear it, since Uncle Leo never gave her a new one.

Liu Song held the mask and ground her teeth, her heart pounding, angry and laden with guilt—she shook her head and wondered why she hadn't cried. What kind of shameful daughter was she? She should be on her knees in a pool of tears, pulling out her hair and screaming. Instead she drifted to her bedroom, unnoticed, a specter in a room full of shadows. She hid the mask in the valise under her bed with her mother's other precious possessions, a photo of her father, her mother's favorite brooch, her brother's empty cologne bottle, and odds and ends from a life she was orphaned from.

When she returned to the living room, her heart sank as she realized the young man was gone; his chair and teacup were empty. She felt more alone than before.

Most of the visitors had left or were in the process of leaving, all but a handful of men that Uncle Leo had selected as pallbearers, toothless men who worked in his laundry. None of them had known Liu Song, or her parents. If they seemed unaffected by their duties, the three wailers more than made up for their stoic expressions. As the casket was slowly closed, the three old women cried and screamed hysterically, their shoulders heaving with a crescendo of violent sobs. Uncle Leo covered his ears and yawned.

Liu Song took one final look at her mother's face and then stepped back.

"Goodbye, Ah-ma," she whispered.

Everyone turned their backs since it was terribly unlucky to watch a coffin being nailed shut. All but Liu Song, who numbly watched a white-haired man in an old suit swing a small hammer again and again. The pounding reminded her of the rhythmic sound of coiled bedsprings.

Liu Song watched each nail sink deeper.

I'm already cloaked in bad luck, what more can be done to me? she thought. *I have no one else—no one left to lose. I have nothing.*

As Liu Song stared at the casket, she imagined her mother inside, her eyes opening again, filled with tears. Her mother's cracked lips, her frail voice urging, pleading, "Run away, Liu Song. Run away."

Big Mother

꒤

(1921)

After Liu Song's mother was lowered into the ground, Uncle Leo went out to dinner with his family and friends. He didn't bother to invite Liu Song, so she stayed at the cemetery and picked wildflowers. She placed them on the tiny slab of marble that marked her mother's grave. As she regarded the elaborate, towering headstones to the left and right of her mother's humble plot, she tried to remember how her ah-ma had looked when she left for her performance—so alive, so vibrant, larger than life; no stage seemed too grand for her. But now there was no audience, no curtain call. Now her ah-ma would remain in the wings, the backstage of a sodden hill, a forgotten bit player, forever.

Liu Song walked home alone in the rain, down King Street, beneath a blizzard of painted signs and hanging lanterns. As she passed the Twin Dragons Restaurant, she could see Uncle Leo and his family through the rain-streaked glass, sitting at round tables, crowded with platters of food on spinning lazy Susans. But instead of eating tofu, boiled white chicken, and *jai choy*, the heavenly vegetables one would normally eat after a funeral, the mourners laughed as they feasted on roast duck with ginger and chives, oily rock cod, served whole, and tureens of oxtail soup. They were enjoying a celebratory dinner. Liu Song smelled sesame oil and heard the sizzle and pinging of a cast-iron wok in the kitchen as more dishes were brought out, but she had no appetite. Her belly was full of grief. She had feasted on the bitter rind of sorrow.

At home, she left the lights off. She donned a nightgown and then crawled into bed, tucking her head beneath the covers. She imagined the blankets were shovelfuls of dirt, burying herself in darkness as her wet hair dampened the sheets. She curled up so tightly she could feel the beat of her heart, her blood pulsing in her legs. She slapped her face and pinched her cheeks, hoping to make herself cry—wishing the knot of grief inside her chest could be expelled, cut off, cauterized. She'd watched her mother slip away, one piece, one touch, and one memory at a time. Liu Song had lived for the past four years in a state of perpetual mourning—maybe she'd already exhausted a lifetime supply of tears.

As she drifted to sleep she thought about the comfort of the earth, the ground, where her family had all been laid to rest. Then her thoughts drifted to the strange young man—her father's under-study. She wondered how old he must be, perhaps in his mid-twenties, too old, perhaps. She doubted he would call on her again. Why would he? Though she certainly entertained the notion of finding him—just to see him perform, of course. She could allow herself that. She knew that a schoolgirl crush was foolish, but the theater community was small, competitive, and well connected—there had even been talk in the newspaper of building a Chinese opera house. If Colin Kwan was in town, she could find him. That wouldn't be too desperate, would it? As she slept, she dreamt of her father, strong and passionate, wearing the mask and gown of a *qing yi*— a noblewoman, exuding grace and virtue. And she fantasized about her parents bringing the young understudy to America as Liu Song's tutor—and suitor, for an arranged marriage that would play out onstage, in three acts plus an encore. But as much as she wanted it to be a hero's story, even in a dream, she knew that tale could only end in tragedy.

With her family gone she was certain no man would want her.

Her parents would have discouraged all of the Chinese-born suitors, knowing that if she married one of them she risked losing her status as an American-born citizen. Plus the students who spoke Mandarin had always looked down on her, while the Cantonese men all wanted wives born in China—versed in the traditions of submission and subservience. They regarded her as too tall, or too skinny, her eyes were too round, or she was too ugly, too modern, too *American*. And no one wanted a shameful performer for a daughter-in-law.

But this is only Act One, she thought, still dreaming.

In a lucid state, she wondered what it might be like to see Colin perform to a packed house—perhaps she'd join him in front of the footlights one day at the Moore Theatre or the Palace up north, in Vancouver, where she first saw her father perform. The notion of klieg lights and plush velvet curtains only made her ache for her mother—for her family. And when she imagined Colin onstage, she also saw her father, and then her uncle. Drunk with sadness, she felt a stranger's breath on her neck and turned her head, sure that she was still dreaming, until she felt the covers pulled back and smelled barley wine, and ginger, and sesame oil. She sensed thick fingers, tugging, rending the fabric of her bedclothes. She felt a calloused hand over her mouth as a man's knees parted hers. *"M`h'gōi bōng ngóh!"* Her scream for help was muffled as she struggled to fight him off. Liu Song stared at the shadowy tin ceiling, horrified. She felt pain and grief, shock and sorrow, and crushing, suffocating humiliation amid the bristling whiskers on his chin, the hair on his legs, and the sweaty folds of his unwashed skin. She felt him tugging on the wide elastic of her sanitary belt, pausing, then pulling it aside. She thrashed with all her might, hysterically, but she was almost as small as her mother. She felt stabbing pain, tearing, but she couldn't cry. She closed her eyes and was someplace else—*someone* else, an actress in a silent film. She was Pearl White in *Perils of Pauline,* tied to a train track as a hulking steam locomotive chugged through a cloud of coal smoke, bearing down on her. Then the scene faded to black.

WHEN THE BED finally stopped shaking, Uncle Leo groaned and stood up, out of breath. He put on his bathrobe and slippers. "Stay in bed. Don't get up until sunrise." He patted her arm and touched her hair as if to make sure she was still there in the dark.

Liu Song closed her eyes and didn't move or make a sound.

As she heard the door close behind him, she lay there, paralyzed, her mind telling herself that it didn't really happen. Her aching body told her otherwise. Finally she pulled the covers up to her face, then smelled Uncle Leo's odor and tossed the bedding aside. She rolled to her side, clutching her pillow. She curled her trembling body around it.

She opened her eyes and saw a waning orb through the curtains, reflecting glittering moonlight around her bedroom, her ceiling, dotting the walls. She looked down and saw that the mirror on her nightstand had tipped over and smashed on the wooden floor. Shiny bits of bad luck lay scattered around her bed as though a tiny shooting star had crashed to Earth, shattering upon impact.

LIU SONG WOKE up startled, terrified. She felt someone kicking her bed, and she opened her tired eyes as someone slapped her face.

"Wake up," a woman's raspy voice said.

Liu Song looked around the darkened room. A faint glow of sunlight was coming through the drawn curtains. *Maybe it was all a dream—a nightmare,* she thought.

"Ah-ma, is that you?" Liu Song whispered.

The woman stepped back.

"Ah-ma?"

The woman shook her head.

"Leo told me how lazy and disobedient you are. No wonder your mother died. She'd still be alive if you'd taken better care of her. Now get up and clean this mess before you make breakfast."

Liu Song sat up slowly, aching. Confused by the portly woman standing in front of her. She wore her dark hair up in a tight bun that barely hid streaks of gray, and her excessive makeup failed to conceal her wrinkles, or her moles and acne scars.

The woman leaned in so close that Liu Song could smell the tobacco on her breath and see the dark stains on her teeth and swollen gums.

"Clean yourself up," the woman said. "And wash the blood off your sheets."

Liu Song wrapped the covers around her waist. "Who are you?"

The woman looked down her nose, proudly.

"I'm Leo's *first* wife—from Canton. *Your* mother was only second wife."

Liu Song struggled to comprehend as the woman held out a thick hand that looked like it belonged to a meat cutter, with stubby, dirty fingernails. She proudly showed off the gold and jade wedding band that had once belonged to Liu Song's parents.

"From now on, *I'm* Big Mother. But you may call me Auntie Eng."

Plucked

(1921)

Uncle Leo sat at the table as though it were any other morning, practicing his English by reading a copy of the *Seattle Post-Intelligencer*. He smoked a bent cigarette and coughed. Then he cleared his throat and leaned over to hawk phlegm into the sink as Liu Song tried to wash dishes while she waited for water to boil for congee. Her mother had always made the sticky rice porridge with onions and slices of pickled tofu, but Uncle Leo liked it plain. He couldn't taste anything but his Chesterfield anyway, Liu Song thought, as she kept quiet, unsure of what to say, suffering in silence, looking over her shoulder for any sign of Auntie Eng.

Meanwhile Uncle Leo read to himself, out loud, and complained about the newspaper. "William Hearst buys paper, then doubles price," he grumbled, not wanting to have to go to the Ning Yeung Association, where he could read the news for free.

As he folded the pages, Liu Song heard a woman in the alley chattering in Cantonese, along with a terrible squawking that ominously fell silent. She heard the creak of the screen door and scrubbed the dishes faster. As her strange new stepmother walked back in, Liu Song noticed that the woman was holding a long carving knife. Her hands and the blade were covered in blood and bits of feathers. Liu Song stepped back as Auntie Eng mumbled and dropped the knife into the dishwater. Then she rinsed her hands before drying them on her baggy pants.

"When you're done with breakfast, you need to boil a big pot of water so you can pluck that chicken. Do it outside, and don't feed any stray dogs."

"Chicken?" Liu Song asked.

"It's hanging in the alley," Auntie Eng said. "Let it bleed out into the bucket, then gut it, boil it, and then pluck, pluck, pluck. Keep the feathers in a bag."

Liu Song had never been to China, let alone Taichan or Canton. She'd been up and down the West Coast of the United States, but not across the mountains to Yakima or Ellensburg—similar farm country, where children her age knew how to properly clean and dress a bird.

"I'll be late for class . . ."

Auntie Eng looked at Leo and cursed in Cantonese.

"No more school," he said. "With your ah-ma gone we can finally put an end to that foolishness. School!" Uncle Leo practically snorted. "You're a girl. The teachers' time is better spent on boys. I called and told them you're not coming back. What do you think you're going to do anyway? Hah?"

"I didn't go to school," Auntie Eng said proudly. "And look at me."

Liu Song wasn't sure if she was expected to answer. She regarded the stern expressions of Uncle Leo and his hardscrabble wife. Then Liu Song stared at the floor.

"When you're done with cooking and cleaning the bird," Uncle Leo continued from behind his paper, "you can go to the music store. I told Butterman—or whatever his name is—that you'd be able to work full-time, for a while at least. Why he was so grateful, I'll never know. Just don't be late to help make dinner."

Liu Song's parents both had eight years of formal schooling, followed by long apprenticeships in the theater. They prized education.

Not going to school—not graduating—had been unthinkable. Plus Liu Song would miss her friends, even the ones who were closed off to her, and especially poor Mildred. Liu Song would miss the teachers, the library, even the gossipy girls in the lavatory. She wouldn't even have a chance to clean out her locker. She wouldn't even be able to say goodbye.

Saddened, Liu Song took a piece of black ribbon and tied it around her right arm—a sign of mourning, for the loss of her mother, her family, her childhood, her innocence.

At least I have a job, she thought, *a place to go, far, far away from here.*

LIU SONG ACHED as she walked to Butterfield's in her mother's old French leather heels. Her insides were sore and her fingers raw from boiling and plucking. She'd barely been able to keep her hands steady enough to apply her makeup. She put on mascara, half-expecting to burst into tears at any moment. She'd been violated by that disgusting, smirking man—robbed of her childhood. Yet all morning she kept wondering what she had done to bring this upon herself. Was she complicit somehow? Did she deserve his attention? She shook her head, struggling to ignore such guilty thoughts. This was *his* doing. She didn't ask for this. And she didn't care how successful he was as a businessman; he wasn't human in her eyes. There were plenty of *yellow cabs* in the neighborhood—loose women who flaunted themselves: flappers, floozies, and painted women who would give any man a ride.

She kept walking, kept grieving. "Who will want me now?" Liu Song asked whatever gods might be listening. All she heard was stray dogs barking in an alley, the brass bells of an electric streetcar, and a man in coveralls who stood on an apple crate shouting about uniting workers, revolution, and Trotskyism. That and the hollow, tinny sound of a piano, coming from a radio display at Grayson's Appliance.

As Liu Song walked, her senses were numb. She couldn't grasp the concept of coming home to the apartment without her ah-ma waiting there. She felt angry, abandoned, but also mournful and longing. Her family had been a whirlwind of chaos, at home, on-stage, backstage, in storefronts, for as long as she could remember. Her heart reeled as she imagined her mother, widowed amid the hysteria of the Spanish flu. But that was why her mother had married Uncle Leo, Liu Song reasoned. She must have been desperate and needed *someone*. He took control of her belongings, her meager savings. And she found a provider—a businessman instead of a showman. But did she know that she was marrying him as second wife? Did it even matter? Some men had spouses back in China whom they didn't see for decades. They took another wife almost out of necessity. All that was important to them was the provision of a son. But her ah-ma took ill and never produced an heir. And by Auntie Eng's age it was evident that she was barren.

As men stopped what they were doing, whipping their heads around to watch her pass, Liu Song looked away, didn't smile. She shimmied to move her dress lower on her hips. She felt naked. She was nothing but a wanton reflection of her mother in a fun house mirror—her ah-ma's grace and simple beauty distorted to hideous proportions as she realized that there were plenty of men who wanted her—for a moment, but not for a lifetime.

At Butterfield's she stopped and stared sadly at her appearance in the window. Her hairstyle, bangs cut across the front, long tresses hanging loose about her face—it was the style of a virtuous unmarried girl. But what was she now? She was nothing. She belonged to Uncle Leo and Auntie Eng.

I have to leave, she thought. *But where can I go? And who but my stepparents would even care?* She was filled with hate, but most of her violent emotions were directed at the lowly person she'd become.

She allowed a glimmer of hope to shine in the corners of her wasted heart. But she knew it was desperation, nothing more. She thought of the strange, gentle man who'd appeared at her mother's wake. Colin still favored her parents. He was the only one who could appreciate her many losses.

"Turn around!" she heard a man's voice shout.

Her heart leapt into her throat, but then she saw his reflection in the glass. A megaphone man in an open-top bus was yelling at her.

"Hey, China-girl, turn around so we can all get a better look!"

Liu Song slowly turned to face a busload of rubberneckers in tiered seats on their way to King Street for a sightseeing tour. They usually didn't stop or walk around. The rich white tourists simply cruised through the neighborhood as a guide pointed out the strange, foreign mysteries of Chinatown, the old lottery and gambling houses on Washington Street, import-export stores, curio shops, and the Japanese settlement. Liu Song touched the buttons on her dress; she felt like a caged zoo animal on display.

"Well, ladies and gentlemen, *this* is something you don't see every day," the tour guide said, "a nifty Chinese girl in a modern dress—isn't that the kitty's eyebrows!"

"She looks like she's dressed for a petting party," one man grumped—the way people often did when they presumed Liu Song didn't understand them.

She turned to go inside but ran directly into Mr. Butterfield, who was blocking the doorway, smoking a cigarillo, slicking back his thinning hair.

"Sing something," he said with an apologetic smile. "Might as well."

"Hey, mister," Liu Song heard a woman on the bus ask, "she speak any English?" It was a question she'd heard often, even though she dressed like an American girl. Her father had heard it too, long after he cut his queue.

"This could put us on the map—the tour map. Stay here and sing." Mr. Butterfield took her coat, and went inside and played the prelude to "When I Lost You."

As Liu Song closed her eyes and started to sing, the chatter faded away. And when she opened her eyes, she noticed the men with their jaws hanging open, and the women—their wives, their sisters and mothers—suddenly looking terribly uncomfortable, but enthralled nonetheless. The onlookers sat in silence as Liu Song crooned through Irving Berlin's hit ballad of death and familial loss.

A newspaperman on the bus stood and held up a flashlamp that ignited as he snapped a quick photo with his Speed Graphic. Liu Song saw colored stars and could smell the smoke and burnt magnesium as he pulled out the film plate and stuffed it into a camera bag before reloading and snapping another.

Even before she'd finished, Mr. Butterfield left the piano and pushed his way onto the bus, hawking copies of sheet music and passing out cards, boasting about how he'd discovered Liu Song's talents in Chinatown and how she'd be a star someday.

Liu Song went inside to collect herself and freshen up as the bus driver ground the gears and revved the engine. As she leaned against the long oaken counter that Mr. Butterfield kept immaculately clean, she realized how safe she felt here, amid the floor-to-ceiling racks overflowing with sheet music and the Craftsman shelving behind the counter with rows and rows of old phonographic cylinders, Pathé disk records, and perforated piano rolls. She looked up at ornately framed portraits of Irving Berlin and Al Jolson, and an old burlesque poster of Marie Lloyd. Mr. Butterfield would tear up whenever he spoke of her. "They tried to deport her for moral turpitude," he'd once said. "But she kept going, even though her voice got weaker and her shows grew shorter." Liu Song blinked as the bus driver honked twice and drove off and Mr. Butterfield returned, giddily counting the money he'd made.

"Well done, sweetheart—you blew 'em away," he said as he

hugged her and kissed her on the cheek. "We must have made thirty whole dollars, and that was just from one song! Imagine if they stop here every day. You're gonna make your uncle awfully proud. Rich too." He stood at the nearest piano and played the first few bars of a victory march as she stepped away.

"My uncle?"

"Leo."

"I know who he is." Liu Song glanced outside, then back at Mr. Butterfield.

She watched as her employer counted out her portion, then tucked the money in a zippered bag that he kept beneath the counter.

"Now that you're working full-time, he wanted me to pay him directly. He said he was saving it for you—that he'd take care of you later."

Liu Song pictured herself in bed, tied down, with ropes around her wrists and ankles, like her mother, her poor, dear *ah-ma*. Liu Song wondered for the first time if Uncle Leo might have poisoned her ah-ma with the camphor oil. She knew he was prone to home remedies. Did it help, or merely hasten the inevitable?

Mr. Butterfield slammed the cash register shut, snapped his suspenders, and relit his smoke. Then his smile faded. "You know— I heard the bad news." He pointed at the ribbon she wore. "I'm very sorry about your mom, that's such a tragedy. I'm sure she was a lovely woman—she had to be, to have had a daughter such as you. If there's anything I can do, if you need time off, you just let me know."

Liu Song thanked him.

"At least you have your uncle. Sounds like he has big plans for you, chickadee."

LIU SONG DREADED going home. She skipped the trolley and slowly walked down Second Avenue like a prisoner heading to the gallows. She shuffled past old nickelodeons that were going out of business and dozens of new movie theaters—the Bijou, the Odeon, the Dream. One marquee that caught her eye showcased *The Red Lantern,* a curious story about the Boxer Rebellion. Liu Song stopped and stared in awe at the poster of a slender woman in an elaborate, flowing gown and Peking-style headdress. *Ah-ma,* she thought, touching the cold glass, inhaling the damp Seattle air. But under close examination it became obvious that the star was a white actress—some Russian named Alla Nazimova. In fact, all of the actors had Western names.

When she was little, Liu Song had dreamed of the stage. Theater was everything she knew. Performing was all her father talked about. Now the stage was changing. It was moving, coming to life in storefront theaters. Even local vaudeville houses like the Alhambra had been converted to showcase moving pictures, which were cheaper. That's where she and Mildred went to watch *The Hazards of Helen* and eat toasted watermelon seeds. Each week the adventurous Helen was nearly burned at the stake, fed to the lions, crushed beneath iron spikes, or cut in half with a buzz saw, yet by some miracle she always got away unscathed.

Liu Song wished she could be that fortunate.

Black and White

(1921)

"You're late."

"We had a very busy day at the music store," Liu Song said. She stopped short of an apology as she watched Uncle Leo hang a red scroll outside their front door. The Chinese characters, painted in gold, were a traditional greeting, inviting the ghost of her mother—welcoming her back before she embarked on her spirit's journey. And on the lintel above the door he'd hung a bundle of dried mugwort and a peeled onion to ward off any wayward demons.

Liu Song knew that Uncle Leo didn't really care about her mother. But he was a slave to appearances and tradition. He was a man who strictly believed his fortunes were wedded to his superstitions, so why take chances? He went through the rituals of mourning even as his first wife had moved in with them. But he was still no family man. He was a businessman—a laundryman, whose hands were always filthy.

"Last night was a good night. Maybe tonight I'll be lucky again." He hiked up his pants, jingling the pockets, which were laden with coins, and wandered off for an evening of drinking and gambling at the Wah Mee Club.

Inside, Auntie Eng was already serving dinner. The chicken Liu

Song had plucked had been roasted and chopped. The savory aroma made Liu Song's mouth water, but her appetite waned when she saw the group of curious strangers who sat around the table eating noisily, chewing, smacking, and picking the meat with their fingers, licking them clean. Liu Song watched as they ate from her parents' celadon double happiness bowls, greedily shoveling rice into their mouths with her mother's favorite chopsticks.

"You don't cook. You don't eat," Auntie Eng said as she sat down at the table.

The visitors looked at Liu Song as if *she* were the stranger in *their* home.

"My sisters and my nephews," Auntie Eng said. "They came up with me from Portland. My sisters will sleep in your room tonight. Their sons will share the couch."

Liu Song stood helpless and hungry as the visitors stared back; then they ignored her and continued eating and chattering about Leo and how fortunate he was that Auntie Eng had been able to finally come to the United States. The Chinese Exclusion Act had limited the flow of Chinese workers from hundreds of thousands twenty years ago to almost none today. Fortunately for Uncle Leo, his immigration records had been destroyed in the fires caused by the great San Francisco earthquake. After a three-day interrogation at Angel Island, he showed up on the steps of the newly rebuilt city hall with hundreds of other Chinese workers and posed as a paper son—claiming to have been born in the United States. Following a lengthy appeal, he was granted full citizenship, which allowed him to eventually bring over his paper wife, who lived with her sisters until Liu Song's mother finally passed away.

The notion of Uncle Leo marking time with each of her mother's seizures, each fevered moment, made Liu Song sick to her stomach. He'd been waiting, barely able to contain his annoyance at having to care for her ailing mother. Liu Song went to her room to collect herself. Then she fixed up her bed and found blankets for the children. After that she went to the living room and sat quietly as Auntie Eng and her sisters played mah-jongg and gossiped and drank *huangjiu* from porcelain teacups that her mother had been given as a wedding present. The women talked about war and famine and the fall of the Manchus, and about family they had left behind and hadn't seen for years. They clucked about Uncle Leo's businesses. He'd opened hand laundries in Portland and Olympia, and had bought a used laundry truck, but still worried about losing business to the new treadle-driven machines. The women talked and smoked and belched and ate boiled peanuts, throwing the wet shells on the floor until the barley wine ran out and they all staggered off to bed, leaving Liu Song to sweep up. She ate the peanuts that remained in the bowl and then changed into her bedclothes. She curled up on the cold wooden floor, next to the hissing radiator, with only a sheet, listening to the children snore. She had terrible dreams, and when she woke in the morning she had strange bruises in hidden places and smelled like Uncle Leo.

MR. BUTTERFIELD WAS right. The next day the rubbernecker bus came by twice. Once in the morning and once in the afternoon, loaded with gawkers who marveled at Liu Song. Some even got off the bus and had her sign their sheet music.

One well-heeled blond woman handed her a small leather book and a pencil. "Just your name, dear," she said. And after Liu Song wrote her name in Chinese, the woman asked again, "No, your *real* name. What's your name in English?"

Liu Song hesitated, confused, then signed *Willow*. She wondered if this was what it had been like for her ah-ma on the evening of her grand performance. She wondered if her mother had had any inkling of how bad things would soon get.

BY DAY'S END, Mr. Butterfield was humming a happy tune and counting the money he'd made. "We'll need to double our orders of sheet music," he said as he sat down on an old leather stool and unscrewed his hip flask. He offered it to Liu Song, who shook her head and smiled politely.

"I haven't played that much since I was your age," he said. "Who knows? We keep this up, kid—I might even sell a few of the new Weltes."

Liu Song took a dusting rag and wiped down one of the enormous pianolas. "Do I get a commission on one of these as well?" she asked.

Mr. Butterfield took another swig. "Missy, if we sell one of the player pianos, I'll give you ten percent, and ten percent of every roll of music that goes with it to boot. Though you might have to shorten your skirt a bit if you expect to attract those kinds of dollars. Your voice isn't your only sales tool, you know."

Liu Song ignored his comment about her skirt and played a few notes on the piano. She didn't know much, just some jazz stingers she'd heard in the neighborhood and had taught herself to play. She plunked away, then left the store on an open chord.

As she walked to the trolley stand, she contemplated earning twenty-five dollars per piano—fifty for a deluxe model, enough to move out on her own, for a while at least. She wondered if she'd be able to enroll in school again, or if she needed a parent, and would Uncle Leo and Auntie Eng even let her leave? She felt tightness in her chest, her gut. She hated the thought of being alone but hated the notion of going home even more. Then she remembered that even if she sold one of the autopianos, the money would probably go directly to her uncle. She slumped onto a cold iron bench next to a man reading a copy of *The Seattle Star*. As she glanced at the paper she recognized the dress on the back page—her mother's dress, the same dress she was wearing. The feature photo was of *her*, singing in front of Butterfield's. The man slowly lowered the newspaper. She recognized his eyes, his gentle smile.

"Not bad for black-and-white," Colin said with his curious accent as he folded the paper and handed it to her. "But you'd look much better in Kinemacolor."

Liu Song had seen only one moving picture in color—*The Gulf Between,* with Grace Darmond. Her father had taken her to a matinee of the sad tale of a young girl who falls in love with a man whose wealthy, disapproving family comes between them. As Liu Song delighted in Colin's presence, her happiness flowing from her beating heart to her aching stomach, she worried about having feelings for someone—anyone—especially after losing so many people who had meant so much to her. She hesitated to hope and dream, unsure if she could take another loss—even a rejection seemed far beyond her capacity to endure.

"Ngóh mh'mìhng?" Liu Song was weary from singing all day, but now her tongue was tied in knots. She switched to English. "Why are you here?" She shook her head. "I'm sorry, that's terribly rude . . ."

"Well, aside from working on my American dialect, I had to see—no, I had to *hear you* for myself. After reading such a flattering write-up in the *Star,* I thought I'd pay you a visit. And to be honest, I think you even outdid your mother—may her spirit rest."

Liu Song's smile faded as she looked down at her empty hands. "I can't believe she's gone. It's better for her, I'm sure. But . . ."

"Again, I'm so terribly sorry, Liu Song."

"My parents . . ."

"Are *proud* of you."

Liu Song heard a brass bell as a streetcar came and went. It was getting late and her stomach was growling, but she didn't want to go home. She felt grateful that Uncle Leo read the *Post-Intelligencer* instead of *The Seattle Star.*

"I knew your parents well enough to know that they would want you to perform, onstage, singing, acting—any way you can. Even here." He touched the newspaper. "This is a good start. I think your mother's spirit has been busy."

Liu Song ached for her ah-ma's presence. A Chinese spirit is said to come back in seven days, before departing. Perhaps her mother *was* looking out for her.

"And what of *your* parents? Your family, back home, your wife?" As Liu Song asked, she could see the discomfort in Colin's face. He frowned and exhaled slowly, staring up at the cloudy sky. She glanced at his finger and didn't see a wedding ring, though they weren't so common in China, where a dowry was more important. The gift of an appliance or a car wasn't unheard of instead of a token piece of jewelry.

"Ah, my parents," Colin said. "My father is a banker. And Mother stays at home. Her skin is so pale—I don't think she ever goes outside. She's too busy tending to my brothers and sisters, and my grandparents. I'm the firstborn son, so I'm expected to take a part in my father's business—to get married, to care for my mother and my siblings . . ."

Liu Song was taken aback as Colin struggled to explain.

"But, you're *here*," she said.

He nodded, slowly. "That I am. I'm here. I always wanted to perform—always wanted to be an actor." The words came out almost as an apology. "First in the opera, like your *lou dou*—he was one of the first performers I had ever met. Your father encouraged me—jokingly of course, but I took him quite seriously. And growing up, I read constantly. I studied English. My father assumed it was to help in business, but I had other plans. While other men my age looked for an obedient wife, I watched every play, photoplay, and moving picture that I could. I wanted to be Chai Hong in *An Oriental Romeo*."

"And then you left your family?" Liu Song asked, astonished that a man his age would break with such traditions. She was different—she was an American. But most of the Chinese-born sons she knew would never think of leaving their families. Who would take care of their mothers when their fathers died?

"My parents said I had been corrupted, that movies were filled with vice and carnality. I'm sorry. You must think dreadful things about me now," Colin said, staring down at his polished shoes. "For my nineteenth birthday my father sent me to America on a business holiday, alone. He bought me a token partnership in a Chinese American business so I could come and go, in and out of the country, as a merchant. I handled his affairs—did everything I was supposed to do. The trip was a success. And then . . . I sent a letter home informing him that I wasn't planning to return, that my younger brother should take my place."

Liu Song saw the sadness wash over him.

"That was two years ago," he said. "I hope to return one day as a famous actor, or at least a successful one. I hope that's enough to save face—to be forgiven. I know. Foolish of me, yes? My father—he is a very wealthy man. But even as his firstborn son I was never afforded the simple luxury of . . . *dreaming*—of doing something on my own. But here, I can live my dream." He wiped his hands on his pants.

"Even on an actor's wages?"

"Even on an actor's wages." Colin laughed. "So I met with your father and he took me on as his understudy. I even met your uncle once. He was there for your mother's performance. He was intrigued—everyone was."

"He's not really my uncle." Liu Song's stomach turned as she thought of the man. "He had another wife in a village near Canton. He only married my mother to try and have a son. Now his first wife is here and I'm the servant, stepchild." *Brood mare.*

"You're like Yeh-Shen." Colin smiled.

Liu Song shook her head. The only thing she had in common with the Chinese Cinderella was the part about the wicked step-mother. There was no golden slipper, no magic fish to clothe her in finery, no spring festival at which to find her prince. "There's no happy ending to my fairy tale."

"Then you should leave," he said, as if it were that simple.

"And go where?"

Colin took a deep breath and exhaled slowly. "I know you're hurting. But you could be like me and just follow your heart—who knows where it will take you?"

Liu Song found comfort and solace in his sympathetic eyes.

"This is Gum Shan. Your father knew this," he whispered. "But the gold isn't in the mountains anymore. It's found on the streets. You saw it yourself—the way those people regarded you. Here, you can be anyone you want to be—it's all about your performance. From the way you sing, the way you act, I think you know exactly what I'm referring to. I never feel more myself than when I'm pretending to be someone else. If I were to follow in my father's footsteps and become a banker—*that* would be the illusion, that would be stage magic and acting, because that's not who I am."

Liu Song hung on his every word.

"Though I must admit I'm truly not much of an opera singer. I don't think I have such a promising future onstage, but that's not where the future is."

Liu Song followed his gaze as they both looked back down Second Avenue.

"The Tillicum, the Clemmer, the Melbourne, the Alaska Theatre—there are eighty movie theaters in Seattle and they're opening more every month, practically every week," he said. "*That's* the future."

The future, Liu Song thought. She imagined those enormous letters as a movie title on a twinkling marquee, with her name featured below. For the first time since her mother died, her timid hopes felt real—it felt possible to be something greater than a stepchild and a source of income for Uncle Leo, or a housemaid and nanny for Auntie Eng and her greedy, slovenly family.

"The future"—Liu Song nodded slowly—"in black-and-white."

The Devil's Claim

(1921)

In the future you can be anyone you want to be.

Those words haunted Liu Song all the way home. That and the thought of Colin forsaking his father and his family for the stage and then giving up the stage for the silver screen—running toward an unknown future, arms outstretched, but alone.

Liu Song had been so alone for so long. She'd been mired in sorrow, been beaten down with despair and hopelessness—to the point of numbness. Now she felt as though she were seeing the world with new eyes, her mother's eyes.

What would my father think? she wondered. Her parents had adored photoplays and motion picture shows even though the audiences were so modern, the themes so unconventional.

The notion of Liu Song performing on-screen seemed as ridiculous, as unseemly, as that of her mother performing onstage. But as she passed a crowd of ticket buyers who patiently waited in line outside a theater showing *The Devil's Claim,* her perspective shifted like a kaleidoscope, and she marveled at the new shapes, colors, and designs of the future that coalesced in her imagination. Especially when she noticed the enormous movie poster featuring the dashing Sessue Hayakawa. Her father had once raved about Hayakawa performing onstage in *The Three Musketeers*—in Japanese.

"He wasn't some coolie actor. His gestures were so dramatic, so poetic, you didn't even need to understand the language—that's great acting," her father had said.

And though Hayakawa must have spoken English with a lingering accent, it didn't matter in silent films. The performance spoke for itself. All that mattered were his handsome looks, his brooding presence, and his piercing eyes, which made even the most matronly of American women swoon. He'd appeared in dozens of films, and Liu Song's father had said he was as famous as Douglas Fairbanks and Charlie Chaplin.

Colin reminded her of Hayakawa, but the similarities went beyond mysterious eyes and a perfect smile. As she daydreamed about Colin, she didn't know what she liked more, his ambition—his willingness to follow his dreams—or his quiet sadness—his reluctance and guilt at having to forsake his familial obligations. His conflict was real. He wore his lament. And he didn't hide the fact that his dreams were burdened with a heavy price. It was a peculiar kind of integrity; it reminded her of her father.

As Liu Song passed the boarded-up remains of the old Opera House, the cold wind carried the smell of rain-soaked soot and ash. The brick structure had survived, but the wooden joists, rafters, and parquet flooring had gone up in a tremendous blaze. Now the building was being rebuilt, repurposed as a parking garage.

Liu Song stopped and stared at one of the brick walls, which still had the pasted remnants of a poster for *Zhuangzi Tests His Wife*. The years had faded the colors, which made the Widow of Zhuangzi look even more heartbroken; the expression of her mask showcased her misery—her tortured soul put to the test. The gown in the painting was the one her mother had worn—the one Liu Song kept beneath her bed. As she stared at the poster, she thought about her mother's presence—her ah-ma's busy spirit, as Colin had said. Liu Song was so grateful to have the mask her mother had worn. In the drizzling rain, Liu Song said a silent prayer to the remains of the theater, as Yeh-Shen had prayed above the bones of her past, hoping for new clothes and a new life. "Ah-ma, you wore the colors of sickness and despair," Liu Song said as she remembered what the colors represented onstage—the symbolism her father had taught her.

As she passed a Buddhist church and a Shinto temple and walked through the Japanese settlement past Cherry Land Florist, Liu Song remembered her mother's favorite tea, made from the seeds of a blue flower. She stopped at the Murakami Store on Weller and wandered the aisles, which were crowded with crates and boxes of dry goods. She was looking for the seeds and perhaps an answer to her prayer. Instead she found something that would suffice—an assortment of ceramic paints. Liu Song carefully selected two small jars, one gold, the other silver. She had just enough money to buy both.

Satisfied, she walked down the alley to her apartment, thinking, *Ah-ma, soon you'll perform again. Soon you'll wear the colors you deserve.*

THE APARTMENT WAS crowded and smelled like cigarettes, flatulence, and sweaty feet. Auntie Eng's sisters were still there. They'd made themselves at home, stringing wet laundry across the alley while their children cut paper dolls out of newspaper, leaving the remains all over the floor. One of them had even bought a turtle from the pet store in the alley and let the reptile creep around Liu Song's room. *If I'm lucky, Auntie Eng will cook it,* Liu Song thought.

Despite this chaos, Liu Song bridled her anger and her fear. She remained silent, and like Yeh-Shen, she did what she was told. She helped cook dinner and doted on Auntie Eng's family. Liu Song played with the children, even though none of them knew how to share and cried when they didn't get their way, drawing stern reprimands from Auntie Eng and her sisters. They blamed Liu Song for being a poor, undisciplined caretaker. Liu Song even went to the store to buy a tin of wet snuff for Auntie Eng's sister, who chewed the ground tobacco and then spat the vile, pungent remains into a Folgers coffee can.

Fortunately for Liu Song, Uncle Leo cared for their slovenly houseguests even less than she did. He popped in to eat, shave, and mask his stench with a splash of bay rum cologne. He'd light prayer sticks in his family shrine, asking for good fortune. Then he would depart for a meeting at the Eng Suey Sun Benevolent Association or catch up to a poker game at the Wah Mee, often returning just before sunrise. Sometimes he would wake her up, but even then she would pretend she was asleep—dead to the world, a part of her dying each time.

Liu Song's routine of domestic drudgery and the late-night visits from Uncle Leo lasted only a few days. Then she followed Auntie Eng and her family to the King Street Station, porting their luggage. She didn't linger at the train terminal to say goodbye. Instead she went home and found Uncle Leo, half-drunk, sprinkling talcum powder on the wooden floor. It had been seven days since her ah-ma's burial. Old-world superstition dictated that they would go to bed and remain in their rooms until the passing of her mother's spirit was complete—until her ah-ma had departed on her final journey. Liu Song accepted this tradition. She embraced it. In fact, she had been counting on it all week.

Alone in her room, she found the valise beneath her bed and dug out her mother's belongings. Liu Song stared solemnly at the opera mask. She had carefully repainted it. The greens, which represented poor judgment, and the blues, which denoted astuteness and loyalty, were now covered by shimmering metallics—silver and gold— the colors of mystery, the colors of an angry god, or a demon, or a vengeful spirit.

Liu Song stared at the mask and waited for Auntie Eng to return and go to bed. She bit her tongue as she heard her stepparents' drunken laughter. They joked as they finished the last of her father's barley wine, the bottles he'd hidden to be uncorked during each New Year's celebration.

When she was certain that Uncle Leo and Auntie Eng were

asleep, Liu Song took out her mother's shimmering white gown, with its long, flowing water sleeves and dramatic red embroidery. She dressed slowly, carefully, reverently, paying attention to every detail as though donning armor for battle. She piled her long hair up high in the style of a married woman. She outlined her eyes with black grease and wrapped a strip of leather around her temple, pulling the cord tight the way she'd seen her father do it, tying the strip in the back so her eyes were held wide open. She covered the cord with her mother's jeweled headpiece, pinning the crown to the leather. Then she tied on the demon mask. She was certain she would laugh when she looked in her vanity mirror. Instead she felt the hairs on the back of her neck stand on end. She didn't see her own reflection. She didn't recognize the red eyes that stared back, flickering in the lamplight. She wasn't Liu Song anymore. Nor was she Yeh-Shen, Cinderella. She wasn't merely her mother's daughter playing a child's dress-up game. She *was* her mother now, if only for one night. And her mother was a very angry spirit.

In the living room she opened the door of the cast-iron stove and stoked the fire. Then she burned a stick of incense and lit all the candles in the room. Finally, she went to the kitchen and found the longest, sharpest carving knife—the one her mother had used for deboning shanks of pork. Liu Song noticed the colors of her gown reflected in the blade. They looked like blood and fire.

Carefully, Liu Song draped a long sleeve over the knife. Then she walked along the wall to the front door. From there she stepped carefully with her bare feet in the talcum, leaving a trail of ghostly footprints from the entrance directly to her stepparents' bedroom. She took a deep breath, heard the popping and hissing of the newly lit candles, and opened the bedroom door. She didn't knock.

Liu Song surrendered to her performance as they walked into the room, mother and daughter together as one, the incarnation of the Widow of Zhuangzi. She let the firelight flood the darkness, casting a spidery shadow over the bed as her long sleeves swept across the floor. Auntie Eng woke first and made an inhuman sound, a squeal like that of a frightened, trapped pig. Then Liu Song, her mother, the Widow, floated to the brass railing at the foot of the bed. She smelled the alcohol on Uncle Leo's breath as he bolted upright, as though waking from an unpleasant dream to a nightmare. His face became a riot of fear, his mouth contorted as his drunken, superstitious mind struggled to reconcile what he was seeing. The Widow slowly pulled back her long sleeve, revealing the blade. She pointed the knife at Auntie Eng's soft belly, then glided around to Uncle Leo. Bulging eyes stared into his. The Widow twirled her sleeve until her hand emerged and grabbed a fistful of hair, lifting his head as the cold edge of the carving knife kissed the soft tissue just below his chin. His face grew pale as he held his breath.

"You will not touch my daughter ever again," the Widow whispered in Cantonese through clenched teeth and the demon's mask. "You will not *speak* to her. You will not *look* upon her," she hissed. "You will give her everything that is *owed* to her—*and more.* And you will *leave . . . my . . . home* before the next moon, or I will tie *you* to this bed and pour oil down your throat every night until you join me in the spirit world. And I promise, on your blood and the blood of your family, that I will never leave this place until you are gone."

The Widow looked at the whimpering mass that was Auntie Eng and sang in a high, shrill voice, *"I'm only second wife."* She reached out, touching the frightened woman's lips with the point of the knife. "But you will call *me* Big Mother."

Liu Song's heart raced as she undressed and sat on the edge of her bed, struggling to collect herself. She lingered on the image of Uncle Leo and Auntie Eng huddled together as she'd left the room. Her bravery had been an act, a put-on that she found exhilarating but emotionally exhausting. She'd removed the mask, which now felt suffocating. She stared at its hollows, which echoed the emptiness she felt, and she gazed forlornly into the darkened corners of her bedroom, half-expecting to see her mother and father, or her brothers, standing there, silently clapping or nodding their approval. Through the walls she could hear Uncle Leo arguing and Auntie Eng crying.

"Well done, Liu Song," her father would have whispered.

Her mother might have gushed, "Encore," while wiping away tears.

As Liu Song lay down and pressed her face into the fabric of the dress she'd worn, she could smell her mother's skin, her lotion, her perfume—her essence. She missed her so much. She clawed at her pillow, wanting to cry, but the tears never came, just a swirling riptide of feeling—anger, abandonment, the fear of being alone, and the weight of the emotional millstone still tied around her neck, submerging her further into the murky depths of stinging, biting solitude. She wished she could wail all night. Instead she curled up in the darkness of her bedroom, listening to her racing heartbeat, which eventually slowed, like the ticking of a clock unwound.

Pitch and Toss

囨

(1921)

When Liu Song woke, Uncle Leo and Auntie Eng were nowhere to be found. Their belongings remained, untouched as far as she could tell. She walked around her apartment barefoot, delighted by her stepparents' absence, finding strange comfort in her solitude. She didn't know if her ruse had actually worked. Her stepparents might attribute the whole thing to bad alcohol. Or in the sobering light of day, they might know what she'd done. It didn't matter. They were gone for now, and the respite was welcome and hard earned. She wistfully hoped that her mother's ghost had actually returned and taken them to the spirit world, kicking and screaming all the way.

Liu Song smiled as she ate a leftover *hum bau* for breakfast. A cold pork bun never tasted better. She drank a cup of hot black tea and then went to work, where she sang such happy tunes for the bedazzled crowds that Mr. Butterfield finally sold a pianola to a wealthy couple—the first sale of many, he hoped. She didn't even have to shorten her skirt. The store owner was so excited and grateful that he paid Liu Song directly, in cash, and sent her home an hour early. As she walked back to her parents' tiny apartment, she imagined a confrontation with Uncle Leo; perhaps he'd kick her out altogether. She half-hoped to find her belongings waiting by the garbage dump, which would be fine by her. Instead, Canton Alley looked the same. The apartment was dark, and the clothesline hung curiously empty of all but a starling that hopped along the wire, flapping its wings and whistling. Liu Song found the front door slightly ajar. As she stepped inside, it was clear that Auntie Eng and Uncle Leo were still gone. Unfortunately, so was everything else— the new radio; the dishes, pots, and pans; most of the bedding; the carpets; and all of the furniture. Everything except for Liu Song's bed had been carted away. Her stepparents had cleaned out the pantry and the cupboards as well. The only food that remained (which wasn't scattered on the floor like garbage) was a half-empty tin of stale saltines. Liu Song stood in the apartment and shook her head, stepping over and around the few empty boxes and crates that remained. She was surprised they didn't take the light fixtures and the wallpaper, or tear out the copper piping beneath the sink.

I got what I wished for, Uncle, she thought. *And you got everything else.*

Then Liu Song remembered her valise and rushed to her room, dropped to her knees, and peeked under the bed. She sat back, then lay on the cool, dusty wooden floor, her heart pounding as she exhaled a huge sigh of relief. Her mother's suitcase was still there. Liu Song pulled it out and opened it, realizing that her superstitious stepfather was probably too afraid to touch it. If he or Auntie Eng had opened it and seen the mask . . .

Liu Song wiped a bead of sweat from her forehead, then leaned back on her elbows, staring into the void that was her closet. She frowned at her clothes, which lay in a heap on the floor. They had thrown out all of her mother's personal belongings and now taken everything of value—all of it gone.

You didn't even leave me a wire hanger, Liu Song thought as she heard a knock on the door and quickly stood up. She reached into the front of her dress to make sure her money was safely tucked away and dusted herself off as best she could. If it was the landlord, she had just enough money to cover a month's rent. Though she wasn't sure how he'd feel about a single girl living alone, which was generally frowned upon. Liu Song was certain the building had a reputation to maintain. It was bad enough that the police regarded any single Chinese woman as a prostitute, but a landlord . . .

"Hello?" A familiar voice called out in Cantonese. "Liu Song?"

She stepped into the living room, ashamed of the terrible mess. "Colin?"

He opened the door and removed his hat, staring at the floor, the empty tinderbox next to the stove, and the vacant cupboards. "May I . . . enter?"

"Please." Liu Song felt flushed with embarrassment. "I'm so sorry. I wish I had someplace for you to sit down, or a cup of tea to offer. I can explain . . ."

"There's no need . . ."

"It's my uncle and his wife, they took . . . everything . . ."

"It's quite all right. Honest," Colin said as he looked around, smiling at the chaos. "I heard all about their sudden departure."

"Heard what?"

Colin turned an old fruit crate up onto its side and offered the wooden box as a seat to Liu Song, who sat down and tried in vain to flatten the wrinkled fabric of her dress. She couldn't take her eyes off the charming young man who knelt on one knee in front of her. His suit seemed perfectly pressed, his hair, miraculously in place, despite the wind outside. He was so close that their toes almost touched. So close she could smell his aftershave. He picked up an empty tobacco tin, brought it to his nose, and then gently set it aside as he regarded the garbage-strewn apartment as though it were a minor inconvenience—a misstep, unfortunate but easily overcome.

"I was at the Wah Mee this afternoon when your stepfather came in and grumbled to all who would listen that he no longer wanted to *be* your uncle."

Liu Song touched her lips, trying not to smirk, remembering

what the man had done to her, how he had mistreated her mother. "Is that so?"

Colin nodded his affirmation. "He came in and talked of how young and beautiful you were—though he used a baser vocabulary. He argued that since there are indeed so few single girls in Chinatown, while there are hundreds, if not thousands of single working men, he ventured you'd be worth something, to someone."

Liu Song's smile vanished. She couldn't believe what she was hearing. She'd known of parents who sold off their extra sons to families that needed the help, but rarely had a daughter changed families—at least not in America and not in her neighborhood. Except in arranged marriages. She swallowed, then asked reluctantly, hesitantly, the way one asked about a fever during the quarantines, "Did he betroth me . . ."

"It was worse than that, I'm afraid."

How can it get any worse? Liu Song thought. *I've been sold like a cow.*

"When no one seemed interested in offering a dowry, he wagered you," Colin said. The words came out hesitantly, as though the truth were a grave insult. "He bet you on a hand of pitch and toss—and he lost."

"Someone won me?" Liu Song asked in stunned disbelief. "In a dice game?"

She watched in horrified astonishment as Colin hesitated and then nodded again, loosening his scarf and fumbling with his hat.

"But that's why I came to see you directly," he said. "The man who won you was an older gentleman from Kwangtung, a widower who seemed eager to have a new, young bride. He spoke of taking you back to China for a traditional wedding."

"I won't do it!" Liu Song protested. "I'll run. He'll never find me . . ."

"You won't have to," Colin said with a modest shrug.

"How can you be so sure?"

"Because." Colin cleared his throat and switched to English as his voice cracked. "*Another* gentleman stepped up and made a better offer. This person offered twice what the winner had wagered, and when that wasn't enough he offered three, four, and then five times the amount. Until that old lecher relented and took the money. Your uncle seemed quite displeased by having bet you for less than your true worth."

My true worth? she wondered. Liu Song wanted to cry, she wanted to scream. She did neither. She stood up, immediately thinking of ways to leave town, but she had so little to her name—even her name now meant nothing. "And who is this"—she spat the word—"*gentleman?*"

Colin rose to his feet and covered his heart with his hat. He whispered softly, "That's why I'm here. I didn't want you to hear about this on the street and labor under some false apprehension. You're free to do as you please, I assure you. And you can be with whomever you choose, whenever you choose to be."

Liu Song shook her head.

"Because that foolish gentleman . . . was me," Colin said.

Liu Song stood speechless for a moment. She wasn't sure what he meant, or to whom she owed what. "I'm . . . sorry . . ."

Colin said, "I couldn't stand idle and let that happen. So I intervened. I hope you don't feel this was an untoward gesture. You're an unmarried girl, and by no means . . ."

"I'm . . ." Liu Song stammered, feeling a rush of gratitude, confusion, and joy hobbled by his hesitant words. "Thank you. I can repay you—I have some money and I'll keep working. I'll pay you back every penny . . ."

"You don't owe me anything. I still have money from my father, despite his disapproval of my career choices. And since I had such respect for your *lou dou*—really, it was the least I could do. I owe him much. Your father gave me my start."

Liu Song was still flushed. Still confused. "I'm not ready to get married . . ."

Colin smiled, wide-eyed. "And I'm not asking. Not that there's anything wrong with you. I'm sure you'll find someone worthy. Speaking of marriage, your uncle sold this along with you." Colin reached into his pocket and then held out his hand. Her mother's ring rested in his palm.

Liu Song felt relieved but also sick to her stomach. She took the ring, grateful to have it but feeling the urge to cleanse it in boiling water. She stared at her muddled reflection in the tarnished gold, then slipped it on the ring finger of her right hand.

Colin changed the subject by offering to help clean up. He went upstairs to find a janitor's closet, returned with a broom and dustpan, and began to sweep up the talcum-covered mess on the floor. He laughed and applauded when Liu Song told him how she had painted her mother's mask and what she'd done to Auntie Eng and Uncle Leo. They joked about Uncle Leo and his old-world superstitions. They talked about music and movies and the families they missed, the good times, and the moments filled with sorrow and regret. And as sunset approached, Colin looked at his watch and let himself out.

"I really shouldn't be here if your stepparents aren't home anymore," he said. "This is a small neighborhood, and I don't want anyone getting the wrong idea. Will you be okay by yourself for a while? Perhaps you'll find a roommate."

Liu Song nodded, though she wasn't sure what that wrong idea was exactly. But she understood by his body language that he was reluctant to be here after dark. Then she looked up and understood as she saw the cherry-red embers of cigarettes that dangled from the hands and mouths of the many men who lived upstairs. The top two floors of her building were occupied by the Freeman Hotel, a flophouse filled with bachelors, cannery workers and lumbermen, laundry hands and fry cooks, who lingered on the fire escape in the evening. The men smoked and talked about money and women, longing for both. Liu Song had for so long been so worried about her mother and preoccupied with avoiding her uncle that she rarely gave the men upstairs a passing thought, and when she did she merely thought of them as neighbors—ones who shared a common tongue, like the other families who lived across the alley. Those innocent notions faded as Liu Song realized that these lonely, unbuttoned men looking down on her probably thought about her quite often. The idea sent a chill up her spine, and she shivered in the cool evening air.

"Does that mean I won't see you again?" she asked Colin, aching for him to stay but not wanting to sound as desperate as she felt.

He paused. "It just means that we probably should see each other in public, to avoid the gossipy hens that cluck around here." He nodded toward the other alleyway apartments and the clotheslines dangling with laundry. "And the vultures." He didn't look up, but she knew who he was referring to.

"How about next Friday?" Liu Song blurted in a way that surprised her. She wasn't sure if it was because she didn't want to let him go, or because she simply enjoyed the protection of his company. "On my way home the other day I noticed an early show playing at the Moore Theatre. It's a new movie, I think you'll like it."

To her delight he didn't even ask what the film was. He immediately said yes.

Liu Song had never been to a first-run theater before. The second-run storefront theaters showing last year's movies were all her family could afford. But she assumed they'd go *qu helan* and was fine with that. Going to the movies and paying her own way wasn't actually a date, and she was comforted by that fact as she remembered her mother's worrisome admonitions about being alone with a man—any man.

Colin tipped his hat. "Perfect. I'll meet you there."

Lovesick

(1921)

When Liu Song arrived at the Moore Theatre, Colin was already there with tickets in hand. He took off his hat and fanned his face, even in the cool air.

"Is that a new dress?"

Liu Song tried to smile demurely, but she nervously blushed instead. "I sold a grand pianola this week, can you believe it? So I went a little crazy and bought a brand-new outfit. Do I look au courant?" She had bought modish stockings and fashionable heels too. They were the first new clothes she'd ever owned—the first to actually fit her in all the right places. She chewed her lip, then stopped when she worried she might be smearing her lipstick. She thought it would make her feel grown-up, but instead it only made her more self-conscious, especially in front of the other theater patrons, none of whom were Chinese. She looked down as the lacy fringe that graced her hips fluttered in the breeze and swayed with each hesitant step.

Colin paused as though speechless. "I . . . don't believe there are adequate words in the English tongue," he said. "All I can say is *nei hau leng.*"

You look beautiful too, Liu Song thought. *I wish I could tell you.*

Liu Song could hardly believe that he saw her as anything other than an awkward, damaged, lowborn girl—someone who spoke her parents' country Cantonese, and was a dropout on top of that.

"You are more than you know," he said. "Your future . . ." He whistled. "I just hope I'm around to see it."

Liu Song remembered something else and asked, "Do you have plans for after the movie?" She then realized how unflatteringly forward that sounded. Her parents had been modern in their vocation and manner of dress, but she'd still come from a traditional household, where girls did not invite boys—let alone men—to anything.

"It's just that I have a commitment," she quickly added. "Mr. Butterfield sold that pianola this week to one of the owners of the Stacy Mansion—he closed the deal by telling them I would perform at its unveiling, which is later tonight. I thought it would be prudent to have someone escort me . . ."

"Ah, of course. That explains the dress," Colin said, nodding in agreement.

INSIDE THE THEATER Colin tipped the usher, who led them with a Matchless flashlight to a pair of first-row balcony seats. Liu Song marveled at the view. Not only was she eye level with the screen but also from that vantage point she could see the packed main floor and look directly into the pit, where a seven-piece orchestra tuned up their instruments and an organist sat stretching his fingers. Colin mentioned that he'd read that the tuxedoed musicians were from Russia and the highest paid in the city.

The audience twittered with excitement when the conductor struck up the opening fanfare and the houselights dimmed. Liu Song stared wide-eyed into pitch black as the music filled the theater. She felt herself being transported elsewhere as her eyes slowly adjusted to the darkness, as the curtain rose and a projector's beam split the void, illuminating particles of dust suspended in the air, gently swirling like glitter in a snow globe. The orchestra moved deftly through the overture, as the words *Bits of Life* appeared on-screen, followed by the opening credits.

"It's an *anthology*," she whispered. It was a new word, one she struggled to pronounce but hoped would impress. "Four movies in one."

Colin nodded and smiled. "You're becoming an expert already."

Liu Song delighted in each short film, occasionally peeking at Colin, who watched with a seriousness beyond the simple entertainment on-screen.

She watched as Colin leaned forward in his seat when he saw the Chinese clothing and Oriental set pieces. Lon Chaney appeared as the main character, Chin Chow. He was a fairly well-known actor, to be sure, but even with his makeup and beard, Liu Song thought he looked awkward and pretentious. Fortunately his fatally flawed wife was played by a new actress, Anna May Wong, who stole the screen from her more famous counterpart.

She leaned over. "They saved the best for last."

As Liu Song watched, she couldn't help but think of her mother—not the sickly woman slowly dying but the proud woman onstage—victorious, if only for one night.

"You know, that could be you up there," Colin whispered. When their hands touched on the armrest, they each pulled away, embarrassed, just as Anna May died on-screen. The radiant Chinese starlet swooned, inhaled dramatically, flaring her nostrils as the orchestra played to a crescendo. Then she batted her eyes and collapsed as the curtain fell and the audience clapped and cheered. Colin gave the show a standing ovation.

AFTERWARD THEY CAUGHT a jitney cab to the Stacy Mansion. Colin led her past the doorman to the parlor, where a few of the younger men recognized him, which surprised and impressed Liu Song. The men in blue blazers spoke of yacht racing and rowing, and of course acting, theater, photoplays, and moviemaking.

"They finance films. Union money," Colin said afterward.

"Are you a member here?" she asked.

"No." He laughed at the thought. "They have certain membership requirements that I am unable to meet. But they do have a splendid pub in the basement, which is open to the public—the Rathskellar. Of course they no longer serve strong spirits, but it's still a nice place *to see or be seen,* if you catch my meaning?"

Liu Song did. And then again, she didn't. Not firsthand anyway. She'd seen places like this only from the outside—the Stacy, the Carkeek Mansion, the Seattle Tennis Club, with their iron fences, topiary, fancy roadsters, and elegant women in diamonds, pearls, and sheared mink boleros. She felt like a pauper in her gauche three-dollar dress. Even the coat-check girls looked more fetching, more becoming. She wouldn't have been surprised if the men and women of the club asked her to run along and find a lint brush, a cigarette lighter, or perhaps the humidor from the gentlemen's smoking lounge.

"Ah, you must be Liu Song—what a clever name. Stupendously appropriate, don't you think?" A man with a finely manicured silver beard and gold spectacles took her hand and touched it to his lips. "I'm Marty Van Buren Stacy. Thank you so much for·agreeing to grace my humble little establishment with your presence."

"I'm . . ." Liu Song was overwhelmed by his hospitality, unsure of how he'd recognized her. Then she felt silly as she realized she was the only Chinese woman in the room—probably the only one ever to have set foot in the club. "Thank you."

"And Master Colin, it's good to see you again. I can't say that I'm surprised to see you here attending to this young songstress. Birds of a feather—as they say."

Liu Song watched in awe while Colin mingled among Seattle's royalty as though he were one of them. It became obvious that behind Colin's modesty lay more affluence than he'd initially let on—

not that it mattered to her. If anything, his lofty status only confirmed the gulf of culture and society that separated them. He had more familial obligations than he'd probably let on as well. Back in China he must have been a prince among men, from a family with generations of servants attending to their every need. She knew that he was well beyond her social status, that to be here with her was a tremendous act of charity. Plus, while he was still regarded as someone of value in a place like this, he would never be fully accepted—which must have been humbling. *To come here,* Liu Song thought—*to be seen with me, he must have owed my father a great deal.*

"We have a special room all set up for you," Mr. Stacy said.

Liu Song looked at Colin, who seemed unsurprised.

"You *will* stay for dinner, won't you?" Mr. Stacy asked. "Then after dessert and all the guests have arrived, you'll favor us with that exquisite voice of yours, yes?"

"We're honored," Colin said. "Thank you for your generosity."

A maître d' led them to a private room near the back that had elegant furnishings and a formal setting for two with flowers and a lit candelabrum. But the wallpaper was old and tobacco-stained, and there were cracks in the wainscoting.

The maître d' held the chair for Liu Song and gently placed a fine lace napkin in her lap. She felt naked for not having worn evening gloves. She looked up at Colin, who was masking a frown as they were left alone with the prix fixe menu.

"Is something the matter?" she asked hesitantly, worried that he was now embarrassed by the dress she wore or that her table manners were somehow flawed.

"It's nothing," he said. "This is splendid."

"No, really. You can tell me . . ."

He set down the menu. "Have you not noticed?"

"Noticed what?" she asked.

"That we're sitting in the servants' dining room." He regarded the wallpaper, the worn carpet with cigarette burns. "We're not normally allowed in a club like this—not out there anyway, so they've fancied up this . . . place . . ."

It wasn't shocking news to Liu Song. She'd hardly believed it when they accepted Mr. Butterfield's offer. But perhaps talent, she'd thought, whatever little she might have, transcended class and social standing—even race, perhaps.

"It's just one evening," she said optimistically. "They get me for a five-hundred-dollar piano. They can keep the piano. You get me for a song."

Colin found his smile, then looked at his menu. "Well, what's for dinner?"

BEING CHINESE, LIU Song thought she had eaten her share of exotic food—compared to the Western palate, at least. She'd grown up on black pickled eggs, on spicy marinated chicken feet, salty dried cuttlefish, and an assortment of dried fungus. But what the waiters at the Stacy Mansion offered on domed silver platters was a continual surprise—one gastronomical dare after another. They dined on green turtle steaks, eel, frog legs, and Liu Song even tried the escargot, which tasted rich, buttery, and delicious until Colin told her what it actually was. She was certain that she must have turned as green as the dish, which was covered in garlic and fresh parsley. She held her napkin to her mouth, trying not to think of the fat banana slugs that left sticky trails of mucus along the alley near her apartment. She felt so ill she hardly touched the thick slice of ginger cream pie that was served for dessert.

Though it was probably just nerves, the thought of performing in such a formal, decadent place, for such seemingly important people, made her palms sweat. She tried not to think of her barren alleyway apartment, where she'd sleep that night beneath a secondhand blanket she'd purchased from a thrift store. A sad, worried, neglected part of her heart feared that this was all just some cruel parlor game—bring in the poor Chinese girl, expose her to such finery, and then laugh over snifters of brandy and glasses of tawny port as she wilted in the spotlight.

"You'll be fine," Colin said. He must have seen her chewing her lip. "You are your mother's daughter. It's your job to set the room on fire."

She felt invigorated at the mention of her mother. She envisioned herself in her mother's gown, with the Widow's mask. Then she felt butterflies in her stomach as she heard a parlor bell ringing down the hall and the muffled sounds of conversation began to settle down. She heard Mr. Stacy speaking to his guests, who were clapping and laughing with excitement.

The waiter returned with a glass of sparkling mineral water. "It's that time," he said.

Liu Song rose to her feet, ran her tongue across the front of her teeth, checked her appearance with Colin, who nodded graciously. She sipped the water and was led down a hallway to the back of the mansion, where the servants' stairs were located. She went up one flight, passed the colored help, who smoked hand-rolled cigarettes and stared at her. Then she came around to make a solo entrance, descending the mansion's ornate formal staircase. There must have been fifty pairs of eyes staring up at her—members, guests, escorts, and assorted relations, all of them sparkling in their formal attire, beaming with the oblivious confidence that comes only from old, gilded wealth. She saw Colin in the back of the room, smiling and waving encouragingly.

"Ladies and gentlemen," Mr. Stacy announced, "all the way from the mystical, magical Orient, Miss Liu Song Eng."

She curtsied and waved, though she was quietly blanching at not only her uncle's surname but also her mistaken homeland. She'd never taken the steamship journey to the Orient, or even been out of the country. She'd barely traveled the West Coast. She noticed Colin, who shrugged and raised his eyebrows as she remembered her father talking of the illusory presence of the stage. Where the unreal becomes real. She smiled, even as the women in the crowd whispered to one another and pointed in her direction.

She drew a deep breath while the audience quieted. Mr. Stacy winked at her, cigar in hand, then walked past an old pump organ and unveiled the grand pianola to the delight of the audience. Liu Song could smell fresh wood soap and see her reflection along the top of the keyless reproducing piano. And Mr. Stacy didn't even need someone to work the pedals. He merely pushed a button and the bellows inflated, moving the cylinder inside as the pianola began playing "A Pretty Girl Is Like a Melody." Liu Song started singing softly but quickly elevated to the top of her range, growing more confident with each chorus. She followed that with "A Good Man Is Hard to Find," staring at Colin as she crooned, "My heart is sad and I'm all alone . . ."

The crowd marveled at her voice and her young age. They begged for one more song, and after a cylinder change, she favored them with a sad, soulful rendition of "Till We Meet Again." She wailed the high notes of each bar as though squeezing every remaining drop of sorrow out of her ruined heart—from the loss of her father through the loss of her mother, and even her innocence. She stared longingly at Colin, so close but so impossibly far away. He was within her reach but seemed forever beyond her grasp.

Afterward she collected praise and compliments, which she modestly received, doubting the authenticity of such kind words—*too much wine,* she thought. They probably had a hogshead hidden somewhere about. Then she remembered Prohibition and found some small validation. Even Mr. Stacy's wife made a point to shake her hand and invited her back to perform anytime—a rhetorical gesture; she didn't really mean it. Then again, she didn't not mean it either. The whole thing left Liu Song happy but confused, accepted but still so alone—the much-adored center of attention while onstage, but a soloist in life.

She rested her voice as she and Colin rode back to King Street Station beneath a cloudy, starless sky. She was unsure of what to make of the whole evening. Did he really want to be with her? Or was this a debt to her father, some strange, forced social obligation? She wanted to ask but was afraid of the answer.

He shared his umbrella as he walked her back to her apartment, past the old Hip Sing Tong building and the new Eastern Hotel. He stopped where the alley met the street. She heard a tomcat wailing in the distance, and a ship's foghorn echoed from somewhere out on the murky blue-green waters of Puget Sound. He lowered the umbrella so they could see each other beneath the flickering streetlights. The rain had let up, dampening their cheeks, their hair, and their eyelashes with a fine mist.

"You are a natural," he said. "I have to study. I have to work at it, but you—it's who you really are. You're like a sunflower. You come alive when you step into that spotlight." He looked at her as though waiting for a reaction. "Did you see the looks on their faces? I think they saw you as a novelty at first—an *amuse-bouche,* but by the end of the night, every man wanted you—and every woman wanted to *be* you."

She looked up into the drizzly night sky, embarrassed that she didn't understand his French but equally charmed by his words. "I didn't really notice all that."

He shook water from his umbrella. "Well, I noticed. Believe me . . ."

She watched as he loosened his tie and stepped aside while a black couple walked by followed by a group of drunken old Chinese men heading back from some gambling den.

"Now I'm frightfully embarrassed to ask you this, especially after the way you wowed everyone tonight." He tipped his hat back with the point of his bumbershoot. "Well, I'm a member of Seattle's Chinese Opera Company, and I love the work there, but I've been trying to find bigger roles, in front of a wider audience. And as luck would have it, I landed a part in a musical at the Empress Theatre. It would mean the world to me if you came and returned the favor—watched me for good luck." He looked at her sheepishly and then handed her a card with his phone number and address. "Maybe you can give me a few pointers afterward."

"I can do that," she teased. "I can watch."

"Liu Song." As he spoke his breath turned to vapor. "I know we didn't meet under the most auspicious of circumstances. And . . . I don't want to overstep my boundaries in any way. It's . . . just that . . ."

That you want to kiss me? She tried to project her thoughts directly into the center of his brain—or his heart, whichever got the message first. Her face felt flushed, and her stomach tightened. It was more than just the cool air that made her hands cold and clammy. She looked up at him hoping, expectant. She felt his hand gently on her arm as he removed his hat with the other hand, leaning in. She could smell his nervousness and feel the welcoming warmth of his skin. Her ears were ringing.

Then he stopped. "Are you all right?"

She felt faint and stepped back. She muttered an apology as she turned, embarrassed. She walked down the alley toward her apartment in such a hurry she nearly broke a heel. She didn't look back as she unlocked the door and slammed it shut behind her, kicking off her shoes. She didn't bother to turn on the lights. She removed her coat and dropped it on the floor en route to the kitchen, where she froze, her muscles tightening violently as she vomited into the sink—the eel, the turtle, the one bite of ginger cream pie. She smelled it all come back up, and she retched again until she was left gagging up nothing but water and stomach acid. She opened the faucet and then melted onto the floor, resting her forehead on the cool piping beneath the sink. She sat in the dark, wiping her chin, staring at the thinly curtained windows, wondering what Colin must be thinking, wondering what in the world had just happened.

A Chinese Honeymoon

꒱

(1921)

"*Pregnant?*" Mr. Butterfield asked. "Are you sure?"

Liu Song had been sick for weeks. At first she thought it had been the food or that the sour stomach she suffered through every morning and into the afternoon was because of her infatuation with Colin. She'd kissed his card and slept with it beneath her pillow every night, hoping it would sweeten her dreams. But as the days passed into weeks, she realized her sickness was much more than that. She felt different, dizzy and fatigued. She was sore in places. And her bleeding had stopped. If her mother were alive, she might have burned a strip of urine-soaked paper, sniffing the fumes for the strange telltale signs of a baby. Liu Song didn't bother. She knew.

She didn't know why she decided to tell Mr. Butterfield, of all people. Maybe it was due to the queasiness she felt while riding on the streetcar to his store every morning. Or perhaps it was because he was the only person who saw her on a daily basis. She knew that at some point she wouldn't be able to fit into her mother's dress— she couldn't hide the truth forever. In the end she realized she just needed to break the news, confess, to tell *someone*—he happened to be there when the dam burst.

Mr. Butterfield sat down on a stool, rubbed his balding pate, and took out a flask of sweet-smelling brandy. He poured the brown liquor into a small cup, and for a moment Liu Song thought he might offer a toast. Then he found his three-finger cigar case, slipped out a Corona, and dipped it into the cup. He cut the tip off, sniffed the wet, rolled tobacco, and then discarded the stub in the trash. "Honestly, I expected better things from you. You didn't strike me as that kind of girl—why would you do an impetuous, careless thing like that? You had such a promising future." He sounded stunned but also saddened. He groaned but more in disappointment than in anger.

The word *had* stung her, reminding her of so many other things in life she had to do—she had to feel regret and embarrassment, she had to pretend she was strong, she had to accept the loss of her parents, her brothers, she had to keep breathing, had to come up for air—because she had her uncle's baby inside her.

You've had me standing in the rain, working for nickels, Liu Song thought. She grew defensive but knew any frustration toward Mr. Butterfield was misplaced. She was his employee, a partner even, if only in a token way. But now she felt small, as though she were shrinking, withering in front of him. She felt used up. She felt like nothing.

"I'm sorry . . ." She wanted to tell him about Uncle Leo but didn't know how. She sank deeper into the pit of shame she had fallen into. "It was only a few times."

Mr. Butterfield grumbled and rolled his eyes. "That's what girls always say." He shook his head and lit his cigar. "And who is this beau of yours? Is he going to do right by you or what? Or is he the kind of lout that skips town as soon as he finds out? You're how old—sixteen? Seventeen? Half the girls in the city are married off at fifteen, dear; there's no shame in the two of you taking care of this down at the courthouse . . ."

"I can't," Liu Song said as she stared at her feet.

"And why is that, pray tell?"

She looked up at Mr. Butterfield's curious, gossipy stare and then looked away. She found the clock on the wall and watched each second slowly tick away. Her face felt hot and her lip trembled. She wanted to cry, but as always, the tears didn't come.

"He's already married," she whispered. Leo's shame was now her shame.

Liu Song watched as her boss stubbed out his cigar, wide-eyed, and shook his head. He leaned forward and said, "I'm just flabbergasted. I did not see *that* coming. Liu Song, sweetheart, you never cease to shock and amaze . . ."

"I'm so, so sorry . . ."

"Young lady, for a lifelong bachelor I consider myself an expert on judging women—*believe me*, but . . . I didn't think you had this kind of moxie in you." He picked flecks of tobacco off the tip of his tongue and then spat into the nearest waste bin. "I just can't believe it. If I were anyone else I'd have to fire you right now, you know that? That's what a practical businessman would—and *should*—do in a situation like this. That's all I need is for the gossips to descend on my store like flies on a dung heap."

Liu Song shook her head. "No one knows, not even him."

She watched as Mr. Butterfield swallowed his brandy in one gulp. He sat back, his cheeks slowly turning pink. He looked as though he were aging before her eyes.

"No sense in telling him now, I suppose. Sadly, you'll only ruin his reputation along with your own." Mr. Butterfield hesitated and then asked, "Are you going to carry this child? There are things that can be done in private to remedy this kind of situation."

Liu Song had considered those options—she'd agonized over them for weeks. She remembered old wives' tales of pregnant women eating small quantities of poison or using knitting needles to keep the seed from taking root. And the only family she had was no family at all—though she worried that if Uncle Leo and Auntie Eng found out, they would want the baby. They just wouldn't want the mother who came along with a newborn. She imagined them taking the child. A part of her wanted that. But another voice called out to her. And as much as she loathed her stepfather-uncle, as much as her skin crawled at the thought of his touch, the other voice knew that this child would still be a part of *her*—part of her mother and father. This child would be her only family—with it, she wouldn't be so alone. She tried to block out the rest, the terrible, ugly truth.

"I'm going to keep it." The decision brought her no comfort.

Mr. Butterfield seemed relieved, as though those words had some quiet, redeeming value. "If only you had shown that kind of will-power earlier, dear, none of this would have happened." He shook his head, still in shock. "Well, when you start to—you know"—he gestured to his stomach and tugged on his waistcoat—"I imagine you won't be able to work here anymore. You've set us back a bit, that's for sure. What a shame that you'll have to take a leave of absence, but necessary, I'm afraid. I certainly can't have my good customers thinking I condone this kind of behavior—appearances are everything, I'm afraid. Who knows, they might think I've been Barney-mugging you behind the counter and that *I'm* the father." He half-chuckled at the notion.

Liu Song blinked, trying not to grimace. She found nothing in their conversation worth smiling, let alone laughing, about.

He offered her a handkerchief. She took it but didn't cry.

"It'll be okay, sweetheart. Somehow, it'll all work out," he reassured her. "And when the time comes, I'll put you in touch with a place that will care for you until the baby arrives. They'll get you through the rough part and help you decide what to do afterward. They'll get you on your feet again."

The rough part, Liu Song thought. The rough part would be explaining this to Colin, whom she hadn't seen or spoken to in weeks.

"Thank you," she said, somewhat relieved—to have told someone but also that her boss had in mind a place that could help her. She knew that none of the white hospitals would admit her.

"I guess this explains why your uncle Leo said to pay you directly from now on." Mr. Butterfield reached beneath the counter and fished out the zippered bag with Liu Song's earnings for the past few weeks. He handed it to her. "Throw you out, did he?"

Liu Song felt the weight of the full bag. This had been her money in the first place. She'd earned every penny. But now it felt like something else—like coins the flower girls earned in the shadowy doorways of Paradise Alley. Now these dollar bills were notes that read: Go away, get lost, good riddance.

"Something like that," she said.

AFTER WORK, LIU Song walked home to save money, and besides, the weather was nice. She strolled by bakeries, inhaling their sweet aromas, and walked past the frying, clinking sounds of greasy spoon diners. She trudged up the broken sidewalks of King Street, passing noodle factories, sausage carts, and the well-stocked window displays of the Yick Fung Mercantile, filled with simple pleasures she could never afford. When she reached Canton Alley, she looked up and down the street, mindful of peeping neighbors and passersby, then slipped toward her apartment. She was famished as she locked the door behind her, and knowing that her cupboards were bare and her icebox empty only made the rumbling in her stomach worse. But her thoughts of food disappeared when she saw an envelope that had been slipped beneath her door. Her heart raced as she read who the fine piece of stationery was from:

Dear Liu Song,

I must apologize for my behavior when last we were together. It was very forward and presumptuous of me, especially after what you've already been through with the loss of your dear mother. I can understand why you haven't called or written. I should have respected your time of grief and mourning. I hope you can forgive my foolishness and perhaps let me make it up to you.

As I hinted, I landed a small part in a revival of *A Chinese*

Honeymoon at the Empress Theatre. It's a very modest
production that will only run a few weeks, but it's a rare
opportunity. And it starts tonight.

I have left a ticket for you at the box office, in your name,
should you decide that you'd like to see me again. Once
more, please accept my sincerest apologies.

Yours truly,
    Colin K.
    FR 324

The note had included his phone number, leaving Liu Song wishing she had a telephone. She slumped to the floor and leaned against
the door, staring at the vacant room, a chronic reminder of her
empty, desolate life. She'd walked through Chinatown every morning, ignoring the stares and whistles from Filipino cannery workers
and Chinese fishmongers. Men twice her age who undressed her
with the soiled fingers of their crude imaginations. And at Butterfield's she drew stares of lust and condemnation, admiration and
hope, expectant supplication. Colin, on the other soft, gentle hand,
seemed like the only person who treated her with tenderness, caring, and respect. He was everything she wanted, needed.

She touched her tight belly and remembered that her life of solitude was about to change. How could she tell Colin? How could
she burden him with that news? She'd wanted to call him the morning after their dinner together. She'd wanted to run to the nearest
phone booth, but she'd been so sick, and her body had ached. And
as each day passed, as each wave of nausea waned, that awful feeling was replaced with doubt, until every time she looked in the mirror she saw nothing of worth. In a roaring society that valued youth
and beauty, her riches were now counterfeit, her innocence bankrupt. She had nothing to offer him but disappointment, embarrassment, and shame.

But even after a few hours of contemplation, a mote of hope refused to go away. That twinkling caused her to rise like a ghost whose labors begin when the sun sets. As night fell, she walked out the door and wandered through the misty rain to the corner of Second Avenue and Spring Street. She stared up at the ornate brass awning that had turned an earthen shade of green, where *A Chinese Honeymoon* had been painted in broad gold lettering. She'd never seen or heard the musical before, but her father had once told her how the production had run in thousands of theaters—a favorite of white audiences all over the world, though he didn't care for it much. She knew the story well—a trumped-up tale of couples who break the law in China by accidentally kissing in public.

Liu Song gave her name to the matron in the box office, who handed her a cardboard ticket. Colin had saved a spot for her in the front row, but she chose to sit in a dark corner near the back of the theater. The Empress playhouse was tiny, but an eager crowd of patrons filled the three hundred seats, chatting and eating roasted almonds from sleeves of pink paper that turned silver when the houselights dimmed. Liu Song watched through the fog of her loneliness and grief as Colin appeared onstage as a servant in the palace of the farcical Hang Chow, the Emperor of Ylang Ylang, a made-up land for a made-up story. A white actor played the part of the Emperor, though he wore makeup to give his skin a yellowish tone. Liu Song thought he looked more like a hairless cat than a man. Still, all eyes were on the Emperor, all but Liu Song's, whose gaze was fixed on Colin. She felt so close to him, a distance measured in heartbeats instead of feet. Colin's role was small, a token at best, but she felt proud.

During intermission Liu Song snatched a program from the trash and found Colin's name at the very bottom. She traced the printed characters with her fingertips. He was the only Chinese performer in the show—even the character of Soo Soo, the peasant girl betrothed to Hang Chow, was played by a white actress. *That could be me,* Liu Song thought. And when the two performers finally kissed at center stage beneath a dazzling spotlight, Liu Song closed her eyes and imagined her and Colin in those roles. Even in a dream, the sight was too much to bear. She wasn't jealous—Colin wasn't hers in any way—but watching their performance only made her want him that much more and, by comparison, made Liu Song feel beyond unworthy. How could a man like Colin accept her? She was the used, the forsaken—the discarded.

After the play ended with a musical fanfare, Liu Song fled. She left amid the clapping and cheering as flowers were thrown toward the footlights, toward the happy couple onstage that appeared like a vision, a mirage in the desert—the embodiment of all she could never be and what she could never have. She was out the door before the first curtain call. She took off her heels and ran home in the rain, shredding her stockings, splashing through mud puddles, dodging motorcars that honked and flicked their lights at her. She staggered to her empty apartment, forever occupied by her persistent companions—shadows of fear, doubt, and regret. She couldn't bear to tell Colin about her condition and she didn't want to torture herself by seeing him again. She tore up the ticket, his card, and his note—all evidence of the man she knew she could never have. She caught her breath and stood in front of the sink, her cold, wet secondhand clothing clinging to her sagging shoulders. She turned on the stove for heat and put on a tiny pot of rice. Then she sat alone on the floor in the dimly lit kitchen, trying not to cry, forcing herself to think of names for her baby, wishing for a boy to call her own.

Dead Letters

꒫

(1934)

William heard clapping and cheering from upstairs as he stared at his glamorously bedraggled mother, this strange weed of a woman, still so young, but weary. *You gave birth to me,* he reconciled all she'd told him. *You loved me, but you gave me away. I guess I know why.* He grimaced at the thought. *My father . . . was your stepfather.* This avalanche of truth wasn't the reunion he had hoped for, but at least their strange relationship was one he could understand. Countless times he'd seen mothers come and go from Sacred Heart, and each time he thought, *If you really cared, you wouldn't leave your child behind, you wouldn't abandon him—no matter what.*

What does that say about me? William wondered. *Or does that merely reflect on my uncle Leo, who was never spoken of, and with good reason?*

"My father was a bad man, then." *Like Charlotte's father.*

"*Father* is too generous a word." She lingered on that thought as though she couldn't find a description worthy of her disgust. But then William saw her glance in the mirror and quickly look away, her eyes cast downward. "I wasn't much better. I didn't know what to do. I wanted what was best for you, but I was young and stupid," Willow said. "But I didn't ever, *ever* want to leave you . . ."

William heard a knock on the door and someone calling Willow's name. They knocked again insistently, and he heard Asa's voice as well.

She held out her hand, admonishing William to stay while she answered. He listened as his mother argued with the comedian and a stage manager, who was saying something about breaking her contract and the legal consequences.

"I have to go, William," she said as she reached for a handkerchief and began wiping the black streaks from her cheeks. "I have to go, but it will just be a few minutes. Promise me you'll stay. I'll be right back . . ."

"I'll stay. I promise."

She closed the door, and William listened to the orchestra in the distance. He waited and wondered if Willow would be performing the same song, or if she had changed her tune as she'd changed her heart so many times. Then he heard another knock and a commotion in the hall.

When he opened the door he saw Charlotte, who looked pale and angry. "I'm sorry, William." Behind her stepped Sister Briganti and two men from Sacred Heart, who grabbed William by the arms and dragged him into the hallway and up the stairs. Then all he felt was shock, and fear, and the urge to run away as fast as he could.

William was deflated—stunned. "That was my mother," he protested to Sister Briganti as she led Charlotte up and out into the alley and then to the sidewalk. He pointed to the marquee. "Willow is my ah-ma!"

Sister Briganti hailed a taxi and frowned. She hesitated and then said, "I know that, William." Her words crashed to the ground like a tree falling, snapping twigs and branches of half-truths and outright lies.

William stammered in disbelief. "What do you mean *you know*?" He watched as the stout woman struggled to express herself. He was used to her expressions of grace and joy, of wrath or condemnation, even pride, but he'd never seen her like this. *What was it?* he thought. *Not sad, but doubtful.*

"I knew you'd be here, William," Sister Briganti said. "From the moment I saw her in the movie theater and then on that blessed poster, I knew you'd do something impetuous like this." She shook her head. "I'm taking you back to the orphanage."

"Why should we go?" Charlotte asked. "He *has* a mother—that was her!"

Sister Briganti paused, shaking her head. "Because, William, your mother is not supposed to see you, nor you her. It's for the best. Come home and I'll tell you why she gave you away."

WHEN WILLIAM ARRIVED back at Sacred Heart, it felt like anything but home. To make matters worse, he was sickened by the thought of his ah-ma returning to her dressing room and finding the place empty. *Would she think I left to pay her back for leaving me? Would she think I didn't care, that I didn't want her back?* He imagined her searching backstage and then giving up, thinking the truth of his father was enough shame for one lifetime. He knew he would have to leave again and find his way back to the theater. The only thing holding him was that Charlotte might be whisked off right then and there—taken to a school for the blind, or some other place far away. Much to his surprise, she was allowed to return to her cottage unaided. She hugged William for what seemed like a whole minute and kissed him on the cheek.

"Thank you," she whispered in his ear.

"For what?"

"For taking me and not taking advantage of me. Thanks for keeping me safe." She smiled, sadly. "I know you're going to find her again—your mother."

How little you know.

"It's only a matter of time now. And now that you know it's really her, do whatever you have to do, with or without me."

William thanked her in return. Charlotte had always been a friend—a good pal, nothing more. But that dynamic had somehow changed, and his hollow heart felt emptier without her. He was surprised that he could feel anything beyond the shock and longing of meeting his ah-ma again. His desperate imagination swirled with joy, anger, and exasperation. *Love? That too.* William felt as though he were treading water to keep from drowning; his emotions and memories swirled like so much flotsam and jetsam.

He was taken directly to Sister Briganti's office in the administrative wing; he walked down the long hallway like a condemned man, passing grim-faced portraits of Abraham Lincoln and Teddy Roosevelt, but none as dour as his headmistress. As William passed Sunny and a handful of others who were mopping the floor, some looked happy at his return, some disappointed, all of them surprised. *Good to see you boys again. I'm afraid I won't be staying long.*

He was ordered to remain in the office with the door closed until she arrived. He sat on his hands and stared at the books on her shelves, unsure if he were in trouble or not—not caring either way. Willow was Liu Song—his ah-ma. He had someplace to go, someone to go to, a reason to leave, even if that reason was only temporary. He hoped they would kick him out—expected it, even. But until then, he wanted answers.

He waited and waited, until he finally heard Sister Briganti arguing with someone in the hallway, in Italian. Then she walked in with an armload of papers and file folders.

William didn't wait for her to sit down. "How did you know that was my mother?" he asked. "How did you know she was alive?"

"Same as you, William," Sister Briganti said with a long, exhausted breath. "I recognized her at the theater, I heard her on the radio—"

"No," William interrupted. "How did you know it was *her*?"

Sister Briganti sat down across from him, collecting her papers and her thoughts. She opened her desk drawer, pulled out a roll of anise Life Savers, and offered one to William. He shook his head and watched as she popped two into her mouth and bit down on them immediately, chewing them to bits. She sat back in her leather chair and absently touched the rosary that draped from her wide collar.

"I knew . . . because it's my sacred responsibility to carry the burden of truth for your families; that duty is not something to be taken lightly." She looked back at William, shifting her weight as though unable to find a comfortable position. "Because of that, I've always known who your mother was."

"How?" William asked. *Don't make me beg.*

He watched her open one of the files that was stuffed with letters. He leaned forward and pawed through the envelopes; all of them had been opened, and all of them were addressed to him. They were from San Francisco, Los Angeles, New York, but mostly—the ones that made his head pound, his temples throb, and his stomach churn—they were from an address right here in Seattle. He brought them to his nose, smelling the paper, hoping to detect a fragrant memory. "She was here." He looked at the postmarks. "That first year . . . here all the time . . ." *She was only miles away. Why didn't she come back for me?* William remembered sweet times with his mother. None of this made sense. *Did she leave to be an actress?*

"I'm sorry, William."

"For what? For lying to me . . ."

"Watch your tone, young man. I never lied to you, William. Not once," she snapped, touching the letters. "But I did withhold the truth. And I did it for your own good, because your mother was ultimately declared unfit to care for you. And she didn't fight those accusations. She willingly gave you up when she signed these papers. She was never coming back, not here anyway." Sister Briganti opened a file of stamped documents. "My deepest regret is that she didn't give you up at birth. She was selfish in thinking she could provide a proper home. All she did was make it worse for you."

"But . . . how . . . why?"

Sister Briganti coughed, cleared her throat, then snapped her fingers, and a novice outside her office brought in a cup of coffee and dishes of sugar and cream. Sister Briganti looked pained as she stirred her coffee with a tarnished silver spoon, the pinging sound punctuating the silence between them. She sat there, not drinking the coffee.

"Why?" he asked, again.

"*She didn't want you,* that's why she gave you up. She's moved on."

He pointed to the cards and letters. "I don't believe you."

William watched as she shook her head, rose, and reached for an old hymnal on the shelf behind her. From behind the volume she fished out an open pack of Fatima cigarettes and a book of matches. She lit one and sat back down, taking a slow drag and blowing the smoke toward the nearest window, which was slightly ajar.

"You can't keep me here," William said. "It's not fair."

Sister Briganti paused to attend to her cigarette. "You can run away again, if that's what you really want. But it's not any easier out there. If the police pick you up without an address to your name, you'll be arrested. You'll go before a judge, perhaps one less caring than me, and you'll be remanded to a reformatory—sent to a place where they take your shoes at night so you don't slip away, where they lock you in a basement and feed you bread and water. Where they label boys like you as *wayward* or *incorrigible* and send you to the *punishment cottage.* A reform school won't treat you with the same courtesies as Sacred Heart. Do you want that? Mother Cabrini always had a soft spot for the Orient; that's why you're treated as well as you are—for that you should be thankful."

For the whippings, being tied down at night, for keeping my mother's words neatly tucked into a folder beside your desk. William stared back, angry, hurt, but most of all, confused. He rested his elbows on the desk and put his head in his hands. He spoke softly, choosing his words carefully. "I just want what anyone would want . . ."

"And what's that, a perfect family? A mother? A father?"

William shook his head. "Willow—my mother—she told me who my father is, what he was. I don't care. I just want the truth."

Sister Briganti leaned back in the chair, which creaked beneath her weight. She blew smoke. "But your mother cared who your father was. That's why she allowed you to come to Sacred Heart in the first place. Because she knew he'd never find you here."

Fathers

꒳

(1934)

William sat with Charlotte on the old porch swing in front of her cottage. The grass had long since turned a dull shade of brown, like the color of unwashed hair. They shared an old wool blanket, warding off the chill air as a flock of geese flew overhead, disappearing in and out of fog, heading south for the winter to places warmer and more inviting. William dangled one foot to the ground, pushing off lazily as the swing rocked back and forth. The rusty hinges squeaked and pinged like the slow tick-tock of a metronome setting the pace, matching the unchanging rhythm of life at Sacred Heart.

"So she was pregnant?" Charlotte asked. "With you?"

William nodded absently, staring toward downtown Seattle and the terra-cotta pyramid atop the Smith Tower that peeked above the horizon. "I guess so. She didn't know right away. Sister Briganti says there's a test they can do now, but back then she had to wait weeks to be sure. Her boss at some music store arranged for her to go to a place for unwed mothers. I was born there.

"Sister Briganti said I was lucky—since Chinese mothers aren't allowed in hospitals, they usually give birth down on the docks. She also said that at the place where I was born, most of the babies are given up or are taken away. But for some reason my ah-ma decided to keep me." *I guess I was the only family she had left.*

"But that explains why she never spoke about my father. I remember being little and listening to President Wilson on the Zenith giving a Father's Day speech. I took out my crayons, sat down, and began to draw a picture for him—I must have thought my father was going to show up or something. When I presented the drawing to my ah-ma, she gushed and told me how beautiful it was. But later that night I saw her take a candle and light it on fire."

Charlotte nodded. "I don't blame her."

"For burning it?"

Charlotte paused. "For not telling you. You're so fortunate that she even kept you. Most unwed mothers would have given you up for adoption right away—they would have had nothing to do with you. There are older girls here who were pregnant once. They've told me frightening stories. She must have really cared about you, William. You must be very special."

At least I used to be, William thought sadly, trying to reconcile his strange circumstances—his unusual parents and the possible outcomes of knowing or not knowing who his father was. *It mattered then. Does it matter now?*

"And Willow told you all this?"

William nodded. "But I'm sure she didn't tell me everything." He didn't know what was real and what was illusory. He'd created fictions in his mind all these years, based on memories and half-truths, mixed with wishes, hopes, and dreams. He'd believed his ah-ma to be dead all along; instead he was dead to her—abandoned, and according to Sister Briganti, he was eventually forgotten. And yet much to Sister Briganti's chagrin and his surprise, William's mother had miraculously reappeared. But the person on-screen, onstage, on the radio, she wasn't his mother either, or at least not the ah-ma he once knew. *His* ah-ma was Liu Song, while Willow was just a facsimile—an actress with makeup and fancy gowns putting on a show.

What kind of bastard am I?

William chewed his lip and then spoke. "Sister Briganti filled in the rest. She told me about how my ah-ma gave birth to me, how she raised me for a few years. She started to explain why my mother seemed to come and go—about other men she dated, about how if my ah-ma couldn't have me, she didn't want her uncle Leo to have me either." He looked down at his empty hands. "She said that's all I needed to know."

"What else is there?"

"Why she never came back for me." *Or was I that much of a burden? Did she give me up so she'd be free to marry someone? Or did she give me up to be an actress?* "She's famous now. I don't think there's room in that spotlight for a bastard."

William felt Charlotte sit up. He turned and saw Sunny running toward them with a note in his hand. His friend stopped and walked the last fifty feet, nearly out of breath.

"Someone's coming for you," Sunny said, wide-eyed.

William, Charlotte—in fact all of the orphans—recognized that tone, like the prickle of electricity that seemed to hum in the air before a lightning storm, the rush of excitement that came only when a parent returned. Most had learned not to get their hopes too high. After all, often parents came back only for a final, wrenching goodbye. But occasionally and often without advance notice (because parents seemed to love being on the giving end of surprises), one of the orphans would hit the jackpot and be told to pack his or her belongings, which meant one thing—going home.

William's heart leapt in his chest, hoping it was Willow—his ah-ma.

"Coming for who?" Charlotte asked.

"It's your father," Sunny said. "Can you believe it?"

"My father? Uncle Leo?" William blurted, bewildered. A surprising tide of anger seeped into his voice. Though truth be told, a queer part of him *was* curious, the same way a newspaper article about a ship sinking makes one curious, or a train wreck, or a gang shooting. "Sister Briganti said he'd never find me here. Why would he . . ."

"Not *your* father," Sunny said as he rested his hands on his knees, out of breath. Then he pointed to Charlotte. "Hers."

William sat back, relieved, disappointed, but hopeful for his friend. He touched her arm as she stared at something unseen. She grimaced and stood up. He noticed that her pale skin seemed to redden and her hand trembled as she reached for her cane.

Charlotte uttered only a single word. "When?"

"In a few days. He's coming to visit, to make arrangements to eventually take you away from here. Can you believe it?"

"I thought your dad was . . ." *How do I say he was a creep, a criminal?* William wasn't sure how much Sunny knew, so he stopped short of saying the word *prison.*

"He must have got out, William," Charlotte said. "All good things come to an end. All bad things go on forever."

"You're not happy about this?" Sunny asked. "This is what everyone hopes for. This is great news—you deserve it."

Charlotte tapped her cane until she brushed Sunny's leg. "That's sweet of you. But you'd understand if you were a girl and you had my father."

"But . . ." Sunny said. "It means you'll get to go home."

"It's okay," William said. *Home is a fairy tale, the kind where children are lost in the woods, found, cooked, and eaten.*

"You can tell Sister B that I don't have a father," Charlotte said. "And that I'm not going anywhere."

AFTER DINNER WILLIAM sat with Charlotte outside the main chapel as the boys' choir practiced some Latin hymn he didn't recognize. Their melodic voices filled the alcove, inspiring a sad reverence. The song had a depressive quality, like a funeral march—intended

to be celebratory, but laden with melancholy. William helped Charlotte light a candle for her mother. He lit one for his own ah-ma
while he was at the altar. And he lit one for Charlotte, though he
didn't tell her that. He had such mixed feelings. He struggled to see
her situation through any lens but the one that magnified his own
loss, his own longing. She had been given a damaged gift, but one
most at Sacred Heart would have been grateful to receive. If his
mother had wanted him back—if only for an afternoon visit, he
would have jumped into that quagmire with both feet. But he knew
their circumstances were different. Their situations weren't merely
apples and oranges. They were oranges and some strange poisoned
fruit.

"Did you tell Sister Briganti that you didn't want to see him?"
William asked. *Because we all know how compassionate that
woman is. She makes cactus cozy.*

Charlotte nodded, then shrugged. "There's nothing she can do.
He's my father. My mother is dead. He has every right. I asked
about my grandmother—I practically begged to go live with her, but
she doesn't have a say in the matter. My father served time for boot-
legging. But now he gets a fresh start. We should all be so lucky."

"But did you tell her?" William asked delicately. He knew that
Charlotte was terrified of her father—something terrible must have
happened between them. She never spoke of it, and William had
always been too afraid to ask.

"Sister B said that perfect parents don't exist and that I was just
being willful and belligerent—that sometimes children get used to
the routine here and don't want to return to the real world. She said
I should be grateful to have him back in my life."

People change, William thought, *Willow certainly did. Maybe
Charlotte's father missed her and would make restitution somehow.*
William wanted to be positive and optimistic, but if Charlotte didn't
want to have anything to do with her father, her reasons were valid
enough, and he believed her.

"Sister B just told me to pray," Charlotte said. "As if that ever helped any of us."

William had tried. But Catholicism, with all of its pageantry, was still a mystery clad in Latin, with ceremonies he didn't understand. Like a mynah bird, William could mimic what was expected of him, but he knew it was merely the price of admission to a strange musical.

Charlotte pulled out a long string of glass beads with a large crucifix at the end. "She gave me a new rosary. Sister B said she gives a special one to every orphan who finds a new family, or every child who is welcomed back into the home they once knew."

William took hold of one end of the long strand. The expensive-looking chain was elaborately woven—a sturdy keepsake, meant to last a lifetime.

Charlotte sighed. "She said this would be the key to my salvation."

William listened to the choir.

"Maybe you should join the order," he said, trying his best to lighten the dour mood. "Become a nun. I bet they'll let you stay then." *Sister Charlotte.*

She didn't laugh. But she didn't frown either. William thought he detected a smile, if only a slight one. He watched as she tucked her long strawberry hair behind her ears. And he noticed for the first time just how pretty she was—maybe it was because she'd be leaving soon. His mother's spotlight had made him see just how far his shadow of sadness had been cast and what that darkness obscured. He realized that Charlotte had always been there, a blind girl hoping he would finally open *his* eyes and see her as more than a friend. He watched her gentle movements, trying to imprint her image on his heart so that he'd never forget what she looked like. He tried to count every freckle. They seemed interesting since they were so uncommon in Chinatown. Most of the people there had birthmarks or moles, if anything, and these were viewed as omens—symbols of good fortune or bad luck. If that were true, then the tan sprinkles that dappled Charlotte's nose and cheeks represented a windfall, of one or the other.

He reached out and laced his fingers through the soft warmth of her hand.

"I'm sorry you're leaving," he said.

She held on tight.

"I'll never leave you, William. I promise."

THE RUMOR OF Charlotte's refusal spread like the plague through the barracks, breeding jealousy and dissent between the older boys and aching confusion among the little ones, who didn't believe such a refusal was even possible.

"Who does she think she is?" Dante asked as the lights went out.

The responses were legion.

"Maybe she's dim as well as blind."

"I heard her father was a bootlegger . . ."

"She's an addlepated pinhead—should be with her own kind anyway."

". . . I told you she was stuck-up."

Hardly, William thought. *She's more accepting than anyone I know.*

"She can't see what she's missing," someone said. And snickering followed.

Sunny threw a sock at William, who was trying to go to sleep. "I think she has yellow fever if you ask me," his friend said quietly.

William ignored him, unsure of what he could, or should, share. Sacred Heart was gossipy enough without him adding more cabbage to the stew.

"I'm just kidding," Sunny whispered. "But the two of you taking off together—it was the talk of the town. You're lucky you've got me, Sunny Truthseer. I heard the girls haven't been as understanding. They've been teasing Charlotte something fierce. Going on about her being with a boy and—you know, an Oriental and all that."

William suddenly felt terrible. He'd never considered the damage he might have done to Charlotte's reputation. He'd never planned for any outcome beyond that afternoon at the 5th Avenue. He realized how self-centered, how preoccupied he'd been. He was still dying to run away again, to find his ah-ma before she left town. Or to muster the courage to demand more answers from Sister Briganti, but Charlotte had to come first, at least for a few days. He owed her that much.

"That's okay. I'm sure they're all just jealous," Sunny said. "Who wouldn't want to spend time on the outside, in the real world? And for a girl that walks with a cane, she's easy on the eyeballs. I'd have done the same."

William didn't feel like talking. He rolled over, hoping his friend would get the hint. He waited in the dark for Sunny to run out of steam.

"I understand why she doesn't want to see her dad."

William rolled back over and opened his eyes. He couldn't see his friend's face in the pale moonlight that spilled through the high windows of the room. But he could see Sunny's faint outline in the bunk next to his. "What are you talking about?"

"It didn't make sense at first," Sunny said. "But I'm in the same boat—I wouldn't want to see my dad either. My mother dropped me off at the library and said she'd be right back. But my dad, he's nothing but trouble—he didn't even go that far. Some dads are like that. I don't remember much . . ."

I don't remember Leo at all. I barely remember the man my mother called Colin.

"You never told me that," William said.

"That's because I never told no one."

"What else is there to tell?"

Sunny paused, and when he spoke again William could hear the change in his friend's voice. Sunny spoke in soft, sniffling bursts.

"My dad took a job out here in the canneries, but then ran off with some woman and we never saw him again. He never wrote. Nothing. My mom, she brought me out to Seattle and we went looking for him. But we ran out of money and no one would take us in, so we had to sleep in the street. She got an infection in her hip from living out-of-doors and couldn't take care of me and had to say goodbye. She said I should forgive him for running away and that I'd understand these things when I got older, but I hated him— I still hate him. I hate his name too—so much that I refuse to say it, even to this day. Growing up on the reservation, I always wished I had a name like Sunny Goes Ahead or Sunny Not Afraid. So when the sisters came for me, I gave up on him and chose a tougher name, Sixkiller, hoping the other kids wouldn't mess with me. I read the name in a book one time. It's Cherokee, but I'm from the Crow res. I'm not from anywhere, anymore. No one around here knows the difference anyway. I'm just another prairie nigger."

William paused to take it all in.

"I'm sorry, Sunny."

"It's okay, Will. You know how it is now. And Charlotte, she probably knows this better than anyone. I mean, her dad went to jail and all, but I heard he was worse than that. I heard he used to do things—kiss her while she was sleeping. How creepy is that?"

William felt sick to his stomach.

"We don't get to choose our parents," Sunny said. "If we did, some of us might choose never to be born at all."

Charlotte's Eyes

(1934)

William woke to another gloomy, drizzly morning, the sun hidden beyond an overcast sky, pale and cadaverous. He shivered as he peered through the October mists of Puget Sound. The horizon was a wet blanket of gray, without any real definition. Just fog and haze. The inverted weather system was perpetually coiled up, ready to sneeze.

When William arrived in his main classroom, someone handed him a note. He recognized Sister Briganti's handwriting immediately. The note was actually an exhaustive list of cleaning duties to fulfill before he could return to class. Evidently he would learn the broom and the coal shovel, and study the washing board and the scrub brush, long before he'd be reconsidered as a suitable candidate for book learning.

Is this to keep me away from the other kids, or to keep me away from Charlotte? William wondered as he found himself mopping the second floor of the main school building, sloshing soapy water about the wooden surface. He thought about his estranged father as he worked on an old, stubborn shoe-polish stain, and he remembered the startled, stricken, distant expression on his mother's face when she'd first seen him. He debated whether she was an actress who occasionally played the role of a mother, or a mother who was given to acting. In his memories she was a lioness, but in reality, she was meek, tamed, caged.

He was wringing dirty water from the mop when he heard excited whispers and the squeaking, rasping sounds of metal chairs on a wooden floor. He peeked into a half-empty history classroom where students had been working on extra-credit projects. They had all left their books open and their papers on their desks and rushed to the windows, crowding in closer for a better look.

"What is it?" William asked anyone who might be listening.

"Get in here and check it out for yourself," Dante answered without turning around. "That must be him down there—the joker's a day early."

"Who?" William asked as he walked toward the window.

Dante looked over his shoulder and said, "Charlotte's papa."

"I heard he's an ex-con that got let out after Prohibition," another boy said. "He just got out of prison, Walla Walla or Sing Sing . . ."

"He doesn't look that scary," a girl added.

William looked down into the courtyard, where he saw a slender man standing next to a DeSoto coupe with white-rimmed tires. The man was chatting pleasantly with Sister Briganti. William thought that he didn't look like a felon or a monster either; he wore a suit and tie but didn't have a hat. In general, he looked like an average father.

William ran downstairs and lingered near the front door with a dozen other onlookers—boys mostly, who'd been fascinated by the thought of a hardened criminal paying a visit to Sacred Heart.

"Don't look him in the eye," one of the boys said.

"He doesn't look that tough," someone retorted.

"Is that him, is that really Charlotte's dad?" William asked, but he didn't need to hear an answer. As the man walked toward the wide double doors, it was clear by his nose, his cheekbones, his hair, even his smile—he was the spitting image of Charlotte, which was comforting and yet disturbing. William had expected a bald, tat-tooed ogre of a man, with visible scars, wearing a blue, sweat-stained work shirt. He had pictured Mr. Rigg with a five-day beard and chewing the unlit stump of an old cigar. Instead, this man was rail-thin and looked quite pleasant. His shoes were old but had new laces. And he carried a plush brown teddy bear beneath his arm.

"You must be William," the man said as he walked up the steps and extended his hand.

William shook it absently. The man's grip was soft and warm and damp.

"Sister here was just telling me all about you—how you're Char-lotte's comrade in arms. Like two blind mice—see how they run."

William wasn't sure if that was a joke or an accusation, until the man smiled. William noticed that one of his front teeth was chipped. Aside from that slight imperfection, he was a handsome fellow, with a gentle, likable carriage.

"Boys and girls," Sister Briganti announced with fanfare, "this is Mr. Rigg—he's come to visit our good Charlotte. And next week, saints be willing, she'll be going home. Let's keep them in your prayers."

I'll be praying that something heavy falls on this man. William thought Sister Briganti looked self-satisfied, as though this news was the fulfillment of her mission—solving familial puzzles, no mat-ter how poorly the pieces fit back together. *What about me?* Wil-liam thought as he stared at the stranger with freckled cheeks and a short, ruddy beard. *What about my family?*

The rest of the orphans looked upon the curious man with the shiny car as though he were Saint Christopher, the Easter Bunny, and Santa Claus all rolled into one. They reached out and touched the mohair bear, petting it as the man passed smiling through the crowded hallway.

But Charlotte wasn't among the happy children who were so eas-ily impressed.

"William," Sister Briganti said, "why don't you run along and tell Mr. Rigg's daughter that her father is here and that he'll be over to visit her shortly?"

Thanks for making me the messenger of misery. William watched as she led Charlotte's father down the hall toward her office. Mr. Rigg looked back and frowned.

William knew that parents had to be interviewed before reclaiming their children. He'd seen quite a few moms and dads fail that part of the process, much to their children's disappointment. Too often parents would show up twitching, lice-ridden, or reeking of booze—demanding their sons or daughters, then leaving emptier than when they'd arrived. And sometimes a home inspection was required as well. But the whole routine seemed ridiculously unfair when compared to fresh adoptive parents, who merely had to show up and sign a few papers before taking their new children to some unknown home where they'd be living with strangers. *They were unfamiliar,* William mused, *but they'd never given up one of their own.* That obviously counted for something.

As William walked down the hall and out the door, he realized that word of Mr. Rigg's arrival had spread faster than William could travel. He overheard dozens of girls gossiping. They all seemed bitter, probably because they were jealous. Mr. Rigg's visit and Charlotte's pending departure were reminders of how much everyone else had lost and how badly they longed to have their loving parents back—their homes, their siblings—to be part of the outside world. Family reunions were fleeting, like sunshine on the horizon, seen from beneath perpetual clouds of cold mist and rain.

As William walked up the hill to Charlotte's cottage, the boys outside seemed giddy. But William didn't smile. He couldn't even fake it. He felt more like a postman delivering the death notice of a loved one. He heard her voice before he knocked.

"The door's open," she said. "Please tell me that's you, William?"

As he walked in he realized that Charlotte's cottage didn't have any lights—no lamps or curtains. She remained in shadow. Her worldview never changed.

"He's here, isn't he," she stated. She'd been standing near the open window counting the beads on her rosary. "It's been years, but I recognized his voice."

William didn't know what to say. "He has a car."

"He shows up in a car and we all get taken for a ride."

William shook his head. Sister Briganti had once shared that unwed mothers received a government stipend each month. William wasn't sure if such a thing applied to fathers—probably not, but perhaps because Charlotte was sightless he would somehow be compensated in her mother's absence.

"He looks nice enough," William said, hoping to ease the tension.

"You don't know him like I do. He's not an honorable person," Charlotte said. "How would you feel if your uncle Leo showed up and wanted you back—wanted to suddenly have a son and be a father and play house after all these years?"

Would it be much worse than this? William didn't have an answer for such a damning question. He'd shared his mother's story about Uncle Leo with Charlotte, but he never considered the possibility of his showing up. He supposed he'd run away again—William planned to anyway, regardless of the hazards. He desperately wanted to reconnect with his ah-ma; even if she didn't want him, he would speak to her, face-to-face. He needed answers. But he didn't want to leave Charlotte either, not now. "Maybe when you leave . . ."

"I told you, William, I'm not leaving."

He corrected himself. "*If* you leave." He paused, waiting for her to argue. "And if you're on the outside, I can come visit you. I'm leaving anyway. I have to see Willow again. If she takes me back, maybe I can help you . . ."

William heard a knock on the door and saw Charlotte's body stiffen.

"Knock, knock. Anybody home?" Mr. Rigg stepped into the room. "There she is, my gingersnap. Look at you—you grew up when I wasn't looking."

"You weren't able to look," she said.

"Well then, that makes two of us," Mr. Rigg said.

William watched as Charlotte took a step back and bumped into an old sofa. She seemed lost in the cottage that she knew so well. She sat down and stared ahead as though recognizing something in a dark corner of her childhood. William stepped toward the door as Charlotte's father handed her the bear.

"I brought you something. It's a Steiff," he said. "You know, this is the best teddy bear money can buy. Its arms and legs move and everything. Here . . ."

She flinched when the stuffed toy brushed her cheek. Then she took the bear and touched its soft fur. She felt along the snout and the head, which gently swiveled back and forth. She caressed the ears and found the silver button punched through one of them as a label of authenticity. William relaxed and exhaled as she brought the teddy to her face and smelled its plush, velvety coat. Mr. Rigg turned to William and frowned again, nodding his head as if to say, *See—a father knows his daughter.* He held the door as William stepped out. William looked back as Charlotte smiled when she found the bear's eyes. Then she gritted her teeth and ripped them out, dropping them to the floor, where they skittered away. The door closed as bits of thread and torn batting floated in the air between father and daughter.

Blackbird

(1934)

William waited at breakfast, pushing his lumpy oatmeal around his bowl, uncovering and reburying cooked weevils as he waited for Charlotte to arrive. The night before, William had watched from the stone steps of the main building, waiting for her or her father to leave. William had stared through the murky twilight as Mr. Rigg finally departed about thirty minutes before sundown, just as Sister Briganti appeared to usher the remaining boys back into their dormitory for the evening. William had hardly slept all night. And when he did he dreamt of dancing shadows, menacing shapes that resembled an imaginary Uncle Leo, a thin-lipped, scowling Mr. Rigg, and the pious yet condemning Sister Briganti. They laughed and twirled while Willow sang a sad lullaby, a haunting melody from his childhood.

"You gonna eat that?" Dante asked.

William shook his head as the larger boy traded bowls with him, then scooped out the bad parts and proceeded to eat the rest in large, heaping spoonfuls. William counted the girls as they walked in one by one. Charlotte was still missing. Maybe she went home? Maybe she ran away in the middle of the night. Either seemed possible. *Maybe Mr. Rigg did something to her . . .*

She walked in as William was struggling to cast those thoughts out of the dark hollows of his imagination. She looked the same as always. She took a bowl and a spoon in one hand and tapped her way to the table, where she sat across from him.

"Are you okay?" William asked. The question seemed ludicrous in the way people can pull someone from a smoldering train accident, bruised and broken, covered in shards of glass, and ask, *Are you okay, mister?*

"I'm blind, William," she said. "But I see what's happening all around me."

"I'm sorry, it's just . . ."

"He's coming back tomorrow," she said. "I'm to pack my things."

William didn't understand—none of this made sense. His ah-ma was Willow Frost—she was a movie star and he wasn't allowed to be reunited with her, let alone see her. Charlotte's only living parent was a convicted creep who'd been sent away for five years. Now he'd shown up with a two-bit haircut and suddenly he was father of the year.

"We should just take off again," William said. "Go someplace where they won't find us. It wasn't so bad the first time . . ." *Minus the bedbugs.*

"They'll find us. Sister B knows exactly where you'd be heading. And I'm too easy to recognize. I don't exactly blend in," she said. "I get along fine here because I know every inch of my cottage. I know the exact number of steps from building to building, from classroom to classroom. But out there . . . I'd just slow you down."

"I'll talk to Sister Briganti. I'll find a way to make this right."

"It's too late, William. What's done is done. My father is coming back and there's nothing I can do to change that. I'm sorry."

"What do you have to be sorry about?"

"I'm sorry that I won't hear your voice as often as I'd like," she said.

William reached across the table and took her hands. He didn't care who might be watching or what the girlish gossips would say. He looked into her pale blue, haunted eyes, watching them quiver. If she were capable, he knew she'd be crying right now.

"You're my best friend, William—my only friend—the one who's never judged me. You're the best person I've ever known. You're kind and generous and thoughtful and you've always given my heart a soft place to land . . . and . . . I guess what I'm trying to say is that . . ."

I'm going to miss you.

She squeezed his hands and then let go. "I hope you see your mother again."

WILLIAM SAT IN Sister Briganti's office. He'd blazed through his chores and shown up early and refused to leave, waiting for two hours until she arrived after teaching class and attending to other meetings. She walked in and set down a large stack of papers.

"Ready for more truth telling, Master Eng?" she asked. "More stories? More answers? I knew you'd be back. Boys are always drawn to the macabre . . ."

William's head was still reeling from Charlotte's kind, anguished, heartbreaking confession. He'd never felt that type of endearment from anyone except his ah-ma—more than fondness or friendship or the pleasure of another's company—this felt real, and true, and now nothing seemed the same. Suddenly the gray clouds had a pinkish hue that wasn't there the hour before; everything smelled better, even the rain. Music sounded richer, as though every high note was written with him in mind. He couldn't wait to fall asleep now, because he looked forward to dreaming of him and Charlotte in a better place, someplace with hope and possibility. But he also couldn't bear the thought of waking up to a school where her desk would be occupied by another girl, or where her porch swing sat vacant, rocking in the lonely breeze.

"It's about Charlotte," he said.

Sister Briganti paused as though recalibrating her thoughts. "What about her?"

"You know her father did something to her." William said those words as a statement of fact, not a question. "You can't send her home with him . . ."

"William, I don't place my faith in gossip. But I do believe that families are complex and that times are hard. I also know that a single father raising a blind daughter is better than the care she would find in most places. I know that you have concerns and she has expressed these concerns as well. But." The conjunction hung in the air between them, like a guillotine about to fall—in front of a mob of urchins and wayfarers who waited for the outcome they knew was inevitable. "There are degrees of evil, William. And as much as I wish the world were a more heavenly place, I, on occasion, and with a heavy heart, must choose the lesser of those evils. In this case, Charlotte is not of age to make her own choices. She has a living parent who, unlike your own, obviously wants her. He has served a great deal of time paying for his past misdeeds, and has assured me that he has nothing but the most benevolent of intentions. And she's almost old enough to marry, should she choose, so hopefully when she's sixteen she'll find a suitor and be on to a better life."

And what in the meantime, should she just suffer in silence? "He's just using her. For money," William said.

Sister Briganti nodded. "That may have been a contributing factor to his renewed interest in his daughter. He tells me otherwise, and I can only do my best to be the judge of the outside of a man. It's not my responsibility to judge the intent of a man's heart—only God knows the sincerity of Mr. Rigg's motives, and only God can judge His children." She droned on and on.

Who are we not to judge? William anguished. *We're taught to obey, to follow, to walk on the path illuminated by those older—*

wiser, experienced, more faithful. But what about parents who leave us—do we, as children, judge them? Am I supposed to regard the empty space in my heart as my own failing—my own inability to stop the bleeding caused by my mother? You can't expect children to sew their own gaping wounds without leaving a terrible scar.

Sister Briganti was still lecturing him as he walked out. She called his name and was saying things in Italian that he didn't understand, nor did he care to.

WILLIAM HAD NO appetite as he waited for Charlotte in the crowded dining hall. The children buzzed about Charlotte's father coming for her—their chatter became a spiteful, jealous chorus. William felt the urge to silence the boys across from him, but she wasn't here yet and surely they'd refrain once she arrived. She was blind, but he knew that she heard all too well, especially the snickering and sarcasm, the biting laughter of children whose only joy came from stealing happiness from others.

William waited and waited, until the last child had been served. And when Charlotte still hadn't appeared, he shook his head, imagining the tragic folly—the audacity of a blind girl running away. He gave what was on his plate to Dante and then went outside, where he picked wildflowers—fawn lilies, camas, and other flowers that purpled the hillside leading to Charlotte's cottage. He hoped she'd be there, sleeping, packing—doing something. Anything was preferable to an empty room, without a goodbye, and her taking to the streets, a sightless girl, all alone. She couldn't see how beautiful she appeared, especially to desperate strangers in the crowded, beguiling city.

Her cottage was silent when William gently knocked on the door, flowers in hand.

She left already. She ran away.

He wasn't ready to let her go. He was ready to plan—to find a way to catch up to her in Pioneer Square when he made his next escape—before or after finding his mother, he didn't know, he didn't care. But he had to see Charlotte. He had to speak with her, to let her know that he wasn't forgetting her, wasn't giving up on her. She might not be able to keep her promise, but that didn't mean he couldn't promise her something more. She'd been wanting, wishing for something that he'd been too blind to recognize.

He called out her name and knocked again, then looked around the courtyard, the garden, the tiny orchard with Italian plum trees, barren of fruit. He peered down toward the grotto. He looked up at a large blackbird that sat atop the cottage, crowing as though mocking him. The bird cocked its head and cawed again, staring at him, then flew away with a loud beating of its wings.

Nervous and hesitant, William opened the door and peeked inside. It was hard to see in the dark interior, but slowly he began to notice Charlotte's things—her balls of colorful knitting yarn, her toys and glass curios—everything remained in place, unpacked, even her shoes. He saw them, her favorite pair—her only pair, patent leather, well worn, with tarnished silver buckles. The shoes were together, dangling inches above the floor. He fell to his knees as he noticed the upturned footstool and the shoes—the tiny shoes that swayed back and forth so slowly it was almost imperceptible. He stared at their quiet, pendulous motion, as though her feet were hands on a clock that had wound down, the gentle ticking, like a heartbeat, stopped, the clockworks frozen, lifeless.

"Charlotte," he whispered in the darkness, dropping the flowers. *Why couldn't you keep your promise?*

Her shoes, her leggings, her dress, the figure of sweet, blind Charlotte, hung from the rafter above, the rosary wrapped around the wooden beam and around her slender neck and around William's broken heart.

Tears

(1934)

William had been to only two funerals that he could remember, and both had been at Sacred Heart. The first was for a sister who died of old age at eighty-eight. The other was for a toddler who had wandered outside, fallen into a fountain, and drowned. William remembered that both of those services, like the one for Charlotte, had a distinct smell of pine, from the lowly casket, hastily fashioned out of seasoned wood hewn from the forest that surrounded the orphanage. As William looked out the window toward a large stand of evergreen, he imagined the trees closing in around all of them, the orphanage as one giant coffin, their existence contained within an open casket for all to see. He wished that the lid had been closed on the vessel that contained Charlotte's body. He didn't like seeing her that way. He couldn't help but regard her lifeless body and recall all the times he'd imagined his mother's funeral. As a little boy he'd feared losing her—feared being alone. Now his ah-ma had returned and yet he'd never felt such loneliness. He never realized it was possible to mourn someone who was still alive.

As he walked by Charlotte's casket to pay his respects, he noticed the black and purple rings around her neck, the indentations where the beads had broken the skin and soft tissue, the damage covered with a thin veil of talcum. Her eyes were half-open because Sister Briganti refused to leave coins on her eyelids to keep them closed.

She'd been afraid someone would steal them. As William glanced at the slivers of milky blue, he realized that Sister Briganti was probably right. Lots of kids felt sorry for Charlotte, but she had no friends. *Just me.*

"I'm sorry, Willie," Sunny said as he followed him past Charlotte and down the steps to the nearest pew, where a group of boys was sitting.

William didn't say anything. He just stared past Father Bartholomew as the stodgy old priest offered a homily about parents and children. William looked past the man in his robes and vestments, through the stained glass behind him, at the shapes of the trees that swayed in the wind, casting shadows on the translucent panes.

"I heard she cried," Sunny whispered.

William nodded. *Blood.* The thought made him grimace as he remembered Charlotte telling him about her inability to shed tears. He wished he could forget looking up at his dear friend, watching dark lines run down her cheeks from the corners of her bulging eyes. The pressure from hanging had ruptured her seared tear ducts.

As William listened to Father Bartholomew, he looked about the chapel. Charlotte's father sat across from them, next to Sister Briganti, who was kneeling reverently, head bowed, hands clasped around her rosary. The closest she ever got to something akin to happiness was during prayer. William stared at her, offended by her serenity. *Look at me. Let me see your eyes,* he wanted to shout. He needed some unspoken confirmation that she felt something for her part in all of this—that she acknowledged some small responsibility, a token of remorse. But the more he swelled with anger, the more that acidlike emotion spilled back onto him. Because William felt lost as well, as though he were floating in the moral backwater between sins of commission and sins of omission.

"Her father looks like a ghost," Sunny said.

News of Charlotte's unspoken relationship with her father had spread about the orphanage, and in the course of hours William had learned new words like *debauchery, molestation,* and *incest*—too many words that struck too close to home. But if there were any doubt about the veracity of Charlotte's story, it had been answered by her death. And no one could help but stare at Mr. Rigg. Not because of the horrible things they imagined him capable of, but because he didn't look like a monster. He looked toothless, de-fanged, and baleful. He was no kind of decent father, he was barely a parent, and now Charlotte would be put into the earth alone, or-phaned forever.

"I can't believe he's here," William said. "She hated him."

As though the man were encumbered by the condemning stares, he stood, wiped tears from his eyes with a handkerchief, looked at his daughter's body once more, without a smile, without a frown, and left without a word, just as the choir in the balcony began to sing.

"I'd love to get my hands on him," Sunny said, shaking his head. "Afterward they'd call me Sunny Sevenkiller."

As the chapel doors closed with a hollow, empty thud, all eyes turned to Sister Briganti; even Father Bartholomew seemed to be addressing her and her alone. Everyone watched as she sat like a statue in her pew, staring ahead stone-faced, regarding the blank space in front of her as though looking for comfort or absolution.

William thought about Willow—his ah-ma. He couldn't con-ceive of any parents utterly abandoning their children. If anything, meeting Charlotte's father had clarified a painful reality—that even monsters can miss their children. Because the uncomfortable truth is that no one is all bad, or all good. Not mothers and fathers, sons and daughters, or husbands and wives. Life would be much easier if that were the case. Instead, everyone—Charlotte, Willow, Mr. Rigg, even Sister Briganti—was a confusing mixture of love and hate, joy and sorrow, longing and forgetting, misguided truth and painful deception.

Indian Summer

囗

(1934)

William kicked off his shoes and stretched out on the soft bed of warm grass over the place where Charlotte lay buried six feet below. A groundskeeper had peeled up the sod for the funeral, rolling it back like a carpet. William drew his feet together, resting his hands across his lap as he tried to imagine the feel of a pine box surrounding him, the smell of seasoned timber, sawdust, and wood glue. He looked up at a pale blue sky, the color of Charlotte's eyes. The sun had returned from its hibernation, and what few clouds William saw were stretched across the heavens like saltwater taffy in a pulling machine. William closed his eyes and felt the heat from the sun teasing his eyelids. But as he heard geese honking and opened his eyes, he saw birds flying south and knew this respite wouldn't last. Charlotte's darkness was permanent. William missed her. He knew this was as close as he'd ever be to her again. He struggled to accept her death, since she'd been holding his hand just a few days ago. He felt as though he'd failed her and that leaving her behind was a betrayal of sorts. Who would remember her? Who would tend her grave? But as Willow had once said, *I didn't have a reason to stay.*

William knew from reading *The Seattle Star* that his ah-ma would be in town for at least another week. But he didn't know where she'd be staying, or who she was with, if anyone, though there was always the theater and the alley and the stage door. If not, there was Chinatown. That's where he hoped he'd find her. Like Charlotte's grave, he knew that neighborhood was where old bones, old skeletons were buried. He suspected that his ah-ma would be drawn there as well, to wallow in the memories, to drown in nostalgia.

His mother's stories had conjured dark thoughts of being seven years old again and waking up in the middle of the night to an empty apartment. He remembered how he used to open the window and sit on the cold iron grating of the fire escape, the breeze chilling his ankles where the feet of his footie pajamas had been cut off as he outgrew them. Back then he would wrap himself in a blanket to ward off the wintery Seattle night, when the wet air permeated brick and mortar, tile and wood, until his fingers and toes looked pale and grayish, translucent in the moonlight. He recalled those nights after the Crash, looking down into the alley and seeing hobos buried beneath piles of coats—reeking men, huddled together, burning garbage for warmth.

Strangely, he never felt alone on those nights, always confident that his mother would return. He'd sit and listen to beats wafting from the clubs and cabaret theaters below. He didn't know what to call that kind of music back then, but he later learned that joyful noise was a piano and a scratchy trombone playing cakewalk and ragtime, and a local version of Tin Pan Alley. The songs would blare and whisper, crashing and receding, coming and going, reminding him of the sound from a Philco radio on a stormy night. As he grew older he realized that the strange rhythm was merely the doorman letting patrons in and out, releasing music into the night like smoke signals. Despite Prohibition, William would watch as men and women staggered into waiting cabs or ambled down the street, straightening their ties and hemlines, stepping to the beat with all the composure of Sunday churchgoers, but listing to the left or right as though the sidewalk were slowly shifting beneath their feet.

He wondered if the clubs were still there. So many things had changed since then. So many places had been boarded up. Fortunes came and fortunes went. William couldn't grasp the concept of health, good or bad, but fortune—that was easy to comprehend. He'd noticed their luck changing as his ah-ma began to receive gifts—bouquets of purple and blue flowers, potted plants, and baskets of ripe fruit. And pink boxes of food—oh, the delicious food. His mouth watered as he remembered the savory, chewy sweetness of wind-dried duck sausage, which to this day was the best thing he'd ever tasted.

And his ah-ma's clothing began to change.

He remembered her blue dress, the one she used to wash in the sink and hang in the bathroom to dry every night—the one she wore every day—was suddenly replaced by a floral number with a lace collar. Then another. And another. And new hatboxes began to stack up in the corner, so high they seemed mountainous. So William would do what any sensible young boy would do; he'd climb them until they tumbled to the floor, then he'd turn them over and beat on them like drums, using his chopsticks.

His ah-ma would scold him, snatching the utensils from his hands. He'd sit down and start to cry until she made funny faces that made him laugh, then handed him a shoe box of empty spools that he used as building blocks.

Then there was the strange man. William vaguely remembered Colin. He recalled, years ago, thinking he must have been his father, or at least a kind fatherly figure. Colin was always smiling and gracious—he never raised his voice, was always joking and laughing. Through the prism of memory, he seemed the perfect gentleman, with a spectrum of manners, decorum, and wealth. William remembered going for rides in Colin's fancy car. William used to sit in the back and watch his mother's scarf whip in the wind. Colin seemed to have been there from the beginning, but William had eventually guessed—by the way this man came and went—that he was not his father, not his true parent. But he was there, just out of frame, in William's earliest childhood memories. And he remained for years. His ah-ma and he seemed to have it all—health, happiness, a sense of belonging.

But then their fortunes changed again. The first thing William noticed was the emptiness in his stomach when their food began to spoil and eventually treats in neatly wrapped boxes stopped showing up and more often than not he went to bed hungry. The flowers had stopped coming as well, and the ones in their vases began to wilt and die; dried petals scattered on the table and blew on the floor when he opened the window. That was when he noticed that his clothes always seemed to be too small—his shoes too. But in retrospect, his ah-ma rarely let on that anything was wrong. Their austerity became a matriarch's virtue, one he had gradually understood. That loving mothers quietly sacrificed their flesh for their children, like ritual suicide, but slowly, one day, one hour, one meal at a time. Which is why he dutifully nodded whenever his ah-ma insisted how full she was—that she wasn't hungry—as he swallowed his guilt each night and ate her portion of the modest dinners she'd prepared.

And he remembered the caustic smell of mothballs as his ah-ma tried to preserve their clothing, which eventually wore thin. She'd patch the knees of his trousers and darn the holes in his socks. He didn't know what bad luck was until their apartment grew colder, even with the windows shut. He remembered sleeping in his mother's bed, huddled against her for warmth. And on nights when she worked, which as he grew older seemed like all nights, he'd take his blanket and pillow and set them on the radiator, which was merely warm instead of hot to the touch. He'd shiver, bouncing back and forth between his feet, waiting for the blanket to heat up. Then he'd wrap the musty fabric around his shoulders and lie on the wooden floor like a caterpillar in a silken cocoon, his back to the bare metal of the radiator, feeling snug and safe once again.

William remembered that when he pressed his ear to the floor, he could hear music playing in the next building—a piano, drums, even a horn section, and people making all kinds of noise, some laughing, some fighting.

Then his ah-ma would return, sometimes sniffling from the cold. "How was work at the club?" he'd ask. "Or were you onstage this time?"

William remembered her shaking her head and frowning, "It was just a party," she said as she curled up on the floor next to him. "With someone I used to know."

William felt her wrap the blanket around the two of them as he moved so she could share his pillow. She smelled strange, like smoke and sweat and old perfume.

"I'd like to go to a party," he said, thinking of birthday parties, dinner parties in the neighborhood. He'd never been to one of the big fancy ones, but he'd seen people celebrating in the restaurants and clubs. "I'll be good . . ."

"It's not a party for little boys," she said, tearing up.

What's the matter, Ah-ma? He remembered thinking those words, but he had been too afraid to ask. Sometimes he made her cry when he spoke, especially when he asked too many questions. He didn't know why.

"It's just the weather, it's just a cold," she said, as though reading his troubled mind. "It's nothing. Everything will be okay." But as she wrapped her arms around him, he could feel her sobs. It was the first time he remembered ever feeling scared.

"Waiting for Lazarus?"

William opened his eyes, looked up, and saw Sunny blocking his view of the sky, which was now streaked with orange and pink. *I must have dozed off,* he realized as his friend lowered himself to the ground and lay perpendicular to William.

"I didn't know her as well as you, but I miss her too," Sunny said, nodding toward the plank of wood that rested in the dirt. The fresh paint bore Charlotte's name.

William didn't say anything. He knew the grave marker was intended to be only temporary, until a family member or a kindly benefactor would pay for a granite slab. But as he looked around the burial ground and counted dozens of similar wooden signs, most of them faded and rotting, he knew those hopes had also been laid to rest.

"You skipped out on Saturday chores," Sunny said. "But I doubt Sister Briganti noticed. She's been in reconciliation all afternoon with Father Bartholomew."

We all have atoning to do, William thought. He felt guilty for leaving Charlotte alone. He regretted his lack of conviction and was prone to fits of guilt and paralyzing bouts of regret. He wasn't certain Sister Briganti felt such emotions.

"You missed supper."

"Not hungry," William said as his stomach grumbled ever so slightly, a faint reminder that he was capable of feeling something other than sadness. He hadn't eaten since before the funeral. And he'd lost what remained of his appetite when he learned that Charlotte's father hadn't bothered to take any of her belongings when he left Sacred Heart. The sisters, in their strange, generous wisdom, had scattered her possessions among the orphans like birdseed. William bit his tongue as he imagined spiteful girls pecking at the remaining bits of Charlotte's existence until there was nothing left.

"I'm sorry, Willie," Sunny said, tearing blades of grass and scattering them in the warm autumn breeze. "But your mother is out there—you don't belong here. I don't want you to leave again and I'll miss having you around. But you need to go. You need to find your mom while you still can. That's what I would do."

William didn't need the reminder, though he wasn't sure how he'd go about leaving again. He'd already spent what little money he had, and without Charlotte's help he wouldn't get far. He'd heard about street kids earning pennies by helping ferry passengers with their luggage at Colman Dock, or standing in line for rich people at movie theaters or the opera. The notion seemed bleak, but possible.

Then he noticed Sister Briganti walking slowly, solemnly across the mossy courtyard toward the grotto. She palmed her rosary.

"Did you hear what I said, Willie? You don't belong here."

William stood, dusted off his trousers, and then helped Sunny to his feet. William stared at the place where he and Charlotte used to meet. The trees were swaying gently in the wind, brown leaves tumbling from the outstretched branches like thistledown.

William walked toward the main gate. "None of us belong here."

WILLIAM SAT ON a bench at the nearest streetcar landing. He had enough money to make it halfway to downtown, but not enough for a transfer. He didn't care. He was done with this place. His mother, his beloved ah-ma, was out there—somewhere. If she wanted him, if she missed him, if she only vaguely remembered the sweet times with him, amid the cameras and glitter and stage lights of her world, none of it seemed to matter. All he knew was that he needed something to fill the pit of emptiness, the cavity that served as a gateway to nothing but raw, exposed nerve—where warmth and cold hurt him in equal proportions.

As he looked back at the school, his residence for these past five years, he saw the stout figure of Sister Briganti walking toward him. He didn't feel like running, or arguing, or supplicating—all he felt was gravity pulling him homeward, to his ah-ma, the person he'd orbited his entire childhood, until she'd given him up. He shrugged and turned his back to Sister Briganti, hoping she'd leave him alone but expecting to feel her wrenching his ear and dragging him back to the orphanage. He listened for the clanging bell of a coachman, the crackle of sparks from the wires overhead, the shimmy of wheels on tarnished rails. But all he heard were footsteps and words in Italian that he recognized as a prayer.

Amen, he thought as he waited. He tensed, his stomach in knots, his heart beating frantically. He remembered the words *Run away, Liu Song. Run away!* And she had. His mother had run away from everything. *She had run away from me.*

Then William heard the flutter of wings as a flock of birds vacated their perch atop the trolley line. The wire shook with the approach of a streetcar. He turned around, and Sister Briganti was staring down at him, her lips pursed. She handed him an envelope containing streetcar tokens and a note.

"The note is from your mother. I debated whether or not to give it to you, but after what happened . . . with Charlotte . . ." She glanced toward the cemetery. "Save a token for the return trip." She turned and walked away. "You can thank me when you come back."

I'll never thank you. And I'm not ever coming back. William swallowed his words and unfolded the note, which read: *Waiting at the Bush Hotel.*

Home

囝

(1934)

William felt reborn to walk the streets of Chinatown again. In his imagination every face was a long-lost relative, every city block was a welcome mat. He relished each sensation, each rediscovered memory, from the sweet, tangy smell of fresh oyster sauce to the magical way fish scales shimmered like flecks of glitter in the gutter as old men in bloodstained aprons hosed down the sidewalks. And King Street had hardly changed in his absence. There was still the familiar yelling and laughing from the alleys, the distant wail of a saxophone, the songs the Japanese Baptist Sunday school children sang as they collected money for the poor, and the splashing of ivory mah-jongg tiles that sounded so much like rain. The only aspect missing was the grip of his mother's gloved hand as they used to walk to the Atlas Theatre. The click-clack of her heels as they stepped around mud puddles dotted with cigarette butts and pigeon feathers.

But this time William was alone. He listened to the lumbering, bellowing trains coming and going from the station two blocks away as he stood outside the Bush Fireproof Hotel, which looked vacant.

The brick façade looked a bit smaller, but the tall building still stood out like a tombstone, marking the death of everything he'd known. He inhaled and smelled diesel and shoe polish and tobacco and the metallic scent of blood from the butcher's stall up the street. And with each scent came a glimmer, a memory of his childhood that had been all but washed away by the wood soap and the lye of Sacred Heart.

As he stepped inside he asked the front desk manager if he could look around.

"Look all you want," the man said, through a haze of cigarette smoke. "Hard to keep tenants these days, after that whole fracas way back when."

William paused for a moment, then remembered reading about Marcelino Julian, a migrant worker who a year and a half earlier went on a rampage in and around the old hotel, killing six men and injuring a dozen more. The hard times had brought out the worst in people. William climbed the stairs, trying not to let his imagination run away with him as he noticed dark stains on the carpet.

He couldn't remember the number of his old apartment, but his feet led the way to the stairs that he used to slide down on, belly-first, leaving a rug burn on his stomach, to the sparkling vinyl flooring in the hallway, which changed from silver to gold with each step. As he walked down the silent hallway, he came upon the door to his former apartment. He felt as though he were merely arriving home from school, five years too late. His life had taken a strange detour, but somehow he'd managed to find his way back. He looked at the note Sister Briganti had given him, out of concern or guilt, he didn't know, nor did he care. It simply listed the Bush Hotel. No apartment number. No other message. But he understood. His ah-ma had known where he was all along. She'd written him before, but those messages had been kept from him, until now, under the right circumstances. *Is that what your death bought me?* William would have asked Charlotte if he could. *Had her final answer to the question of her father softened Sister B's pious heart?*

William didn't knock. Instead he felt for the cold brass of the doorknob and opened the unlocked door. Inside, the place was barren, save for an old carpet and a few empty beer bottles strewn in a corner. The apartment smelled like dust and cat urine, and judging by the cobwebs on the ceiling, no one had lived here for some time, maybe since they'd left. Without the benefit of furnishings, pictures on the wall, curtains, blue flowers in a vase, it looked larger than he'd expected—an empty box that a home, a life, a family had once fit into comfortably. Now devoid of the tokens and touchstones of life, the place felt like a mausoleum, a rotting cavity, mirroring the pit in his stomach. The only home he'd ever known was now a forgotten void where even the ghosts had grown bored and weary and fled to more comforting surroundings.

"Hello," William said softly, hearing nothing in reply.

The only sound came from his leather soles on the creaking wooden floor as he peeked into the bedroom. The space was nothing but blank walls and an open wardrobe with a single coat hanger. The wire frame looked so still, William could have sworn the hanger had been painted there. Daylight poured in through a cracked window, illuminating a swirl of soot and grime that made him want to sneeze.

Maybe she isn't here. Maybe this is Sister Briganti's idea of a joke.

"Willow?" William asked, sniffling. He saw a shadow move, but the shape was only a flight of pigeons that had nested on the fire escape. They fluttered and squawked, dancing about one another, oblivious to his presence.

He swallowed and slowly opened the bathroom door. The overhead light socket was empty, and it took the better part of a minute for his eyes to adjust to the darkness. His heart froze when he saw the outline of a figure draped within the confines of the claw-foot tub. The shadow was that of a woman—her head tilted back, the peaks of her bare knees rising above the dirty, mildewed lip of the basin.

"Ah-ma?"

The shadow woman inhaled, which caused no small relief to William as he stepped closer. She was clothed in a pale blouse and skirt. The tub was dry. It was as though she were bathing in memory alone. Her fur stole covered her chest like a blanket. Her hat sat in the bottom of the tub, near the drain. William could hear a baby crying in another apartment, somewhere down the hall, though the haunting, desperate sound was gone so fast he might have imagined it.

"Ah-ma?" he asked again.

She didn't say a word. William watched as she blinked, the whites of her eyes seeming to glow in the dimness of the room. That faint glow was wet with tears.

"I'm sorry I wasn't there when you got back," William said, suddenly realizing that those were the words he'd hoped to hear from her. Instead she said nothing as she sat in the tub, staring at the blank wall in front of her as though watching an old movie.

Finally she spoke. "This is where it happened."

I know what happened here. William swallowed the words.

"This is where our lives changed," she said. "This is where I lost you."

Will

(1924)

In a dreamlike fog, Liu Song stumbled out of bed and to the crib where her two-year-old son was standing up on wobbly legs, crying. In the darkness she felt his small hands reaching out to her. She picked him up, put one arm beneath the baby fat of his chunky thighs, and curled him toward her, her nose pressed into the fluff of his hair, which smelled like lilac soap and fresh shea butter from his nighttime bath.

"Ah-ma," he said in a toddler's voice.

"Shhhhh . . ." she whispered as she felt his tiny sausage fingers touch her cheek, her nose, and her lips. She knew he could recognize her voice, her smell, but he always had to touch her face, especially in the dark, just to make sure. Liu Song felt him draw a long breath and then peacefully exhale. His entire body went limp, as though he'd been running in a dream and the sandman had finally caught up to him.

Liu Song swayed back and forth for a moment, debating whether to return him to his crib. She loved rocking him when he was so peaceful, such a contrast to the first time she'd held him, warm and wet and screaming, at the Lebanon Home for Girls.

She delighted that he'd been born eight pounds, eight ounces, two lucky numbers in a row to a mother wedded only to sadness and misfortune. During her pregnancy she'd worried about her ability to care for him, but once she had him in her arms—once she felt his breath, heard his whispered cry—motherhood felt right, felt complete, and she knew she never wanted to let go.

She'd told the midwife, "His name is William." Then Liu Song had reclined in the birthing chair, her newborn in her arms, wondering what the spirits of her mother and father would think of such a Western-sounding name. She wished she'd been able to hire a fortune-teller to evaluate William's date of birth, to confirm which of the five elements complemented his name. And she gazed heavenward, looking for a portent, an omen, or a sign, but all she noticed were brown water spots and the rust on the cracked tin ceiling, and vacant cobwebs in every dusty corner.

Looking back, Liu Song could still hear Mr. Butterfield's voice ringing in her ears. He'd warned her that most people viewed that run-down home in North Seattle as *a repository for weak-willed women*. So to Liu Song the name *Will* seemed a natural, suitable argument to the contrary. Plus, that simple word was close to *Willow*, the Anglicized version of Liu Song. Will would be a family name. And when the nurses had moved Liu Song to a tiny recovery room, she'd lain nearly elbow to elbow in a row of matching beds with six other girls and their newborns. Liu Song remembered everyone looking exhausted, delirious with drug-spawned resignation, many still bleeding or in horrendous pain. But *weak-willed* wasn't a description that applied to any of them. Not anymore. Like the others, Liu Song had come this far. She'd staggered, fallen, and then crawled across some unspoken maternal finish line where a new challenge was set to begin—one measured in days, weeks, months, and years. But there was satisfaction in the prize swaddled at her breast, then and now.

Worried that she'd wake him, Liu Song walked about her apartment and then sat on the edge of her bed. She scooted beneath the covers, then lay back, slowly reclining, hoping not to rouse him. She stroked the soft fabric of his flannel pajamas and felt a bit of wetness on her cheek as he drooled ever so slightly.

"William Eng," she whispered. "What am I going to do with you?"

She hated the last name they'd both been branded with. And even though she'd lied and told the midwife that she didn't know who the father was, Liu Song vaguely recalled screaming Leo's name during her labor—cursing him and Auntie Eng, crying for her ah-ma as she gave birth to a boy in a cloud of righteous pain and a haze of ether. The doctor wrote Leo Eng's name on the birth certificate in loco parentis, in place of a parent, a festering blister on an otherwise pristine and celebratory document.

"Someday I'll give you a real birthday party," Liu Song whispered.

Because of fluid in his lungs, William had not been allowed to leave the Lebanon Home for weeks that spilled into months. Liu Song remained as well, so that he could be fed without a bottle or a wet nurse—so he could fully recover.

During Liu Song's extended stay, she'd been expected to help out with the new girls as they arrived, each of them terrified and alone. None seemed to mind that Liu Song was Chinese as she tried her best to light the path that she had just traveled. But that light grew darker as Liu Song watched delirious new mothers be told that their tarnished reputations would only burden their children—that an unwed mother was unfit to *be* a mother. She listened in as they were compelled with unrelenting guilt, goaded, and ultimately swindled, into signing away their children. She looked on in sadness and confusion as mysterious couples arrived each week, then left with newborns, often pried from the grasp of wailing, hysterical young girls. But those infants seemed luckier than the forsaken—the babies no one wanted. Those few without prospects, from mothers who truly didn't want them, from mothers who had died during childbirth, those born sightless or without arms, those children were taken away by grim-faced caretakers to places unknown. Liu Song watched this strange tragedy performed over and over again, quietly wondering why no one had chastised *her* for weaknesses of the flesh, for bringing shame to her family and being a blight on public morality—she wondered why no one came to try to take William from *her*. At first she thought it was because of her son's sickly condition; then she caught her reflection in the polished tin of a bedpan and realized the truth of the matter—that no one would adopt a Chinese baby.

As Liu Song closed her eyes, she realized that her misfortune had been William's good luck. Her sorrow had given birth to joy. She would celebrate one day. But due to William's poor health when he'd been born, Liu Song had been unable to give him a proper red egg and ginger party. Even now the thought was sadly comforting. If she had been sent home from the Lebanon Home on time, that celebration, with chewy *yi mein* commemorating thirty days of life, would have been a lonely occasion. Because she knew that her family would only have been able to be present as ghosts. At least if she threw a party now, she reasoned as she fell asleep, William would be old enough to eat the longevity noodles by the fistful.

LIU SONG WOKE promptly at 6:05 A.M.—she didn't have a choice. Each morning the Shasta Limited chugged into the Oregon and Washington Station, alerting the neighborhood of its arrival with a stout blast of its whistle. The steam horn was so loud the bellowing sound rattled Liu Song's windows from two blocks away. She peeked at William, who merely smiled and yawned. He stretched as she pinched his nose and changed a wet diaper. Then Liu Song carried him to the kitchen, where he played on the floor while she reheated a pot of rice, mixing last night's sticky clumps with sweetened condensed milk and a drop of vanilla extract. An hour later their bellies were full, their teeth were brushed, their hair was combed, and they were out the door.

As Liu Song pushed William along King Street in a secondhand Sturgis carriage, she couldn't help but notice that the city had become a blooming flower as Chinatown extended its petals in all directions. But she still stood out from the crowd on every street corner. In Chinatown she was a girl out of place—young, unmarried, yet with a child. And as she headed uptown, toward Butterfield's, she was an Oriental face in a city of white strangers who marveled when she spoke such fluent English. They gushed over her accent, which she'd always apologized for. Somehow her voice had become exotic, sophisticated, and mysterious. Though that might have been because of Mr. Butterfield's relentless promoting. After she returned to work he'd given her a raise, doubling her commission on sheet music, providing income that she desperately needed. The Lebanon Home had helped her apply for a pension for unwed mothers, but she'd answered the questionnaire honestly and said that she had no plans for William to attend Sunday school. As a result, she'd been denied, which was unfortunate because Liu Song didn't even know what Sunday school was. She put down how she intended for William to attend Chinese school in the afternoons when he was old enough to enroll in public kindergarten, but that didn't help her cause. That, and the fact that single Chinese women were still viewed with suspicion.

To make things worse, she'd lost her apartment while at the Lebanon Home, but Mr. Butterfield had generously found her another place. He'd moved her few belongings to a partially furnished room at the Bush Fireproof Hotel, on the corner of Sixth and Jackson. Liu Song felt safe there because William Chappell, who had once been a volunteer fireman, had built the seven-story hotel. The modern building had 255 rooms, 150 of which had private baths. Liu Song had lived there for nearly two years, paying $1.25 per day. The tiny one-bedroom unit was smaller than her old place in Canton Alley, but at least it was a home without bitter memories etched into every wall, every floorboard, and every ceiling tile.

"You can repay me by coming back to work, dear," Mr. Butter-field had said. "As soon as you're able. Patrons have been asking about you for months. I lied and told them you were in California working on a vaudeville circuit."

Liu Song had planned to repay Mr. Butterfield by William's first birthday but managed to settle her debt in half that time by taking a weekend job as a dancer at the Wah Mee Club. The popular speakeasy in Maynard Alley was the one place where her reputation worked to her advantage. She'd hoped to get an opportunity as a singer, but the pay was good in the meantime. On a Saturday night, after payday at the docks, she made more money selling dances than she earned all week at the music store. But at the music store, her employer let her bring William to work. Mr. Butterfield had even cleared a space in the back where William could take naps while she hustled songs on the street. And when he wasn't tired, the music store was a toddler's wonderland.

"Ready to play a song for your mama?" Mr. Butterfield asked William, who loved sitting on his lap, William's tiny feet on top of Mr. Butterfield's wingtips as they worked the foot pedals of a small upright pianola. "Pedal faster," Mr. Butterfield said. "Now slow through this part . . . then we'll hit it hard for a big finish." The ped-als not only drove the manual piano but also accented and shaped the music. The keys moved like magic, but in a small way, William *was* playing the song. Then he'd pop down, run outside, and throw himself into Willow's arms. "I did it," he'd say. "I played it for you."

That's how Willow spent her days, fifteen minutes on, fifteen minutes off—enough time to earn a living and care for her son. That was a unique advantage her day job had over her weekend gig at the club, which required special arrangements, from special friends.

Liu Song sipped a cup of tea as she watched William close his heavy eyelids and doze off. Then she heard the front door open. She smiled as Mildred came inside.

"Look at you in that dress!" Mildred said in Chinese.

Liu Song stood and straightened the seams of her cheongsam. The long dress might have seemed modest on someone else, but the formfitting silk hugged her curves in a way that demanded attention. "Too Oriental? Too garish? Too revealing?" she asked.

"Too bad." Mildred shook her head. "I wish I was as tall as you."

Her old friend doffed her coat and hat and peeked at William, who was now snoring lightly. "He's getting so big," she said. Mildred's eyes were wide and expressive, even more so with the heavy green eye shadow she wore.

Liu Song nodded proudly and poured Mildred a cup of tea.

The rumor at Franklin High was that Liu Song had gotten pregnant and been forced to drop out. Mildred had fought that rumor and was the only person who came and visited Liu Song at the Lebanon Home, against the wishes of her mother. And when Liu Song took the job at the Wah Mee, Mildred offered to babysit William. She said she'd do it for free, just to help out, but Liu Song insisted on paying her. Liu Song avoided asking Mildred if her mother knew that they were friends again. She wished Mildred could be equally adept at avoiding questions.

"How was your date last week?"

Liu Song took a deep breath and tried not to express her disgust. Mildred had fixed her up on a blind date last Thursday with a recent high school graduate, a boy named Harold from a prominent Chinese family. But, like so many men—young or old—Harold didn't want a date as much as he was hoping for a night to remember.

"Same as the others," Liu Song said.

Ironically, William was the only reason most men asked her out, not because they wanted anything to do with him but because, as Harold had intimated, "Hey, the field has already been plowed—why not till the soil once in a while?"

"You're too picky," Mildred said as she took out a Marlboro. Like most women, Mildred favored them because of the red band around the filter that hid her lipstick stains. She went to the stove, bent down, and lit the cigarette on the pilot light. "Have you looked in the mirror lately? You could have any man you want . . ."

"I don't want *any* man."

Mildred smiled but rolled her eyes in a way that seemed to say *Suit yourself.*

A moment of silence lingered between them as Mildred took a long draw on her cigarette. She looked at her painted fingernails, then back at Liu Song.

"So are you ever going to tell me who the father is?"

Liu Song found her clutch and gloves. "William doesn't have a father."

"Oh, that's right," Mildred said, teasing. "You discovered him under a mountain of rocks, like the Monkey King. When he learns to fly on a cloud, could you let me know? I could save a lot of money on streetcar tokens."

"He has me," Liu Song said. "That's all anyone needs to know." She kissed her sleeping boy on his tiny, pursed lips. Then she looked at Mildred, resting one hand on her hip. "And no boyfriends allowed. Your mother wouldn't approve . . ."

"My mother wouldn't approve of a lot of things." Mildred giggled and blew a perfect smoke ring into the air. It hung between them like an unfulfilled wish.

Liu Song poked her hand through the center, dissipating the smoke. She looked at her friend with one eyebrow raised.

"Fine. No boyfriends will come over. I promise," Mildred said, cursing in Chinese as she plopped down on the worn davenport. "I'll read a book or something."

The Wah Mee

口

(1924)

The Wah Mee Club was only one block over, tucked neatly into the belly of Maynard Alley. But to Liu Song the whiskey-soaked club seemed a world away from the rest of the city—from the rest of Chinatown for that matter. Because unlike the stately (and dry) Luck Ngi Music Society, or the Yue Yi Club, which had bright neon signs on the outside and handsome musicians on the inside—men from Hong Kong, with slicked-back hair who wore matching jackets and stood in a gold-leafed band box playing the stringed *yi wuh* and the tenor saxophone—the Wah Mee could easily be missed. In fact, if it weren't for the steady stream of patrons one might never know the nightclub was there at all. And tonight the men were out in droves, some in traditional brocade dragon jackets, but many more in Western suits and ties, with fedoras and homburgs.

As Liu Song passed a beat cop who stood at the T where the alley met the street, tipping his hat at passersby, she was reminded of a story Mr. Butterfield had told her. The tale was about a local distributor named Roy Olmstead—Seattle's Rum King, who made his fortune bringing cases of alcohol down from Canada. Rumor had it that his wife, Elsie, hosted a popular children's radio program that also carried hidden messages about where the action was each night. As Liu Song passed dozens of people coming and going from the alley, all beneath the watch of the local police, she surmised that

Miss Elsie must have been spinning one of her yarns about the Celestials of Chinatown.

When Liu Song walked past the club's only window, made of frosted glass bricks, she could make out the opaque silhouettes of bodies moving inside. The figures were muted and distorted, as though the patrons were underwater. When she reached the entrance, Liu Song turned the key that rang the doorbell. She peered through the one transparent block and waved as a large shadow blocked the light. A second later a squat fireplug of a man opened the heavy wooden door. Liu Song heard music and laughter wafting out into the evening on a warm current of cigarette smoke and the overpowering smell of stale beer.

"Sweet Willow." The man spoke in Cantonese with a thick, farm-country accent. He was clad in a dark green suit, wearing white leather shoes, and he said her name as though it were more of a statement than a greeting. He waved a few Chinese and Filipino patrons in as well, then looked up and down the alley before locking the door.

Liu Song checked in with the manager and then signed her dance card, just below the time and date. The club's three-piece band was already playing a familiar tune as a pair of white sailors lined up for a dance, a nickel apiece, though some tipped more. Liu Song obliged the servicemen, making small talk and trying her best to create the illusion that she cared. On the nights when she grew tired of pretending, she acted like she didn't speak English. She didn't think of herself as a dancer. She thought of herself as an actress playing a part for an audience of one. That simplified things.

As the second sailor led her through a fox-trot, she shuffled backward in a wide, lazy circle, circumnavigating the dance floor. On a second pass she caught a frightening glimpse of an older, balding man in Oxford bags, who stood at the rail of the club's tiny, hand-painted craps table. The man's shirtsleeves were rolled up, and his suspenders hung below his waist. An unlit cigarette dangled precariously from his lower lip as he bounced a pair of dice off the far wall of the gaming table again and again, until finally the other players groaned and the man threw his hands up, cursing in Cantonese and then louder in English, as though one language wasn't enough to express his outrage.

Uncle Leo, she thought. Liu Song had seen him on the street once or twice from far away and always managed to avoid running into him, until now. But as she watched the stickman rake the chips from the table and begin stacking them into neat piles of green, black, and red, the gambler looked up and Leo was gone. In his place was some other man, a simple patron who looked especially down on his luck.

As the dance ended, Liu Song thought of how she dreaded the inevitable reunion with her drunken stepfather. She'd often pictured him turning from the craps table toward the wooden dance floor, fishing in his baggy pants for a cigarette lighter. In her nightmares he would demand that she light his cigarette. He'd regard her slender ankles and leer at her curves until he made eye contact.

Liu Song looked at the stranger, this man who was not her uncle. She still felt terrified—of what? She wasn't sure. That just by Uncle Leo's presence, people might know her shame. Or that he'd follow her—drag her off to wherever he lived now? That he'd find out about William. Her stomach tightened.

She stood, frozen in place as the man approached. In her heels she was an inch taller than he was, even in his fancy leather shoes. As he looked up at her and frowned, she felt a wave of nausea and was reminded of Uncle Leo's smell. His pungent body odor reeked of bad dreams. He blew smoke as he walked by, though she remained frozen in something akin to sleep. A hostess handed him his coat and hat, and Liu Song felt the room spinning as she watched Uncle Leo snap his suspenders into place and then reach into his suit jacket and pull out a billfold. He opened the leather wallet and showed her how empty it was. Then he reached into his pants pocket and fumbled around a bit before he pulled his hand back out and held up an empty silver money clip.

"My bad luck at dice is your good fortune," he said with a shrug. "If I had known the dancers were as lovely as you, I would have saved a dime or two. Because that's all you're worth." He spat on the floor. "I don't care about the spirit of your mother, and I don't care about you. All I care about is . . ."

Liu Song blinked and Uncle Leo was gone; a confused-looking man stood in his place. He shrugged and tipped his hat. She watched him stagger away, past the doorman and into the night without a second glance. As sensation returned to her frozen limbs and she could breathe normally again, she felt as though she'd woken from a nightmare, leaving her to wonder what had happened. She always thought that if she ran into her stepfather, things would be different, that she'd be stronger, that she might find satisfaction in his failings. But even brushing up against his memory left her feeling neither strength nor joy. She was shaken by how much she still feared him, how paralyzed and helpless she felt—frightened but detached. The last few times she'd seen him, Uncle Leo had been drunk, and if she had a choice she hoped he'd be drunk forever. She remembered him being angrier when sober.

Liu Song left work early that night. She didn't even care that she still had names on her dance card. She couldn't put her mind at ease until she saw William. She ran home as fast as she could in high heels, almost slipping on the wet, oily pavement. She bolted up the stairs and burst into her apartment, much to Mildred's surprise.

Her friend had fallen asleep reading a copy of *Picture Play* magazine. Mildred blinked and stretched as she sat up, fixing her hair and looking at the clock. "You're home early. Slow night, or did you forget something? Something bad happen?"

"Nothing happened," Liu Song lied. "I just had a strange feeling . . ."

"I told you I wouldn't bring any boyfriends over," Mildred said, yawning. "And this time I really meant it. I promised . . ."

Liu Song walked past Mildred to the bedroom, where she found William sleeping soundly in his crib, half-covered by a blanket. He looked so peaceful, without a care or a worry in the world. She watched him breathe as she touched his cheek, which felt soft and warm, comforting.

She exhaled a weary sigh of relief. "I'm sorry, William."

He snored gently and pursed his lips as though dreaming.

"I'm sorry I can't be here all the time. But I won't let anything bad happen to you. I'll do anything to keep you safe."

Dance Card

(1924)

It took Liu Song months to stop worrying about Uncle Leo on a daily basis—to stop having paralyzing dreams each night. For weeks she slept with William at her side and looked over her shoulder everywhere they went. And her next few shifts at the club had been tense, nervous affairs. But her stepfather had never returned, at least not on the nights she had worked. Maybe he'd channeled his misfortune elsewhere, Liu Song thought. Or perhaps he'd been too busy with his laundry business—who knew? She'd seen him again on the street but managed to turn and walk the other way before he noticed. She was grateful for his absence, because even if she never saw his face again, a part of him would always be close by. How she could hold William, bathe him, sing to him, love him in every way and not allow nightmares from the past to occupy her waking hours had been a miracle—*William* had been a miracle. His gentle temperament, his sparkling eyes, his tiny spirit had a way of returning all the love she had for him tenfold. The more she adored him, the more she felt adored. She wondered if that was how her ah-ma felt about her *lou dou*. Then she thought of her ah-ma marrying Uncle Leo, how she had sacrificed herself upon the altar of marriage a second time, as a second wife. *She did it all for me,* Liu Song thought, as eddies of guilt and gratitude pooled in the corners of her eyes. That's what love is. Not the gushing, eye-rolling high drama of movie stars, but the real, heartbreaking, unconditional kind—like the love she had for William.

Liu Song smiled as she felt his tiny, mittened hand in hers. She'd cut a hole in his other mitten, and he'd put it to good use. She smiled as he bumbled along, sucking his thumb while they walked to the market, a tuft of black hair sticking out from beneath his cap. She'd left the carriage at home, hoping the added exercise would wear him out. The long walk on his tiny legs was the best way to ensure he'd sleep through the night—or at least slumber through the first hour. Mildred had a big date and wouldn't be able to come over until later. Liu Song didn't like the arrangement, but she had no choice. She would have to put William to bed and leave him alone until Mildred arrived.

Liu Song dreaded the thought of leaving him, but she'd left him alone once before when Mildred had called and said she was running a few minutes behind. And besides, the Wah Mee was only a block away, and her neighbor, a solemn, grandmotherly widow, said she would call the club if William woke up and wouldn't settle himself back to sleep. Liu Song would have asked her to watch her son for the hour, but the old woman was a bit touched in the head.

So as the fat moon rose above the waters of Puget Sound, Liu Song fought against her guilt and her worry as she put William to bed. She removed curlers from her hair and did her makeup and then left with her regrets. She lingered in the hallway, expecting to hear him calling her name from behind the locked door, but the only sound she heard was a rush of water through the exposed plumbing as someone upstairs flushed a toilet. She waited a minute longer, searching the silence, then sighed and walked to the club.

"Sweet Willow, you're popular tonight," the doorman said. "A gentleman booked you for the whole evening."

She paused and peered into the dimly lit club, which was packed with Chinese men and women, even a few Japanese couples, plus a few Korean drinkers and gamblers. The tables and bars were crowded. "One of the regulars?" she asked as she touched the pearl buttons on her blouse.

"Someone called in advance." The doorman shrugged. "He said that he wanted to fill your entire dance card. I told him it would cost a pretty penny—he said okay."

Despite working in a speakeasy that sold illegal booze and offered fan-tan, faro, blackjack, and birdcage, the Wah Mee's owners prided themselves on running a *straight* club. Dancers caught offering a little "something on the side" were immediately fired. Though Liu Song knew that those types of girls quickly found steady work elsewhere.

"I don't understand," she said.

"He was very specific," the doorman told her. "And he had a strange accent but seemed harmless enough. He's sitting at the bar right now, see for yourself."

Liu Song looked up, scanning the Wah Mee for Uncle Leo, remembering his thick Cantonese accent, searching her mind for an excuse to tell her boss why she had to flee the club—she'd quit if she had to. But as she looked through the haze of cigar smoke, she recognized the gentleman. He was dressed for the occasion, in a black shirt, white tie, and canvas spats, and his hair was slightly longer. She was overwhelmed with relief to see Colin's wide smile. Her heart soared with delight and then sank with embarrassment. She'd avoided the local movie theaters and even the new China Gate Opera House for fear of crossing paths with him. She felt ashamed for having left so many things unspoken, unresolved. And she felt so awkward and unsure of how she could explain the secret she had waiting for her back home, a secret that wore tiny footie pajamas and called her ah-ma.

But as Colin waved and seemed genuinely happy to see her, the awkwardness subsided, leaving her with the ringing echo of doubt—and impending disaster. It was as though she were standing aboard a yacht on a sunny day but feeling water lapping at her feet as the ship begins to sink beneath the waves. She tried not to chew her lip as he sauntered toward her. She hated the thought of letting him down again, but when she took the job at the club she'd expected such strange reunions would happen sooner or later. Chinatown was a small place—a tiny village within a city. She'd been lucky to hide in the shadows this long.

"I keep going to the movies week after week, expecting to see your face smiling back at me," Colin said. "It's been a long time. I thought you left town. Mr. Butterfield said you went to California for a while."

Hardly, she thought. "I thought the same of you. I've been . . . here," she confessed sadly, pointing about the room. "I've had some changes in my life . . ." Liu Song couldn't continue. She fidgeted, struggling to find the words.

"Congratulations," Colin said, gently touching her arm as though to alleviate the worry that must have been evident on her face. "I saw you on the street last week, through a storefront window. You were like the beautiful ghost of your ah-ma, pushing a carriage. At first I thought you might have been hired as someone's nanny, but then I saw the way you held that baby." He took her hand in his. "I know true love when I see it."

Liu Song could barely breathe.

Someone cranked up the Victrola behind the bar, and an old song, a lazy two-step, began to play amid the sound of tumbling dice, the clinking of stemmed glassware, and the chatter of men and women in various languages, tongues, and dialects. Their exclamations roared with each turn of luck, some good, some bad. She was grateful for the noise, which drowned out the ringing in her ears.

"I was sad at first," Colin said. Then he sipped his drink. "But at least I understood why you disappeared. Though I never see a husband . . ."

"I'm not . . ." Liu Song hesitated. "I'm not married—never was."

"It's okay, I understand—believe me. Life is complicated. I know . . ."

"I wanted to tell you, but I just couldn't figure out how." Liu Song gushed her apology as though it would be less painful to get it all out at once. "I went and saw you that night at the Empress, when you were appearing in *A Chinese Honeymoon*. I was so sick, and so saddened. There really isn't any proper way to explain it . . ."

"You don't have to, Liu Song. Or is it Willow? That would make a terrific screen name, by the way." He ordered another Bronx martini and a grape soda for her. "I just wanted to see you again. I've been in Vancouver and Idaho, taking walk-on rolls as a half-breed in a pair of Nell Shipman films. She's opened her own studio over near Coeur d'Alene, which is quite impressive. And I also got a job in a Streamliner called *Balto's Race to Nome*. The movie is supposed to be set in Alaska, but we shot it near Mount Rainier and I'm supposed to be an Inupiat Eskimo. Close enough for the silver screen, I guess. It's all quite exciting."

Liu Song sat at the bar, her knees touching his as they talked. When her manager cruised by, Colin handed him Liu Song's dance card and a ten-dollar bill. Colin smiled and told her about his hopes and joys. They talked for an hour and two more drinks, until a trio of musicians arrived and began playing a homespun version of ragtime. Colin led her to the dance floor, and Liu Song delighted in doing the fox-trot with someone other than a total stranger or a sailor on leave, or a rich man who liked to talk about himself and his money. She didn't have to force herself into the pit of polite conversation. She didn't have to pretend like an actress onstage or on the screen. She danced until her feet hurt. Then Colin removed her shoes and held them behind her as she wrapped her arm around his waist and leaned into his chest, feeling him carry her weight and all of her burdens. They slowly circled the crowded dance floor, even as the band played something faster. She could almost have slept in that position, surrounded, enveloped. She understood how William felt being gently, lovingly rocked to sleep, and she understood now why he slept so soundly, so utterly content. She'd never felt so safe, so protected, so wanted. Though a part of her wondered why Colin didn't ask about William.

After the band's first set, Colin suggested they get some fresh air, so they hung out in the alley as men and women came and went from the club, some laughing and smiling, others tripping and staggering away.

"It's a nice night. We could go for a drive," Colin suggested. "Unless . . ."

Liu Song looked around the club.

"I'm sorry," he said. "Is there someone else—"

"No," Liu Song interrupted. "Not at all. It's just that my shift . . ."

"I paid for all of your dances. You can leave anytime."

Liu Song glanced at the doorman, whose nod confirmed Colin's statement.

Colin offered to drive her home in his new enclosed Chrysler even though she lived only a stone's throw away. "We'll take the scenic route," he said as he opened the door for her and wrapped a motor robe around her shoulders to ward off the chill, despite the fact that the car had a built-in heater. He drove away from Chinatown, past the Aiko Photographic Studio and Ceasare Galleti's Boot and Shoe Repair. She looked back as the neon faded. Mildred would be with William by now, so Liu Song relaxed as they drove north, circling Green Lake, cruising by fine neighborhoods of newly built Tudor homes. They drove as though they were in a parade and he were proudly showing her off, the grand marshal and the Narcissus Queen. She felt such joy, but also worry. She'd never been this far away from William.

She asked him to turn back, and so they drove toward downtown, past the grand Coliseum Theatre. "This is the first theater built exclusively for movies. I'd like to take you sometime. It's incredible," he said casually. "One day you'll be up on that screen. Breaking hearts with just a glance—of that I have no doubt."

She tried to be coy at first, aloof, but could resist only so long before she surrendered to the shower of his praise. But as they returned to Chinatown, she grew nervous, expectant, as though this time together was a social contract and she would be obliged to fulfill it all night long. And she grew more hesitant, block by block, street by street, because she knew in that moment that she would do anything if he asked. But when they arrived at the Bush Hotel, he didn't ask anything at all.

As he came around and opened her door, she leaned up and kissed him on the cheek, thanking him for the ride home and the splendid evening. He didn't push, or grab, or hint, or suggest, he merely smiled in the street light as revelers staggered by and music played from the dozens of clubs that were still open, the sounds pouring out in all directions amid the perfumed air. He pointed to the waning moon that peeked from behind the top of the Smith Tower, which rose above the Seattle skyline like an obelisk.

"I'd like to take you there sometime."

"The moon?"

"The observatory at the top of the building." He laughed. "I've never been, but I hear the view is extraordinary. Would you like to go? Not just you, but you and . . ."

"William," she said proudly. "My son's name is William. He's two—almost two and a half now. He's walking . . . talking . . ."

"Would you and William like to join me?"

Liu Song was somewhat confused. Was this a date? Was this a strange gesture of friendship? Most single men of Colin's age and stature wanted nothing to do with a woman burdened by a fatherless child.

"You're a package deal. I don't see how I could possibly invite one without the other. I'd like to meet him. If that's okay with you?"

Liu Song wanted to cry. She felt so much emotion and adoration that it surprised even her. Her cheeks were flushed and hot. She smiled and nodded, trying not to burst with joy and excitement. She'd sworn she'd keep William away from any men she dated, but suddenly she couldn't remember why. "I'd love to."

"How about next Saturday? I'll pick you up at noon."

She watched as he tipped his hat and drove off, wondering why she'd avoided him for so long, her heart quietly breaking as she wished she could go back and reclaim the years they'd been apart.

The Wishing Chair

回

(1924)

On Saturday, Liu Song gave William a sudsy bath in the kitchen sink. She washed his hair with baby shampoo and taught him to blow bubbles, which drifted on the tide of warm air from the radiator, then popped on the cold glass of their living room window, leaving behind round, soapy rainbows. She couldn't help but smile as William splashed and laughed whenever another soap bubble popped.

She dried him off and kissed his tiny, perfect feet as she sang an old Chinese lullaby. She barely remembered the lyrics, which was fine with William, who made up his own words as he tried to sing along. Then she dressed him in his nicest outfit, navy blue coveralls and a white shirt, and leather baby shoes with double-knotted laces. Oddly enough, she was more concerned with William's appearance than with her own, though she had tossed and turned the night before with curlers in her hair. She hoped to make a good impression outside the club, but she was even more concerned that William be presentable. She wanted to be taken seriously as a proud, responsible parent—an attempt to avoid her misgivings about being an unwed mother and shed the yoke of degradation that came with such perceived failings. Liu Song had grown accustomed to the stigma of being a performer—she'd been prepared her whole life for that strange mix of adoration and blatant disrespect. But being an unwed mother was a shame not easily hidden or erased. And Liu Song had not discussed the details of William's paternity with anyone. Not Mr. Butterfield and not even Mildred.

Liu Song looked in the mirror and pinched her cheeks, smiling as she heard a knock, and William began to chatter and call her name. She lifted him in her arms, resting his plump bottom on her hip. She looked into the mirror one last time and then opened the door. Colin stood hidden behind a bouquet of morning glories.

"I saw your father give flowers just like these to your mother, after her big performance. I think they were her favorite."

Liu Song nodded. "You're so thoughtful. Moonflowers like these were a joke between my parents. When they met as apprentices they had so little money—they'd pick water spinach and eat it for dinner nearly every night. Those swamp cabbage flowers look the same, but these smell so much better."

"I'll trade you." Colin smiled as he handed her the flowers and took William from her arms, who seemed to marvel at the stranger. She brought the sweet-smelling petals to her nose and found a vase as she watched Colin put his hat on her son. His tiny head disappeared beneath the felt of the wide brim as his smile peeked out from below.

When they stepped outside Colin explained that he'd driven from his rented home on Beacon Hill, but the weather was nice and warm and suitable for walking, so he gallantly pushed the carriage as they walked down the street. Liu Song couldn't help but notice their reflections in the shop windows. At a glance they looked like a perfect family. She had chosen to wear her mother's jade ring on her right hand, and in the glass the mirror image looked as though she were a virtuous, married woman.

As she regarded her reflection, Liu Song noticed that she wasn't smiling. She realized she was wary of getting her hopes up. Happiness in her lifetime had been a scarce commodity, and she mistrusted not so much Colin's intentions as her own turn of fortune. She'd been unlucky most of her life, the only exception being the smiling, raven-haired boy who sucked his thumb and waved at strangers as they passed. So Liu Song made small talk, trying not to reveal how deeply she cared, how complete she felt, even as they huffed and puffed up First Hill, which the locals called Profanity Hill because the street was so steep that men would curse their way to the top. Colin pushed the carriage, whistling a happy tune as he easily navigated the arduous incline.

When they finally arrived at Smith Tower, Liu Song stared up and felt a wave of vertigo as clouds slowly drifted past the tip of the tallest building west of the Mississippi. She steadied herself and then reached into her purse. Colin stopped her and paid for their tickets with a twenty-dollar bill.

The visit to the tower was William's first time in an elevator. His eyes grew wide and he held Liu Song's hand tightly as they peered through the windows of the latticed brass elevator doors, watching each floor disappear, revealing another level of smoke-filled offices, lobbies, suites—filled with busy, important-looking executives.

Liu Song felt faint as they stepped off the elevator car onto the thirty-fifth floor. She'd never been higher than atop a seven-story building. The breathtaking views of the city, the Puget Sound, and the Olympic Mountains on the horizon made her knees go weak.

"Just look at that," Colin said. "Thirty years ago an aeronaut named Professor Pa Van Tassell floated out over the water beneath a balloon powered by the Seattle Gas Company. He jumped from two thousand feet up, with a parachute."

Liu Song thought he was teasing her, making up stories.

"No, really. He landed safely near the shore." Colin wrapped his arm around hers and pushed the carriage with one hand as an usher in a bright red uniform with gold epaulets welcomed visitors into the famed Chinese Room. "Sometimes you just have to go where the wind blows you."

As Liu Song stared in surprise and fascination at the Chinese furniture and the hand-carved ceiling, she asked Colin, "Did you know about all this?"

"I did." He nodded. "But I had to see it to believe it."

"Would you like to sit in the Wishing Chair?" another usher asked as he pointed to an ornate throne in the center of the room that had a gorgeous view of Mount Rainier. When Liu Song approached, she could see the intricate carving of a dragon swallowing the world on the backrest, while the armrests were serpents. A pair of fierce, crouching lions, carved from polished rosewood, flanked the throne. "Everything you see here was a gift given to the Smith family," the usher said. "From Her Royal Highness Tzu-hsi the Empress of China, but I'm sure you know that."

Liu Song smiled politely. She didn't know much Chinese history but did remember that, according to her father, the Dowager Empress had once been a concubine, elevated by the status of her son— the Emperor's rightful heir. And she supported the Chinese Opera. Tzu-hsi had been hated and loved for that, among countless other reasons. Liu Song understood how that felt.

Colin turned to Liu Song and said, "After you, Your Majesty," but William had finally grasped the reality of how high they were and wanted to be held by his mother.

"You first," she said. "I insist. Besides, I'm hardly of noble birth."

She watched as Colin bowed, waved to the tourists out on the observation deck as though they were his honored guests. Then he sat down as the usher smiled.

"Why is it called the Wishing Chair?" Liu Song asked. She set William down, and he walked around the room, timidly stepping toward the wraparound deck with its polished brass railings and the fresh, salty air. He came back and held her hand as she looked at Colin.

"It's called the Wishing Chair," the usher said, "because legend has it that whoever sits in the chair will be married within a year.

The Smiths' daughter was the first to sit there. She ended up getting married a year later, in this very room."

Liu Song tried not to blush as Colin stared back at her, unblinking.

"But," the usher said, puncturing the awkward silence, "since you two are *already* married, perhaps some other good fortune will come your way."

Liu Song looked at Colin, and he smiled; neither said a word until William spoke, furrowing his brow and pointing at Colin as he blurted, "Dadda?"

AFTERWARD THEY ATE lunch at the Brooks Brothers restaurant, which drew stares from the other patrons, but Liu Song didn't mind. Then Colin walked them back to the Bush Hotel. Liu Song invited him up for tea, but he declined with a polite smile.

"I would love to, honestly, but you're an unmarried woman with a child. I don't want to overstay my welcome. Besides, it's probably his nap time."

Liu Song was somewhat crestfallen when he kissed her on the cheek and waved goodbye. She felt slightly rejected after such a lovely time together—a perfect afternoon—but she knew he was right. He was looking out for her, worrying about her, because in a careless moment she might create more problems than she could handle. She remembered when she'd first moved into the hotel, how the gray-haired Chinese manager had assumed she was a rich man's mistress. In retrospect she supposed that was the only reason he agreed to rent her the room. Either way, she was thankful that he let them live there, despite having to turn down his numerous advances and offers of opportunities to *work off her rent*.

A single mother in a neighborhood filled with Chinese bachelors, she was grateful to have William, whose mere presence generally managed to keep those with less than honorable intentions at bay, as his smile softened hearts everywhere he went.

As Liu Song walked down the hallway, she noticed that the door to her apartment was slightly ajar. She thought about going back downstairs and fetching the manager in case there was a burglar, but then she remembered the only other person who had a key. Liu Song slowly opened the door and breathed a sigh of relief when she saw Mildred standing in the bathroom. Her friend had her face to the mirror as she painted her lips a bright shade of raspberry. Mildred smacked her lips together and then tucked the metal lipstick tube into a tiny sequined clasp. She turned to Liu Song and puckered her lips to show off a perfect Cupid's bow.

"Sorry, Willow. I didn't mean to bust in, but I have another date and my mother wouldn't let me out of the house if I had makeup on. How do I look?"

Mildred was the only person who called her Willow outside the club. She was a senior in high school now and thought the moniker was such a modern name—a grown-up name, as if having a child wasn't grown-up enough. Liu Song inspected Mildred's thick eyeliner and eyelashes, painted black. She reached up and smoothed out the pinkish tone of her friend's rouged cheeks.

"Do I know the lucky fellow?" Liu Song asked in Chinese.

"His name is Andy Stapleton," Mildred answered in English. "In case you were wondering. Not that you need to know." She smiled and batted her eyelashes. "He's an incredible dancer—he knows the Charleston, the Lindy, *and* the tango."

Liu Song checked William's diaper and then put him down for a nap. She turned back to Mildred and looked her up and down appraisingly. "And you thought your mother would be upset with just the *makeup*?" Liu Song knew that many girls Mildred's age had already been betrothed by their parents. Dating, not to mention dancing, was a Western concept that good Chinese girls didn't entertain.

"So he's a *gwai lo*." Liu Song addressed the obvious as if saying it out loud, confronting Mildred with the truth, would somehow force her friend back to a point of reason.

Mildred put her hands on her hips and cocked her head. "Oh, Willow, don't be so crude. He's not a round-eyed devil. He's a *sai yan*. He's an American. You dance with gentlemen just like him every weekend."

"I waltz—that's a big difference. And I don't have parents to condemn me for it. Plus I have a child to feed and clothe."

"I'm just having fun. Aren't I allowed? I would think that you of all people wouldn't chastise me for this. I'll be more careful . . ."

"You can never marry him," Liu Song stated. She didn't want to argue, but she did hope to talk her dear friend away from the edge of the emotional cliff she was standing on. Both of them knew that there were laws preventing mixed-race marriages. Her parents had told her stories of wayward Chinese girls running off with their *sai yan* boyfriends. Even in states like Washington that didn't have provisions preventing such marriages, the judges or justices of the peace could arbitrarily throw out requests for a marriage license at any time, for any reason. In a small community where a girl's reputation was everything, Mildred was wading into the deep part of the ocean. She was a teenage girl splashing about, unaware of the big waves that could sweep her away. Which was why Liu Song was so grateful for Colin. He was perfect for her. He accepted who she was, where she'd been, and what she wanted to become one day. In fact, he encouraged her—he championed her every step.

"Did you hear what I said?" Liu Song asked. "You can never marry a *sai yan*."

Mildred smoothed out her lipstick with a tissue. "Good!" She laughed. "Because I'm never getting married—ever. Look around you. It's 1924, not 1824. I'm American-born and so are you. I'm going to be a modern girl and live it up. All I want is to let my stockings down and have fun and do what I please, whenever I please, with whomever I please. I don't care what my parents think. They're stuck in the past. I'm not. That makes all the difference in the world. Don't you think?"

Like Mildred, Liu Song had been born here but raised in a family steeped in tradition. She was a citizen, Colin wasn't. But in many ways he was more modern than she. Their relationship was all so confusing. She thought about the Wishing Chair and marriage, remembering that he was foreign-born. She wouldn't be able to marry him either, without losing her citizenship. If that happened (as she dared to dream), what would become of William? What price might he have to pay?

A WEEK LATER the hotel manager stopped Liu Song in the hallway as she was heading off to work and handed her an envelope. She felt dread in her stomach as she opened it beneath the man's stern gaze. She'd lived with the lingering fear that her living arrangement would result in her eviction, or worse. She breathed a sigh of relief and even giggled as she held up a pair of movie tickets to the Coliseum Theatre. The tickets were for a Wednesday showing of *The Thief of Bagdad,* starring her favorite actress, Anna May Wong. There wasn't a note, but Liu Song knew who they were from. She showed off the tickets to the manager, who grumbled and scratched his head as he walked away.

On Wednesday night she had Mildred stay with William once again. In exchange, she let her friend use the telephone in the hallway to call her boyfriend, a suitable arrangement for both. Liu Song kissed William as he sat on the floor playing with a shoe box full of mismatched blocks. She helped him spell C-A-T and B-I-R-D. He was such a cheerful boy, given to only an occasional tantrum, which just made Liu Song laugh. To her that was the truest definition of a man, so stubborn but needy at the same time—he didn't know what he wanted, and even when he did, he wouldn't recognize it if it came up and bit him.

Liu Song walked past the desk clerk of the hotel, down the steps, and out the door. She practically ran into Colin, who stood next to his car. She'd planned to walk, but like on so many of their occasions together, he'd planned ahead, leaving little to chance.

"You didn't have to," Liu Song said.

"I could drive alongside, serenading you through the window. Or you could rent a Packard across the street and follow me."

She shook her head as he opened the door for her. The car was already warm, and the leather seats felt supple and smooth.

"Who's watching the man of the house?"

"A friend."

The comment hung between them like an uninvited passenger, lazing in the backseat, snoring, kicking, and distracting them from their pleasant evening.

Liu Song spoke before he did. "Her name is Mildred Chew. I took correspondence courses and graduated not long after William was born. But she's still in school. We stayed in touch, and we've become quite close. She watches William, but that's not really what you wanted to ask me, is it?"

"What do you think I want to ask?"

The car stopped at a red light. Liu Song looked longingly out the window toward men and women, couples, families, all of them walking about with purpose, with hope, with places to go where they were wanted, even loved.

"Well, I've wondered why you've never asked who William's father is." Liu Song felt regret that she'd steered the conversation in this direction, but she knew the delicate subject had to come up sooner or later. She'd thought about this dilemma and preferred to scare Colin away now, rather than spend these weeks titillating each other. "You've never asked if he's still around. You've never asked anything . . ."

"I won't ask. It's obvious that whoever it was, he isn't around now. You have a handsome, healthy baby boy who fills you with pride. You're a good mother. You have talent and youth and a future that I'm excited to watch unfold. Some things are best left in the past. It's clear that you've left that part of your life behind. I see no need to dig up the bones of another man. And it's not really any of my business . . ."

"But . . ." Liu Song spoke, knowing that with each word she was giving him an opportunity to pull the car over, to let her off on some side street and drive away without looking back. "You come from a family of means. You're kind. You're more handsome than you realize. You're a performer—there are plenty of girls out there who'd love for you to fill up their dance cards. Why . . ."

"Why you?" He answered her question with a question. "Why not you?"

For the first time Liu Song realized why her parents had been so close. They'd both been actors, products of the stage. They'd lived in a world that few appreciated. Liu Song thought about her own disconnection from her peers, from her traditional Chinese community, and knew that Colin must feel the same way. *But what about William,* she asked herself, *what kind of reputation would he inherit? What am I burdening him with?*

Liu Song's worries vanished when they arrived at the Coliseum, which was like no movie palace she'd ever seen. She marveled at the ornate lobby, filled with brass cages that hung from the vaulted ceiling. Dozens of songbirds chirped and cooed as the orchestra tuned their instruments to the biggest pipe organ she'd ever seen, or heard.

"It's the largest musical instrument in the world," Colin said as they found their seats. "It's only appropriate for the most expensive film ever made. They spent two million, if you can believe it."

Liu Song couldn't. That much money seemed unfathomable. Colin came from wealth. Perhaps this whole business could impress his family after all.

In the dark they listened to the rhapsodic score, which filled the house and swept them to someplace far away where men climbed magic ropes, horses flew, and a shirtless Douglas Fairbanks rode through the air atop a magic carpet. But the best part, the most memorable moment, etched into Liu Song's imagination, was the first scene, when she felt Colin's arm around her. She could smell the woolen fabric of his suit and the spice of his cologne. She felt joy, but also tremors of doubt and tendrils of dread, as she watched an old mage on-screen who sat on a hillside directing smoke into the heavens, where the aphorism "Happiness must be earned" lay written in the stars.

Stand-Ins

꒱

(1924)

Liu Song inhaled, trying not to worry. The strange neighborhood she found herself in was redolent of pine trees, gasoline, and bleach—lots of bleach. The pungent smell tickled her nose and reminded her of Uncle Leo's laundry business—a memory she didn't care to relive as she waited for Colin to arrive. For the past two weeks he'd seen her off and on, though lately more off than on. He'd been haunting a local film production and had finally landed a small role and invited her to join him on the set—extras were always needed and he'd talked her up as some kind of seasoned performer, even though her venue had merely been a sidewalk and her audience, passing motorists.

Liu Song waited on the corner of Virginia and Third Avenue, looking away and fidgeting as men drove by and tooted their horns, until Colin finally arrived.

"Ah . . . can you smell that?" Colin said, smiling as delivery trucks rattled by.

Liu Song wrinkled her nose. She'd never been to Seattle's Film Row, which was located in the northern tip of Belltown, where the streets were lined with long rows of cozy brick offices and small warehouses.

"That's our future," Colin said, breathing it in, savoring the chemical stench, and exhaling slowly.

Liu Song had hoped their future together was something less toxic.

"Nitrocellulose film. That's what money smells like. A few small production companies are located here," Colin said as they walked. "But most of these buildings are just administrative offices and film exchanges—where the larger studios house their movie reels, all except the U.S. Army Motion Picture Service and the Kodascope Library, which are located on Cherry Street. Local authorities felt it was safer to group these places together in one part of the city—film is a fire hazard, you know."

Liu Song noted the exchange offices for Columbia Pictures, Universal, and MGM, among others, nestled between the William Tell Hotel and the Jewel Box Theatre. She stopped counting after twenty.

"What's the matter?" Colin asked as he noticed the concern on her face.

Where do I begin? Liu Song thought. Her doubts had taken root. "I'm not certain that I'm cut out for this kind of work." She thought about her mother. "I've grown up around the stage, but this moviemaking is all so strange."

"On the stage you get one chance to get your lines right—to get your dance moves just perfect," Colin reassured her. "With movies, they can roll the camera again and again until they get it just so. Trust me. You'll do fine."

Liu Song wished she felt as confident. Colin had found bit parts here and there all over the Northwest. He'd encouraged her to audition. But he knew what to expect. Liu Song put on a brave face. "Is the studio you're working for around here?"

"It's not a studio, exactly," Colin said. "The local unions produce small movies and shorts to further their cause. Ever since Upton Sinclair signed on to write screenplays for the railway unions, labor films have been all the rage. This one is called *The New Disciple*. It's a political film in the form of a love story. I'm just a walk-on, but it's a real photoplay—a real movie. Even if it's not quite a real set. It's a wonderful place for you to learn the ropes, I think."

As they turned the corner Liu Song saw a throng of people crowding the sidewalk in front of a large display window. The painted marquee read, ALL ROADS LEAD TO RHODES. The retailer's storefront was so crowded Liu Song could hardly see inside. At first she assumed that the store must have received a new shipment of console radios, which were growing in popularity, but as they crossed the street and got closer, she saw that the window display had been decorated like a living room with sofa, chairs, lamps, potted plants, and even a high-walled backdrop with curtained windows and a wooden fireplace. Instead of mannequins, a film crew in shirtsleeves and hanging suspenders were setting up lights and giant reflectors. A cameraman stretched a measuring tape from the lens of a large movie camera to the middle of the set. Liu Song stared wide-eyed as Colin led her inside and through the housewares department to where a small corner of the store had been roped off. A security guard stopped them until he found Colin's name on a clipboard, then he stepped aside and tipped his hat. A production assistant ushered them to a busy area behind the set where they sat on a bench with other extras and bit players.

Liu Song pointed to a pair of tall folding chairs in front of them. The canvas chair backs faced in their direction as a makeup artist attended to the occupants.

"Those are the stars: Pell Trenton and Norris Johnson," Colin whispered.

Liu Song read their names, which were written in grease pencil on the backs of the chairs. Even from behind she could admire Pell's dashing, broad-shouldered physique and Norris's elegantly styled hair and long gown.

"I'm so grateful you're here," Colin said. "You calm my nerves."

Liu Song felt the opposite. She wished he could return the favor as she forced a smile. "How many movies have you been in now?"

"Five," Colin said. "Each time as an extra. Today I play a servant in a rich man's house. I don't get a credit, but at least I appear on-screen quite a bit—that is, if I don't end up on the cutting room floor when they edit everything together. And of course I get another notch on my résumé."

The production assistant wandered back and shouted for standins. Liu Song had no idea what he meant. Colin smiled and took her hand as he stood up, waved, and quickly volunteered the two of them.

"What are we doing?" Liu Song felt lost. "I have no idea what . . ."

Colin whispered in her ear as they were being led onto the set. "The director has called for stand-ins. They need two extras in front of the camera for a practice run. We'll just be in for a few minutes so the camera operator can adjust the timing and measure the lens's focal length. We stand in until they're ready to roll film. This way the stars look fresh for the camera instead of melting. It's fun, you'll see. Just mind that you don't look directly into the lights—they can do permanent damage. Miriam Cooper burned her eyes by looking into the lights on the set of *Kindred of the Dust*."

Liu Song hardly understood a word he said. She wondered if this was what it was like for her mother, stepping onstage for the very first time. But this audience was a film crew who seemed unimpressed. To the crew, she and Colin were merely placeholders, living statues that they casually regarded as they moved lights, adjusted reflectors, and took measurements.

Liu Song felt heat radiating from the lights. Then her heart skipped a beat as she saw the director, a tall man with a tiny megaphone, take his seat next to an olive-skinned gentleman with a pencil-thin mustache who peered through the camera.

"Hey, Chop Suey, you do speak English, don't you?" the director asked.

"And French, Latin, and a little bit of Italian," Colin said. *"Va bene?"*

"Great, an aristocrat," the cameraman said. "Take two steps back, Your Majesty."

Colin smiled and pointed to two Xs on the floor marked with tape. "This is where we stand," he told Liu Song. They moved back as five other extras stood in the background, pretending to talk and laugh politely.

"The camera's not rolling," Colin said. "This is playacting, so you have nothing to worry about. But it's good practice for a bigger opportunity that's coming up."

Liu Song had sung before busloads of strangers. She'd wandered backstage during many of her father's productions, so she'd grown accustomed to that type of performance. Filmmaking, on the other hand, was new, foreign, and yet deliriously intriguing. She drew a deep breath, swallowed, and nodded, wondering what else Colin might have in store.

"Just another performance," Colin said as he touched her arm and smiled reassuringly. "For now. This is the beginning for us. Someday William will see you on the screen in a real movie. Imagine how proud he'll be."

Welfare

(1924)

When Liu Song arrived at Butterfield's the next morning, she found a peculiar woman playing the piano and humming a strange hymn. Her hair was tinted a light shade of pink and pulled up so tightly that her eyebrows seemed to be jerked back in a look of perpetual surprise. Her eyes were blue, like ice, and her unpainted lips were like a slit that divided the vertical wrinkles on her face into northern and southern halves. The song she played was a lullaby, but to Liu Song the melody was a funeral march.

"Hello, I'm Mrs. Peterson," the woman said as she stepped from the piano and extended a limp, white-gloved handshake to Liu Song, letting go quickly as though she didn't appreciate the touch of others. "I'm with the Child Welfare League and I'd like to ask you a few questions, if I may?"

Liu Song felt ambushed and woefully unprepared. Was this Uncle Leo's doing? Had he found out about William? "Do I have a choice?"

"No." Mrs. Peterson gazed back without emotion. "You don't."

Mr. Butterfield parted the curtain that separated the showroom floor from the storeroom. He smiled and held up a cup of tea on an unmatched saucer. "Ah, Liu Song, I see you've met our special guest." He offered the cup to Mrs. Peterson, who squinted at the coffee-stained china. She took one polite sip and then set the cup aside.

"If this is about William," Liu Song said in her best English, "I assure you, he's doing very well. He's very healthy, very fat. A happy boy."

The woman looked around the store, then back at Liu Song. "This is strictly routine. It's my job to follow up with all single mothers when the child gets to an age of moral viability. It's not just the feeding and clothing and diaper changing that the state worries about, but the social environment, the condition of the mother." Mrs. Peterson cleared her throat. "And her circumstances."

"I can certainly vouch for her character," Mr. Butterfield said. "Liu Song here is quite responsible. She's both industrious and thrifty."

"And I'm sure you'll appreciate that as one who profits from her talents." Mrs. Peterson opened up a ledger and began writing in tiny, perfect penmanship. "Your testimony is appreciated, in direct proportion to how biased it is."

Liu Song looked at her employer and blinked, hoping he would understand how thankful she was, for the job, and for the effort.

"You are an Oriental. Chinese, I presume. Where were you born?"

Liu Song explained how she'd been born at home, in Seattle, with a midwife at her mother's side. Liu Song didn't have a copy of her birth certificate, but her mother had registered her at the King County Court House two months after she'd been born.

"And do you have any family? Any relatives whom I could speak with? People who support you and how you intend to raise young . . ." The woman looked at her notes.

"William," Liu Song said. "And no, my mother died before William was born. The rest of my family . . . all of them are gone, taken by the flu, or moved away." As she spoke, Liu Song realized just how terribly alone she was. William was everything to her. She felt such affection for Colin, but what she felt for her son was beyond comparison. She would live for Colin, but she would die for William.

Liu Song sat up straight, smiling—not too broadly, but not too meekly. She suddenly wished she'd dressed more modestly. She did her best to answer each probing, leading, condemning question without revealing something that would be sharpened and twisted and used against her. Her English was good, but she still had to stop and ask Mrs. Peterson to repeat the questions, again and again, not because she didn't understand the wording but because she was afraid that she might answer incorrectly. Mr. Butterfield chirped up twice more, and twice he was politely dismissed.

"Well, it's nice to see that a girl like you can earn an honest living. It's not entirely reputable, but it's legal. And from the news clippings that your employer shared with me before you arrived, it appears you have a knack for this type of thing." Mrs. Peterson spoke with grudging approval as she shook her head.

Liu Song thanked her, feeling slighted but relieved.

"Now." Mrs. Peterson stood up and closed her ledger. "Seeing as how you are gainfully employed, all that's left is a home interview and inspection. I'll need your address. And how soon can I meet your son?"

Liu Song had been afraid of that. She'd been able to support herself, to buy food and clothing, but she had little else—a bed, a lamp, an old davenport sofa with holes and tears that she'd tried to patch with what sewing supplies she could afford. William had a third-hand crib, a dresser with unmatched drawers, missing all but one knob, and a few toys.

"How about next week?" Liu Song asked.

"How about tomorrow?" Mrs. Peterson rebutted. "The sooner, the better."

Partially Pregnant

꿔

(1924)

Mrs. Peterson arrived the next day, twenty minutes early. Fortunately, Liu Song had expected she might and prepared accordingly. She had splurged on half a duck, and the bird was roasting in the oven, filling the tiny apartment with a comforting, savory aroma. Her furniture and decorations looked somewhat mismatched, but quaint, modest, and ordinary—exactly the image she wanted to portray.

"You'll do fine," Colin had reassured her. "Just be yourself."

"And what if I'm not good enough?" Liu Song had asked.

"You're an actress—just play the part."

Liu Song wasn't sure what would be more nerve-racking, standing in front of a packed theater or playing to an audience of one. But she smiled and invited the woman in nonetheless, just as the teakettle began to whistle. Liu Song didn't ask, she went ahead and poured two cups and placed them on the newly installed coffee table, along with some black bean tea cookies, before offering Mrs. Peterson a seat on the sofa. Liu Song noticed an old theater handbill sticking out from behind the cushions and stuffed it back down just as William walked into the room. One shoe was untied, but aside from that he looked darling in his handsome blue coveralls.

"Hi," he said cheerfully as he waved and sat down on the floor where Liu Song had placed a brand-new toy train. She'd bought it after work today, specifically for William to have something new to play with while the home inspector visited.

If Mrs. Peterson enjoyed children, it was hard to tell as she glanced at William with the same polite detachment that she used toward the furniture. Liu Song noticed that the woman kept her white gloves on and peeked at her fingertips whenever she touched something, searching for evidence of dust or dirt.

"You have a lovely home," Mrs. Peterson said in a blunt, matter-of-fact manner that made it seem as though she felt otherwise. "Just the two of you then?"

Liu Song nodded and explained her arrangement with Mildred Chew, who was practically a part-time nanny, and how they'd once been classmates. Liu Song made sure to reference her own high school diploma, which she'd earned a year early.

Liu Song followed Mrs. Peterson as she opened her ledger and walked about the tiny apartment, inspecting the bathroom, the screened-off bedroom Liu Song shared with William, the magazines— *Life, Vogue, Collier's*—that were arranged on an end table. She seemed particularly interested in the Chinese curios and decorations that sat on a bookcase, the small family altar where Liu Song lit candles, burned incense, and offered bits of embroidery to honor her parents, and the mask Liu Song's mother had worn. The woman touched it and flinched as though it might bite. She went on to check the windows, the radiator, the icebox; she even opened the oven, but she didn't write anything in her book.

"You're welcome to stay for dinner," Liu Song offered.

"Are you currently married?" Mrs. Peterson asked, ignoring Liu Song's gesture of hospitality. "And if your husband is not around, have you been legally divorced?"

William was crashing his wooden train into the leg of the table, making train noises and giggling. Liu Song picked him up, resting him on her hip, train and all, as he spun the toy's wheels.

"No," she blurted. "Of course not. I'm not sure I understand . . ."

Mrs. Peterson stared at her. "I am aware that you have been seeing someone."

"I have a friend. His name is Colin Kwan. I'm not sure how serious he is."

"Dadda," William said, looking at the two women with rapt, curious eyes.

A moment of silence lingered among the three of them. Liu Song smiled nervously and rocked her son, but she was painfully aware of Mrs. Peterson's condemning gaze.

"So, who is the father, exactly?" Mrs. Peterson looked into her ledger. "The birth certificate states that a Mr. Eng . . ."

"It's hard to explain," Liu Song said. *Please don't ask me this.*

"It always is, dear."

William dropped the train and wiggled his feet to get down.

"He's not exactly anything . . ."

"You can't be partially pregnant, young lady. This Leo Eng is either the father or not the father. It would appear that he is your husband since you share the same last name, but it seems like this Colin fellow has a certain place in your life as well . . ."

"Why do you need to know this?" Liu Song asked. "You can see that my son is perfectly healthy. I have a home. He is cared for . . ."

"It's not his physical well-being that we care about. It's the morality of those he is raised by. You claim to be unmarried. You don't want to talk about the father. You sing, act, and dance for a living. It's not beyond reason to think that you're compromised . . ."

"I'm not."

"But you can see how it looks. You're lucky that you're an Oriental woman. In most situations a woman like you would lose the child immediately. But, seeing as how no one would adopt a yellow baby, well . . ."

William walked over to Mrs. Peterson and offered her his train. He smiled and batted his eyes.

The woman drew a deep breath and took the toy, thanking William. "Look, Miss Eng, I'm going to have to recommend the removal of your son until we can determine who the father is. You must respect his paternal rights."

William looked back at Liu Song and waved.

"But if you could cooperate and tell me who this man is, the judge might be lenient in his final decision. What can you tell me? Or I could just go find this Mr. Eng and get his side of the story—that's how it works in many instances. You could still invoke the tender years doctrine, which would allow you to care for your son until he's of age to be returned to his rightful father. But the problem is that if you don't tell me who the father is, someone might assume you have other things to hide, that you're not who you say you are, which may complicate things as far as your citizenship, and that of your son."

Liu Song swallowed hard as she watched William. "When my father died, my mother remarried another man, out of necessity—out of desperation. But later she fell ill as well and passed away. And this fellow, this man my mother married, he kept me for a while as a servant . . ." Liu Song looked down at her empty hands, her fingers appearing aged and wrinkled beyond her years. "He was my stepfather. His last name was Eng."

The point of Mrs. Peterson's pencil broke, and she stared at the broken lead and the blemish on her paper. She adjusted her spectacles and wrinkled her nose. "And as far as you know this Eng person doesn't even know he's fathered this . . ."

"His name is William," Liu Song said. As she watched Mrs. Peterson, awaiting her reaction, she noticed that the woman's hands seemed to shake and her fingers trembled ever so slightly. "And no, I don't think he knows, nor do I think he cares."

Mrs. Peterson closed her ledger and drew a deep breath. She reached for the nearest teacup and took a long sip. Then she removed her glasses and folded them carefully, stowing them in a brass case. "Well, when your mother died he stopped being your stepfather and you stopped being his stepdaughter. Legally, I'm going to have to tell him. He's still the father, and he still may want the child."

The woman frowned at William as though he were a stain on the carpet, a mess she had to clean up. Liu Song chewed her lip as the social worker removed her gloves and placed a hand on William's head, brushing his dark cowlick to one side. The stern woman cocked her head as she observed him playing, then looked up and wiped her hand on her knee. "He's the spitting image of you."

Liu Song wasn't sure if that was a compliment or an insult. She glanced at her reflection in the mirror and saw how pale she looked. Her hands were wet and clammy, and her eyes welled up with hot tears, but she refused to cry in front of this woman; she didn't want to be pitied and she didn't want to beg.

"I think we're done here. I have all I need," Mrs. Peterson said as she donned her gloves and stood up. "I wish you the very best of luck. I'll let you know as soon as I hear back from Mr. Eng. But, considering the circumstances, I don't think he'd want the child. Most men don't—at least until the diapers are done with."

But Uncle Leo wasn't like most men. Liu Song thanked her and picked up William, who waved goodbye. "But what if he does?"

"Then I would offer a suggestion, Miss Eng, the same one I offer to all girls in your situation, though usually I do it right after the child is born." Mrs. Peterson paused at the door. She looked down at her ledger and then at Liu Song. "It's an unfair world, filled with vile men and hapless women, but none of that matters to me at this point. I just want whatever is best for the child, and in this case, your son is still very young."

"What does that mean?"

"It means a child doesn't always have to know who his mother is—but a boy needs a father," Mrs. Peterson said bluntly. "You've made your bed. I suppose you'll just have to lie in it. But William doesn't have to lie there with you. Good day."

The Eyes of the Totem

꒡

(1924)

Chinatown had always been a place of comfort for Liu Song, despite her detours around Uncle Leo's laundry and the gaming halls where she feared his shadow. But now that fear had an aspect of inevitability. He would know about William. Liu Song shuddered. *He won't want anything to do with us,* she'd reassured herself. He was a superstitious fool, and her mother's ghost had scared him away. But in broad daylight she felt less certain. She had tried not to panic. Instead, she took Colin's encouragement to heart and followed him to every casting call, every audition, every chance possible, from films for the Communist Workers' Theatre to government-sponsored shorts like *Fit to Fight* that warned soldiers about the perils of venereal disease. She lingered with Colin outside local studios hoping to be seen and suffered through bullpens of extras hoping for a few dollars for a day's work. She hoped to find work that would take her and William away from this city. And with each outing she gave serious consideration to changing her name. Not creating a stage name. The name she found herself desperately pining for was Liu Song *Kwan*. She thought the name had a magical ring to it, and if Collin married her, he could adopt William. But she also knew that as much as he cared for her, and she for him, marriage could present other problems. How long could he stay in this country under the pretense of being a merchant? And when he left, she and William would have to go with him. But even that was better than losing her son.

She tried not to think those thoughts as she walked along, holding William's hand while he stumbled over cracks in the sidewalk. But each morning she dreaded going to work. Butterfield's was a steady source of income and safer than dancing at the Wah Mee, but the music store was the one place Uncle Leo would know to find her.

She breathed a sigh of relief when she found Colin waiting for her at Butterfield's. She'd shied away from having him stop by in the past because his presence while she performed made her nervous—more timorous than singing before a busload of tourists. Yet here he stood in a linen suit, hat in hand, chatting amiably with her employer, much to her surprise and slight embarrassment. In the crook of his arm, Colin held another bouquet of bright blue flowers. *That's what a wish fulfilled looks like,* Liu Song thought as she walked in and said hello; the two men smiled, beaming conspiratorially at the sight of her and then at each other.

"Good morning, *Willow,*" Mr. Butterfield said. "Master Colin was just telling me about your stage name. I think it's wonderful—simply marvelous. Much easier for the locals and tourists to understand. We should use it here at the store, don't you think?"

Colin nodded in agreement. "He does have a point."

She set William down, and he went to plunk away on a tiny piano. "I didn't know that I needed a stage name."

"You do now." Colin winked. "I finally did it. I got you a part in a movie. It's a small part, but it's a huge production, called *The Eyes of the Totem*. It's starring Wanda Hawley—she's as big as Gloria Swanson. And best of all, we'll appear on-screen together. I was just working out the details—"

"Your beau here . . ." Mr. Butterfield cheerfully interrupted, almost blushing.

Liu Song's imagination tripped over the word *beau*, which

sounded official—committed. The word carried with it a sense of belonging, of possession. She thoroughly enjoyed the sound of that word.

Mr. Butterfield kept yammering, waving his hands as he spoke. "Master Colin wanted to make sure you were available for the days they need you on the set. I thought it was a fabulous idea. This is great publicity for the store. And who knows, dear, this could be the start of something—*something big.*"

Liu Song suspected a polite form of collusion between her boss and her *beau* as she watched the men glance at each other knowingly.

"Well, I'll leave you two alone," Mr. Butterfield said as he stubbed out his cigarillo and disappeared into the storeroom, humming a cheerful tune.

Colin handed her the flowers. "How did your meeting go?"

"Fine." She hated lying but couldn't bear to tell Colin about Uncle Leo. She didn't want to scare him away, burden him with her shame, or lure him into something more than he was capable of. But she didn't stop hoping.

"I'm sorry. What's this about a movie?" she asked, changing the subject. "And how did you convince Mr. Butterfield . . ."

Colin confirmed what Liu Song already knew—that her boss had earned much at her expense. She was the songbird that kept laying golden eggs. As much as she worried about losing her job, Mr. Butterfield was much more concerned about her leaving him, especially with radio sales booming and music sales on the decline. She wondered if Butterfield's could even sell a player piano these days without her promised performance as the kicker. Having her around was more than just a point of pride—it kept the store going. She had more power than she realized—more freedom and more opportunities. Why not make the most of them? Why not try new venues? She didn't have to hide anymore. Leo would find out about her sooner rather than later.

"The entire production is being filmed in Tacoma," Colin explained. "Most of the scenes have already been shot at the new H. C. Weaver Studios. They spent fifty thousand dollars building that place—you should see it; there are fifteen star dressing rooms, separate greenrooms for extras, a projection room; it's quite amazing. I went to the dedication earlier in the year. But the best news is that part of the movie takes place at a Chinese cabaret. I pulled a few strings at the China Gate Theatre, offering props, silk costumes, and set pieces to the studio in exchange for a minor role. That's where we come in. I'm on-screen for most of the scene, but there's a great opportunity for you as well. More than a stand-in, more than an extra. We have a scene together. It's a small part, but it could be the start of something greater." He smiled. "And since Mr. Butterfield is your employer and your second-biggest fan, I thought it was only proper form to make his acquaintance and ask for his blessing."

"Blessing?"

"I'm sorry," Colin said. "Perhaps it's my English. I wanted to ask for his permission. Is that how you say it?"

Liu Song furrowed her brow, smiling.

Colin switched to Chinese. "I have something important to ask you."

Liu Song suddenly felt underdressed, unprepared. She knew that Colin was a modern fellow, but tradition and convention called for some sort of gesture—a proposal, perhaps? She tried not to hope, but her thoughts ran away with her.

She imagined standing in the dark, behind a velvet curtain, listening as a packed house falls silent when the orchestra begins playing a rousing overture. She can almost feel the breeze on her bare shoulders as she envisions the curtains parting.

Liu Song held her breath as she watched Colin fumble with something in his suit pocket. He looked nervous and flustered.

From the stage all she sees are the footlights as her eyes adjust to the gloaming.

Colin paused and took a deep breath.

She feels the warmth of the spotlight, brighter than the noon-day sun.

Colin held up a telegram from Western Union. "My father is coming next week."

Suddenly Liu Song is standing alone onstage as the houselights come on. She hears the solemn clapping of a single man, a janitor, wedded to his broom.

Liu Song tried not to look crestfallen as she regarded the paper. She'd lingered on the periphery of his affection, his attention, their shared passions, lost in the hopeless decorum, waiting for Colin to declare his intentions, which seemed plainly, painfully obvious. Yet they had been perpetually unstated.

"I've waited a long time for this moment," Colin said as he took her hands in his. They felt warm, soft, gentle. "I've waited to speak with my father, for him to see what I've become, and for him to see what's possible. I want to introduce you as well. This is the start of something big for both of us, in every way possible."

"But what about your . . . duties . . ."

Liu Song watched his every gesture, trying to decipher meaning from every word, every pause, seeking answers to questions her pride wouldn't allow her to ask.

Colin hesitated as though he were considering his past obligations for the first time. It was as if he'd been so engaged in his career that the possibility of failure, of rejection, had never once been considered. "I'm sure he'll have some critical things to say, but when he sees me on the set, when he sees me with you—I know he'll come around. He's always wanted me to take the reins of the family business, to settle down and give him grandchildren. This is as close as I can get. Please tell me you'll be there."

Liu Song hesitated. She was a young girl in a city of lonely men—outnumbered ten, twenty, one hundred to one. She knew that even as a single mother she could find a suitor if she really tried. But she also knew that she didn't want any of them. She didn't want to be the wife of a cabdriver, the mother of a laundry runner, the step-mother of grown children who would regard her as a maid and a short-order cook. She had William's unconditional love—she wanted more but refused to settle for the warmth of some strange man's bed. She didn't want to be a subservient wife, a silent prisoner. If there was anything she had learned from her mother, it was the painful understanding that cages come in all sizes—some even have white picket fences, four walls, and a front door. Liu Song loved performing—that was her true self. The lonely girl who danced with strangers was the actress. Deep inside her bruised and battered heart she knew that she wanted what her mother wanted, what her father dreamt, what they sacrificed for. She wanted to perform, not just onstage but in the arms of someone who would truly love her. She didn't care what she had to endure. She only cared whom she'd be sharing that spotlight with.

"Please tell me you want this as much as me," he asked.

She looked at Colin, wondering where her hesitation had gone. "I do."

IF COLIN WAS nervous about seeing his father for the first time in nearly five years, Liu Song couldn't tell. She wasn't sure if his optimism was a by-product of his uncanny acting ability or a reckless brand of fearlessness—the kind she suspected she would need to succeed in this business. Her mother had possessed that kind of courage, before illness stole her resolve, along with her husband, her dignity, and her dreams. Or was that courage all an act too? Liu Song wondered how flexible the truth must be to performers who were always pretending to be someone else.

She felt Colin's arm around her as he bought two tickets for the

Puget Sound Electric Railway's trolley to Tacoma. She felt warm and safe as she leaned into him. She reached up and straightened his tie, wondering how long it would be until he kissed her. She was certain that meeting Colin's father was some sort of vetting process. But she also suspected that she was a buffer between the two men. They were meeting on location, in a public place, where the condemning eyes of a disappointed, angered father might be distracted by the grandiose spectacle of filmmaking, where his stern voice might be softened by Liu Song's polite smile. *If all goes well,* Liu Song thought, *there will be nothing between Colin and me. And sweet William will have the father he deserves.*

As they traveled the southern spur of the interurban line, Liu Song counted the minutes and the miles, growing more anxious. She took deep breaths, exhaling slowly, relaxing her shoulders and calming her mind—the way her father had shown her once before he took the stage. She was so excited about being on the set of a major production, but still worried about meeting Colin's father. She knew so little about the man, but she expected him to be a traditional Chinese father, more entrenched in old-world customs than her uncle Leo. She imagined Mr. Kwan as the opposite of her own father in every possible way, which left her perplexed as to how Colin could be so hopeful. Then again, she thought, *maybe Colin isn't hoping for reconciliation—for acceptance.* Maybe this would be Colin's last goodbye—a cutting of the cords, where he'd declare the two great loves of his life. Three if he counted William. She hoped. She indulged her imagination. She dreamt shamelessly.

She was still daydreaming as they stepped off the train at Tacoma's Union Station. Colin led her across the busy street and around the corner, past ticket scalpers working the alley by the sparkling Pantages Theatre. Two blocks up the steep hill she saw a line of people outside the Rialto, waiting for the evening show. But by far the largest crowd had amassed in the street to the north.

"Most of the filming will take place at Weaver's big studio near

Titlow Beach," Colin said. "But tonight they're shooting at the Grand Winthrop Hotel."

Together they waded through the throng of people—hundreds of onlookers hoping to catch a glimpse of Wanda Hawley. Liu Song recognized the starlet immediately. She was hard to miss as she stood on the front steps of the hotel, wearing an enormous fur coat, flanked by two stout policemen, who kept the horde of autograph seekers at bay. The uniformed officers had to shout to be heard over the thrumming of a generator truck parked in the alley. Long cables snaked up and through a pair of open second-story windows. Enormous movie lights stood like sentinels, illuminating the lobby of the hotel. Liu Song marveled at the elaborately constructed façade, which had transformed the stately hotel into the Golden Dragon— a palace of indulgence, a den of temptation, where they'd be performing alongside dozens of other actors and Chinese extras. The setting was daunting.

"Now I know why you told your father to meet you here," Liu Song said as they showed their IDs to a production assistant who kept track of actors and scenes on a blackboard. The man directed them to where parts of the hotel had been repurposed as staging areas for crew members and makeup artists, and a storage pen for assorted props.

"My father is a rich man," Colin said. "But still, how can he not be impressed by all of this? They hired the scene painters from the World's Fair." Colin paused as they saw the main set, where the hotel's grand ballroom had been turned into a glittering Oriental nightclub, complete with fine linens, bamboo trees, hanging lanterns, and tuxedoed waiters. "Weaver's studio is the third largest motion picture production stage in the United States. The other two are in Hollywood. This business is no trifle—no passing fancy. I'm not an opera singer traveling from town to town hoping for a free meal." He smiled at Liu Song. "And how can he not be impressed by you?"

Liu Song tried not to take his words as a slight toward her father. She knew Colin was merely excited—lost in the moment. She wished she shared his confidence. And as a seamstress guided her to the ladies' dressing room in the basement and Liu Song was fitted with an elaborate ball gown, she felt emboldened by the dress, by the part, by the memory of her parents. She thought about Mildred and William sitting at home—she wished they could see her now, but then she remembered that they'd be able to. One day she'd take them to the nearest movie house and she'd surprise them.

Liu Song studied her part as a makeup artist dusted her face, complimented her smooth skin, and outlined her eyes with thick, black eyeliner. Their scene was simple the way Colin had explained it on the ride down from Seattle. He was the dashing young proprietor of the club, and she was his wife. She'd flit about the scene, speaking with Colin and other guests before being sent away for her protection as the stars of the film made their grand entrance and Colin was subsequently arrested. Liu Song knew that her part was small, but she found comfort in that. She preferred to dip her toe into the tepid pool of cinema instead of plunging in headfirst.

Then the waiting began.

"This is all part of the process," Colin said, as he looked at his wristwatch and glanced at the door. "We wait and wait and wait . . ."

Liu Song nodded. She'd learned to associate Colin with the virtue of patience. She watched as he was called to the set on three different occasions. Each time he took his scenes in stride. She stared spellbound as he reacted to the lights, the camera, even the other big-name stars like Tom Santschi and Violet Palmer, who seemed beyond the reach of the rest. *He fits in. He belongs here. He's born for this. Surely his father will see this. Such talent is obvious.*

Then she heard her name called. She didn't even recognize it at first.

"Willa Eng," a man said. "Is there a Willa Eng on the set?"

"It's Willow," Liu Song called out, grimacing at the sound of her last name. She stepped into her heels and found her place beneath the lights. The last time she and Colin had done this it had been a silly affair—all in nonsensical fun, playacting, like charades. But now the cameras would roll on them.

"Are you ready?" she teased Colin as he slicked his hair back and buttoned his suit jacket. She noticed him looking nervous for the first time as he glanced at the clock.

"He'll be here," Liu Song said. "He's probably here already, out in the crowd . . ."

"You don't know my father," Colin said. "He'd be early to his own funeral."

Liu Song touched his arm as she looked into his eyes and then toward the camera, where she saw a strange, upside-down figure reflected in the lens. Then she noted that the director, the cinematographer, the bulk of the crew were all looking toward the entrance, wide-eyed. Liu Song glanced up at Colin and saw him grow pale. She turned around and saw a beautiful Chinese girl, not much older than herself. The girl wore a tight-fitting cheongsam made of shimmering red silk. She appeared nervous and strangely out of place. Liu Song presumed the girl to be an extra, lost in the confusion. Until she saw the way the girl looked at Colin—searching, recognizing. Her eyes were filled with something Liu Song knew all too well—longing.

"This is a closed set," a producer snapped. "Miss, you can't be here. Somebody get her out of frame. If we need more Chinese extras, honey, I'll let you know."

"Colin." Liu Song looked up, not wanting to ask.

"I can't believe she's here," he whispered. "I can't believe he sent her."

Liu Song felt a crushing weight on her heart as the director shouted, "Places!"

She stood before him, listening to the clatter and din of cast and crew.

"It was . . . an arranged . . . marriage," Colin muttered, distant, as though he were speaking to himself, reminding his conscience of forgotten labors.

Liu Song felt her heart bend across the anvil of his words. The blows of the hammer kept coming, kept pounding.

"Arranged . . . by my father. I haven't seen her since she was maybe fourteen years old—so long ago. I thought that she would be married by now—that my father would have released me from that obligation. That everyone had just moved on without me."

Obligation. Liu Song thought she knew the meaning of the word. She looked down, not wanting to see the girl, or the regret—the guilt in Colin's eyes.

"She's my . . . fiancée," she heard him whisper. The words were ice.

Liu Song felt his hands on her shoulders. He was speaking, but she didn't hear a word as his lips moved like an actor's in a silent film. Then he let go and she watched the scene unfold from the inside out. She watched Colin walk toward the comely visitor as crew members threw up their hands in frustration. Liu Song blinked as he touched his fiancée's hand, exchanged words, and then the girl left. By the look on Colin's face as he returned, Liu Song knew that something terrible had happened, and not just to her.

Colin looked horrified, fearful—the way Liu Song felt. "My father is on his deathbed," he said. "And my brother has become a drunk and a gambler. My mother sent my fiancée here to bring me back. I'm so sorry, Liu Song. I have to go home. I have to leave tomorrow. I'll return if I can. I promise. This isn't how I planned to . . ."

"Quiet on the set!" the director yelled. "We've got a movie to shoot."

As the camera rolled, Liu Song looked at the stranger Colin had become beneath the halcyon lights. And in her place, Willow made her appearance. Her ears were numb, ringing, silencing his dialogue—his heartfelt gestures that he somehow managed to perform. Willow stared up at him, her eyes welling with hot tears, her lower lip trembling as she tried to patch the cracks in the emotional dam that was bursting with each of Colin's gestures, with each silent soliloquy. She struggled with how she'd explain this to William. He was little, he would adjust, but he'd feel Colin's absence. Perhaps more keenly, more completely than she'd feel the emptiness in her own heart as she cried helplessly for the first time in years.

Colin kissed the tears on her cheeks, then he touched his lips. He looked at the wetness on his fingertips as if the warm residue were blood from a weapon. Then he kissed her lips, gently, before exhaling, catching his breath, and walking out of the scene as Liu Song heard the director mumble something about keeping the camera rolling—that this was a golden moment. She heard the flickering of the shutter, the hum of the lights, and the silence punctuated by the sound of Colin's footsteps, fading.

Lullaby

(1924)

Liu Song paid sixty cents for a return ticket and sat by herself in the back of the 525 Limited, bound for Seattle with short stops in Kent and Auburn. She didn't wait for Colin, nor did she bother to look for him. She didn't know if he had another scene or another unscheduled performance with his long-lost fiancée—she chose not to linger and find out. All she wanted now was her son and the comfort of her tiny home.

As she sat in the near-empty railcar, watching the gray-green blur of another train zoom past the arched windows, she tried to think of nothing but William, but she couldn't forget the look on Colin's face or the tears that finally caught up to her. She could have cried for hours. All of her pain and struggles and loneliness had overwhelmed her the way Colin's fiancée—his past—had caught up to him, crashing his big night. Liu Song struggled to reconcile the secret he'd kept, the growing list of commitments he'd run away from—his father, his family's business, the responsibilities of a first-born son, and a betrothal. That was the worst. But the girl in the red cheongsam, his fiancée—none of this was her fault. He'd been unfair to that poor girl as well. She was merely an innocent bystander, but now Colin was standing by her, leaving with her, conscripted into marrying her. *Where does this leave me?* Liu Song anguished. *I'm alone at the bottom of a deep well of doubt.* And at the murky

bottom of that cold spring, Liu Song realized that it wasn't just
Colin who had misled her—she had betrayed herself. She'd followed her heart, her hopes, without questioning him. Now those
hopes were tangled. She remembered learning about the Greeks
back at Franklin High—about the Gordian knot. That was her
heart, a thicket of longing, misgiving, rejection, and disbelief. There
was no way to untie so many twists and coils. The only solution was
to do what Alexander the Great had done, and cut through the
mess, severing all ties—all but William.

He said he'd come back for me. Liu Song was haunted by his
words. *He said he'd come back for me* if *he could. Not when.* Reality stripped of the armor of optimism was nothing but naked truth—
pale and weak.

Liu Song cursed herself for needing someone. She hated herself
for introducing William to a man who had run away from his family. Her hopes were an emotional mistake, burdened with a heavy
price, one that she couldn't afford to pay again.

As she gazed despondently out the window, she saw the moon's
reflection ripple across the Duwamish River and felt the train begin
to slow. She heard the coachman ringing the bell at each street crossing, warning pedestrians and drivers alike. Liu Song stared through
the glass at the blinking radio towers that seemed to be everywhere,
the sparkling marquees. The city had been reborn during her short
lifetime as streetlights and electricity transformed each block into a
carnival of neon. Men walked the streets with purpose, with lacquered canes and polished shoes, and women crossed the streets in
bobbed hair and sequined gowns that shone pink, lilac, and peri-
winkle beneath gas lamps and the sweeping headlights of shiny au-
tomobiles. The city had grown up around her; she was a mother,
but she still felt like a lost little girl.

As she walked from the train station, her heels clicked on polished marble. She passed wives who threw their arms around their
husbands, but all she embraced was the creeping loneliness of to-

morrow. Her only comfort was in knowing who waited for her—her baby boy, who would always wait for her, always welcome her with outstretched arms that reached beyond petty judgment and unmet expectations. As she waved to the manager at the Bush Hotel, she thought she detected something strange in the man's eyes. Was it surprise, or sorrow? She felt her cheeks, where her tears had long since dried, realizing that her makeup—her mascara-streaked face—must be the calling card of the newly brokenhearted.

When she reached her door, she fumbled in her purse for the key, stopping as she heard Mildred slide back the dead bolt.

When the door opened, her friend nearly jumped. "It's you," she exclaimed in Chinese. "You're back early. I wasn't expecting you for hours . . ."

"I told you," Liu Song huffed as she saw Mildred's guilty expression. "I don't want you bringing any boyfriends over while I'm away. It's not just for William's sake. The man downstairs is always giving me sideways looks—I can't chance . . ."

"There's no one here but me."

"And William," Liu Song said with a weary, accusatory tone. *I just want to curl up with my boy and sleep for a million years, Liu Song thought.* "I'm too tired to argue . . ." She looked in the mirror near the door. Her mascara wasn't too bad.

"No," Mildred said as she fidgeted with her tiny wristwatch. "It's just me. William isn't here. Your uncle came by for a visit—he offered to take William out for ice cream. He was dressed nice and seemed like such a likable fellow . . ."

Liu Song dropped her purse and hurried to the room she shared with her son. His crib was empty. His carriage was gone. She felt light-headed and held on to the doorjamb. She'd never told Mildred who William's father was—just that he was a married man, out of reach and beyond her reckoning. And she'd never shared the details of how she and her stepparents had parted ways.

"I'm so sorry, Liu Song." Mildred grew pale as she gushed her apology in English and Chinese, as though for emphasis of her sincerity—her anguish. "I didn't see the harm. He said he was just going down to the soda counter at Owl Drug. But . . ."

Liu Song noticed the kerchief in Mildred's hands—the linen was a damp clump of worry. "How long ago—when did he leave?" Liu Song was practically shouting. She was standing on the precipice of panic, trying not to look into the abyss.

Mildred's eyes glossed over. Her mouth began to tremor, but the words wouldn't come. Liu Song held her friend's hands, which were cold and shaking. She spoke slowly, acting as calm as she could. "Mildred. This man, when did he leave . . . with my son? How long ago?"

"I'm so sorry." Mildred shook her head. "It was four hours ago. I'm so sorry, Liu Song. I'm so sorry. I didn't think anything bad would happen. He said he'd be right back, but when he didn't come back I ran up and down the street looking for them. I even went to the drugstore and asked the clerk and the soda jerk, but they hadn't seen them. I don't know where they went, or why he'd take your boy. You're family . . ."

Liu Song's estrangement from Uncle Leo must have weighed upon Mildred more with each passing hour. The discord of strained familial relations—of things left unspoken—must have been blaring like a police siren by the time Liu Song had returned. Stepparents were often the villains in fairy tales, and Liu Song had rarely mentioned Uncle Leo or Auntie Eng. Now she wished she had, as a warning.

"Please, don't tell my mother," Mildred pleaded. "Please . . ."

"Go," Liu Song said. "Go and look everywhere you can. If you find them call for the police until I get there. Do you understand? Look as long as you can." She watched as Mildred nodded through her tears and ran out the door. Then she noticed her mother's opera mask hanging on the wall. The painted heirloom had been moved, slightly.

IN THE HOTEL lobby Liu Song begged to use the telephone. She spoke with the local operator and asked to be connected to Leo Eng, but no one picked up on the other end. So she ran out the door and into the darkness in the direction of the Jefferson Laundry on South Jackson, a place she'd avoided for two years. Leo's father had lost the original business when the white unions boycotted all of the Chinese laundries twenty years ago. And if that wasn't enough, the Knights of Labor ran everyone else out of town. But like a cockroach, Leo had returned ten years later with fifty cents in his pocket and won a two-thousand-dollar lottery, enough money to reopen the laundry. This time he named it after an American president. Now he made a handsome living taking in the sheets and the towels of the local workingman's hotels—the Northern, the Panama, the Milwaukee, and the Ace. Liu Song knew the laundry would be open until at least midnight—she'd start there. Then visit the gaming parlors, one by one, until she found her stepfather. She doubted William would be with him, but finding Uncle Leo was the key to finding where he lived; then she'd deal with Auntie Eng if she had to. Liu Song pictured blood dripping in the alley, but there would be no feathers this time.

Liu Song found her uncle at the laundry, smoking and chatting with a handful of workers. He didn't seem surprised to see her. In fact, she detected a wry smile as he stubbed out his cigarette and cleared his throat. She winced as he spat on a brick wall in the alley. His excrement slowly crawled down the side of the building. He shooed away his employees and removed the white laundryman's cap he wore. He tossed it in a bin.

"Where's my son! Where is William! You had no right to take . . ."

"He's not here," Uncle Leo said. He spoke in a casual tone—as though this were a poker game and he already had the winning hand. "But I do have every right to take my son. When I got the letter from the Peterson woman, I just had to see for myself. I saw you parading that carriage up and down the street months ago—little did I know you had a surprise in there for me. I didn't believe it at first. But then I saw him, so handsome, so strong—he takes after your mother and me. I even went to the King County Clerk's Office, just to be certain. When I saw my name on the birth certificate . . ."

"What do you want?" Liu Song said. "You can have anything I have—anything but him. He's *my* son. I gave birth to him. I nursed him. He will never know who you are—he'll have nothing to do with you—I promise . . ."

"You have *nothing* to give but the boy, well, almost nothing," he said. "You can keep wet-nursing my son for a few months. And then I'm sure we can work out some arrangement where we both get what we want. But know this—I can take him from you anytime I wish. A son belongs to his father and the law is on my side. If you do your job well, I'll keep you around. I might even let him live with you."

"I'm his mother, he's only two years old . . ."

"No, you're his nanny. And if you leave town, I will come for you and take him away and you will *never see him again*. I promise you this."

Liu Song drifted between the shores of relief and horror. *I can keep him for now.* She watched as her stepfather lit another cigarette, blowing smoke.

"Your auntie Eng is walking him back to the Bush Hotel right now. You should run along. He'll need his diaper changed." As he spoke he unconsciously scratched himself inside the waistline of his trousers.

Liu Song slipped away, rubbing her arms for warmth. She wanted to take William and run—despite Uncle Leo's warnings. But she had nowhere to run to.

When she arrived back at her apartment, she found the place eerily quiet. Auntie Eng was nowhere to be seen, a stubbed-out cigarette on the floor outside her door and the accompanying smell were the only evidence of her having been there.

Liu Song trembled with relief when she found the carriage parked in the middle of her apartment, William inside, fast asleep. He looked so still, she worried that something was amiss—she couldn't help but lift him from the carriage and clutch him to her chest, feeling his warmth, his breathing, his moment of joyful, satisfied, comforted wakefulness as he smiled and touched her face. Then she smelled tobacco in his hair and on his clothing. She undressed him and drew a hot bath, wanting to scrub away every fingerprint, every odor, every taint Uncle Leo and Auntie Eng had left on her precious child.

As she dried him off, William looked up at her and smiled. Her heart was awash in hurt and anger, disappointment and fear. She wanted to take him and disappear, run away. Instead she smiled through her tears and sang a lullaby. She tickled his belly button, pretending everything would be okay.

Parting

(1925)

When Liu Song woke in the morning, she lit an old candle for her parents and solemnly placed a tea offering in her family shrine, next to the statue of Ho Hsien-ku, the only woman among the eight Chinese Immortals. Liu Song understood that kind of isolation, that loneliness. She couldn't bear to sing or act or perform or even smile. Just putting on a brave face for William when he woke up took all the emotional energy she had left from a hollow, empty, sleepless night. She'd called Mr. Butterfield from a pay phone and told him she was ill and couldn't string two notes together, and it wasn't far from the truth. As she watched William in his high chair, eating mashed carrots and taro root, she wondered what kind of life she could provide him without Colin's help, material and emotional. Her answer came with a knock on the door.

She knew it would be Colin. She'd run off, half-hoping he would go without saying goodbye but half-dreaming he'd come back and never leave.

His expression as he stood spoke his heart even before he opened his mouth. He looked like he hadn't slept, and he was still wearing the same clothes he'd had on the day before. He didn't come bearing flowers. The only thing he held in his hand was his hat.

"Cowin," William said, as he smiled with a mouth full of carrots.

Liu Song invited Colin in, but he hesitated, absently waving at her son.

"I'm sorry, Liu Song." He cleared his throat. "I had no idea that would happen last night. I knew my father was ill. My mother had sent a telegram months ago, but my mother worries too much. And they've been begging me to come home, offering any excuse for me to give up my dreams. I've ignored them for so long—too long, I guess. I didn't know my father was near death—I'm told he may not even live long enough to see me return. But I have to go."

Liu Song looked away, glanced at the clock. He must have read her mind.

"We sail today, in a few hours."

Liu Song heard William saying hello and laughing in his singsong voice. She stepped back as Colin took a step toward her. She stood between him and her son.

"If you asked me to stay . . ." Colin hesitated. "I would . . ."

"I would never ask that," Liu Song said, even as her heart screamed: *Ask!* "Family is too important. I could never impose . . ."

She watched as his posture, his face, his eyes, relaxed. He seemed relieved, as though a weight had been take off his shoulders. *But is he happy I didn't ask him to stay or happy that I understand why he has to leave?*

"You must wait for me then."

Liu Song stared back at him. *As if I have a choice.*

"But what about your . . . fiancée?" Liu Song hated saying the word. "I know I'm a single girl, without a real family, with a child—not high on anyone's list of candidates for marriage, but I thought we shared something special. I thought I meant more to you. More than just kindred spirits on the stage, before the cameras . . ."

Colin chewed his lip, then spoke. "I'm sorry, Liu Song. I never mentioned her because I never thought I would have to. I figured she'd find someone else and free me from that commitment. She was so far away . . . just a forgotten memory. You know I'd rather be here—with you, with William. I mean that. I want *you*. But I guess a part of me knew that I could only run for so long. I could only avoid my obligations back home for so many seasons. I was afraid to declare myself for you because I knew the past would eventually catch up to me. I hoped for better things . . ."

Liu Song couldn't believe what she was hearing. Her heart swelled with his unvarnished adoration—his words confirmed what she'd always felt but was afraid to believe. And yet, now he was leaving. With another woman, a girl much like herself. And none of them knew if or when he might be coming back.

"I can fix this, Liu Song. There is so much happening in America— so much we can accomplish. You know what you want and how to get there. You are your mother's daughter in every way. Keep going without me, keep singing and acting and auditioning. Don't give up on your gift—your talent is large enough to fill the screen. I'll come back as soon as I can. You have to wait for me." He reached into his billfold and handed her a wad of twenty-dollar bills. She refused, but he placed the cash on the table. It was more money than she'd ever had.

"It's all I have," he said. "Buy yourself something nice, something to remember me by, something for William, save it for a rainy day."

Liu Song smiled, sadly, because she never knew guilt had such a price; besides, it seemed that every day was rainy in Seattle. But in the end there was no one else, Liu Song realized. Just William. She'd wait for Colin as long as she could. There was no one else worth waiting for. And she didn't want to settle for less. She nodded, and Colin wrapped his arms around her, holding her closer than he ever had. She reached up, touched his shoulders, then smelled another woman's perfume and stepped away. She couldn't reconcile his words with his obligations, not yet. He tried to kiss her, but she turned her cheek and saw William smiling and laughing. She felt like crying but laughed back at him. The absurdity of her life was made apparent as he dumped his bowl on the floor. The ceramic didn't break, it merely wobbled to a halt.

"Keep singing, keep acting," Colin said. "Don't ever stop. Because that's how I'll find you when you're famous and have moved on."

Liu Song tried to ignore his flattery, yet savored every word. "I will."

"Keep performing."

My whole life is make-believe, she thought. "Always."

"I'll send a telegram as soon as I can. I promise I'll write. I'll take care of this and return and it'll be as though I'd never left."

Liu Song looked at her son and then at Colin. She collected herself and put on the performance of her life. She swallowed her tears. Then she held Colin's hand and touched his face; his cheek was warm, his skin soft. She smiled bravely and wished him safe travels and every happiness, which she could never have.

Living Arrangements

꒰

(1925)

By late winter Liu Song realized she might be waiting forever. She'd counted the days it took for Colin's steamship to reach Hong Kong and then Canton and the time it would take for a telegram to arrive letting her know that he'd made it home safely and when he might be coming back. Each evening she waited for a messenger boy from Western Union to knock on her door, and each evening she went to bed disappointed. She knew that telegrams were expensive, especially from overseas, so she didn't expect much, a few words at best, but she didn't expect silence either. When weeks of silence stretched to months, she learned to accept that quiescence as another kind of message, one she received loud and clear.

She tried to forget about Colin by staying busy at the music store, but even that happy distraction proved to be short-lived as months rolled by without selling a single player piano, even during the holiday season, when all she sang were songs like "Greensleeves," "The Twelve Days of Christmas," and "Silent Night."

William loved the holiday songs. He played inside, where it was warm, peering through the window and waving while Liu Song stood outside as it rained and rained. She smiled and kissed him through the cold glass.

Despite her street performances, which still drew large crowds, Mr. Butterfield had struggled to sell even a quarter of the sheet music he'd ordered. Everything about Butterfield's seemed old now, used, unwanted, everything collecting dust. Hand-painted advertisements and discounts hadn't helped.

William clapped and said, *"Sheng dan kuai le."* Liu Song looked at him and raised an eyebrow until he switched to English. "Merry Cwismas," he said as she walked into the store to take her break. She was proud of William's English but tired of feeling so alone during such a festive season. She sat down across from her employer.

"I'm afraid we're done for, dear," Mr. Butterfield announced as he pored over his ledger and emptied his flask into a crystal tumbler with a cracked bottom.

Liu Song looked at the clock, unsure of what he meant. It was only one in the afternoon, too early to call it a day, she thought, even though the sightseeing buses were done for the season. The days had been slower than usual, but the rainy weather always hurt business. Especially since she'd been fighting a cold and sniffling all morning. She sipped a cup of hot jasmine tea to warm her throat and soothe her voice.

"We're going the way of the dodo." Mr. Butterfield cursed as he closed his ledger and dropped the thick bound book into the trash. He waved to the financial record of his store as though parting from a lifelong friend. Then he fished out a handkerchief and dabbed at the corners of his eyes, blowing his nose as he stared out the window.

Liu Song looked across the street toward a new electronics store that had opened just in time for the holidays. That was where their business had gone. Radios had become all the rage, with three new stores opening up within blocks of the music shop. And new radio stations were popping up as well, offering more hours of live music. No one wanted player pianos anymore, especially the expensive Weltes. They were bulky and had to be tuned and watered, and the song rolls were expensive compared to the free music on the radio that could be found live in the evening hours, seven days a week.

Liu Song had thought radio might be a fad, but RCA and Crosley tube units were everywhere, even outselling the expensive Zeniths that had worried Mr. Butterfield the most.

"What now?" Liu Song asked, wanting to know the answer.

Mr. Butterfield hesitated and then loosened his tie. "I'm sorry, dear. It's been a pure joy while it lasted, but I'm afraid I can't pay you commission on what we aren't selling. You've got a magnificent voice, and you can act, and half the women in the city would kill for your cheekbones, but looks can't keep the lights on. We gave it a good fight, but I'm selling everything for half price starting tomorrow—all through the holidays. And I'll post going-out-of-business signs after New Year's. It'll probably take most of January to clear things out and settle with the bank. Then I'll close the doors for good. If you need a letter of recommendation, I'm happy to oblige."

It took a moment for Liu Song to process what she was being told. Business had always been up and down, but the city seemed to be booming, people were buying Plymouths and Pierce-Arrows, and the furriers were as busy as ever. She had thought that Mr. Butterfield would be able to adapt to the changing times. Somehow she'd hoped this was a lull, a calm before the storm of holiday business. Little did she know that that calm was a last breath, a death rattle before the end of her day job.

Mr. Butterfield handed her two dollars in change but couldn't look her in the eye as he wiped away a tear. That was all she'd made in the last week. Then he handed her a five-dollar bill on top of that. "I'm going to miss you, Liu Song. You'll always be my Willow. And I'll miss William too." Before she could thank him he'd already turned. "Please be a dear and lock up when you leave," he said as he walked away. "I've got some more drinking to do." She watched as he snapped his suspenders and disappeared into the back room. He was gone before she had time to say goodbye. She lingered in the awful silence of the music store, a permanent rest. Then she called for William, who had been playing with a windup tap dancer in the piano repair room, which sat empty. She smiled as he held up the well-worn toy. The coil had been shot from overuse, and now the tin figure hardly moved at all, but William bounced the little man along.

As they walked down the street, Liu Song searched for help-wanted signs, but she knew that jobs for women were few and far between. The only place hiring was the Jefferson Laundry. She gritted her teeth as she walked by, imagining what it would be like working as a waste girl, picking up fetid laundry, stained sheets, and soiled rags. She didn't bother walking the long way home, circumnavigating that particular business. There was no use engaging in that folly since her uncle Leo had made his presence felt on a weekly basis.

When she arrived at the Bush Hotel, she found a bundle of fresh linens from the Jefferson Laundry, neatly twined, resting on her doorstep. The sheets she found waiting each week delivered an unspoken message: *I'm watching. I'm waiting.*

Appetites

꿈

(1926)

"I'm hungry," William said, pointing to his belly button, which stuck out below a faded blue shirt that he'd all but outgrown. "I'm hungry, Ah-ma."

We never have breakfast, Liu Song wanted to remind him. She'd been out of work for months and hoped he'd be used to that fact by now. She was, but she knew he didn't understand that they'd nearly exhausted their savings, including the money Colin and Mr. Butterfield had given them. As she heated up yesterday's rice and mixed in an egg and some sprouting onions, she thought about how her mother had slowly wasted away. *Is that what's happening to us?* She skipped supper, again, and watched William eat. Her mouth watered as the thought of leftovers made her stomach ache. Once William was down for a late nap, she ate the bits he'd left behind and counted the remaining coins in her purse. She might be able to rummage for used clothing, but with what little she had she'd never be able to pay rent. They barely had enough to buy food. Mildred had left town with a boyfriend—that Andy-something. Mildred had planned to elope somewhere in California, earning money along the way by entering dance marathons. Liu Song pictured her friend with a sign on her back that read: DRINK MALTED OVALTINE, sleepwalking her way through forty days on the dance floor—for glory and one thousand dollars in prize money. *Good for you,* Liu Song thought, *but bad for me*. Without Mildred, Liu Song struggled to find someone she trusted to watch William so she could work at the Wah Mee Club. She'd tried auditioning for several small theater roles but couldn't seem to get a break without Colin's connections. And what few jobs there were for women seemed unattainable. To the white establishments, she was too Oriental, and to the Chinese establishments, she was too modern, too Western. She was tainted with a child born out of wedlock and no other family to vouch for her. And by the time she returned to what was left of the music store to ask for a recommendation, Mr. Butterfield had already left town.

She sat on the floor in William's room, listening to him snore while she read a copy of Seattle's *Screenland* newspaper. There were new shows listed, new productions advertised, new movies being filmed, but nothing that called for a Chinese actress. In desperation she woke William and dressed him in his warmest clothes. She held his hand as he sleepily walked alongside her toward the Stacy Mansion.

"Why are we here?" William asked.

Liu Song wiped his runny nose with her sleeve and rubbed his hands, his cheeks, his ears, trying to keep them warm. "Ah-ma is here to ask about a job; understand?"

William shrugged and stared up in awe at the sprawling manse; a lopsided formation of snow geese flew overhead. The birds honked as they winged their way toward Tacoma and warmer climes to the south.

Liu Song drew a deep breath. She felt guilty for bringing William along, but she didn't want to leave him alone. She was desperate, but she didn't want to appear so needy—yet she was willing to do anything for her son. Mrs. Van Buren had once said Liu Song was welcome to come back and perform. But the exclusive club looked cold and uninviting now that the grass had turned brown and the trees had lost their leaves, all but the evergreens that flanked the wrought-iron gate, which was open to let sleek cars cruise in and out. The drivers looked bored while the passengers looked elegant, giddy, and half-drunk. As Liu Song looked at the club ladies in their white gloves and mink stoles, the men in their car coats and their velvet hats, she thought that now seemed like as good a time as any.

She felt invisible as she walked to the mansion's entrance. Until the doorman said, "Hey, the servants' entrance is on the east side of the building. Go out the gate and circle around the block . . ."

"I don't work here," Liu Song said.

"Well, you sure ain't a member."

"I was hoping to speak with Mr. or Mrs. Van Buren if they're here. My name is . . ." She held William's cold hand as he leaned toward the open door, the warmth, and the smell of garlic, onions, and roast beef. "Tell them Willow is here. Willow Frost. I once performed here for the members."

The doorman looked her up and down and then told her to wait while he checked. When he returned, he presented Mrs. Van Buren, who seemed confused.

"I'm sorry, do I know you?" the woman said as she raised a cigarette holder to her lips. The doorman flashed a lighter, and Mrs. Van Buren blew a long stream of smoke into the cool air that swirled as she absently touched the string of pearls around her neck.

Liu Song felt naked in her faded dress and tattered shoes that had once barely passed for elegant. "I'm . . . Willow. Willow Frost. I performed here once . . ."

Liu Song watched as the woman's eyes narrowed when she saw William. Her pleasant smile disappeared. "You were with that Colin fellow, weren't you? He left abruptly last year for the Orient. I know some of the members here had unfinished business dealings with him. Looks like he left you in the lurch as well. I'm afraid if you're a friend of his, there's nothing we can do for you . . ." The woman shook her head and glanced at the doorman, who took Willow's arm.

"But you said I could perform here anytime," Willow said as she and William were led away. "I need work. I'm begging you. You said . . ."

"I say a lot of things. Now I'm saying goodbye."

THAT NIGHT LIU Song curled up in bed, hungry and cold; her body ached. And her threadbare sheets were old and dirty. She couldn't bear to put the fresh linens from the Jefferson Laundry on her bed. Her denial wasn't merely her pride. She'd tried the sheets once and had terrible nightmares; unlike William, who slept peacefully, his head resting on her shoulder, his arm across her belly, his tiny fingers moving slightly as though he were catching butterflies or tadpoles in his dreams. She regarded her son's sweet face as he snored—so relaxed, so untroubled, so perfect.

IN THE MORNING she bathed William and fed him the last of their rice, which had previously been an offering in their family shrine. She still felt ill and run-down from not eating enough, not sleeping well enough, from worrying, or perhaps just from loneliness and a broken heart. Whatever her maladies might be, she knew she couldn't provide for William. So she stared into the mirror and cried. For years she hadn't been able to cry, and now she couldn't seem to stop. She sobbed until the muscles in her stomach hurt and her nose was red and her cheeks were wet and her collar damp. She cried until she was exhausted. Then she sat on her worn sofa, breathing, trying not to think, trying not to feel anything anymore. The only time she let her guard down was when William would look at her and smile. He walked over, arms outstretched, and she knelt on one knee, hugging him. When she let go, he regarded her tears and asked, "Ow, Ah-ma?" He touched her tears. "Owie?"

When her nose was no longer puffy and her eyes no longer swollen from crying, she let William play as she dressed, slowly, meticulously, as though preparing for her own funeral. She regarded her tiny apartment and her son. She held William's hand and walked down the stairs, descending slowly into the cold. Out on the street she wrapped her arm around William—they needed winter clothing. They needed a lot of things.

"Where going?" William asked. His breath fogged the air.

Liu Song didn't answer as she led her son across the street.

"Ah-ma?" William asked again. "Bakey?" He pointed to the Mon Hei Bakery.

Liu Song feasted on the heavenly scent of fresh pork buns. Months had passed since she'd tasted something so delicious. She led William down the street. She couldn't speak. She was afraid that she'd burst into tears, and it took all of her energy to contain her sorrow. She stopped at a flower cart and, with trembling fingers, handed over the last of their money and pointed to a bouquet of white peonies.

The man who was selling the flowers said, "I'm sorry for your loss—death is a terrible thing," as he handed her the symbolic arrangement. Liu Song thanked the man with a stoic whisper and slowly walked away. She led William down the street, past a music store that was playing a sad song she didn't recognize. From there they cut through an alley and ended up in front of the Jefferson Laundry.

"Smell bad," William said as he pinched his nose. "I go home."

They walked inside, and Liu Song rang the service bell on the counter quickly, as though doing so would lessen the discomfort— like swallowing a spoonful of rotten cod-liver oil. She tried not to recoil when Auntie Eng stepped through a pair of wooden swinging doors. The stout woman smelled of detergent and yesterday's sweat. She snorted and forced a smile, revealing a graying tooth that had died at the root. Then she took the flowers and barked out something in Chinese, but her farmland accent was so thick even Liu Song had no idea what the woman had said.

She turned and walked into the back of the laundry, and Liu

Song heard a conversation erupt, quickly turning into a heated argument.

Liu Song looked at William, who was fidgeting as he held her hand, looking back toward the door and the restaurant across the street. As she waited she hoped the desperation and surrender in her eyes weren't as contagious as her cold. She tugged on William's hand. "I'm your ah-ma. I will always be your ah-ma. Do you believe me?"

William nodded, but he was confused. He probably would have nodded at anything if it meant going to the bakery on the way home.

When Liu Song looked up again, Auntie Eng had stepped out and was untying her waist apron, cursing at her in Cantonese as she threw it on the floor. She paused for a moment as she looked up at Liu Song, then spat in her face. Liu Song recoiled and closed her eyes while the warm, foul-smelling spittle ran down her cheeks and nose. She heard Auntie Eng storm out as she felt a rough hand place a soft towel in her hand. She wiped her face clean, trying not to gag as the disgusting smell lingered.

When she opened her eyes, Uncle Leo was standing there. He slicked his thinning hair to one side. His face was wet from perspiration and steam. He took the towel, sniffed the cotton, wiped his forehead and cheeks, and then neatly refolded it. He placed the soiled cloth atop a stack of fresh towels. He didn't say a word. He just smiled at Liu Song as if to say, *I knew you'd come back.*

Sing-Song

꒐

(1926)

A week later Liu Song stood on a cracked slab of mossy sidewalk outside the Bush Hotel, urging William to avoid the landscape of mud puddles and overflowing gutters. The heavy rain had stopped an hour ago. The afternoon sun was shining, but the water was still flowing downhill from Washington Boulevard all the way to Pioneer Square, washing away a week's worth of litter, cigarette butts, and vermin.

William laughed as he tossed a pinecone into the muck and followed it downstream until an emerald-colored automobile ran it over.

Liu Song felt as though she were watching a ghost as the old tree-green landaulet glided up to the curb. "It's time to go," she said to William as she checked her reflection in a compact mirror. She looked like her mother, the young woman she'd once seen in an old sepia photograph. But the sadness in Liu Song's eyes echoed the pain her mother had been burdened with in the years before she'd died.

This is just another role. I'm just playing a part, Liu Song thought as she put on a brave smile while William hopped up and down with excitement.

"Horses?" he asked. "We go ride them?"

Liu Song shook her head. "No, we just watch. It'll be so much fun, I promise." She looked at the new suit William was wearing. New shoes as well—a pair that fit, instead of having to squish his little toes into old, worn leathers with holes in the soles.

William frowned as he pulled at his tie and stiff, starched collar.

The driver honked, and Liu Song quickly opened the door and nodded as if in agreement to Uncle Leo. Then she helped William into the back before she sat down next to her former stepfather. He spat out the window and then grumbled, "We're late." He patted her thigh and revved the engine, pulling away before she'd even closed the door.

Liu Song felt trapped, speeding along from Chinatown to George-town, past the Rainier Brewery, which was on its last legs, relegated to bottling soda and near beer. And she felt a crushing wave of lone-liness as they passed King County Almshouse and Hospital, which sat on a one-hundred-acre stretch of farmland. Liu Song remem-bered her family being turned away on the stone steps of that brick building. But back then the property had been packed with tents. She touched her nose as she recalled the entire greenbelt redolent of wet canvas and night soil as people lay dying of the flu. She missed her family. A part of her wished she had died at home along with her father and her brothers, and in a way, part of her had. With every mile, she sank further into her regrets, but she'd thought about her desperate straits, and like her mother, she had no choice. She was doing this for William, who sat in the back and laughed and smiled as if this were the best day he'd had in forever, and sadly, it probably was. He smiled all the way to Meadows Race Track.

"I will introduce you as Liu Song—no last name," Uncle Leo informed her.

That's fine with me. I'm finally free of your name, but now I belong to you again.

"We'll be meeting with men—colleagues from the Chong Wa As-sociation, a hotel owner, a labor foreman for the Alaskeros, all very important men."

Liu Song nodded.

"You'll come and go with my permission," Uncle Leo said. "You might sing for them sometime, but you'll perform for me and no one but me."

That was their arrangement, which even Auntie Eng had accepted. Liu Song had agreed to be Uncle Leo's *xi sang*. She'd escort him to social occasions, grace the room for his business meetings, and entertain his associates at his pleasure. But she knew that wasn't all that was expected of her. She was his, a sing-song girl in every way.

She watched William's head bob in the backseat as he nodded off. She drew a tired breath, struggling to keep her composure. She'd given herself to Uncle Leo in order to keep William fed, clothed, cared for—this was what she had to do to keep him by her side. She was like Margarita Fischer in *The Sacrifice*, taking someone else's burden to protect a member of her family.

Liu Song had been to the Meadows only once, as a little girl. She recalled trainloads of people, dressed in their weekend finery, packed into open cattle cars. She remembered the smell of grass and hay and the sight of the muddy, mile-long track, surrounding a placid pond, cattails swaying in the breeze. There must have been ten thousand people in the grandstand that day, screaming, cheering. Everyone had been so excited on the way down but seemed drunk and dejected on the ride back.

She walked holding Leo's arm, about to direct William to the grandstand when Leo barked, "This way!" He pointed to the opulent clubhouse and then cleared his nose, wiped his hand on his pants, and straightened his tie. He looked out of place as they sat on the lower porch at a wicker table where tuxedoed waiters brought them pitchers of ice water, peeled oranges, and lemon slices with honey. Two white men and a Filipino man joined them and talked about his laundry, unions, contracts, promises, and the startling beauty at Leo's side. Liu Song smiled politely and kept an eye on William as he stood behind a painted rail near the track, watching horses parade by before heading to the starting gate.

Liu Song listened and regarded the wealthier patrons as they passed Leo's table and headed upstairs to the veranda. These men and women were all furs, jewels, laughter, and smiles—not haughty, just oblivious to those with less. Though a few men paused and smiled at Liu Song, kissing her hand and chatting with Uncle Leo as he smiled back and nodded. That was when she understood the value of a *xi sang*. Leo was too controlling to give her to other men (she hoped), but he wasn't above using her to attract their favor. Leo grinned and was about to speak when all eyes turned to the entrance, where everyone was fawning over a handsome couple as they made a dramatic entrance. Even Liu Song recognized them as they swept into the clubhouse and ventured upstairs, pausing for photos and autographs.

Uncle Leo furrowed his brow.

"That's Molly O'Day and Richard Barthelmess," Liu Song gushed to Leo and his associates. "I read that they're filming *The Patent Leather Kid* at Camp Lewis, south of Tacoma." The other men smiled and pointed, in awe of the stars and somewhat impressed with her knowledge, which only seemed to irritate Uncle Leo.

As the commotion faded, a bugler played the Call to the Post. Everyone double-checked their betting slips and waited for the bell to ring and the horses to come thundering out of the gate. All but Liu Song, who glanced at William and then back toward Richard Barthelmess, who was watching the race unfold from the staircase. She remembered his piercing eyes and his cleft chin from *The Yellow Man and the Girl*. He'd played Cheng Huan, a Buddhist who cared for Lillian Gish, his broken blossom—the unwanted and abused daughter of a prizefighter. Liu Song had read about a reporter so upset by the scenes of abuse that he'd left the set to vomit.

Liu Song shook her head solemnly as she remembered the tragic ending, where Lillian was beaten to death. Cheng Huan had built a shrine in her honor before taking his own life.

As a wave of cheering swept across the clubhouse, Liu Song turned her attention to the track. Spectators rose to their feet for the finish. Some bettors screamed with joy; others swore and tore their tickets, pitching them into the air, where the pieces rained down like confetti at a parade. She watched as William stood with his hands outstretched, trying to catch the bits of paper as they flitted about. He caught a handful and smiled at her. She clapped for him, blowing him kisses.

Then behind William she saw the triumphant jockey riding his Thoroughbred to the winner's circle. The small man was clad in leather and silk, with whip in hand. Liu Song grimaced when she saw the welts on the horse's back and foreleg. She ached for the exhausted horse as she watched its muscles twitch and could smell the sweat and fear. She felt Leo's hand on her backside and was jealous of the blinders the horse wore. She wished she had something similar to shut out the world.

Mother's Daughter

(1934)

William walked alongside his mother, who had had enough of the Bush Hotel and the memories that came with it. He followed her across the street, past a man on the corner of Jackson who was passing out pamphlets and yelling, "The Russians did it!" while a muralist painted a scene with George Washington in it on the opposite street. They stepped around families who huddled for warmth near gushing steam vents and avoided policemen who looked weary of another night of having to relocate vagrants.

"But what happened to Colin?" William asked as they walked. He wasn't sure how much more he wanted to know about his father—Uncle Leo. There had been such unspoken sadness throughout his childhood. He'd assumed—no, he'd hoped—that the man he'd seen off and on had been Colin. Now it dawned on him that the man in his life must have been someone else. "Did he ever come back for us?" *Did he come back for you?*

Willow nodded. "The morning after his fiancée had showed up he packed his things and then came to see me. He was a wreck of apologies and excuses and prior commitments. My heart hurt to see him. He came to say goodbye. He finally professed his adoration, but his actions didn't match his words. He left the same day. He had to go—even I understood that. He had a mother to take care of and a family business to save, a beautiful fiancée to share his life with—

all of his ambitions here, all of his plans were an escape—the spotlight faded and the curtain fell upon all of his hopes and my dreams of a life with him, a better life for us. But I didn't give up acting."

William listened to his mother, who seemed like a shadow of the woman she portrayed on-screen. She rubbed her thin arms to ward off the chill in the air.

"I was so hurt, so angry with him, but also so desperate and frightened of the possibility of losing you." Willow shook her head. "Colin left me heartbroken. But he promised to come back for me. He left me with money, some money anyway. He promised to set things right. He said that he'd find a partner to run his father's business, or force his brother to fill his shoes. He said that the woman who had shown up was a problem he would resolve. That he wanted me to carry on as best I could. That we would fix this whole mess and start over—he begged for me to have patience. He wrote to me and said that he was a dragon and I was his phoenix. And that one day we would be together again and my life would change, I'd transform."

"When did he come back?"

William watched his mother for a long time. She didn't answer, then finally shook her head. "It took him a year to write that, and by that time I'd given up all hope. Then the letters came, quite often. And in those letters he said that he'd return as soon as he could—six months more, perhaps—a year at the most." William watched as she drew a ragged breath and exhaled slowly. "But those months became five long years."

The same amount of time I've been at Sacred Heart. William recognized the irony. *Right after you said you'd be right back.*

"I'd lost my job when the music store closed. I was an unwed mother, a dancer, and no man in his right mind would have anything to do with me. Besides, if I married a Chinese man, I'd lose my citizenship and might have to go to China—a place I'd never been. I had no idea what that would mean for you. But I couldn't marry a white man either, not that anyone wanted me for more than . . ." She trailed off. "My reputation was in the gutter. I lived in fear of losing you permanently to the state at best and Uncle Leo at worst. For months I went to bed every night weary, hungry, sick, and fearing a knock on the door. I woke every morning rushing to your bed to make sure you were still there. Your third birthday came and went. I didn't even celebrate it."

William stopped his mother, who was so lost in the story that she almost walked into traffic. When the light changed, he walked her across the street. They passed a familiar alley, and William heard music and boisterous sounds from the Wah Mee Club—gamblers cheering on a winning streak, and a collective groan when someone rolled an unlucky seven.

"I worked two, sometimes three jobs—everything temporary, singing, dancing, and acting a little, when I could, which wasn't very often," his ah-ma continued. "But as my mother found out years earlier, women's jobs don't pay very much, hardly enough to live on. I even went back to the Stacy Mansion, hoping to find work as a singer, but I had been a novelty, yesterday's news. They barely remembered me, and nobody cared. As a last resort I approached Mrs. Peterson for a mother's pension. I even let some local priest splash water on your head so you'd qualify. I tried desperately to better my English so you could speak like an American. But she turned me down. She said I wasn't old enough to be a pensioner and that if I loved you I should just give you up. I left her office and never went back. In the end, I had a tiny bit of money tucked away. That got us by for a while. I made it last as long as I could."

As they walked, William wondered where they were going. In the darkness his ah-ma seemed more ghost than human, more shade than substance, more of a memory than a mother. He watched as she touched an old movie poster that had been pasted to a brick wall; the paper was cracked and chipped, peeling. As they walked the air seemed fresher, the sounds of motorcars and club music more familiar. He'd walked King Street before with his ah-ma, years ago. They'd walked this avenue often.

"I was only a girl," she said as tears streamed down her cheeks. "But as Colin always pointed out, I was my mother's daughter and I could always act—always put on a performance. So I took on a new role as a *xi sang*. Leo had always wanted a sing-song girl— a pretty girl to accompany him, someone he could show off. And I wanted you. So I pawned my dignity, for whatever it was worth." She paused as though she were waiting for a reaction, one of anger or rejection. William didn't know how to feel or what to say, so he said nothing and kept walking.

"I went to meetings and socials, and sang and performed opera for Leo and his clients. I was his . . . *companion*. And he paid my rent and let me keep you. He even let you come along on some of our outings," she said as she stared into the darkness. "I . . . made the best of the worst of things. I kept going. For three long years, I kept playing my part, always thinking I would get away—that I'd take you and we'd disappear. But I could never save up enough money to be sure. And I was afraid that if we fled and failed to escape, I'd lose you forever. Then the world fell apart."

"The Crash?" William asked as he looked around the street and saw boarded-up buildings and a man sleeping on a park bench, cradling a half-empty wine bottle like a mother holding a child. The rounders were everywhere, men who worked all summer and drank all winter, drifting from one mission home to another.

His ah-ma paused for a moment, then kept walking. "That too."

Gilded

꿈

(1929)

Liu Song opened the fine silk robe Uncle Leo had given her and turned sideways in front of the bathroom mirror. Her hands contoured her belly, which two months earlier had been smooth, flat, and soft to the touch. Now her belly felt as firm as a green winter melon. Her stomach protruded as though she'd gorged herself on an eight-course meal, taking extra helpings of dessert. After years of being careful and taking every precaution, of surviving close calls and drinking the bitter root tea prescribed by the old, white-bearded man at the Hen Sen herb shop, her worst nightmare had repeated itself. Liu Song didn't look as though she was carrying a child, yet, but she certainly felt pregnant. Her nausea hadn't been as bad as it had been with William. She drank ginger ale and smoked clove cigarettes, which helped to keep her food down. But she was sore, seemingly everywhere. Her sensitive parts felt more sensitive. She found that she could cry for hours for any reason and sometimes no reason at all, though she certainly had her pick of subjects to rue, the least of which was simply remembering who the father was. Liu Song shuddered and rubbed the goose bumps on her arms.

Mercifully, she hadn't seen Uncle Leo in weeks. It took months for the Crash to reach Seattle, but when it did everyone, including her former stepfather, felt its arrival. When regular orders at the laundry had disappeared in a wave of cancellations, he'd fired all of his longtime workers and replaced them with cheaper labor, which in Chinatown was saying something. And as she had watched some of those workers move out of the Bush, American, and Northern hotels and into flophouses, she wondered how long it might be before she was out on the street as well. *Would he force us to move in with him?* she wondered. *Or will I work folding sheets and duvet covers instead of accompanying him to the horse races and the Wah Mee on Saturday nights?* If only she could be that fortunate. The end of Prohibition was nowhere in sight, but even if it was, there wasn't enough gin and whiskey in the world to make her forget the price she'd paid for the sordid life she'd created for herself.

Liu Song tried to read the newspaper. She didn't know much about the stock market, or speculating, or buying on margin, or any of the complicated terms that headlined *The Seattle Star* these days. But she knew what dying slowly was all about, and everyone was struggling to hang on, each neighborhood was slipping away bit by bit as each new bank would fail to open its doors. The runs on the banks got so bad that People's North End Bank equipped their storefront with tear-gas nozzles. And when the sawmills began to lay off leathernecks by the thousand, the world of workingmen toppled to the ground like falling timber. Liu Song tried to be grateful for her gilded cage, but the bars were everywhere she looked.

"I'm going to school now," William said from somewhere in the kitchen. He was so much older now, a bit taller, more adventurous. Ready for school.

Liu Song closed her robe and tied it around her waist. She wandered to the front door, where William was ready for another week as a first grader at the Pacific School on Twelfth and Jefferson. "Don't forget you have Chinese school today." She handed him a wooden writing slate with Cantonese characters etched into the frame.

She raised an eyebrow as he frowned. "Yes, you have to go. I know it means you're going to two schools, working twice as hard—that just means you'll be twice as rich. Don't be late—for either school." William had been learning city Cantonese at the new Chong Wa building, but he preferred English to Chinese. As a boy of seven years, he spoke English almost as well as she did.

"Do you have another date this weekend?" William asked.

"I don't think so," Liu Song lied. She had hidden most of her dates with Uncle Leo from William, including the one this weekend. But she wasn't sure how much longer she could maintain that charade. She'd taken William out with them on occasion, to the Jun-bo Seafood Restaurant, the Sunken Garden in Lakewood, and the Coal Miners' Picnic, but he was older now and they were more discreet. Years had passed since the last time Uncle Leo visited her apartment, and even then they'd had a terrible argument about him showing up unexpectedly. Her shame, her sacrifice, couldn't remain hidden forever. And perhaps she wouldn't have to hide anymore.

Liu Song looked at the clock and then slipped to the bedroom as excited as a child before the Lunar New Year celebration. She peeked beneath her bed and found her mother's valise—a familial treasure chest with all that remained of the person she used to be and might still be again.

As she opened the valise, she regarded the slip of yellow paper that sat atop her keepsakes. She touched the telegram that had come the week before—it was real. She sighed with relief. She wasn't dreaming. The message sent via Western Union hadn't vanished in the night along with her hopes. She read the telegram again; it was unbelievably long. At twenty-five cents a word, it must have cost a small fortune to send, so she savored each letter, each punctuation mark. The sender had never been one to spare any expense. Even during times of hardship. He poured out his heart, laced with apologies for being gone so long.

Liu Song lay on the floor, clutching the note to her chest. Today was the day. Today, Colin was coming back for her.

Seconds

丂

(1929)

Liu Song stood apart from the crowd that waited at Pier 36. She heard seabirds and wrinkled her nose as murky green seawater lapped at the pilings, which were crusted with barnacles, tube worms, and the occasional fat, purple starfish. The waterfront normally smelled its best when the tide was high, even if those smells were laced with diesel fumes or reeked of old nets filled with Dungeness crab. But as Liu Song looked southward, to where the Skinner & Eddy shipyard lay eerily quiet, she noticed squatters in tents and cardboard shacks dumping pails of yesterday's night soil into the Puget Sound. Her stomach turned as she watched seagulls swoop down into the muck, until the blast of a horn scared them away, if only for the moment.

She watched as the steamship *Tantalus* edged along the pier with the help of a tugboat. The ship's towering blue smokestacks blasted billowing clouds of white steam that swirled and eventually became one with the overcast sky. She remembered her parents mentioning the Blue Funnel Line, speaking of the China Mutual Steamship Company with affection. It was the same way she felt as she watched passengers descend the gangplank after pursers punched their tickets.

Liu Song hardly recognized Colin, even as he waved and smiled. He'd gained weight, especially around the middle, and wore a dark suit that made him look more serious than she remembered. She expected him to hold her, to hug her neck, or kiss her on the mouth as the Caucasian travelers did, but he merely shook her hand, though he didn't seem to want to let go.

"You look exactly as I remember." He spoke in Chinese with a thicker accent than before. His English had faltered during his absence.

"You look . . . better," Liu Song said sweetly.

They had lunch at the elegant King Fur Cafe even though Liu Song could hardly eat. Colin was quick to complain about the food and the service. "The waiters are so much better in Hong Kong—much more efficient. They dress nicer and can ladle your soup and light your cigarette at the same time."

Liu Song thanked him as he paid the bill. "You must be tired," she said. "I'm still at the old place. Come over and relax. You can take your shoes off—" Liu Song caught herself. She didn't want to appear too forward—too desperate.

As Colin walked her back to the Bush Hotel, both of them relaxed and Liu Song found herself swept away all over again, even as his belongings were taken to the Sorrento, a fine hotel she'd only seen from the outside. It didn't matter; Chinatown was their city—it was where they belonged. Though she wished so much time hadn't passed.

He sat on her new sofa while she made oolong tea and put fresh almond cookies on a small ceramic dish. "You must be doing well despite these times of strife," Colin said, but the words came out as more of a question. "You have many nice things. New couch. New carpets, I see."

Liu Song explained how the music store had gone out of business and how she'd picked up a few jobs here and there that paid the bills. She nibbled on a semiburnt cookie as she fought a wave of nausea and tried to sit so her stomach didn't show. Colin's last few letters had mentioned that his father's bank had struggled like everywhere else, but that he thought the worst of it was over. He'd found new investors, who were buying lumber equipment and shipping it back to China. He'd come to close the deal, but most of all, he wanted to see her.

Liu Song didn't want to ask, but the question lingered between them like a ghost. "And how is your . . . wife?" In the few letters she'd written she'd never once asked about his fiancée and he'd never surrendered that information. She assumed the subject was settled and wasn't worth talking about.

Colin loosened his tie ever so slightly. He looked at Liu Song and half-smiled, half-frowned. "Good Chinese wife, made me nice and round." He patted his stomach. "And she's given me two children, a boy and a girl—both healthy and strong. I named my daughter after you. I named her Willow."

Liu Song drifted between disappointment and denial, but still managed to smile and laugh, not quite believing him about the name. "Does she know about me?" *Do I still mean anything to you, and should she worry—should I?* "Does she know that you're here with me right now?" Considering her arrangement with Uncle Leo, Liu Song felt hypocritical questioning Colin about his intentions, but she had to know.

"I've told her everything." He hesitated, fidgeting, and then looked into her eyes. "I've even told her that I want to marry you."

Liu Song almost dropped her teacup.

"I came here on business," Colin said, "but I had something else to attend to—a proposal to make, to you, Liu Song. I wouldn't be so crass as to ask in a letter, or a telegram. I don't even know about your life now, I may have no right to ask such a thing. But I had to see you, had to see how you're doing, had to see if you're still pursuing the dream that I had to give up. And I had to ask if you'd take me as your husband."

Liu song's heart leapt while her stomach turned.

"I . . . I don't know what to say," she stammered. "All these years I've hardly allowed myself to dream such a thing." The room was spinning. "But what about your wife—you'd leave her behind? You'd leave your children?" The thought was abhorrent to Liu Song. She'd done the worst of things to keep William. She could never envision giving him up, even if Colin offered her the world to return to China, she would not consider that option without her son.

Colin sat back and rubbed his forehead. "I don't think you fully understand . . ."

"I don't." Liu Song felt flattered, but confused more than anything. "What else is there to understand? What aren't you telling me?" *That you love me?*

"I love *us,*" Colin said as he touched her hand. "I've saved my father's business. I'm a wealthy man. I would split my time between Canton and Seattle. I can afford both families. I gave up my dreams, but that doesn't mean I have to give you up."

Liu Song closed her eyes and tried not to cry. Not this way. Not again. She tried to process what Colin was saying. She opened her eyes and looked at his pained, sincere face. She finally understood. "You would take me as a second wife?"

He seemed to shrink before her eyes. He looked hurt at the accusation, but the statement was true. "I . . . already have a *second* wife—that's how I've always seen her, Liu Song. She's an obligation, a promise that I had to keep. I do my best by her. But I want *you* as my first wife. That's why I've come all this way, to ask you this in person."

Liu Song stared back in disappointment, in disbelief. She did love him, she wanted to be with him, not just for William's sake but to satisfy every unfulfilled wish she'd ever had. But he wasn't the same man as the one who'd left. He'd changed from an actor to a tap dancer. He was Daddy Rice with metal plates on his wingtips. He was Al Jolson in *The Jazz Singer.*

Colin kept dancing. "Plenty of businessmen do this, Liu Song. It makes sense. I could provide for you—you could pursue your acting and singing and anything your heart would desire. I can take care of William as well."

Compared to the sorry life she had now, his proposal was beyond reasonable. And their marriage wouldn't be recognized here, so she wouldn't have to leave with him. Mildred would have leapt at the chance with arms wide open. But Liu Song would be no different than the person she was yesterday, party to another compromised arrangement to another man. *You are your mother's daughter.* The words spun in her head.

Liu Song felt her stomach turn again, this time with cramping instead of nausea. She held her breath and counted until the pain went away, but her thoughts were reeling. She heard small footsteps and saw the door open. She'd forgotten what time it was. William walked in smiling.

"Hello," William said as he set down his book bag and asked his mother if he could have a cookie. She gave him hers.

"This must be William," Colin gushed. "Look at you—you've grown so much!"

"William," Liu Song said, "say hello to Mr. Kwan."

"You remember me, don't you?" Colin asked.

William nodded and smiled politely, but his eyes betrayed his confusion. Colin didn't seem to notice. He kept complimenting William.

Liu Song excused herself to the bathroom, unsure if she were going to throw up. Her stomach ached and her forehead was pale and damp. She splashed water on her face and breathed as slowly and deeply as she could until the pain subsided.

When she returned she asked her son to do his chores and went downstairs with Colin. They chatted about William until they reached the street. She had to see the neighborhood for what it was, poor, broken, and infested with hopelessness. Starving immigrants from barren farms who had arrived years earlier to work in the canneries now sat on the sidewalk banging their chopsticks on empty rice bowls. And there was heavy black smoke billowing into the sky in the distance, in the direction of Hooverville. Liu Song wondered if the army had gone in again and burned everything down. Despite all the hardships, she was grateful to have been born here, but she still had to acknowledge the raw, unvarnished life she had and compare it to the one Colin was offering her. She'd waited five years for him, never truly expecting him to return—it had seemed better that way. To forever be longing was better than to forever be disappointed.

"Can I take you to dinner? You and . . ."

"William." *Have you forgotten his name already?*

"Actually, you and the president of Blanchard Lumber, and perhaps a few others."

Liu Song paused. "You want me to join you for a business meeting?"

"Oh, you make it sound like an execution at dawn. I promise it won't be that bad. And afterward we can sneak away and talk about our future."

I want to be more than a sing-song girl. "I . . . don't think we have a future." Liu Song couldn't believe what she was saying.

Colin seemed dumbfounded, as though rejection were a possibility he had never considered. He opened his mouth as if to speak, then closed it again.

Liu Song looked at Colin and for the first time in her life felt sorry for him. It didn't diminish what her heart felt, but her head was telling her something else. He'd been headstrong in his pursuit of acting, headstrong in his father's banking business, headstrong in everything he wanted. He was kind and from a family of means and still so handsome. But he was someone else's father, someone else's husband. Liu Song had sacrificed everything for William— *everything*. Colin had sacrificed nothing for her.

She watched as the severity of her words found purchase in his heart. He pointed to an old man with one arm, selling bruised apples on the street. "Look around you. You have nothing. I can give you everything. You can pursue your dreams. Why deny yourself what you deserve?"

What do I deserve? Liu Song thought long and hard as she stared at the despair of the street, the depravity of the laundryman down the avenue. She looked up at Colin and for once wasn't acting—she was her true self. That person, her mother's daughter, had been absent a very long time. She welcomed her back.

"I just realized that I'm perfect for you," she said as Colin turned to her and smiled with relief. "It's just that you're not perfect for me."

SHE DIDN'T EXPLAIN to William where Colin had gone and, fortunately, he didn't ask. He listened to *Let's Pretend* on the radio while she heated up a tin of tofu with pimiento and green onions. And while they ate she wondered how much money she had saved up and if it was enough to move to someplace far away from Uncle Leo.

"How would you like to go to California?" she asked William. "To live."

William spoke with his mouth full. "Why? What's wrong with right here?"

"I'm serious. They say it's sunny all the time in California. And there are sandy beaches everywhere. There's a Chinatown in Los Angeles that's twice as large as our neighborhood. There's more acting jobs. More things to do."

Liu Song watched her son as he kept eating, sucking on the ends of his chopsticks, unsure if he believed that she was serious. She wondered how hard it would be for him to leave his school, his friends, everything he'd known.

"Okay," he said.

"Okay what?" she asked.

William shrugged and kept eating. "I'm okay with moving . . ."

"You wouldn't miss your friends, miss your home?"

William looked at her and smiled, somewhat confused, as if she'd just asked the most ridiculous question. "Home isn't my school. Home is wherever you are."

Liu Song smiled and gave William her bowl. She couldn't eat. Her stomach was still aching. But her heart felt full. She realized that she'd been waiting here for Colin, and with that tether gone she was adrift. She was saddened, free, and ready to risk the storm that might follow her if she fled Seattle.

But first she needed to get through the night, because the sewing needles in her stomach were unrelenting. She tucked William into bed and drew a hot bath. She touched her belly and wondered why this was happening now. Was it Colin? Or was her body merely deciding to leave Uncle Leo, rejecting all that remained of him, of her old, broken life, even before her heart and mind had decided?

She remembered her mother talking about losing a baby once. She tried to remain calm as she slowly undressed, tied her hair up high with a broken chopstick, and slipped into the tub, feeling the warmth envelop her, soothing the pain, which came in waves, like the backbeat rhythm of a heartbeat. She watched the water turn a ruddy pink and felt hot and light-headed one moment, then so chilly that her teeth were chattering the next. Her cheeks felt cold as warm tears cascaded to her chin and dropped into the bathwater.

She closed her eyes and saw her parents. She saw her future, far away from here, beneath spotlights with cameras and cheering fans. She heard music to songs that she'd never had the courage to sing. She tried to open her eyes, but she felt sleepy, and when she did raise her eyelids, her vision was blurry, shadowy, as though she were staring through a tunnel, a portal that was closing. She tried to call for help, to call for William, to call for anyone, but her eyelids refused to stay open. Finally the pain subsided as warmth surrounded her and she allowed the darkness to swallow her whole.

Sanitarium

(1929)

Liu Song woke to the sound of stiff leather shoes upon a polished wooden floor. She opened her eyes, but all she saw was white: a white ceiling, white walls, white linens, and white skin. Her eyes ached and her lips felt dry; the tender skin was coarse and chapped, peeling. She was burning up with fever.

With her eyes slowly adjusting to the light, she winced as a grim-faced nurse slipped something cold and metallic into her mouth. The nurse glanced up at the clock on the wall, but Liu Song's vision was still too blurry for her to read what time it was. Then the nurse snatched the thermometer, read it quickly, shook it, and stepped to the next bed, where she slipped the thermometer in the mouth of another patient.

Liu Song slowly turned her head and tried to count the beds. It seemed as though she was sharing the room with six other women: one black, one Indian, the rest white, one feebleminded—all of them young, all of them looking better than she felt.

The black woman smiled and waved. Liu Song tried to wave back but found that her arms and legs had been bound to the bed by thick leather straps. Horrified, she strove not to panic. She felt suffocated, every part of her body aching, itching, her skin crawling. She tried to escape, the only way she could, by running to the darkest, safest corner of her mind. The place Uncle Leo could never find.

"Do you understand English?" the nurse asked.

Liu Song vaguely remembered where she was and nodded. "Yes."

"Then I can tell you it's for your own good, dearie," the nurse said as she pointed to Liu Song's restraints from two beds away. The nurse kept wending her way around the room with the thermometer in hand. "That way you don't get all restless and pull out the stitches in your sleep."

Liu Song tried to move but was too dizzy and weak; her body didn't respond as though it belonged to her. She looked down and discovered stains on her shirt from where she'd thrown up on herself. Someone had cleaned her up, but she still smelled of ripe stomach acid and a hint of onion. She looked toward her belly but couldn't see past the covers. And whenever she shifted her weight or moved her hips, she felt stabbing pains near her belly button.

She heard the nurse again. "Take it easy over there, you've had surgery."

Liu Song blinked, confused. "Surgery?" She looked around, slowly realizing that she was in a hospital of sorts, a recovery room.

"You've been sterilized."

Liu Song didn't understand the word. "Where's my son?"

"You lost the baby, hon," the nurse said without looking up. Liu Song watched as the woman made notes on a clipboard before hanging the slab of wood on the wall. "Maybe it's God's way of saying you're not cut out for motherhood," she said without even a shrug of concern. "Are you still in pain?"

Liu Song remembered William and shook her head, but hot tears began to run down her cheeks. She bit her tongue, trying to hold in her emotions.

The nurse disappeared from view for a minute, then came back with a sponge and a bottle of something that smelled like dreaming.

Liu Song shook her head as the nurse sprinkled a few drops on the sponge and put it in a mask, then wrapped the mask around Liu Song's head. She didn't want to breathe. She was afraid they were trying to kill her, poisoning her, afraid she'd never wake up. In a fit of panic she looked around the room and saw that the black woman had pulled up her gown and was touching the scar above her belly button.

Liu Song closed her eyes again. Her last conscious thoughts were of William.

WHEN LIU SONG woke it was morning. She could tell that her fever had passed. The only warmth she felt now was from the sun shining through the barred window. As her stomach reminded her that she hadn't eaten, she looked around, but all she saw was a bowl of broth next to her bed with a thin soup skin on the top. She couldn't help thinking that if her mother were here she would have made her *gai jow* with dried wood ears and tiger lily buds. Her mother had credited the chicken-wine soup with saving Liu Song from the flu. If only the concoction had saved the rest of her family.

Liu Song noticed that two of the other patients were up and a nurse was helping them out the door and down the hallway. That gave her hope that this ordeal would soon be over. But then a familiar woman walked in and stared at Liu Song with pinched lips and a wrinkled forehead, as though she were a riddle to be solved, a social equation with an empirical answer.

"Mrs. Peterson," Liu Song said. The woman's presence was not a comfort.

"So you do recognize me? That's good I suppose. That just means you can trust me and what I'm about to say."

Liu Song felt her stomach ache again—whether from the lack of food, nerves, or the surgery, she couldn't be sure. She reached toward her nightstand and found a glass of water. She emptied the glass in two large gulps.

"When can I go home? Where's my son?"

Mrs. Peterson looked at a folder in her lap. "You can go home when we decide what to do with your son."

Liu Song tried not to panic, tried not to tell herself stories with unhappy endings. She needed to be calm, rational. She needed to be a good mother.

"Right now, the plan is to contact the father and have him take William, permanently. You've never married. You've gotten pregnant, again. You were found in the bathtub, in terrible shape, doing deplorable things . . ."

Liu Song didn't understand. The woman spoke too fast.

"My only regret is that your son wasn't taken from you at birth. Who knows what damage you've done to him. It's better that he's with his father. It's not too late . . ."

"His father doesn't want him. Please . . ." Liu Song knew that wasn't true. Leo might not want the burden of raising a son, but it was common for childless couples to adopt or buy a child outright. Such arrangements weren't entangled with love or actual emotion. They were solely practical. If a child was adopted into a Chinese family and given a good name, that name came with the responsibility to care for his elders—a social debt that was expected to be paid. After all, a child owed everything to his parents. And in the meantime, Leo might relish free help in the laundry. Or Auntie Eng might have use for William as a house servant. Liu Song shook her head.

Mrs. Peterson looked at the other patients in the recovery room. "Well, considering your estranged relationship with Mr. Eng, I suppose we could make an exception. Think of it as an act of charity— grace, if you will. The sisters at Sacred Heart could take your son, but understand that this would be permanent. You'd be giving him up for adoption, and odds are, *no one* will adopt him. But at least he'll have a moral upbringing and there will be plenty of other kids his age. He might even make friends."

Liu Song desperately wanted to see her son, to hold William, to run away. "Are those my only options?" she asked, trying not to cry.

"Give him up to Mr. Eng," Mrs. Peterson said, "or take your chances with an orphanage. It's a moot point to me."

Liu Song stared at her empty hands for what seemed like hours. Scared and alone, again, she felt her heart pounding, her hopes and dreams bent across an anvil, waiting to be hammered. *I can't give him anything, not even my name,* Liu Song thought. *But I'll never give him to Leo.* She looked up at Mrs. Peterson and whispered, "The orphanage. Where do I sign?"

When the papers were read and signed through a fog of disbelief, disconnection, Liu Song gave Mrs. Peterson an hour's worth of parental instruction—William's favorite food, favorite toy, favorite bedtime story, and she resigned herself to fatigue and her bottomless well of sadness. She didn't ask if he'd be allowed a photo of her or if he might know who his family was. She couldn't bear to hear the answers. She could hardly breathe through her tears.

"You could at least thank me," Mrs. Peterson said as she was about to leave. "I've done you, and your son, a tremendous favor."

The woman stood in the doorway as the clock on the wall ticked away a lonely minute. She tapped her foot on the wooden floor.

"Thank you," Liu Song whispered as she cried softly.

Liu Song listened to the woman's footsteps as she walked away. She heard the door at the end of the long hallway open and close. She sat motionless as an orderly came and went. She watched the man help each of the other women into a wheelchair and take them away. When he left with the last woman, the black woman, Liu Song took a deep breath and then screamed. She screamed until she tore her stitches and the sheets dotted red. She screamed and flailed her bare legs, tearing out her hair as nurses and orderlies stormed into the room and fell upon her, wrenching her to her side, a meaty hand shoving her head into a pillow as she wailed until she felt a pinch in her thigh and her tears were the only things that moved.

Daughter of the Dragon

回

(1934)

William didn't fully understand his ah-ma's plight, but he knew that whatever she'd done, she'd done it for him, which left him feeling loved and guilt-ridden at the same time. As he searched his memories, he vaguely remembered Colin and Uncle Leo, but he never forgot his mother's sadness. The only time he remembered her feeling truly at ease was during the Lunar New Year's celebration. They'd dress in red and watch the parade on Seventh Avenue, waiting for the *liu bei* to look their way. The actors who dressed up as the black and gold lion would strut and bob, weave and lunge, as musicians banged drums, gongs, and cymbals. Some would even light strings of firecrackers that flashed and echoed between the brick buildings, filling the air with smoke. His ah-ma would hand him a red envelope wrapped in a lettuce leaf to feed the lion, pacifying the beast and sparing him for another year.

Then they'd return to their apartment, where they would sweep away yesterday's grime, the dirt, and dust. Only after she had cleaned every corner would his ah-ma relax, completely exhausted. It was as though she were sweeping away the past, the cobwebs, the spiders, and the dead things in her mind.

As he followed her along Second Avenue toward midtown, William stared up at the Smith Tower, which was closed. The only light came from the glowing pyramid at the top, a beacon rising high above the garbage-strewn streets.

"Taking me to the Wishing Chair?"

His mother didn't smile. She merely shook her head. "I want to show you something. I want you to see who I am." She pointed to the small building next door, the Florence Theatre, with its new, glittering sign that advertised talkies. William had never been to the second-run theater, which was showing *Daughter of the Dragon*.

William had heard of Sax Rohmer's books and movies featuring the nefarious Dr. Fu Manchu, but Sister Briganti had never approved of them. Still, that didn't keep his classmates from drawing on handlebar mustaches and pulling their eyes back in an attempt to look mysterious and dangerous.

William stood in line as his ah-ma bought two tickets. They sat together in the middle of the theater, whispering through the newsreel and a cartoon of *Flip the Frog*.

"Is that why you gave me up?" William finally asked. "To keep me away from Uncle Leo? If so, it's not your fault. I understand." He watched the flickering cartoon reflected in her eyes.

"In hindsight, I should have taken you and fled when I had the chance, but I was weak. You don't understand, William. I never wanted to give you up. How could I do such a thing? Instead I chose the lesser of two evils. I gave you up to keep you from him. And gave myself up in the process. I never expected to leave the Cabrini Sanitarium. I didn't want to leave. I stayed and wrote to you. I know I wasn't supposed to, but I knew where you were. I hoped you'd get my letters and understand."

William thought about the trove of cards and correspondence that Sister Briganti had kept hidden from him all these years. He shook his head as a Morton pipe organ played a happy melody. William felt sick to his stomach. The song faded and the lights grew dimmer and the feature film began. This time the music was more ominous.

As the credits rolled, William recognized the names of Sessue Hayakawa, Anna May Wong, and Warner Oland as the evil Dr. Fu Manchu. He searched his memories and remembered himself and his young mother in the company of a much older man. He vaguely remembered his ah-ma calling him her uncle.

William remembered his mother in the bathtub.

"Uncle Leo would have wanted nothing to do with a pregnant woman. But the baby—I worried that if I had a girl this time, he and Auntie Eng would make me sell her, or worse. And if I had a boy they might take the newborn and call it their own. Or keep the two of you, eventually tossing me aside."

William listened to his mother's confession, which was more painful than any he'd ever stumbled through with Father Bartholomew. He looked at the screen and heard Sessue say, "It is the supreme irony—that the only person I have ever deeply loved, should be born of blood that I loathe."

That's who I am, William thought.

"They wouldn't let me leave the sanitarium until I gave you up one way or the other. I asked about you, begged for you. But they said you had been taken away to a temporary home—that it was what was best for you. And in a sad way, I knew that was the truth. I couldn't take care of us. I was about to be evicted from my apartment because of how they found me. I couldn't take care of you. So I signed you away—permanently. That was the only sure way to keep Uncle Leo from finding you. I had lost you, but I could never lose you to him."

William looked at the screen and saw a familiar face. It was his ah-ma, it was Willow. His mother appeared as a handmaiden to Anna May, who was playing the villainous daughter of Fu Manchu. "But, how did you get *here*?" William asked, pointing toward the screen.

"Who would have thought that *Eyes of the Totem* would be my big break? The movie wasn't even released for two years, and by then no one wanted silent films—they all wanted talkies. H. C. Weaver went out of business, and two years later the studio burned to the ground. But Asa saw the film in a second-run theater, while half-drunk. He'd spent time in an institution as well. I think he recognized sorrow when he saw the tears, the sadness, the pain, which was real—I never had to act to make myself cry, William. I was never one of those actresses who rubbed salt or glycerin in her eyes. I only had to think of you and the tears would come."

William looked at his mother, who was crying as she spoke.

"Asa found a producer who tracked me down and vouched for me. The studio gave me a screen test. Everyone was looking for the next Nina Mae McKinney—they already had a black Greta Garbo, now they needed an Oriental one as well. That led to a contract. I stopped being Liu Song and I became Willow Frost. The studio even paid to have my name legally changed. They gave me a monthly stipend. They paid to have my back teeth removed to improve my smile. They fixed my crooked nose. Then my big moment came with a role originally written for Anna May. She was allergic to the cornflake snow they were using on the set, so I got the part. But I never forgot you, William. Each year on your birthday, I'd have Mr. Butterfield ask about you at the orphanage, and check on the whereabouts of Uncle Leo—hoping, praying, that if something happened to him, if he died, I'd somehow be able to return as your ah-ma. That was my foolish hope. A hope that slowly vanished as I realized the studio would never embrace the scandals of my past, especially when they were keeping me busy doing three movies a year. Besides, as far as Mrs. Peterson and the state were concerned, I stopped being your mother the moment I signed those papers."

William watched as his ah-ma swallowed and caught her breath.

"And later, when the studio found out I could sing, they sent me on the road, which was a relief. For me, performing onstage is more enjoyable and safer than standing in front of a camera making movies all day."

"Why?" William asked as he watched his ah-ma on-screen. She seemed so glamorous in a jeweled gown with a glimmering head-piece that looked like something from the Ziegfeld Follies.

"Because after each movie, among the cards and fan mail, I would inevitably receive a telegram from Uncle Leo."

William froze as the hero, played by Sessue, shot her.

"And because I die in all my films, William—every single one."

William watched his mother's collapse on-screen. Her movie-star voice was raspy and deeper than in real life, more dramatic, pure make-believe. He listened as the music swelled to a rolling cre-scendo. He watched as she closed her tearful eyes, her shoulders drooped, and she fell silent, lifeless.

When he turned to speak, his ah-ma was gone, her seat empty as an apology.

Old Laundry

(1934)

William knew his mother wasn't coming back. He didn't hold out hope that she would return with a bucket of popcorn or a handful of Tootsie Rolls, or even the toasted watermelon seeds and dried cuttlefish they had snacked on when he was younger. She'd brought him here to make her confession, to say goodbye, and he knew that, in her own strange way, she was hoping for forgiveness. But she didn't bother to wait around. As for William, for her, rejection wasn't something to be withstood—it was something to be avoided.

As he sat back in the theater, he looked at the stage. The tiny venue had once hosted vaudeville comedians. The lobby was filled with signed posters featuring Fay Tincher, Buster Keaton, and Charlie Chaplin, from their days as traveling performers. William had plenty of answers, but he still felt empty; the joke was on him it seemed. He wished he could have seen his grandparents, wished he had known them, before those days surrendered to silent films and the talkies that were now everywhere.

He didn't know why he sat there until the film was over. He knew his mother was dead on-screen, he wasn't hoping to catch another glimmer of the only true family he'd ever known, but maybe it was simply because he had a single streetcar token left to his name and nowhere else to go. So he sat, in darkness, while the audience clapped politely and the organist played a happy waltz as patrons drifted to the exits. William was the last to leave the empty theater as an usher began to sweep up.

Outside, the air had a bite to it that hadn't been there before. He pulled his collar up to ward off the chill, thinking of where he could go at this late hour. He knew the train station would be open—and warm. He headed back in that direction, but even from a block away he could see police officers dragging homeless men and squatters out of the station, tossing them into the streets along with their belongings. The officers were yelling at the men and pointing in the direction of Hooverville. William considered flowing south with the rising tide of misery until his curiosity got the better of him—up the street, one block away, sat the Jefferson Laundry.

William couldn't bring himself to look away. His cold feet seemed to move on their own as he found his way past street musicians and fruit vendors packing up for the day and to the window of the laundry, where a faded picture of Zhong Kui hung in a golden frame. William recognized the demon slayer from childhood stories—fairy tales to him, but revered superstitions to Uncle Leo, his father. William peeked inside and saw a lumpy old woman taking in bundles of sheets and passing out claim tickets. *Auntie Eng,* he thought. Not his real aunt. Not his real anything. She was hardly family. *Sunny is more family than that old woman.*

Then William glimpsed a strange yet familiar face as it emerged from the back room. The stern-looking man had lost more hair since the last time William had seen him. But his clothes looked the same, just older and more out of fashion. He'd gained weight too, which William found odd, considering the city was filled with so many hungry mouths. The man looked to be twenty, maybe thirty years older than Willow. William gritted his teeth at the thought.

What you did, Ah-ma, you did for me. William understood why Willow never came back for all those years. She was helpless here, laden with too many bad memories. He wondered when Uncle Leo had finally seen his ah-ma, in the newspaper, or on-screen, or heard her familiar voice on the radio. Did he recognize her right away? And was he more interested in Willow now, or in Liu Song? Would he have some claim to her? *And if he did,* William realized, *the only way to collect on that debt would be through me.*

Then the man looked up, directly at William. He glanced at his watch and came around the counter. He untied his apron, tossed the dirty linen in a bin, and opened the door. William was overwhelmed by the smell of detergent and a wave of moist heat that steamed into the frigid air.

"No jobs today. Come back next week," Leo said in Cantonese.

William stared back at him.

"Do I know you?" Leo asked.

William kept staring, examining the man's face, his nose, his receding hairline. William shook his head slowly. *No. And you never will.*

Prodigal

〖卐〗

(1934)

Despite his daydreams, William was no character in a Horatio Alger story. He wasn't Ragged Dick or Ben, the Luggage Boy. Nor did he envision being rescued from the street by Daddy Warbucks and transported to a mansion on Capitol Hill, where he'd spend the waning years of his childhood with tuxedoed servants and a scruffy dog.

Gee whiskers, he thought sadly. He gave up on those dreams and accepted all the reality that a streetcar token could afford. He picked up the broken pieces of his childhood and carried them inside him all the way back to the gates of Sacred Heart.

When he entered the main school building, he went to Sister Briganti's office. She was there, smoking, drinking black coffee, and reviewing a ledger.

"I'm back" was all he could say.

"Welcome home, William," the nun replied, hardly looking up. She didn't say *I told you so.* She didn't say anything at all. She just turned the page. And so did William.

When he wandered back into the dorm he shared with the other boys, there was a rousing cheer, as though he had left like Pinocchio, ventured to Pleasure Island, and returned home as a real boy. He didn't feel like a boy. He still felt like an orphan, but he no longer ached for what he'd lost; now he ached for what he'd never have.

"I didn't want to see you again," Sunny said. "But I'm really glad you're back."

William knew what he meant. Orphans didn't regard each other as family, they could never be that close, but they shared each other's pain, each other's loneliness. There was small comfort in just knowing that someone else understood.

"I saved you something," Sunny said. "Just in case." He reached under his mattress and pulled out a newspaper. He unfolded it, turned to the back, and handed it to William, who looked at a full broadside of Seattle's finest.

"Why are you giving me the Society Page?"

"Look closely," Sunny said, pointing with his chin.

The page was covered with dozens of dolled-up portraits of Seattle's cultured women, in satin tennis dresses and floral gowns. They seemed gaudy considering the poverty on the streets. In the lower right-hand corner was a tiny photo, the smallest on the page, no bigger than his palm. The image was his ah-ma. The caption read: "Weepin' Willow Frost returns to Seattle. Is she the latest member of Hollywood's sewing circles?"

"A Chinese woman on the Society Page," Sunny gushed. "Can you believe it?"

I don't know what to believe anymore. Just that I'll spend a few more years here, and then become another vagrant on the street.

"Thank you," William said.

At dinner the food tasted the same—stale bread with the tiny divots where the mold had been cut out, and turnips. But there was a benign comfort in blandness. The voices were the same too. The jokes were the same. Everything was the same except for the warm place in his life that had previously been filled with the glow from Charlotte. Now that emptiness felt cavernous, without her, without

Willow—without his ah-ma. William tried not to dwell in that sad place. He tried his best.

After dinner, when the other boys were studying or horsing around playing Broadsides with pad and pencil, the girls knitting or roller-skating outside, William fished out the old, dog-eared photo of his mother, the one he'd carried around like a holy relic. He took that scrap of smelly, tattered, faded yellow paper and the newspaper Sunny had given him, and walked out into the creeping darkness of the evening. The new moon lit his way to the cemetery where Charlotte lay buried. He brushed fallen pine needles from her wooden marker and dug a small hole next to her resting place with his bare hands. The ground was cold and wet and smelled of rotting leaves. When the hole was large enough, deep enough, William gently placed the images of his mother at the bottom. He regarded her Hollywood smile for a quiet moment and then covered her glamorous, wrinkled, longing face with handfuls of dirt until the hole was filled. He wished the same could be said of the one in his chest. As he smoothed the dirt above his mother's makeshift grave, he said, "I forgive you." Then he walked back to the dorm, crawled beneath his covers with his muddy hands and dirty fingers, his clothes still on, and buried his head beneath the pillow.

The Actress

(1934)

Willow hated airplanes. She wasn't afraid of flying and the noise didn't bother her. What she loathed was the tedium. Her last flight from Los Angeles to New York City had taken fifty-six hours, not counting an extended stop in Kansas City. But as much as she disliked the miracle and modern convenience of air travel, trains were worse. Even the fastest passenger trains were burdened with freight—bags, cargo, and memories. Because she had grown up near a train station, their comings and goings reminded her of the person she used to be.

During the last four months she'd arrived in each new city to a throng of reporters, theater and movie columnists, cameramen, and even autograph-seeking fans—*she had actual fans,* which always surprised her. Most were Caucasian men, older than she was—much older. They brought flowers and gifts, always more lavish than what she would have chosen for herself. No Chinese people came, which didn't surprise her. Few things had changed in that regard. She was still a female performer, unmarried. Being in movies didn't mollify that shame. It only put her seemingly tawdry career under a spotlight for all to see. Most Western moviegoers saw a glamorous Oriental delight. Her former neighbors in Chinatown, however, saw a corrupted woman, exploiting their sacred traditions for gain—for filthy lucre. In Willow's mind, both were right. But still, the crowds came and showered her with unfiltered adoration. One well-meaning man even gave her a basket filled with pomegranates. He seemed offended when she refused to accept it. But she couldn't bear to explain that his gift symbolized the bearing of many children. For Willow, the sweet-sour fruit would always taste bitter.

But leaving by train was the hardest part of traveling. Leaving was different. Arriving to a new crowd was a heralded event. But leaving was like becoming yesterday's news—no one cared. *Is that how we'll all leave this business?* she wondered. She didn't like the answer that came to her. Even Stepin and Asa felt the discord—the emptiness of rising on a tide so high that when it ebbs everything of value is sucked away. From the loving eyes of thousands to the confused stares of a few.

Willow stayed close to the rest of the performers who would be making the trip on the Empire Builder to Spokane, then on to Minneapolis, and Chicago—another city, another venue, another puppet show where her strings were golden shackles.

"That was your boy, wasn't it?" Stepin asked. He was the only one who knew. Asa might have suspected, but he'd been so drunk he hardly remembered what day it was. He'd already missed the train twice on this leg of the tour.

Stepin put his arm around her shoulder. "The things that we do, that make us so black, and leave us feeling so blue." He hummed a sad tune.

Willow couldn't bear to speak of the boy she'd left behind, again. She merely nodded and looked away, hoping not to cry. She'd been teased on many occasions about her weeping moniker. Some said it was because she was a woman, that she played it up for dramatic effect—her one trick, used over and over to melt the hearts of stubborn men. But the truth was, Willow did it because she had to. If she didn't, something inside her would burst.

Willow checked her ticket as the train chugged into the terminal. She stood back watching stewards and handlers load their luggage.

All she kept with her was her mother's valise. Willow left Stepin and Asa to find a bench and sat, the old case in her lap. She stared at her empty hands. The lines on her palms had always been her road map, leading her far away, in her mind and eventually in the flesh. She'd followed that lonely path because she had lost her family, everyone dear to her, and had nowhere else to go. Now that road had brought her full circle. She did have someone. She always had.

"That's our train, Frosty," Stepin said as he adjusted his hat. He signed an autograph for the train's purser and shook hands with other passengers in line.

Willow didn't answer.

"You gonna catch the next one, maybe?" He didn't press the issue. There would be other trains carrying crew and wardrobe carts and musical instruments and the rest of the traveling road show that her life had become. The moviemaking was pleasant, shallow work. But traveling, performing, the ups and downs, had taken their toll.

Willow watched as Stepin and Asa and the ladies of the Ingénues boarded one by one. The purser punched their tickets and tucked them into their seatbacks as stewards helped the women with the cases that contained their musical instruments. Most of the cast and crew ignored her. But Stepin knew. He tipped his hat and waved goodbye. She wondered if she'd ever see him again, perhaps on-screen in some first-run theater. ·

While she still sat in the station, the final bell rang and the train pulled away. She'd never felt more alone, even as hundreds of people walked by. No one recognized her, and she began to treasure her anonymity like a gift. She certainly didn't feel like anyone special. Far from extraordinary. She sat and thought about her parents taking these same trains. She thought about all the years she wanted to take William and run away. But she'd been young and scared. Now she was older and frightened—of the person she'd allowed herself to become. She'd become her mother's daughter, the compromised woman with a crushing sadness, and the brave performer—all of it. But now she would try to be someone else. The mother to a son.

As she left the train station she wasn't sure if going back for William would make things better or worse. She would be giving up everything to be with him. And whatever attention or publicity that came with it, good or bad, she was ready to embrace it all. And there was still the chance that Leo would swoop down like a vulture and take him away. *Let him try*, she thought. She would throw *kai ching* in his path. She would distract him with devil money. She wouldn't give up so easily this time. She wouldn't tell herself stories. She would fight if she had to. She wouldn't compromise. She couldn't anymore.

Five years ago Liu Song had given up her son, her beautiful boy. Today, as she stepped off the Laurelhurst trolley and strode through the cold iron gates of Sacred Heart, she didn't know if it was even possible for Willow Frost to adopt a child, but she would give anything in the world to find out.

As she walked past the offices, searching, she saw the teachers, cooks, custodians, and sisters—the surrogates she'd allowed to look after her son. They didn't appear to be bad people, though they didn't look like family. The children, *they* looked like family. As she searched, Willow knew she must have stood out at Sacred Heart, not because she was a Chinese movie star but because she was a living, breathing parent. The orphans stared at her as though she were some strange apparition from a hopeful dream. They whispered among themselves and looked around, searching.

Willow turned and followed the smell of boiled cabbage and powdered milk to the crowded lunchroom, where she saw a woman in charge. Willow recognized the nun as a figure of authority by the deference shown to her by the other teachers. And the way the orphans stood aside as the woman roamed, ruler in hand. When Willow's eyes met hers, they exchanged startled, knowing glances. The sister nodded and pointed to the courtyard past the window, where

Willow saw dozens of excited children surrounding a truck that was open on one side, carrying racks of books.

Outside, Willow could smell the diesel fumes from the truck and hear the chatter of happy, hopeful children as each ran off, a book in hand. She didn't see the boy she was looking for, but a few of the older kids noticed.

"You must be Willow," a boy said, unblinking.

"And who would you be?" she asked.

"I'm a friend of William's. I'm Sunny," he said. Then he pointed up the hill, toward a knot of pine trees. "If you're looking for him, you'll find him there."

She thanked him and waved to the children whose sad, curious eyes were all now on her. As she turned and walked past the trees, she saw a clearing filled with old stone pillars—headstones. She noticed the dates that had been etched into granite and painted on stone, calculating the ages of those buried there. Some had lived well into their teens, but just as many had died at three, four, most before their tenth birthdays.

She searched for her son and sighed with relief as she saw William sitting in the grass next to a wooden marker. He'd arranged a cup of tea, an orange, an apple, and two sticks of incense. Curlicues of agar wood smoke rose above his makeshift funeral offering. He sat with his back to her, reading out loud from a book called *Cast upon the Breakers,* pausing to engage in conversation with a girl named Charlotte. Willow watched as he paused as though sensing the presence of another, or perhaps he caught her perfume on the breeze. He closed the book and rose to his feet, turning toward her.

"William . . ." Liu Song was barely able to speak his name.

He stared back incredulously. "Ah-ma?"

She nodded and drew a deep breath. "Your friend told me where to find you."

William glanced at his offering, then rubbed smoke from his

eyes. He looked back up at Willow, wide-eyed. "Charlotte told you?"

She shook her head. "The boy down the hill. Your friend . . ."

"You mean Sunny."

Willow nodded again.

William stepped toward his ah-ma. He paused and regarded her, hesitant, as if he were unsure she was really there, then threw himself into her open, waiting arms. He looked down the hill toward the orphanage and then off toward the horizon. "His name is Sunny." William smiled. "Sunny Dreams Come True."

Willow held her son close. She touched his cold cheek, ran her fingers through his hair, felt happiness welling up in her eyes as she softly whispered, *"In your dreams whatever they be, dream a little dream of me."*

Author's Note

My writing career began when I wrote my parents' eulogies. I was an aspiring writer, fumbling for years with this thing called *fiction*, but too often I had nothing of substance to write *about*. It was only after I'd collected enough scars that I found the expository canvas on which to paint my stories, like the one of Willow Frost.

Willow is less a figment and more of an amalgam; a beautiful golem animated by the pain, suffering, and sacrifices of others—from my own mother, who had a tumultuous life of joy and abandonment; my Chinese grandmother, who was an alpha female at a time when most women were unwilling to pay the price for that kind of independence; and even a nod to famed actress Anna May Wong, who found success in Hollywood but could never find *amour*.

William's story, on the other hand, is not so unique. His began as an exploration of familial relationships during the Great Depression when thousands of children were consigned to places like Seattle's Sacred Heart Orphanage. These "orphans" (among them, the author Wallace Stegner) were left behind by destitute parents who promised to return. Sometimes they did. But some promises are harder to keep than others.

Yet amid this ramshackle, tar-paper, threadbare landscape was a literal light in the dark—the fledgling film industry, which hadn't yet coalesced in Hollywoodland.

So at a time when escape entertainment was redefining itself on a monthly basis, when pianolas were outselling pianos, when radios were outselling them both, silent films were becoming the unwanted orphans of talkies. And film studios were popping up everywhere, in places like Minnesota, Idaho, and even Tacoma, Washington, where the long-forgotten H. C. Weaver built the third-largest film stage in the U.S. and produced three movies, which are now lost.

William and Willow's tale is also a reflection of an early China-town, where minority mothers were not allowed in "white" hospitals. The late Ruby Chow, one of Seattle's famous activists and restaurateurs (who once hired a skinny college kid named Bruce Lee), was born with the help of a midwife on a Seattle fish dock.

These are the things we don't remember, but there are also things we wish we could forget, like Seattle's Wah Mee Club, where in 1983 fourteen people were gunned down, thirteen losing their lives. The Wah Mee Massacre devastated families and decimated the China-town economy. Yet, this iconic place was once a cultural hub, where on a rainy night a handsome young blackjack dealer met a coat-check girl with a perfect smile. They later exchanged vows and eventually celebrated sixty years of marriage. I should know—I'm their grandson.

But encircling this story is the fact that this novel *is* fiction. And while I, by accident or with deliberate intent, have played God with dates, geography, and personages, this is still a story infused with generations of hope and tribulation. The characters of William, Willow, and Charlotte are made up but hopefully you'll find that my intentions are true.

Acknowledgments

I find myself in karmic receivership for the aid and comfort received from the following, for helping me tell this story, in ways seen and unseen:

So I'm blowing good-night kisses to Julie Ziegler, Kari Dasher, Andrew Wahl, and the staff and volunteers at Humanities Washington for inviting me to read something new at Bedtime Stories, their annual fund-raiser. Little did we know that those twelve hastily scribbled pages I read that night would turn into the book you're now holding.

I'm offering a rousing standing ovation to the staff of Seattle's Wing Luke Museum for your acceptance and encouragement, and for allowing me to put on those cool white gloves and step into the basement archives. I felt like Howard Carter breaching the doorway to King Tut's treasure room, candle in one hand, chisel in the other. But instead of gold statuary I laid eyes upon dozens of silver cases and trunks, filled with costumes and scripts that once belonged to the Cantonese opera star Ping Chow.

A wide-eyed wave, as I press my nose to the window of the Museum of History & Industry (MOHAI). I'm the kid. You're the candy store.

A shout-out to the Tacoma Public Library (as much as one can shout in the library), whose collection of photographs by art director Lance Gaston are the only tangible records of the films: *Hearts & Fists, The Eyes of the Totem,* and *Heart of the Yukon.* These silent films have vanished, along with the hopes and dreams of the long-forgotten H. C. Weaver Studios.

An aperitif to the late Bill Cumming, one of the Northwest's best painters and most charming raconteurs, who also happened to be one of my favorite instructors back when I was a know-nothing art student. Bill's memoir, *Sketchbook,* was the next best thing to a time machine.

A salute to the Pacific Northwest Labor and Civil Rights Projects based at the University of Washington and directed by Professor James Gregory. (Go Huskies!)

And a front-row ticket to the enigmatic J. Willis Sayre, who passed away in 1963 after dedicating his life to chronicling Seattle's theatrical history. His collection of photographs, theater programs, and related ephemera is nothing short of astounding, also obsessive.

Plus lifetime achievement awards for the immortals Anna May Wong, Sessue Hayakawa, and Lincoln Perry: brave minority actors who paved the way for the next generation, only to be marginalized and often ridiculed for their labors.

Then there are the books that were helpful along the way and which I eventually need to return to the public library: Stephen O'Connor's *Orphan Trains,* Eric L. Flom's *Silent Film Stars on the Stages of Seattle,* Hye Seung Chung's *Hollywood Asian,* Nell Shipman's *The Silent Screen & My Talking Heart,* Mel Watkins's *Stepin Fetchit: The Life and Times of Lincoln Perry,* Graham Russell Gao Hodges's *Anna May Wong: From Laundryman's Daughter to Hollywood Legend,* and Gypsy Rose Lee's *The G-String Murders* (yes, it's actually called that).

And of course there needs to be a moment in the spotlight for my überagent, Kristin Nelson. I was once told that if you're a nice guy you need a jerk for an agent, and if you're a jerk you need a nice agent to clean up your messes. Kristin is the exception to that rule. Or, maybe I'm a jerk and don't realize it . . .

To my team at Ballantine: Libby McGuire, Kim Hovey, Jennifer Hershey, Theresa Zoro, Kristin Fassler, Quinne Rogers, Susan Corcoran, Scott Shannon, Matt Schwartz, Toby Ernst, Jayme (nice name) Boucher, Kelle Ruden, and last but not least my amazing publicist, Lisa Barnes, who makes me seem smarter, look taller, appear handsomer and more charming than I actually am. One of these days I'll come and serenade you all with the karaoke version of "Wind Beneath My Wings." I'll pass out earplugs and Asahi. You'll love it . . . when I stop singing . . .

And to my saintly editor, Jane von Mehren, who believed in Willow and William from the start and strove valiantly at times to save me from myself. Jane, we did it.

But as always, the person I owe the most is my wife, Leesha, my partner in this never-ending pas de deux, for allowing me to spend extended periods of time in a place that we have learned to affectionately call Storyland. And with that in mind, I have to nod my appreciation to my intrepid teens for understanding that when Dad is in Storyland, they need to ask someone else for a ride to the mall, to volleyball practice, to drum lessons, to the Emergency Room . . . (103° is not a fever, right?)

Songs of
Willow Frost

JAMIE FORD

A Reader's Guide

A Conversation with Jamie Ford

Random House Reader's Circle: Your first novel, *Hotel on the Corner of Bitter and Sweet,* has been described as "a wartime-era Chinese-Japanese variation on *Romeo and Juliet*" (*The Seattle Times*). In what ways is *Songs of Willow Frost* a different kind of love story, and why did you want to turn to this narrative next?

Jamie Ford: If I were to create a perfume, it would come in a cracked bottle and be called "Abandonment." That's how *Songs of Willow Frost* opens. It's another love story—and while there are boy-meets-girl aspects to the tale, the real love story is about a mother and her son, and about how two people can be so close yet so far away from each other, and ultimately so misunderstood. I don't think we ever really understand our parents until they're gone—at least that's been my experience. William feels that loss, and it affects him profoundly. But then he has something many of us don't get—the opportunity to find his mother again, to see her through new eyes.

RHRC: William is on a birthday outing with the Sacred Heart Orphanage when he sees a film star whose face and voice remind him of his long-lost mother, Liu Song. What was the role of orphanages during the Great Depression? Why would he suspect that she is still alive?

JF: When I began researching orphanages during the Great Depression, I was blown away by how many orphans still had living parents (because that sort of defies the definition of an orphan, right?).

What I discovered was that two thirds of the kids in Seattle's orphanages had at least one parent still living. Parents who could no longer support them would take their kids to places like the Sacred Heart Orphanage, or in a few tragic cases abandon their children in public buildings, knowing they would eventually be remanded into state custody. Author Wallace Stegner was one of these orphans. His mother left him and his brother at Sacred Heart—the orphanage featured in *Songs of Willow Frost,* which still stands today—and returned a year later.

So it's not at all unusual for William to suspect that his mother might be out there, somewhere. Whether that hope makes it easier or harder for him and his fellow children in the long run—that's the question.

RHRC: William has to venture into Depression-era Seattle in order to find her—and he travels there in a creative way. Did you always intend for William to escape from Sacred Heart in a bookmobile?

JF: Sometimes reality is too wonderful to be denied. In this case, Seattle's first bookmobile hit the streets in 1931 with six hundred books, and it actually visited Sacred Heart, so it became the perfect getaway vehicle, both literally and metaphorically. Sadly, the Depression caught up to the bookmobile, and the program was cut near the end of 1932. (Has there ever been an era when libraries *haven't* had their budgets cut?). Bookmobile service resumed in 1947.

RHRC: Based in part on the first Chinese American movie star Anna May Wong, Liu Song—or Willow Frost, as she comes to be known—stands at a nexus point between Chinese and American culture and identity, between generations, and between the deep history of traditional Chinese theater and the newer landscape of American movie houses. What sorts of choices and challenges does she face as an Asian American woman navigating life in the 1920s and the early American film industry? To what extent does her path mirror and diverge from that of her mother's?

JF: Anyone who is the child of immigrants eventually gets caught in a whirlpool of personal hopes, dreams, familial expectations, cultural mores, misconceptions, and at times, outright discrimination.

Willow comes from a culture that traditionally values women as mothers and little more—where women were banned from the theater, where men performed female roles onstage, and women associated with this form of entertainment were seen as less than chaste. But she's also American-born, with opportunities within her reach but forever beyond her grasp. She's too American for her Chinese suitors, but to men in the U.S. she's viewed as an oddity at best and an object of desire at worst.

By becoming Willow, Liu Song is able to achieve the unfulfilled dreams of her parents, who were actors on stage—especially her mother—but even as Willow she's limited. Like Anna May Wong, she can never be more than an exotic extra, condemned to be the villainess or victim. She always dies in her films, and is unable to find love on screen as well as in real life. For Lui Song, the success of Willow comes at a steep price.

RHRC: Willow breaks into the movie industry at a studio in Tacoma, Washington. What was the state's role in early American film? Does it still bear the footprint of that era?

JF: Before the film industry coalesced in Southern California, there were viable studios in unusual places like Minnesota, Idaho, and even Tacoma, where H.C. Weaver Productions has long been forgotten.

Early in the research process I called the Washington Film Office, and they told me the first film shot in Washington State was *Tugboat Annie* (1933). I'd read about movie crews on Mt. Rainier around 1924, so I knew the film office information was off. I kept digging and found press clippings that led to the H.C. Weaver production stage, which at the time was the third-largest freestanding film space in America (the larger two were in Hollywood).

H.C. Weaver produced three films, *Hearts and Fists* (1926), *Eyes of the Totem* (1927), and *The Heart of the Yukon* (1927). These silent films were tied up in distribution and unfortunately released when talkies were overtaking their silent predecessors. The studio closed its doors as the Roaring Twenties stopped roaring. The building was converted into an enormous dance hall, which burned to the ground in 1932. The films have all been lost, though the Tacoma Public Library has a wonderful collection of production shots by Gaston Lance, the studio's art director.

RHRC: Film is a constant artistic presence throughout the novel, but music—obviously—also runs through *Songs of Willow Frost*. What importance do you see music having for William and Liu Song? Did music play a role in your writing process?

JF: Liu Song is suffering in silence. In fact, women in general didn't have a collective voice until the Nineteenth Amendment, when women were guaranteed the right to vote. So music is transcendent for Liu Song—it literally and metaphorically becomes her voice. And because of that, because of her singing, William recognizes her.

As far as music playing a role in the writing process, I always try to write for all five senses, so music becomes part of the tapestry of storytelling—plus, certain songs mark the time and echo the backstory of my characters. Like Irving Berlin's "When I Lost You."

RHRC: You have said that Liu Song/Willow is also an amalgamation of your own mother and Chinese grandmother. Are there particular real-life experiences that worked their way into your story, and what was it like to write with them in mind?

JF: I come from a family of big families. Both of my Chinese grandparents had more siblings than you could count on one hand, yet my father was an only child. The reason for that is because my Chinese grandmother had a backroom "procedure" that left her unable to bear more children.

And yet my grandmother was fierce. She was an alpha female at a time when it was perhaps culturally and socially unacceptable, but in America, as a U.S. citizen, she could become something different. That said, as a Chinese woman, she was still a minority within a minority, and unable to receive proper medical care.

My mom, on the other hand, was Caucasian. But she was dirt-poor—so poor that when she became pregnant with my oldest sister, she could only dream of giving birth in an actual hospital. That dream went unfulfilled, as her husband at the time gambled away the money she'd saved for the delivery. But, like my grandmother, she picked herself up after every setback, after every sacrifice.

There are elements of both of them in Willow—in the kinds of challenges she faces, and the determination with which she faces them and survives.

RHRC: *Songs of Willow Frost* provides "the kind of ending readers always hope for, but seldom get" (*The Dallas Morning News*). What do you think is the secret to a great ending?

JF: I see storytelling as making a contract with the reader. I'm promising a certain journey, and good or bad, happy or sad, I need to deliver in a satisfying way—completing the story. But I'm also a big fan of redemptive endings and the type of endings where it feels as though a new story is just beginning, one that belongs to the reader's imagination.

RHRC: Your touring has taken you into a wide variety of venues—bookstores, libraries, literary festivals, community reads programs, walking tours, museums, Asian American organizations, ESL classes, high schools and colleges, writing workshops with faculty and inner-city youth, even men's and women's prisons. What are some of your favorite ways to connect with your fans both through and beyond events?

JF: I'm always up for unusual events, whether it's meeting with a homeless book group or visiting a men's medium security prison. But beyond that I thoroughly enjoy social media. The writing life is somewhat monastic, so it's great to connect via Twitter, Facebook, Instagram—*the usual suspects*—and at jamieford.com, naturally.

RHRC: What do you hope readers take away from *Songs of Willow Frost*?

JF: I hope they're equally entertained and enlightened. I hope they value their time spent with Willow and William. And I hope they see growth in me as a writer. Is that too much to hope for? I mean, before the Beatles wrote *Abbey Road* they were singing, "She loves you, yeah-yeah-yeah."

We all have to start somewhere.

RHRC: Your novels are so richly detailed and clearly evoke Seattle in different historical periods. What does your research process for each novel look like? How do you bring each era to life?

JF: I collect a lot of ephemera, which is a fancy way of saying I have a very messy office filled with old maps, newspapers, magazines, theater handbills, postcards, and even old high school yearbooks (it's amazing what you can find on eBay).

But I also spend time in places like the Wing Luke Museum and the Museum of History and Industry in Seattle. I get to put on the white archivist gloves and sift the historical sand, and every once in a while I'll find a bone—some little obscure detail that will work its way into the story.

RHRC: *Hotel on the Corner of Bitter and Sweet* sold over 1.3 million copies, was on the *New York Times* bestseller list for more than two years, won the Asian Pacific American Award for Literature, and was even transformed into a popular stage play. Why do you think it resonated so deeply with readers across the country? Are there any particularly memorable or surprising reactions that you'd like to share?

JF: At its core, *Hotel* is a love story—or actually a love-lost-and-then-found story, which I think everyone can relate to on some level. There's a reason why people try to lose twenty pounds before class reunions. There are just some people in our lives whom we love, and lose, and unfailingly long for. They orbit our hearts like Halley's Comet, crossing into our universe only once, or if we're lucky twice, in a lifetime.

Hotel also deals with race relations during an oft-forgotten period in U.S. history. As a researcher and storyteller, I like turning over rocks and looking at the squishy things underneath. I think others do, too.

As far as memorable reactions, here are three that immediately come to mind:

1. Being invited to the Minidoka Reunion (Minidoka was an internment camp outside Twin Falls, Idaho), where former internees had a karaoke night and sang "Don't Fence Me In."
2. Going to Norway and speaking to high school students who were assigned the book, which was surreal.
3. A sansei (third-generation Japanese American) woman sharing that she had read the book to her mother, a former internee, while she'd been in hospice, and that the book was the first time they'd talked about "camp."

RHRC: What's next for Jamie Ford?

JF: I'm currently working on a new novel about a boy who was raffled off at the 1909 World's Fair in Seattle.

Oh, and I need a nap. I think I have one scheduled for next year.

Questions and Topics for Discussion

1. William's life at Sacred Heart is, he feels, a hard one. Do you agree? In the long run, do the caregivers at Sacred Heart do more to help or harm their young wards?

2. The orphans at Sacred Heart share a collective "birthday," one for boys and one for girls. What would it be like to celebrate such an event? Would it feel less special without a focus on the individual, or even more joyful to share it with a community?

3. On May 4, 1931, the first bookmobile hit the streets of Seattle, where it did indeed visit the historical Sacred Heart Orphanage (as well as Boeing Field). Why do you think there was such a need to bring the library to its patrons, rather than allowing those patrons to visit the library as they chose?

4. What qualities does Liu Song share with her mother? How are their lives similar or different?

5. Does Liu Song's mother represent strength, weakness, or a little of both? Do you think she knew she was a second wife?

6. Why doesn't Liu Song study Cantonese Opera instead of pursuing a career in film and stage?

7. What do you think happened to Mr. Butterfield after the loss of

his music store? Personally and professionally, how would he react to Liu Song's newfound fame as Willow?

8. Imagine that you are Liu Song and pregnant under her circumstances. What would you do? Who might you tell? And would you keep the baby?

9. The novel explores the subject of abandonment, whether by willful desertion or by circumstance. What forms does such abandonment take among contemporary families?

10. In the time period the novel is set in, economic and social classes were clearly defined, and while change was desired by some, it was feared by others. Do you think the time we live in today is more just and fair, or are we in fact worse off?

11. The social worker Mrs. Peterson represents an outside authority at a time when mothers had fewer rights to their children than fathers. When did that begin to change and why?

12. During the early years of the silent-film era, studios and production companies could be found in most states. So why had much of the film industry congregated in Hollywood a decade later?

13. What factors contributed to the eventual demise of the grand movie palaces of the 1920s and '30s?

14. Willow always knew where her son was, so why didn't she come back sooner, especially as she gained success?

15. Why does Willow die in all of her films?

16. How do you think Charlotte's death impacted Sister Briganti?

17. In the end, Willow comes back for William. What do you think happened to them after the novel's conclusion? What happened to her career?

18. Overall, do you think the story is one of hope and promise or suffering and sacrifice?

The son of a Chinese American father, JAMIE FORD is the author of the *New York Times* bestselling novel *Hotel on the Corner of Bitter and Sweet*, which won the Asian/ Pacific American Award for Literature. Having grown up in Seattle, he now lives in Montana with his wife and children.

www.jamieford.com

Jamie Ford is available for select readings and lectures. To inquire about a possible appearance, please contact the Random House Speakers Bureau at 212-572-2013 or rhspeakers@randomhouse.com.